John Connolly was born in Dublin in 1968. His debut – *Every Dead Thing* – swiftly launched him right into the front rank of thriller writers, and all his subsequent novels have been *Sunday Times* bestsellers. He is the first non-American writer to win the US Shamus award. To find out more about his novels, visit John's website at www.johnconnolly.co.uk

Praise for *The Black Angel*

'Connolly has made a name for himself specialising in darkness, and *The Black Angel* is no exception. Five Star.' *Daily Mirror*

'Connolly has virtually no match when it comes to chilling his readers. This is heady stuff, dispatched with all the casual brio that is Connolly's stock in trade . . . those willing to take the journey will find that the rewards are considerable.' *Daily Express*

'Seldom has a thriller writer been so adept at turning the screw yet further and evoking a sense of awful dread among his landscapes and tormented characters. Colourful but visceral grand guignol, and definitely not to be read at night.' Maxim Jakubowski, *Guardian*

'There is a precision to the horrors in Connolly's books that make them one of the few sequences to have found anything interesting to say about serial killers since Thomas Harris.' *Independent*

'John Connolly writes beautifully about a world that is desolate, pain-filled and seeming hopeless, with the powers of darkness always threatening to rent the fabric of reality and bring chaos. But he also has a keen eye for the underbelly of modern American life, a good ear for current street argot, and his violent set pieces are satisfyingly exciting and vibrantly realised.' Myles McWeeney, *Irish Independent*

'Great narrative talent packed with vivid scenes and sequences. An impressive feat of storytelling.' *Irish Times Weekend Review*

'Satisfying and literate thrill ride.' *Evening Herald*, Dublin

Also by John Connolly

Every Dead Thing

Dark Hollow

The Killing Kind

The White Road

Bad Men

Nocturnes

John Connolly

THE BLACK ANGEL

HODDER

First published in Great Britain in 2005 by Hodder and Stoughton
A division of Hodder Headline

1

A CIP catalogue record for this title is available
from the British Library

ISBN 0 340 83767 5

Typeset in Sabon by
Palimpsest Book Production Limited,
Polmont, Stirlingshire

Printed and bound by
Clays Ltd, St. Ives plc

Hodder Headline's policy is to use papers that are natural, renewable
and recyclable products and made from wood grown in sustainable
forests. The logging and manufacturing processes are expected to
conform to the environmental regulations of the country of origin.

Hodder and Stoughton Ltd
A division of Hodder Headline
338 Euston Road
London NW1 3BH

For Sue Fletcher, with gratitude and affection.

Grateful acknowledgement is made for permission to reprint from the following copyrighted work:

Pinetop Seven: lines from "Tennessee Pride" (lyrics: Darren Richard) from *Pinetop Seven* (Self-Help/Truckstop Records, 1997), © Darren Richard, reprinted by permission of Darren Richard and Truckstop Audio Recording Company. *www.pinetopseven.com*

1

No one can know the origin of evil
who has not grasped the truth about
the so-called Devil and his angels.

Origen (186–255 A.D.)

Prologue

The rebel angels fell, garlanded with fire.

And as they descended, tumbling through the void, they were cursed as the newly blind are cursed, for just as the darkness is more terrible for those who have known the light, so the absence of grace is felt more acutely by those who once dwelt in its warmth. The angels screamed in their torment, and their burning brought brightness to the shadows for the first time. The lowest of them cowered in the depths, and there they created their own world in which to dwell.

As the last angel fell, he looked to heaven and saw all that was to be denied him for eternity, and the vision was so terrible to him that it burned itself upon his eyes. And so, as the heavens closed above him, it was given to him to witness the face of God disappear among gray clouds, and the beauty and sorrow of the image was imprinted forever in his memory, and upon his sight. He was cursed to walk forever as an outcast, shunned even by his own kind, for what could be more agonizing for them than to see, each time they looked in his eyes, the ghost of God flickering in the blackness of his pupils?

And so alone was he that he tore himself in two, that he might have company in his long exile, and together these twin parts of the same being wandered the still-forming earth. In time, they were joined by a handful of others who were weary of cowering in that bleak kingdom of their own creation. After all, what is hell but the eternal absence of God? To exist in a hellish state is to be denied forever the promise of hope, of redemption, of love. To those who have been forsaken, hell has no geography.

But these angels at last grew weary of roaming throughout the desolate world without an outlet for their rage and their despair. They found a deep, dark place in which to sleep, and there they secreted themselves away and waited. And after many years, mines were dug, and tunnels lit, and the deepest and greatest of these excavations was among the Bohemian silver mines at Kutná Hora, and it was called Kank.

And it was said that when the mine reached its final depth, the lights carried by the miners flickered as though troubled by a breeze where no breeze could exist, and a great sighing was heard, as of souls released from their bondage. A stench of burning came, and tunnels collapsed. A storm of filth and dirt arose, sweeping through the mine, choking and blinding all in its path. Those who survived spoke of voices in the abyss, and the beating of wings in the midst of the dust clouds. The storm ascended toward the main shaft, bursting forth into the night sky, and the men who saw it glimpsed a redness at its heart, as though it were all aflame.

And the rebel angels took upon themselves the appearance of men, and set about creating an invisible kingdom that they might rule through stealth and the corrupted will of others. They were led by the twin demons, the greatest of their number, the Black Angels. The first, called Ashmael, immersed himself in the heat *of battle, and whispered empty promises of glory into the ears of ambitious rulers. The other, called Immael, waged his own war upon the church and its leaders, the representatives upon the earth of the One who had banished his brother. He gloried in fire and rape, and his shadow fell upon the sacking of monasteries and the burning of chapels. Each half of this twin being bore the mark of God as a white mote in his eye, Ashmael in his right eye and Immael in his left.*

But in his arrogance and wrath, Immael allowed himself to be glimpsed for a moment in his true, blighted form. He was confronted by a Cistercian monk named Erdric from the monastery at Sedlec, and they fought above vats of molten silver in a great foundry. At last, Immael was cast down, caught in the moment of transformation from human to Other, and he fell into the hot ore. Erdric called for the metal to be slowly cooled, and Immael was trapped in silver, powerless to free himself from this purest of prisons.

And Ashmael felt his pain, and sought to free him, but the monks hid him well, and kept him from those who would release him from his bonds. Yet Ashmael never stopped seeking his brother, and in time he was joined in his search by those who shared his nature, and by men corrupted by his promises. They marked themselves so that they might be known to one another, and their mark was a grapnel, a forked hook, for in the old lore this was the first weapon of the fallen angels.

And they called themselves "Believers."

1

The woman stepped carefully from the Greyhound bus, her right hand holding firmly on to the bar as she eased herself down. A relieved sigh escaped from her lips once both feet were on level ground, the relief that she always felt when a simple task was negotiated without incident. She was not old — she was barely into her fifties — but she looked, and felt, much older. She had endured a great deal, and accumulated sorrows had intensified the predations of the years. Her hair was silver gray, and she had long since ceased making the monthly trek to the salon to have its color altered. There were horizontal lines stretching from the corner of each eye, like healed wounds, mirrored by similar lines on her forehead. She knew how she had come by them, for occasionally she caught herself wincing as if in pain while she looked in the mirror or saw herself reflected in the window of a store, and the depth of those lines increased with the transformation in her expression. It was always the same thoughts, the same memories, that caused the change, and always the same faces that she recalled: the boy, now a man; her daughter, as she once was and as she now might be; and the one who had made her little girl upon her, his face sometimes contorted, as it was at the moment of her daughter's conception, and at other times tattered and destroyed, as it was before they closed the coffin lid upon him, erasing at last his physical presence from the world.

Nothing, she had come to realize, will age a woman faster than a troubled child. In recent years, she had become prone to the kind of accidents that bedeviled the lives of women two or three decades older than she, and took longer to recover from them than once she had. It was the little things that she had to look out for: unanticipated curbs, neglected cracks in the sidewalk, the unexpected jolting of a bus as she rose from her seat, the forgotten water spilled upon the kitchen floor. She feared these things more than she feared the young men who congregated in the parking lot of the strip mall near her home, watching for the vulnerable, for those whom they considered easy prey. She knew that she would never be one of their victims, as they were more afraid of her than they were of the police, or of their more vicious peers, for they knew of the man who waited in the shadows of her life. A small part of her hated the fact that they feared her, even as she enjoyed the protection that it brought. Her protection was hard bought, purchased, she believed, with the loss of a soul.

She prayed for him, sometimes. While the others wailed "Hallelujah" to the preacher, beating their breasts and shaking their heads, she remained silent, her chin to her chest, and pleaded softly. In the past, a long time ago, she would ask the Lord that her nephew might turn again to His radiant light, and embrace the salvation that lay only in relinquishing violent ways. Now she no longer wished for miracles. Instead, as she thought about him she begged God that, when this lost sheep at last stood before Him for the final judgment, He would be merciful and forgive him his trespasses; that He would look closely at the life the man had lived and find within it those little acts of decency that might enable Him to offer succour to this sinner.

But perhaps there were some lives that could never be redeemed, and some sins so terrible that they were beyond forgiveness. The preacher said that the Lord forgives all, but only if the sinner truly acknowledges his faults and seeks another path. If this was true, then she feared that her prayers would count for nothing, and he was damned to eternity.

She showed her ticket to the man unloading the baggage from the bus. He was gruff and unfriendly to her, but he appeared to be that way to everyone. Young men and women hovered watchfully at the periphery of the light from the bus's windows, like wild animals fearful of the fire yet hungry for those who lay within the circle of its warmth. Her handbag gripped to her chest, she took her case by its handle and wheeled it toward the escalator. She watched those around her, heedful of the warnings of her neighbors back home.

Don't accept no offers of help. Don't be talking to nobody seems like he just offerin' to assist a lady with her bag, don't matter how well he dressed or how sweetly he sings . . .

But there were no offers of help, and she ascended without incident to the busy streets of this alien city, as foreign to her as Cairo or Rome might have been, dirty and crowded and unforgiving. She had scribbled an address on a piece of paper, along with the directions she had painstakingly transcribed over the phone from the man at the hotel, hearing the impatience in his voice as he was forced to repeat the address, the name of the hotel near incomprehensible to her when spoken in his thick immigrant accent.

She walked the streets, pulling her bag behind her. She carefully noted the numbers at the intersections, trying to take as few turns as possible, until she came to the big police building. There she waited for another hour, until a policeman came to talk to her. He had a thin file in front of him, but she could add nothing to what she had told him over the phone, and he could tell her only that they were doing what they could. Still, she filled out more papers, in the hope that some small detail she provided might lead them to her daughter, then left and hailed a cab on the street. She passed the piece of paper with the address of her hotel through a small hole in the Plexiglas screen. She asked the driver how much it would cost to go there and he shrugged. He was an Asian man and he did not look pleased to see the scribbled destination.

"Traffic. Who knows?"

He waved a hand at the slow-moving streams of cars and trucks and buses. Horns honked loudly, and drivers shouted angrily at one another. All was impatience and frustration, overshadowed by buildings that were too high, out of scale with those who were expected to live and work inside and outside them. She could not understand how anyone would choose to remain in such a place.

"Twenty, maybe," said the cabdriver.

She hoped it would be less than twenty. Twenty dollars was a lot, and she did not know how long she would have to stay here. She had booked the hotel room for three days, and had sufficient funds to cover another three days after that, as long as she ate cheaply and could master the intricacies of the subway. She had read about it, but had never seen it in reality and had no concept of its operations. She knew only that she did not like the thought of descending beneath the earth, into the darkness, but she could not afford to take cabs all the time. Buses might be better. At least they stayed above ground, slowly though they seemed to move in this city.

He might offer her money, of course, once she found him, but she would refuse any such offer, just as she had always refused it, carefully returning the checks that he sent to the only contact address that she had for him. His money was tainted, just as he was tainted, but she needed his help now: not his money, but his knowledge. Something terrible had happened to her daughter, of that she was certain, even if she could not explain how she knew.

Alice, oh Alice, why did you have to come to this place?

Her own mother had been blessed, or cursed, with the gift. She knew when someone was suffering, and could sense when harm had come to anyone who was dear to her. The dead talked to her. They told her things. Her life was filled with whispers. The gift had not been passed on, and for that the woman was grateful, but she wondered sometimes if a faint trace of it had not found its way into her, a mere spark of the great power that had dwelt in her mother. Or perhaps all mothers were cursed with the ability to sense their children's deepest sufferings, even when they were far, far from them. All that she could say for sure was that she had not known a moment's peace in recent days, and that she heard her daughter's voice calling to her when sleep fleetingly came.

She would tell that to him when she met him, in the

hope that he would understand. Even if he did not, she knew that he would help, for the girl was blood to him.

And if there is one thing that he understood, it was blood.

I parked in an alleyway about fifty feet from the house, then covered the rest of the distance on foot. I could see Jackie Garner hunched behind the wall bordering the property. He wore a black wool hat, a black jacket, and black jeans. His hands were uncovered, and his breath formed phantoms in the air. Beneath his jacket I made out the word "Sylvia" written on his T-shirt.

"New girlfriend?" I said.

Jackie pulled open his jacket so I could see the T-shirt more clearly. It read, "Tim 'The Maine-iac' Sylvia," a reference to one of our local-boys-made-good, and featured a poor caricature of the great man himself. In September 2002, Tim Sylvia, all six-eight and 260 pounds of him, became the first Mainer to compete in the Ultimate Fighting Championship, eventually going on to take the Heavyweight Championship title in Las Vegas in 2003, knocking down the undefeated champion, Ricco Rodriguez, with a right cross in the first round. "I hit him *hahd*," Sylvia told a post-match interviewer, making every Down-Easter with flattened vowel sounds feel instantly proud. Unfortunately, Sylvia tested positive for anabolic steroids after his first defense, against the six-eleven Gan "the Giant" McGee, and voluntarily surrendered his belt and title. I remembered Jackie telling me once that he'd attended the fight. Some of McGee's blood had landed on his jeans, and he now saved them for special wear.

"Nice," I said.

"I got a friend who makes them. I can let you have some cheap."

"I wouldn't take them any other way. In fact, I wouldn't take them at all."

Jackie was offended. For a guy who might have passed for Tim Sylvia's out-of-condition older brother, he was pretty sensitive.

"How many are there in the house?" I said, but his attention had already wandered onto another subject.

"Hey, we're dressed the same," he said.

"What?"

"We're dressed the same. Look: you got the hat, the same jacket, the jeans. Except you got gloves and I got this T-shirt, we could be twins."

Jackie Garner was a good guy, but I thought that he might be a little crazy. Someone once told me that a shell accidentally went off close to him when he was serving with the U.S. Army in Berlin just before the Wall came down. He was unconscious for a week, and for six months after he awoke he couldn't remember anything that happened later than 1983. Even though he was mostly recovered, there were still gaps in his memory, and he occasionally confused the guys at Bull Moose Music by asking for "new" CDs that were actually fifteen years old. The army pensioned him off, and since then he had become a body for hire. He knew about guns and surveillance, and he was strong. I'd seen him put down three guys in a bar fight, but that shell had definitely rattled something loose inside Jackie Garner's head. Sometimes he was almost childlike.

Like now.

"Jackie, this isn't a dance. It doesn't matter that we're dressed the same."

He shrugged and looked away. I could tell he was hurt again.

"I just thought it was funny, that's all," he said, all feigned indifference.

"Yeah, next time I'll call you first, ask you to help me pick out my wardrobe. Come on, Jackie, it's freezing. Let's get this over with."

"It's your call," he said, and it was.

I didn't usually take on bail skips. The smarter ones tended to head out of state, making for Canada or points south. Like most PIs, I had contacts at the banks and the phone companies, but I still didn't much care for the idea of tracking some lowlife over half the country in return for five percent of his bond, waiting for him to give himself away by accessing an automated teller or using his credit card to check into a motel.

This one was different. His name was David Torrans, and he had tried to steal my car to make his getaway from an attempted robbery at a gas station on Congress. My Mustang was parked in the lot beside the station, and Torrans had wrecked the ignition in a doomed effort to get it started after someone boxed in his own Chevy. The cops caught him two blocks away as he made his getaway on foot. Torrans had a string of minor convictions, but with the help of a quick-mouthed lawyer and a drowsy judge he made bail, although the judge, to his small credit, did set bail at $40,000 to ensure Torrans made it to trial, and ordered him to report daily to police headquarters in Portland. A bondsman named Lester Peets provided the coverage for the bond, and then Torrans skipped out on him. The reason for the skip was that a woman who had taken a knock on the head from Torrans during the attempted robbery subsequently lapsed into a coma in some kind of delayed reaction to the blow she had received, and now Torrans was facing some heavy felony charges, and maybe even life in jail if the woman died. Peets was about to go in the hole for the forty if Torrans didn't show, as well as sullying his good name and seriously irritating local law enforcement.

I took on the Torrans skip because I was aware of something about him that nobody else seemed to know: he was seeing a woman named Olivia Morales, who worked as a waitress in a Mexican restaurant in town and had a jealous ex-husband with a fuse so short he made volcanoes look stable. I had spotted her with Torrans after she finished her shift, two or three days before the robbery went down. Torrans was a "face" in the way that such men sometimes were in small cities like Portland. He had a reputation for violence, but until the robbery bust he had never actually been charged with a serious crime, more through good fortune than any great intelligence on his part. He was the kind of guy to whom other lowlifes deferred on the grounds that he had "smarts," but I had never subscribed to the theory of comparative intelligence where petty criminals were concerned, so the fact that Torrans's peers considered him a sharp operator didn't impress me much. Most criminals are kind of dumb, which is why they're criminals. If they weren't criminals they'd be doing something else to screw up people's lives, like running elections in Florida. The fact that Torrans had tried to hold up a gas station armed with only a pool ball in a sock indicated that he wasn't about to step up to the majors just yet. I'd heard rumors that he'd developed a taste for smack and OxyContin in recent months, and nothing will scramble a man's intelligence faster than the old "hillbilly heroin."

I figured that Torrans would get in touch with his girlfriend when he found himself in trouble. Men on the run tend to turn to the women who love them, whether mothers, wives, or girlfriends. If they have money, they'll then try to put some ground between themselves and those who are looking for them. Unfortunately, the kind of people who went to Lester Peets for their bond tended to be pretty desperate, and Torrans had probably used all of his available funds just rustling up his share of the money. For the moment, Torrans would be forced to stick close to home, keeping a low profile until another option presented itself. Olivia Morales seemed like the best bet.

Jackie Garner had good local knowledge, and I brought him in to stay close to Olivia Morales while I was taking care of other business. He watched her buying her food for the week, and noticed her including a carton of Luckys in her buy, even though she didn't appear to smoke. He followed her home to her rented house in Deering, and saw two men arrive a little later in a red Dodge van. When he described them to me over the phone, I recognized one as Torrans's half brother Garry, which was how, less than forty-eight hours after David Torrans had first gone off the radar, we found ourselves hunched behind a garden wall, about to make a decision on how to deal with him.

"We could call the cops," said Jackie, more for form's sake than anything else.

I thought of Lester Peets. He was the kind of guy who got beaten up by his imaginary friends as a child for cheating at games. If he could wheedle his way out of paying me my share of the bond, he would, which meant that I'd end up paying Jackie out of my own pocket. Calling the cops would give Lester just the excuse that he needed. Anyway, I wanted Torrans. Frankly, I didn't like him, and he'd screwed around with my car, but I was also forced to admit that I was anticipating the surge of adrenaline that taking him down would bring. I had been leading a quiet life these past few weeks. It was time for a little excitement.

"No, we need to do this ourselves," I said.

"You figure they have guns?"

"I don't know. Torrans has never used one in the past. He's small-time. His brother has no jacket, so he's an unknown quantity. As for the other guy, he could be Machine Gun Kelly and we wouldn't find out until we hit the door."

Jackie considered our situation for a time.

"Wait here," he said, then scuttled away. I heard the trunk of his car opening somewhere in the gloom. When he returned, he was clutching four cylinders, each about a foot in length and with the curved hook of a coat hanger attached to one end.

"What are they?" I asked.

He held up the two cylinders in his right hand—"Smoke grenades"—then the two in his left—"and tear gas. Ten parts glycerine to two parts sodium bisulfate. The smokes have ammonia added. They stink bad. All homemade."

I looked at the coat hanger, the mismatched tape, the scuffed pipes. "Wow, and they seem so well put together. Who'd have thought?"

Jackie's brow furrowed, and he considered the cylinders. He lifted his right hand. "Or maybe these are gas, and these are smoke. The trunk's a mess, so they've been rolling around some."

I looked at him. "Your mom must be so proud of you."

"Hey, she's never wanted for anything."

"Least of all munitions."

"So which should we use?"

Calling on Jackie Garner was looking less and less like a good idea, but the prospect of not having to hang around in the dark waiting for Torrans to show his face, or trying to gain access to the house and facing down three men and one woman, possibly armed, was certainly attractive.

"Smoke," I said at last. "I think gassing them may be illegal."

"I think smoking them is illegal too," Jackie pointed out.

"Okay, but it's probably less illegal than gas. Just give me one of those things."

He handed a cylinder over.

"You sure this is smoke?" I asked.

"Yeah, they weigh different. I was just kidding you. Pull the pin, then toss it as fast as you can. Oh, and don't jiggle it around too much. It's kind of volatile."

Far away from Portland, as her mother made her way through the streets of an unfamiliar city, Alice emerged from a deep sleep. She felt feverish and nauseous, and her limbs and joints ached. She had begged, again and again, for a little stuff just to keep her steady, but instead they had injected her with something that gave her terrible, frightening hallucinations in which inhuman creatures crowded around her, trying to carry her off into

17

the darkness. They didn't last long, but their effect was draining, and after the third or fourth dose she found that the hallucinations continued even after the drug should have worn off, so that the line between nightmare and reality became blurred. In the end, she pleaded with them to stop, and in return she told them all that she knew. After that, they changed the drug, and she slept dreamlessly. Since then, the hours had passed in a blur of needles and drugs and periodic sleep. Her hands had been tied to the frame of the bed, and her eyes had remained covered ever since she was brought to this place, wherever it was. She knew that there was more than one person responsible for keeping her here, for different voices had questioned her over the period of her captivity.

A door opened, and footsteps approached the bed.

"How are you feeling?" asked a male voice. It was one that she had heard before. It sounded almost tender. From his accent, she guessed that he was Mexican.

Alice tried to speak, but her throat was so terribly dry. A cup was placed to her lips, and the visitor trickled water into her mouth, supporting the back of her head with his hand so that she did not spill any upon herself. His hand felt very cool against her scalp.

"I'm sick," she said. The drugs had taken away some of the hunger, but her own addictions still gnawed at her.

"Yes, but soon you will not be so sick."

"Why are you doing this to me? Did he pay you to do this?"

Alice sensed puzzlement, maybe even alarm.

"Who do you mean?"

"My cousin. Did he pay you to take me away, to clean me up?"

A breath was released. "No."

"But why am I here? What do you want me to do?"

She remembered again being asked questions, but she had trouble recalling their substance, or the answers that she gave in reply. She feared, though, that she had said something bad, something that would get a friend into trouble, but she couldn't recall her friend's name, or even her face. She was so confused, so tired, so thirsty, so hungry.

The cool hand passed across her brow, brushing the damp hair from her skin, and she almost wept in gratitude for this brief moment of solicitude. Then the hand touched her cheek, and she felt fingers exploring the ridges of her eye sockets, testing her jaw, pressing into her bones. Alice was reminded of the actions of a surgeon, examining the patient before the cutting began, and she was afraid.

"You have nothing more to do," he said. "It's nearly over now."

As the taxi neared its destination, the woman understood the reasons for the driver's unhappiness. They had progressed uptown, the area growing less and less hospitable, until at last even the streetlights grew dark, their bulbs shot out and glass scattered on the sidewalk beneath. Some of the buildings looked like they might have been beautiful once, and it pained her to see them reduced to such squalor, almost as much as it hurt her to see young people reduced to living in such conditions, prowling the streets and preying on their own.

The taxi pulled up in front of a narrow doorway marked with the name of a hotel, and she paid the driver $22. If he was expecting a tip, he was now a disappointed man. She didn't have money to be giving people tips just for doing what they were supposed to do, but she did thank him. He didn't help her to get her bag from the trunk. He just popped it and let her do it herself, all the time looking uneasily at the young men who watched him from the street corners.

The hotel's sign promised TV, AC, and baths. A black clerk in a D^{12} T-shirt sat behind a Plexiglas screen inside, reading a college textbook. He handed her a registration card, took her cash for three nights, then gave her a key attached to half a brick by a length of thick chain.

"Got to leave the key with me when you go out," he told her.

The woman looked at the brick.

"Sure," she said. "I'll try to remember."

"You're on the fourth floor. Elevator's on the left."

The elevator smelled of fried food and human waste. The odor in her room was only marginally better. There were scorch marks on the thin carpet, big circular black burns that could not have come from cigarettes. A single iron bed stood against one wall, with a space between it and the other wall just large enough for a person to squeeze through. A radiator sulked coldly beneath a grimy window, a single battered chair beside it. There was a sink on the wall, and a tiny mirror above it. A TV was bolted to the upper right-hand corner of the room. She opened what appeared to be a closet and discovered instead a small toilet and a hole in the center of the floor to allow water from a shower head to drain away. In total, the bathroom was about nine feet square. As far as she could see, the only way to shower was to sit on the toilet, or to straddle it.

She set out her clothes on the bed, and placed her toothbrush and toiletries by the sink. She checked her watch. It was a little early. All that she knew about where she was going she had learned from a single cable TV show, but she guessed that things didn't start to get busy there until after dark.

She turned on the TV, lay on her bed, and watched game shows and comedies until the night drew in. Then she pulled on her overcoat, put some money in her pocket, and descended to the streets.

Two men came to Alice and injected her again. Within minutes her mind began to cloud. Her limbs felt heavy, and her head lolled to the right. Her blindfold was removed, and she knew that it was coming to an end. Once her vision had recovered, she could see that one of the men was small and wiry, with a gray pointed beard and thinning gray hair. His skin was tanned, and she guessed that this was the Mexican who had spoken to her in the past. The other was an enormously fat man with a belly that wobbled pendulously between his thighs, obscuring his groin. His green eyes were lost in folds of flesh, and there was dirt lodged in the pores of his skin. His neck was purple and swollen, and when he touched her, her skin prickled and burned.

They lifted her from her bed and placed her in a wheelchair, then wheeled her down a decaying hallway until she was brought at last to a white-tiled room with a drain in the floor. They transferred her to a wooden chair with leather straps to secure her hands and feet, and there they left her, facing her reflection in the long mirror on the wall. She barely recognized herself. A gray pallor hung behind her dark skin, as though her own features had been thinly overlaid on those of a white person. Her eyes were bloodshot, and there was dried blood at the corners of her mouth and upon her chin. She was wearing a white surgical gown, beneath which she was naked.

The room was startlingly clean and bright, and the fluorescent lights above were merciless in their exposition of her features, worn down by years of drugs and the demands of men. For a second, she believed that she was looking at her mother in the glass, and the resemblance made her eyes water.

"I'm sorry, Momma," she said. "I didn't mean no harm by it."

Her hearing became acute, a consequence of the drugs pumping through her system. Before her, her features began to swim, mutating, transforming. There were voices whispering around her. She tried to turn her head to follow them, but was unable to do so. Her paranoia grew.

Then the lights died, and she was in total darkness.

The woman hailed a cab, and told the driver where she wished to be taken. She had briefly considered taking public transport, but had made the decision that she would use it only during daylight hours. By night she would travel by taxi, despite the expense. After all, if something were to happen to her on the subway or while waiting for a bus before she spoke to *him*, then who would look for her daughter?

The cabdriver was a young man, and white. Most of the others were not white, from what she had seen earlier that evening. Few were even black. The races that drove the cabs here could be found only in big cities and foreign lands.

"Ma'am," the young man said, "are you sure that's where you want to go?"

"Yes," she said. "Take me to the Point."

"That's a rough area. You going to be long? You're not going to be long and I can wait for you, take you back here."

She didn't look like any hooker that he had ever seen, although he knew that the Point catered to all tastes. The cabdriver didn't like to think about what might happen to a nice gray-haired lady moving among the bottom dwellers of the Point.

"I will be some time," she said. "I don't know when I'll be coming back, but thank you for asking."

Feeling that he could do nothing more, the driver pulled into traffic and headed for Hunts Point.

He called himself G-Mack, and he was a playa. He dressed like a playa, because that was part of what being a playa was all about. He had the gold chains and the leather coat, beneath which he wore a tailored black vest over his bare upper body. His pants were cut wide at the thigh, narrowing down to cuffs so small he had trouble getting his feet through them. His cornrows were hidden beneath a wide-brimmed leather hat, and he kept a pair of cell phones on his belt. He carried no weapons, but there were guns close to hand. This was his patch, and these were his women.

He watched them now, their asses barely hidden beneath short black imitation-leather skirts, their titties busting out of their cheap bustier tops. He liked his women to dress alike, felt like it was kind of his brand, m'sayin? Anything worthwhile in this country had its own recognizable look, didn't matter you was buying it in Buttfreeze, Montana, or Asswipe, Arkansas. G-Mack didn't have as many girls as some, but then he was just beginning. He had big plans.

He watched Chantal, this tall black hooker with legs so thin he marveled at how they could support her body, teeter on her heels as she headed over to him.

"Whatchu got, baby?" he asked.

"Hunnerd."

"Hunnerd? You fuckin with me?"

"It's slow, baby. I ain't had but some blow jobs, and a nigga try to stiff me in the lot, makin like he goan pay me soon as I'm done, wastin my time. It's hard, baby."

G-Mack reached out for her face and held it tightly in his fingers.

"What'm I goan find and I take you down that alleyway and check you out, huh? I ain't goan find no hunnerd, am I? I goan find bills hidden in all them dark places, ain't I? You think I'm goan be gentle with you, huh, when I go lookin inside? You want me to do that?"

She shook her head in his grip. He released her, and watched as she reached under her skirt. Seconds later, her hand emerged with a plastic Baggie. He could see the notes inside.

"I'm goan let you get away with it this once, y'hear?" he said as he took the Baggie from her, holding it carefully with his fingernails so as not to sully his hands with the smell of her. She gave him the hundred from her handbag too. He raised his hand as if to strike her, then let it drop slowly to his side and smiled his best, most reassuring smile.

24

"That's just cause you new with me. But you fuck with me again, bitch, and I will fuck your shit up so bad you be bleeding for a week. Now get yo ass back out there."

Chantal nodded and sniffed. She stroked his coat with her right hand, rubbing at the lapel.

"Sorry, baby. I just—"

"It's done," said G-Mack. "We clear."

She nodded again, then turned away and headed back onto the street. G-Mack watched her go. She had maybe another five hours before things got quieter. He'd take her back to the crib then and show her what happened to bitches who fucked with the Mack, who tried to embarrass him by holding back on him. He wasn't about to discipline her on the street, because that would make him look bad. No, he'd deal with her in private.

That was the thing with these hos. You let one get away with something, and the next thing they were all holding out on you and then you weren't nothing better than a bitch yourself. They needed to be taught that lesson early on, else they weren't worth having around. Funny thing was, you fucked them up and they still stayed with you. You worked it right and they felt needed, like they was part of a family they'd never had. Like a good father, you disciplined them because you loved them. You could screw around on the ones who were sweet on you and they wouldn't say boo, because at least they knew the other whores you were seeing. In that sense, a pimp beat a square any day. It was all okay as long as you kept it in the family. They were your women, and you could do with them what you pleased once you gave them a sense of belonging, of being wanted. You had to get psychological with these bitches, had to know how to play the game.

"Excuse me," said a voice to his right.

He looked down to see a small black woman in an overcoat, her hand inside her bag. Her hair was gray, and she looked like she might break in two if the wind was strong enough.

"What you want, Grandma?" he said. "You a little old to be trickin."

If the woman understood the insult, she didn't let it know.

"I'm looking for somebody," she said, taking a photograph from her wallet, and G-Mack felt his heart sink.

The door to Alice's left opened, then closed again, but the lights in the corridor beyond had also been extinguished and she was unable to see who had entered. A stench assailed her nostrils, and she found herself retching. She could hear no footsteps, yet she was aware of a figure circling her, appraising her.

"Please," she said, and it took all of her strength just to speak. "Please. Whatever I done, I'm sorry for it. I won't tell nobody what happened. I don't even know where I am. Let me go, and I'll be a good girl, I promise."

The whispering grew louder now, and there was laughter intermingled with the voices. Then something touched her face, and her skin prickled and her mind was bombarded with images. She felt as though her memories were being ransacked, the details of her life briefly held up to the light and then discarded by the presence beside her. She saw her mother, her aunt, her grandmother . . .

A house full of women, set on a patch of land by the edge of a forest; a dead man lying in a casket, the women standing around him, none of them weeping. One of them reaches for the cotton sheet covering his head, and when it is removed he is revealed to be near faceless, his features destroyed by some terrible vengeance wrought upon him by another. In a corner stands a boy, tall for his age, dressed in a cheap hired suit, and she knows his name.

Louis.

"Louis," she whispered, and her voice seemed to echo around the tiled room. The presence beside her withdrew, but she could still hear its breathing. Its breath smelt of earth.

Earth, and burning.

"Louis," she repeated.

Closer than brother to me. Blood to me.

Help me.

Her hand was clasped in the hand of another, and she felt it being raised. It came to rest upon something ragged and ruined. She traced the lineaments of what once was a face: the eye sockets, now empty; the fragments of cartilage where once was a nose; a lipless gap for a mouth. The mouth opened, taking her fingers inside, then closed softly upon them, and she saw once again the figure in the casket, the man without a face, his head torn apart by the actions of—

"Louis."

She was crying now, crying for them both. The mouth upon her fingers was no longer soft. Teeth were erupting from the gums, flat yet sharp, and they tore into her hand.

This is not real. This is not real.

But the pain was real, and the presence was real.

And she called his name in her head once again—
Louis—as she began to die.

G-Mack kept his face turned from her, taking in his women, the cars, the streets, anything to divert his attention and force her to go elsewhere.

"Can't help you," he said. "Go call Five-O. They be dealin with missing persons."

"She worked here," said the woman. "The girl I'm looking for. She worked for you."

"Like I said, can't help you. You need to be movin on now, else you goan get into trouble. Nobody want to be answering yo questions. People here want to make money. This is a business. This like Mickey D's. It's all about the dollar."

"I can pay you," said the old woman.

She raised a pathetic handful of ragged bills.

"I don't want yo money," he said. "Get out of my face."

"Please," she said. "Just look at this photo."

She held up the picture of the young black woman.

G-Mack glanced at the photograph, then tried to look away as casually as he could, the sick feeling in his stomach growing suddenly stronger.

"Don't know her," said G-Mack.

"Maybe—"

"I *said* I ain't never seen her."

"But you didn't even look prop—"

And in his fear, G-Mack made his biggest mistake. He lashed out at her, catching her on the left cheek. She staggered back against the wall, a pale spot against her skin where his open hand had struck her.

"Get the fuck out of here," he said. "Don't you be comin round here no more."

The woman swallowed, and he could see the tears starting, but she tried to hold them back. Old bitch had some balls, he'd give her that. She replaced the photograph in her bag, then walked away. Across the street, G-Mack could see Chantal staring at him.

"The fuck you lookin at?" he shouted to her. He made a move toward her and she backed away, her body eventually obscured by a green Taurus that pulled up alongside her, the middle-aged business type inside easing down the window as he negotiated with her. When they'd agreed on a price, Chantal climbed in alongside him and they pulled off, headed for one of the lots off the main drag. That was another thing he'd have to talk about with the bitch: curiosity.

Jackie Garner was at one side of the window, and I was at the other. Using a little dentist's mirror I'd picked up, I'd seen two men watching TV in the living room. One of them was Torrans's brother Garry. The drapes on what I took to be a bedroom nearby were drawn, and I thought I could hear a man and a woman talking inside. I signaled to Jackie that he should stay where he was, then I moved to the bedroom window. Using the raised fingers of my right hand, I counted three, two, one, then hurled the smoke canister into the occupied bedroom. Jackie tossed his through the glass of the living room, then followed it with a second. Instantly noxious green fumes began to pour from the holes. We backed away, taking up positions in the shadows across from the front and back doors to the house. I could hear coughing and shouting inside, but

I could see nothing. Already, the smoke had entirely filled the living room. The stench was incredible, and even at a distance my eyes were stinging.

It wasn't just smoke. It was gas too.

The front door opened and two men spilled out into the yard. One of them had a gun in his hand. He fell to his knees on the grass and began to retch. Jackie came at him from out of nowhere, put one big foot on the gun hand, and then kicked him hard with the other. The other man, Garry Torrans, just lay on the ground, the heels of his hands pressed to his eyes.

Seconds later, the back door opened and Olivia Morales stumbled out. David Torrans was close behind her. He was shirtless, and a wet towel was pressed to his face. Once he was away from the house he discarded it and made a break for the next yard. His eyes were red and streaming, but he wasn't suffering as badly as the others. He had almost made it to the wall when I emerged from the darkness and swept his feet from under him. He landed hard on his back, the wind abruptly knocked out of him by the impact. He lay there, staring up at me, tears rolling down his cheeks.

"Who are you?" he said.

"My name's Parker," I said.

"You gassed us." He vomited the words out.

"You tried to steal my car."

"Yeah, but . . . you *gassed* us. What kind of sonofabitch gasses someone?"

Jackie Garner shambled across the lawn. Behind him, I could see Garry and the other man lying on the ground, their hands and legs bound with plastic ties. Torrans's head turned to take in the new arrival.

"This kind," I told him.

Jackie shrugged.

"Sorry," he said to Torrans. "At least I know it works."

G-Mack lit a cigarette and noticed that his hands were shaking. He didn't want to think about the girl in the picture. She was gone, and G-Mack didn't never want to see the men who took her again. They found out someone was asking after her, and then another pimp would be taking care of the Mack's team, because the Mack would be dead.

The Mack didn't know it, but he had only days left to live.

He should never have hit the woman.

And in the white-tiled room, Alice, now torn and ruined, prepared to breathe her last. The mouth of another touched her lips, waiting. He could sense it coming, could taste its sweetness. The woman shuddered, then grew limp. He felt her spirit enter him, and a new voice was added to the great chorus within.

2

The days are like leaves, waiting to fall.

The past lies in the shadows of our lives. It is endlessly patient, secure in the knowledge that all we have done, and all that we have failed to do, must surely return to haunt us in the end. When I was young, I cast each day aside unthinkingly, like dandelion seeds committed to the wind, floating harmlessly from the hands of a boy and vanishing over his shoulder as he moved onward along the path toward the sunset, and home. Nothing was to be regretted, for there were more days to come. Slights and injuries would be forgotten, hurts would be forgiven, and there was radiance enough in the world to light the days that followed.

Now, as I look back over my shoulder at the path that I have taken, I can see that it has become tangled and obscured by undergrowth, where the seeds of past actions and half-acknowledged sins have taken root. Another shadows me along the path. She has no name, but she looks like Susan, my dead wife; and Jennifer, my first daughter, who was killed beside her in our little house in New York, walks with her.

For a time I wished that I had died with them. Sometimes that regret returns.

I move more slowly through life now, and the growth is catching up with me. There are briars around my ankles, weeds brush my fingertips as I walk, and the ground beneath my feet crackles with the fallen leaves of half-dead days.

The past is waiting for me, a monster of my own creation.

The past is waiting for us all.

I awoke to darkness, with dawn impending. Beside me, Rachel slept, unknowing. In a small room next to ours, our infant daughter rested. We had made this place together. It was supposed to be a safe haven, but what I saw around me was no longer our home. It was some composite, a collision of remembered places. This was the bed that Rachel and I chose, yet it stood now not in a bedroom overlooking the Scarborough marshes but in an urban landscape. I could hear street voices raised, and sirens crying in the distance. There was a dresser from my parents' house, and on it lay my dead wife's cosmetics. I could see a brush on the cabinet to my left, over Rachel's sleeping head. Her hair is red. The hairs caught in the brush were blond.

I rose. I entered a hallway in Maine, and descended stairs in New York. In the living room, she waited. Beyond the window, the marshes shone with silver, incandescent with moonlight. Shadows moved across the waters, although there was a cloudless night sky above. The shapes drifted endlessly east, until at last they were swallowed up by the waiting ocean beyond. There was no traffic now, and no sounds of the city broke the fragile quiet of the night. All was stillness, but for the shadows on the marsh.

Susan sat by the window, her back to me, her hair tied with an aquamarine bow. She stared through the glass at a little girl who skipped on the lawn. Her hair was like her mother's. Her head was down as she counted her steps.

And then my dead wife spoke.

You have forgotten us.

No, I have not forgotten.

Then who is that who sleeps beside you now, in the place where I once slept? Who is it that holds you in the night? Who is it that has borne you a child? How can you say that you have not forgotten, when the scent of her is upon you?

I am here. You are here. I cannot forget.

You cannot love two women with all of your heart. One of us must be lost to you. Is it not true that you no longer think of us in the silences between every heartbeat? Are there not times when we are absent from your thoughts while you twine yourself in her arms?

She spit the words, and the power of her anger sprayed blood upon the glass. Outside, the child stopped her skipping and stared at me through the pane. The darkness obscured her face, and I was grateful.

She was your child.

She will always be my child. In this world or the next, she will always be mine.

We will not go away. We will not disappear. We refuse to leave you. You will remember us. You will not forget.

And she turned, and once again I saw her ruined face, and the empty sockets of her eyes, and the memory of the agonies that she endured in my name were brought back to me with such force that I spasmed, my limbs extending, my back arching with such force that I heard the vertebrae crack. I woke suddenly with my arms curled around my chest, hands upon my skin and hair, my mouth open in agony, and Rachel was holding me and whispering — "Hush, hush" — and my new daughter was crying in the voice of the old, and the world was a place that the dead chose not to leave, for to leave is to be forgotten, and they will not be forgotten.

Rachel stroked my hair, calming me, then went to attend to our child. I listened to her cooing to the infant, walking with her in her arms until the tears ceased. She so rarely cried, this little girl, our Samantha. She was so quiet. She was not like the one that was lost, and yet I sometimes saw a little of Jennifer in her face, even in her first months. Sometimes, too, I thought I caught the ghost of Susan in her features, but that could not be.

I closed my eyes. I would not forget. Their names were written upon my heart, along with those of so many others: those who once were lost, and those whom I had failed to find; those who trusted me, and those who stood against me; those who died at my hand, and those who died at the hands of others. Each name was written, carved with a blade upon my flesh, name upon name, tangled one unto another, yet each clearly legible, each subtly engraved upon this great palimpsest of the heart.

I would not forget.

They would not let me forget.

The visiting priest at Saint Maximilian Kolbe Catholic Church struggled to articulate his dismay at what he was seeing.

"What . . . what is he *wearing*?"

The object of his dismay was a diminutive ex-burglar, dressed in a suit that appeared to be made from some form of NASA-endorsed synthetic material. To say that it shimmered as its wearer moved was to underestimate its capacity for distorting light. This suit shone like some bright new star, embracing every available color in the spectrum, and a couple more that the Creator Himself had presumably passed over on the grounds of good taste. If the Tin Man from *The Wizard of Oz* had opted for a makeover at a car valeting service, he would have emerged looking something like Angel.

"It seems to be made of some kind of metal," said the priest. He was squinting slightly.

"It's also reflective," I added.

"It *is*," said the priest. He sounded almost impressed, in a confused way. "I don't think I've ever seen anything quite like it before. Is he, er, a friend of yours?"

I tried to keep the vague sense of embarrassment out of my voice.

"He's one of the godparents."

There was a noticeable pause. The visiting priest was a missionary, home on leave from Southeast Asia. He had probably seen a great deal in his time. It was flattering, in a way, to think that it had taken a baptism in southern Maine to render him speechless.

"Perhaps we should keep him away from naked flames," said the priest, once he had given the implications some thought.

"That might be wise."

"He will have to hold a candle, of course, but I'll ask him to keep it outstretched. That should be all right. And the godmother?"

Now it was my turn to pause before continuing.

"That's where things get complicated. See the gentleman standing close by him?"

Beside Angel, and towering at least a foot above him, was his partner, Louis. One might have described Louis as a Log Cabin Republican, except that any self-respecting Log Cabin Republican would have bolted the doors, pulled the shutters, and waited for the cavalry to arrive rather than admit this man to his company. He was wearing a dark blue suit and sunglasses, but even with the shades on he seemed to be trying hard not to look directly at his significant other. In fact, he was doing a pretty good impression of a man without a significant other at all, hampered only by the fact that Angel insisted on following him around and talking to him occasionally.

"The tall gentleman? He seems a little out of place."

It was an astute observation. Louis was fastidiously turned out, as always, and apart from his height and his color there was little about his physical appearance that would seem to invite such a comment. Yet somehow he radiated difference, and a vague sense of potential threat.

"Well, I guess he would be a godfather too."

"Two godfathers?"

"And a godmother: my partner's sister. She's outside somewhere."

The priest did a little soft-shoe shuffle to emphasize his discomfort.

"It's most unusual."

"I know," I said, "but then, they're unusual people."

It was late January, and there was still snow on sheltered ground. Two days earlier, I had driven down to New Hampshire to buy cheap booze in the state liquor store in preparation for the celebrations after the christening.

When I was done, I walked for a time by the Piscatqua River, the ice still a foot thick near the shore but webbed by cracks. The center was free of encumbrance, though, and the water flowed slowly and steadily toward the sea. I walked against the current, following a wooded berm, thick with fir, that the river had created over time, cutting off a patch of bog land where early-budding blueberry and blackberry, and gray black winterberry and tan winter maleberry, coexisted with spruce and larch and rhodora. At last I came to the floating area of the bog, all green and purple where the sphagnum moss was interwoven with cranberry vines. I plucked a berry, sweetened by the frost, and placed it between my teeth. When I bit down, the taste of the juice filled my mouth. I found a tree trunk, long fallen and now gray and rotted, and sat upon it. Spring was coming, and with it the long, slow thaw. There would be new leaves, and new life.

But I have always been a winter person. Now, more than ever before, I desired to remain frozen amid snow and ice, cocooned and unchanging. I thought of Rachel and my daughter, Sam, and those others who had gone before them. Life slows in winter, but now I wanted it to cease its forward momentum entirely, except for we three. If I could hold us here, wrapped all in white, then perhaps everything would be fine. If the days advanced only for us, then no ill could come. No strangers would arrive at our door and no demands would be made upon us other than those elemental things that we required from one another, and that we freely gave in return.

Yet even here, amid the silence of the winter woods and the moss-covered water, life went on, a hidden, teeming existence masked by snow and ice. The still-ness was a ruse, an illusion, fooling only those who were unwilling or unable to look closer and see what lay beneath. Time and life moved inexorably forward. Already, it was growing dark around me. Soon it would be night, and then they would come again.

They were visiting more frequently, the little girl who was almost my daughter, and her mother who was not quite my wife. Their voices were growing more insis-tent, the memory of them in this life becoming increas-ingly polluted by the forms that they had taken in the next. In the beginning, when first they came, I could not tell what they were. I thought them phantasms of grief, a product of my troubled, guilty mind, but grad-ually they assumed a kind of reality. I did not grow used to their presence, but I learned to accept it. Whether real or imagined, they still symbolized a love that I once felt, and continued to feel. But now they were becom-ing something different, and their love was whispered through bared teeth.

We will not be forgotten.

All was coming apart around me, and I did not know what to do, so I sat instead among snow and ice on a rotted tree trunk, and willed clocks to stop.

It was warmer than it had been in many days. Rachel was standing outside the church, holding Sam in her arms. Her mother, Joan, was beside her. Our daughter was wrapped in white, her eyes tightly closed, as though she were troubled in her sleep. The sky was clear blue, and the winter sunlight shone coldly upon Black Point. Our friends and neighbors were scattered before us, some talking, smoking. Most had dressed up for the occasion, happy for an excuse to break out some color-ful clothes in winter. I nodded greetings to a few people, then joined Rachel and Joan.

As I approached, Sam woke and waved her arms. She yawned, looked blearily about, then decided there was nothing important enough to keep her from another nap. Joan tucked the white shawl under Sam's chin to keep out the cold. She was a small, stout woman who wore minimal makeup and kept her silver hair cut short against her skull. After meeting her for the first time that morning, Louis had suggested that she was trying to get in touch with her inner lesbian. I advised him to keep those opinions to himself, or else Joan Wolfe would try to get in touch with Louis's inner gay man by reaching into his chest and tearing his heart out. She and I got on okay, most of the time, but I knew that she worried about the safety of her daughter and her new grandchild, and this translated into a distance between us. For me it was like being within sight of a warm, friendly place that could be reached only by traversing a frozen lake. I accepted that Joan had cause to feel concerned because of things that had happened in the past, but that didn't make her implicit disap-proval of me any easier to bear. Still, compared to my relations with Rachel's father, Joan and I were bosom buddies. Frank Wolfe, once he had a couple of drinks inside him, felt compelled to end most of our encoun-ters with the words "You know, if anything ever happens to my daughter . . ."

Rachel was wearing a light blue dress, plain and unadorned. There were wrinkles on the back of the dress, and a thread hung loose from the seam. She looked tired and distracted.

"I can take her, if you like," I said.

"No, she's fine."

The words came out too quickly. I felt like I'd been pushed hard in the chest and forced to take a step back. I looked at Joan. After a couple of seconds, she moved away and went to join Rachel's younger sister, Pam, who was smoking a cigarette and flirting with a group of admiring locals.

"I know she is," I said quietly. "It's you I'm concerned about."

Rachel leaned against me for a moment and then, almost as if she were counting the seconds until she could put space between us once more, broke the contact.

"I just want this to be done," she said. "I want all of these people to be gone."

We hadn't invited very many people to the christening. Angel and Louis were present, of course, and Walter and Lee Cole had come up from New York. Apart from them, the bulk of the little group was made up of Rachel's immediate family and some of our friends from Portland and Scarborough. All told, there were twenty-five or thirty people present, no more, and most would come back to our house after the ceremony. Usually, Rachel would have reveled in such company, but since Sam's birth she had grown increasingly insular, withdrawing even from me. I tried to recall the early days of Jennifer's life, before she and her mother were taken from me, and although Jennifer had been as raucous as Sam was quiet, I could not remember encountering the kind of difficulties that now troubled Rachel and me. True, it was natural that Sam should be the focus of Rachel's energy and attention. I tried to help her in every way that I could, and had cut back on my work so that I could take on some of the burden of caring for her and give Rachel a little time to herself, if she chose. Instead, she seemed almost to resent my presence, and with the arrival of Angel and Louis that morning it appeared that the tension between us had increased exponentially.

"I can tell them you're feeling ill," I said. "You could just take Sam upstairs to our room later and get away from everyone. They'll understand."

She shook her head. "It's not that. I want *them* gone. Do *you* understand?"

And in truth, I did not, not then.

The woman arrived at the auto shop early that morning. It stood on the verge of an area that, if it was not quite gentrified, then at least was no longer mugging the gentry. She had taken the subway to Queens and been forced to change trains twice, having mistaken the number of the subway line. The streets were quieter today, although she still could see little beauty in this place. There was bruising to her face, and her left eye hurt every time she blinked.

After the young man had struck her, she had taken a moment to recover her composure against the wall of an alleyway. It was not the first time that a man had raised his hand to her, but never before had she endured a blow from a stranger, and one half her age. The experience left her humiliated and angry, and in the minutes that followed she wished, perhaps for the first time ever, that Louis were near at that moment, that she could reach out and tell him what had occurred, and watch as he humiliated the pimp in turn. In the darkness of the alleyway, she placed her hands on her knees and lowered her head. She felt like she was about to vomit. Her hands were shaking, and there was a sheen of sweat upon her face. She closed her eyes and began to pray until the feelings of rage went away, and as they departed her hands grew still and her skin became cool once again.

She heard a woman moan close by, and a man spoke harsh words to her. She looked to her right and saw shapes moving rhythmically beside some trash bags. Cars drifted slowly by, their windows lowered, the drivers' faces rendered cruel and hungry by streetlights and headlamps. A tall white girl teetered on pink heels, her body barely concealed by white lingerie. Beside her, a black woman leaned against the hood of a car, her hands splayed upon the metal, her buttocks raised to attract the attention of passing men. Close by, the rhythmic thrusting grew faster, and the woman's moans increased in pitch, false and empty, before finally fading entirely. Seconds later, she heard footsteps. The man emerged from the shadows first. He was young and white, and well dressed. His tie was askew, and he was running his hands through his hair to tidy it after his exertions. She smelled alcohol, and a trace of cheap perfume. He barely glanced at the woman against the wall as he turned onto the street.

He was followed, after a time, by a little white girl. She looked barely old enough to drive a car, yet here she was, dressed in a black miniskirt and a cutoff top, her heels adding two inches to her diminutive stature, her dark hair cut in a bob, and her delicate features obscured by crudely applied cosmetics. She seemed to be having trouble walking, as though she were in some pain. She had almost passed the black woman by when a hand reached out, not touching her, merely imploring her to stop.

"Excuse me, miss," she said.

The young girl paused. Her eyes were very large and blue, but already the older woman could see the light dying inside. "I can't give you money," she said.

"I don't want money. I have a picture. I'd like you to take a look at it, maybe tell me if you know the girl."

She reached into her bag and removed the photograph of her daughter. After some hesistation, the girl took it. She looked at it for a time, then handed it back.

"She's gone," she said.

The older woman stepped slowly forward. She didn't want to alarm the girl. "You know her?"

"Not really. I saw her around some, but she went away a day or two after I started. I heard her street name was LaShan, but I don't think that was her real name."

"No, her name is Alice."

"Are you her mother?"

"Yes."

"She seemed nice."

"She is."

"She had a friend. Her name was Sereta."

"Do you know where I can find her friend?"

The girl shook her head.

"She left too. I wish I could tell you more, but I can't. I got to go."

Before the woman could stop her, she had stepped out into the stream and was taken up by the flow. She followed her, watching her go. She saw the girl cross the street and hand some money over to the young black man who had hit her, then take up position once again with the other women lining the street.

Where were the police? she wondered. How could they let this continue on their doorsteps, this exploitation, this suffering? How could they allow a little girl like that to be used, to be killed slowly from the inside out? And if they could permit this to happen, how much could they care about a lost black girl who had fallen into this river of human misery and was dragged down by its currents?

She was a fool to believe that she could come to this strange city and find her daughter alone. She had called the police first, of course, before she had even decided to come north, and had given them what details she could over the phone. They had advised her to file a report in person once she came to the city, and she had done so the previous day. She had watched the policeman's expression alter slightly as she spoke to him of her child's circumstances. To him, her daughter was another addict drifting through a dangerous life. Perhaps he meant what he said when he told her he would do his best for her, but she knew that the disappearance of her little girl was not as important as a missing white girl, maybe one with money or influence, or simply one without puncture holes in the flesh between her fingers and toes. She had considered returning to the police that morning, and describing the man who had struck her and the young prostitute with whom she had spoken, but she believed that it would make little difference if she did. The time for the police was gone now. She needed someone for whom her daughter would be a priority, not merely another name on an ever-growing list of the disappeared.

Although it was Sunday, the main door to the auto

shop was half raised, and music was playing inside. The woman crouched down and edged her way into the dimly lit interior. A thin man in coveralls was bent over the interior of a big foreign car. His name was Arno. Beside him, Tony Bennett's voice came from the cheap speakers of a small, battered radio.

"Hello?" said the woman.

Arno turned his head, although his hands remained hidden in the workings of the engine.

"I'm sorry, lady, we're closed," he said.

He knew he should have pulled the shutter down fully, but he liked to let a little air in, and anyway he didn't expect to be here for too long. The Audi was due to be picked up first thing Monday morning, and another hour or two would see it done.

"I'm looking for someone," she said.

"The boss ain't around."

As the woman approached, he saw the swelling on her face. He wiped his hands on a rag and abandoned the car for the time being.

"Hey, you okay? What happened to your face?"

The woman was close to him now. She was hiding her distress and her fear, but the mechanic could see it in her eyes, like a scared child peering out of twin windows.

"I'm looking for someone," she repeated. "He gave me this."

She removed her wallet from her bag and carefully extracted a card from its folds. The card was slightly yellowed at the edges, but apart from this natural aging it was in pristine condition. The mechanic reckoned that it had been kept safe for a long time, just in case it was ever needed.

Arno took the card. There was no name upon it, only an illustration. It depicted a serpent being trampled beneath the feet of an armored angel. The angel had a lance in his right hand, and its point had pierced the reptile. Dark blood flowed from the wound. On the back of the card was the number of a discreet answering service. Beside it was a single letter *L,* written in black ink, along with the handwritten address of the auto shop in which they now stood.

Few people had such cards in their possession, and the mechanic had never seen a card with the address of the shop added by hand. The letter *L* was the clincher. In effect, this was an "access all areas" pass, a request — no, an *order* — to extend any and all help to the person who possessed it.

"Did you call the number?" he asked.

"I don't want to talk to him through no service. I want to see him."

"He's not here. He's out of town."

"Where?"

The mechanic hesitated before answering.

"Maine."

"I'd be grateful to you if you'd give me the address of where he's at."

Arno walked to the cluttered office that stood to the left of the main work area. He flicked through the address book until he came to the entry he needed, then took a piece of paper and transferred the relevant details to it. He folded the paper and gave it to the woman.

"You want me to call him for you, let him know you're on your way?"

"Thank you, but no."

"You got a car?"

She shook her head.

"I took the subway out here."

"You know how you're going to get up to Maine?"

"Not yet. Bus, I guess."

Arno put on his jacket and removed a set of keys from his pocket.

"I'll give you a ride to Port Authority, see you safely onto the bus."

For the first time, the woman smiled.

"Thank you, I'd appreciate that."

Arno looked at her. Gently, he touched her face, examining the bruise.

"I got something for that, if it's hurting you."

"I'll be fine," she said.

He nodded.

The man who did this to you is in a lot of trouble. The man who did this to you won't live out the week.

"Let's go, then. We got time, I'll buy you a cup of coffee and a muffin for the trip."

Dead man. He's a dead man.

We were gathered around the font in a small group, the other guests standing in the pews a little distance away. The priest had made his introductions, and now we were approaching the meat of the ceremony.

"Do you reject Satan, and all his empty promises?" asked the priest.

He waited. There was no reply. Rachel coughed discreetly. Angel appeared to have found something interesting to look at down on the floor. Louis remained impassive. He had removed his shades and was focused on a point just above my left shoulder.

"You're speaking for Sam," I whispered to Angel. "He doesn't mean you."

Realization dawned like morning light on an arid desert.

"Oh, okay then," said Angel enthusiastically. "Sure. Absolutely. Rejected."

"Amen," said Louis.

The priest looked confused.

"That would be a yes," I told him.

"Right," he said, as if to reassure himself. "Good."

Rachel shot daggers at Angel.

"What?" he asked. He raised his hands in a "What did I do?" gesture. Some wax from the candle dripped onto the sleeve of his jacket. A faintly acrid smell arose.

"Awwww," said Angel. "First time I've worn it, too."

Rachel moved from daggers to swords.

"You open your mouth again, and you'll be buried in that suit," she said.

Angel went quiet. All things considered, it was the smartest move.

The woman was seated by a window on the right side of the bus. In one day, she was passing through more states than she had previously visited in her entire life. The bus pulled into South Station in Boston. Now, with thirty minutes to spare, she wandered down to the Amtrak concourse and bought herself a cup of coffee and a Danish. Both were expensive, and she looked with dismay at the little wad of bills in her purse, adorned by a smattering of change, but she was hungry, even after the muffin the man from the garage had so kindly bought for her. She took a seat and watched the people go by, the businessmen in their suits, the harried mothers with their children. She watched the arrivals and departures change, the names clicking rapidly across the big board above her head. The trains on the platform were silver and sleek. A young black woman took a seat beside her and opened a newspaper. Her suit was neatly tailored, and her hair was cut very short. A brown leather attaché case stood at her feet, and she wore a small matching purse upon her shoulder. A diamond engagement ring gleamed upon her left hand.

I have a daughter your age, thought the old woman, but she will never be like you. She will never wear a tailored suit, or read what you read, and no man will ever give her a ring like the one that you wear. She is a lost soul, a troubled soul, but I love her, and she is mine. The man who had her upon me is gone now. He is dead, and he is no loss to the world. They would call what he did to me rape, I suppose, for I surrendered to him out of fear. We were all afraid of him, and of what he could do. We believed that he had killed my older sister, for she went away with him and did not return home alive, and when he came back he took me in her place.

But he died for what he did, and he died badly. They asked us if we wanted them to rebuild his face, if we wanted to keep the casket open for a viewing. We told them to leave him as he was found, and to bury him in a pine box with ropes for handles. They marked his grave with a wooden cross, but on the night he was buried I went to the place where he lay and I took the cross away, and I burned it in the hope that he would be forgotten. But I gave birth to his child, and I loved her even though there was something of him in her. Perhaps she never had a chance, cursed with a father like that. He tainted her, polluting her from the very moment she was born, the seed of her destruction contained within his own. She was always a sad child, an angry child, yet how could she leave us for that other life? How could she find peace in such a city, among men who would use her for money, who would feed her drugs and alcohol to keep her pliant? How could we have let that happen to her?

And the boy — no, the man, for that is what he is now — tried to look out for her, but he gave up on her, and now she is gone. My daughter is gone, and nobody yet cares enough about her to seek her out, nobody except me. But I will make them care. She is mine, and I will bring her back. He will help me, for she is blood to him, and he owes her a blood debt.

He killed her father. Now he will bring her back to this life, and to me.

The guests were scattered through the living room and the kitchen. Some had found their way outside and were sitting beneath the bare trees in our yard, wearing their coats and enjoying the open air as they drank beer and wine and ate hot food from paper plates. Angel and Louis, as always, were slightly apart from the rest, occupying a stone bench that looked out over the marshes. Our Lab retriever, Walter, lay at their feet, Angel's fingers gently stroking his head. I went over to join them, checking as I went that nobody lacked for food and drink.

"You want to hear a joke?" said Angel. "There's this duck on a pond, and he's getting really pissed at this other duck who's coming on to his girl, so he decides to hire an assassin duck to bump him off."

Louis breathed out loudly through his nose with a

sound like gas leaking under near-unendurable pressure. Angel ignored him.

"So the assassin arrives, and the duck meets him in some reeds. The assassin tells him that it will cost five pieces of bread to kill the target, payable after the deed is done. The duck tells him that's fine, and the assassin says, 'So, do you want me to send you the body?' And the duck says, 'No, just send me the bill.'"

There was silence.

"Bill," said Angel again. "You know, it's—"

"I got a joke," said Louis.

We both looked at him in surprise.

"You hear the one about the dead irritating guy in the cheap suit?"

We waited.

"That's it," said Louis.

"That's not funny," said Angel.

"Makes me laugh," said Louis.

A man touched me on the arm, and I found Walter Cole standing beside me. He was retired now, but he had taught me much of what I knew when I was a cop. Our bad days were far behind us, and he had come to an accommodation with what I was, and with what I was capable of doing. I left Angel and Louis to bicker, and walked back to the house with Walter.

"About that dog," he said.

"He's a good dog," I said. "Not smart, but loyal."

"I'm not looking to give him a job. You called him Walter."

"I like the name."

"You named your *dog* after me?"

"I thought you'd be flattered. Anyway, nobody needs

to know. It's not as if he looks like you. He has more hair, for a start."

"Oh, that's very funny. Even the dog is funnier than you."

We entered the kitchen, and Walter retrieved a bottle of Sebago ale from the fridge. I didn't offer him a glass. I knew that he preferred to drink it by the neck when he could, which meant anytime he was out of his wife's sight. Outside, I saw Rachel talking with Pam. Her sister was smaller than Rachel, and spikier, which was saying something. Whenever I hugged her, I expected to be pierced by spines. Sam was asleep in an upstairs room. Rachel's mother was keeping an eye on her.

Walter saw me follow Rachel's progress through the garden.

"How are you two doing?" asked Walter.

"Three of us," I reminded him. "We're doing okay, I guess."

"It's hard, when there's a new baby in a house."

"I know. I remember."

Walter's hand rose slightly. He seemed on the verge of touching my shoulder, until his hand slowly fell away.

"I'm sorry," he said, instead. "It's not that I forget them. I don't know what it is exactly. Sometimes it seems like another life, another time. Does that make sense?"

"Yes," I said. "I know just what you mean."

There was a breeze blowing, and it caused the rope swing on the oak tree to move in a slow arc, as though an unseen child were playing upon it. I could see the channels shining in the marshes beyond, intersecting in places as they carved their paths through the reeds, the waters of one intermingling with those of another, each changed irrevocably by the meeting. Lives were like that: when their paths crossed, they emerged altered forever by the encounter, sometimes in small, almost invisible ways, and other times so profoundly that nothing that followed could ever be the same again. The residue of other lives infects us, and we in turn pass it on to those whom we later meet.

"I think she worries," I said.

"About what?"

"About us. About me. She's risked so much, and she's been hurt for it. She doesn't want to be afraid anymore, but she is. She's afraid for us, and she's afraid for Sam."

"You've talked about it?"

"No, not really."

"Maybe it's time, before things get worse."

Right then, I found it hard to imagine how much worse circumstances could get. I hated these unspoken tensions between Rachel and me. I loved her, and I needed her, but I was angry too. The burden of blame slipped too easily onto my shoulders these days. I was tired of carrying it.

"Doing much work?" asked Walter, changing the subject.

"Some," I said.

"Anything interesting?"

"I don't think so. You never can tell, but I've tried to be selective. It's pretty straightforward stuff. I've been offered more . . . *complicated* matters, but I've turned them down. I won't bring harm upon them, but—"

I stopped. Walter waited.

"Go on."

I shook my head. Lee, Walter's wife, entered the

kitchen. She scowled as she saw him drinking from the bottle.

"I turn my back for five minutes, and you abandon all civilized behavior," she said, but she was smiling as she spoke. "You'll be drinking out of the toilet bowl next."

Walter hugged her to him.

"You know," she said, "they named the dog after you. Maybe that's why. Anyway, lots of people want to meet you because of it. The *dog* wants to meet you."

Walter scowled as she grabbed him by the hand and pulled him toward the garden.

"Are you coming outside?" she asked me.

"In a moment," I said.

I watched them cross the lawn. Rachel waved to them, and they went to join her. Her eyes met mine, and she gave me a small smile. I raised my hand, then touched it to the glass, my fingers dwarfing her face.

I won't bring harm upon you and our daughter, not by my choosing, yet still it comes. That's what I'm afraid of. It has found me before, and it will find me again. I am a danger to you, and to our child, and I think you know that.

We are coming apart.

I love you, but we are coming apart.

The day drew on. People left, and others, who were unable to make the ceremony, took their places. As the light faded, Angel and Louis were no longer speaking, and were more obviously maintaining their distance from all that was taking place around them than before. Both kept their eyes fixed on the road that wound from Route 1 to the coast. Between them lay a cell phone.

Arno had called them earlier that day, as soon as he had seen the woman safely onto the Greyhound bus from New York.

"She didn't leave a name," he told Louis, his voice crackling slightly over the connection.

"I know who she is," said Louis. "You did right to call."

Now there were lights on the road. I joined them where they sat, leaning slightly on the back of the bench. Together we watched the cab cross the bridge over the marsh, the sunlight gleaming on the waters, the car's progress reflected in their depths. There was a tugging at my stomach, and my head felt as though hands were pressed hard against my temples. I could see Rachel standing unmoving among the guests. She too was watching the approaching car. Louis rose as it turned into the driveway of the house.

"This isn't about you," he said. "You got no reason to be concerned."

And I wondered at what he had brought to my house.

I followed them through the open gate at the end of the yard. Angel stayed back as Louis walked to the cab and opened the door. A woman emerged, a large, multi-colored bag clasped in her hands. She was smaller than Louis by perhaps eighteen inches, and probably no more than a decade or so older than he, although her face bore the marks of a difficult life, and she wore her worries like a veil across her features. I imagined that she had been beautiful when she was younger. There was little of that physical beauty left now, but there was an inner strength to her that shone brightly from her eyes. I could see some bruising to her face. It looked very recent.

She stood close to Louis and gazed up at him with

something almost like love, then slapped him hard across the left cheek with her right hand.

"She's gone," she said. "You were supposed to look out for her, but now she's gone."

And she began to cry as he took her in his arms, and his body shook with the force of her sobs.

This is the story of Alice, who fell down a rabbit hole and never came back.

Martha was Louis's aunt. A man named Deeber, now dead, had fathered a child upon her, a girl. They called her Alice, and they loved her, but she was never a happy child. She rebeled against the company of women, and turned instead to men. They told her that she was beautiful, for she was, but she was young and angry. Something gnawed deep inside her, its hunger exacerbated by the actions of the women who had loved her and cared for her. They had told her that her father was dead, but it was only through others that she learned of the kind of man he was, and the manner in which he had left this world. Nobody knew who was responsible for his death, but there were rumors, hints that the neatly dressed black women in the house with the pretty garden had colluded in his killing along with her cousin, the boy called Louis.

Alice rebeled against them and all that they represented: love, security, the bonds of family. She was drawn to a bad crowd, and left the safety of her mother's home. She drank, smoked some dope, became a casual user of harder drugs, and then an addict. She drifted from the places that she knew, and went to live in a tin-roofed shack at the edge of a dark forest, where men came to take turns with her. She was paid in narcotics, although their value was far less than what the johns had paid to sleep with her, and so the bonds around her tightened. Slowly she began to lose herself, the combination of sex and drugs acting like a cancer, eating away at all that she truly was, so that she became at last their creature even as she tried to convince herself that this was only a temporary aberration, a fleeting thing to help her deal with the sense of hurt and betrayal that she felt.

It was early one Sunday morning, and she was lying on a bare cot, naked but for a pair of cheap plastic shoes. She stank of men, and the hunger was upon her. Her head hurt, and the bones in her arms and legs ached. Two other women slept nearby, the entrance to their rooms blocked by blankets hung over ropes. A small window allowed the morning light to seep into her room, sullied by the dirt upon its pane and the cobwebs, freckled with leaves and dead bugs, that hung at its corners. She pulled the blanket aside and saw that the door of the hut was open. Lowe stood in its frame, his giant shoulders almost brushing either side of the doorway. He was shirtless, his feet bare, and sweat glistened upon his shaved head and trickled slowly down between his shoulder blades. His back was pale and hairy. He had a cigarette in his right hand, and was talking to another man, who stood outside. Alice figured it was Wallace, the little "high yellow" man who ran his hookers and his small-time narcotics trade from out of this hut in the woods, with a little illicit whiskey for those of more conservative tastes. A laugh came, and then she saw Wallace as he moved across the large window at the front of the hut, zipping up his fly and rubbing his fingers upon his jeans. His shirt was open and hung loose upon his pigeon chest and his little belly. He was an ugly man, and rarely bathed. Sometimes he asked her to do things for him, and it was all that she could manage not to choke on the taste of him. But she needed him now. She needed what he had, even if it meant adding to her debt, a debt that would never be paid.

She put on a T-shirt and skirt to cover her nakedness, then lit a cigarette and prepared to pull the blanket fully across. Sundays were quiet. Some of the men who used this place would already be preparing for church, and they would sit in the pews and pretend to listen to the sermon, even as they thought of her. There were others who had not darkened a church door in many years, but even for them Sundays were different. If she could work up the energy, she might go to the mall, pick up some new clothes with the little money that she had, maybe some cosmetics too. She had been meaning to do it for a couple of weeks, but there were other distractions here. Still, even Wallace had recently commented on the state of her dresses and her underwear, although the men who came here weren't too particular. Some even liked the squalor of it, for it added a certain spice to their sense of transgression, but Wallace generally preferred to pretend that his women were clean even if their surroundings were not. If she went out early she could get her business done, then come back and relax for the afternoon. There might be some work for her in the evening, but it would not be as demanding as the night before, not by any means. Fridays and Saturdays were always the worst, with the threat of alcohol-fueled violence ever present. True, Lowe and Wallace protected the women, but they couldn't stay with them behind that curtain while the men were being serviced, and it didn't take more than a split second for a man's fist to reach a woman's face.

There came the sound of a car approaching. She could see it through the doorway as it turned. Unlike most of the cars that came to this place, this one was new. It looked like one of those German cars, and the chrome on its wheels was spotless. The engine growled briefly as it came to a stop. She saw doors opening, front and back. Wallace said something that she could not hear, and Lowe tossed his cigarette on the ground, his other hand already reaching behind his back to where the butt of the big Colt emerged from his jeans. Before he could grasp it, his shoulders exploded in a red cloud that billowed briefly in the sunlight, then fell wetly to the floor. Somehow he remained standing, and she saw his hands clutch at the door frame, holding himself upright. Footsteps crunched on the gravel outside, then the second shot came and part of Lowe's head disappeared. His hands relinquished their grip, and he fell to the ground.

Alice stood frozen, rooted to the spot. Outside, she could hear Wallace pleading for his life. He was backing toward the hut, and she could see his body grow larger and larger as he neared the window. There were more shots, and the glass shattered into thousands of pieces, the remaining shards in the frames edged with blood. Now she could hear the other girls responding. To her right, Rowlene was screaming repeatedly. She was a big girl, and Alice could almost picture her on her bed, her sheet pulled up to her chest, her eyes drowsy and flecked with red as she tried to make herself small in the corner of her bunk. To her left, she could hear Pria, who was half Asian, strike the wall as she struggled to clear her head and find her clothes. Pria had partied with two johns the night before, and they had shared some of their buy with her. She was probably still high.

The figure of a man appeared in the door frame. Alice briefly glimpsed his face as he entered, and the sight gave her the impetus she needed. She allowed the blanket to fall gently, then climbed on her bunk and pushed at the window. At first it would not move, even as she heard the man moving through the hut, coming closer to the whores' quarters. She hit the frame with the base of her palm, and it swung out with barely a sound. Alice pulled herself up and squeezed herself through the gap, even as the next shot came from the stall beside her own and splinters burst from the wall. Rowlene was gone. She would be next. Behind her, a hand grasped the blanket and pulled it to the floor as gravity took hold and Alice tumbled to the ground. She felt something snap in her hand as she fell awkwardly, and then she was running for the cover of the trees, fallen branches snapping beneath her feet as she ducked and weaved into the forest. The shotgun roared again, and an alder disintegrated barely inches from her right foot.

She kept running, even though her feet were cut by stones and her clothing torn by briars and thorns. She did not stop until the pain in her side was so great that she felt as though she were being ripped in half. She lay against a tree and thought that she heard, distantly, the sounds of men. She knew the face of the man at the door. He was one of those who had taken Pria the night before. She did not know why he had returned, or what had led him to do what he did. All that she knew was that she had to get away from this place, for they knew who she was. They had seen her, and they would find her. Alice called her mother from a phone at a gas station, the pumps locked and the station closed, for it was still early on Sunday morning. Her mother came with clothing, and what money she had, and Alice left that afternoon and did not ever return to the state in which she was born. She called in the years that followed, mostly with requests for money. She called weekly at least, and sometimes more often than that. It was Alice's one unfailing concession to her mother, and even at her lowest she always tried to keep the older woman from worrying more than she already did. There were other small kindnesses too: birthday gifts that arrived early, or more often late, but arrived nonetheless; cards at Christmas, a little cash included in the early years, but later only a signature and a scrawled greeting; and, very occasionally, a letter, the quality of the script and the color of the ink varying in accordance with the lengthy process of the missive's completion. Her mother cherished them all, but mostly she was grateful for the calls. They let her know that her daughter was still alive.

Then the calls ceased.

Martha sat on the couch in my office, Louis standing to one side of her, Angel seated quietly in my chair. I was by the fireplace. Rachel had looked in on us briefly, then left.

"You should have looked out for her," Martha again told Louis.

"I tried," he said. He looked old and tired. "She didn't want help, not the kind I could offer her."

Martha's eyes ignited.

"How can you say that? She was lost. She was a lost soul. She needed someone to bring her back. That should have been you."

This time, Louis said nothing.

"You went to Hunts Point?" I asked.

"Last time we spoke, she said that was where she was at, so that was where I went."

"Is that where you got hurt?"

She lowered her head.

"A man hit me."

"What was his name?" asked Louis.

"Why?" she said. "You gonna do for him like you done for others? You think that will find your cousin? You just want to feel like a big man, now it's too late to do what a good man would have done. Well, that don't wash with me."

I intervened. The recriminations would get us nowhere.

"Why did you go to him?"

"Because Alice done told me she was working for him now. The other one, the one she was with before, he died. She said this new one was gonna take care of her, that he was going to find wealthy men for her. Wealthy men! What man would want her after all she'd done? What man . . . ?"

She started to cry again.

I went to her and handed her a clean tissue, then slowly knelt down before her.

"We'll need his name, if we're to start looking for her," I said quietly.

"G-Mack," she said at last. "He calls himself G-Mack. There was a young white girl too. She said she remembered Alice, but she was calling herself LaShan on the street. She didn't know where she'd gone to."

"G-Mack," said Louis.

"Ring any bells?"

"No. Last I heard she was with a pimp called Free Billy."

"Looks like things changed."

Louis stood and helped Martha from her chair.

"We need to get you something to eat. You need to rest up now."

She took his hand and gripped it tightly in her own.

"You find her for me. She's in trouble. I can feel it. You find her, and bring her back to me."

The fat man stood at the lip of the bathtub. His name was Brightwell, and he was very, very old, far older than he seemed. Sometimes he acted like a man who had recently woken from a deep sleep, but the Mexican, whose name was Garcia, knew better than to question him about his origins. He recognized only that Brightwell was a thing to be obeyed, and to be feared. He had seen what the man had done to the woman, had watched through the glass as Brightwell's mouth closed on hers. It had seemed to him that some grave knowledge had shown itself in the woman's eyes at that moment, even as she weakened and died, as though she realized what was about to occur as her body failed her at last. How many others had he taken in this way, Garcia wondered, his lips against theirs as he waited for their essence to pass from them? And even if what Garcia suspected of Brightwell was not true, what kind of man would believe such a thing of himself?

The stench was terrible as the chemicals worked on

the remains, but Brightwell made no attempt to cover his face. The Mexican stood behind him, the lower half of his face concealed by a white mask.

"What will you do now?" said Garcia.

Brightwell spit into the tub, then turned his back on the disintegrating body. "I will find the other one, and I will kill her."

"Before she died, this one spoke of a man. She thought he might come for her."

"I know. I heard her call his name."

"She was supposed to be alone. Nobody cared."

"We were misinformed, but perhaps nobody cares anyway."

Brightwell swept by him, leaving him with the decaying body of the girl. Garcia did not follow him. Brightwell was wrong, but Garcia did not have the courage to confront him further on the issue. No woman, as death approached, would cry out over and over again a name that meant nothing to her.

Someone did care.

And he would come.

II

He that hath wife and children,
hath given hostages to fortune.

Francis Bacon, *Essays* (1625)

3

The celebration of Sam's christening continued around us. I could hear people laughing, and the startled hiss of bottles opening. Somewhere a voice began singing a song. It sounded like Rachel's father, who tended to sing when he was in his cups. Frank was a lawyer, one of those hearty, hail-fellow-well-met types who liked to be the center of attention wherever he went, the kind who thought that he brightened up people's lives by being loud and unintentionally intimidating. I had watched him in action at a wedding, forcing shy women to dance on the grounds that he was trying to take them out of their shells, even as they trembled awkwardly across the dance floor like newborn giraffes, casting longing glances back at their chairs. I supposed it could be said of him that he had a good heart, but unfortunately he didn't have a sensitivity toward others to go with it. Aside from any concerns he might have had about his daughter, Frank seemed to regard my presence at such convivial events as a personal affront, as though at any moment I were going to burst into tears, or beat someone up, or otherwise rain on the parade that Frank was trying so hard to put in place. We tried not to be alone together. To be honest, it wasn't too difficult, as we both put our hearts into the effort.

Joan was the strong one in the marriage, and a soft

word from her could usually make Frank take things down a notch. She was a kindergarten teacher, and an old-style liberal Democrat who took very personally the way the country had changed in recent years under both Republicans *and* Democrats. Unlike Frank, she rarely spoke about her worries for her daughter directly, at least not to me. Only occasionally, usually when we were leaving them at the end of another sometimes awkward, sometimes mildly pleasant visit, would she take me lightly by the hand and whisper: "Look after her, won't you?"

And I would assure her that I would take care of her daughter, even as I looked into her eyes and saw her desire to believe me collide with her fear that I would be unable to fulfill that promise. I wondered if, like the missing Alice, there was a taint upon me, a wound left by the past that would somehow always find a way to infect the present and the future. I had tried, in recent months, to discover a means of neutralizing the threat, mainly by declining offers of work that sounded like they could involve any serious form of risk, my recent evening with Jackie Garner being the honorable exception. The trouble was that any job that was worth doing necessitated risk of some kind, and so I was spending time on cases that were progressively sapping my will to live. I had tried to walk this path before, but I was not living with Rachel when I followed it, and I did not last long upon it before I found the lure of the dark woods impossible to ignore.

Now a woman had come to my door, and she had brought with her her own pain, and the misery of another. It was possible that a simple explanation would arise for her daughter's disappearance. There was little merit in ignoring the realities of Alice's existence: her life at the Point was dangerous in the extreme, and her habit made her more vulnerable still. The women who worked those streets disappeared regularly. Some were fleeing their pimps or other violent men. Some tried to leave the life before it consumed them entirely, sick of robbery and rape, but few of those women succeeded, and most trudged back to the alleys and the parking lots with their hopes of escape now entirely gone. The women tried to look out for one another, and the pimps monitored their movements too, if only to protect their investments, but these were gestures and little more. If someone was determined to hurt one of these women, then he would succeed.

We brought Louis's aunt into the kitchen and entrusted her to the care of one of Rachel's relatives. Soon she was eating chicken and pasta and sipping lemonade in a comfortable chair in the living room. When Louis went to check on her a little later, he found her asleep, exhausted by all that she had tried to achieve for her daughter.

Walter Cole joined us. He knew something of Louis's past, and suspected more. He was more knowledgeable about Angel, as Angel had the kind of criminal record that merited a sizable file to itself, although its details pertained to the relatively distant past. I had asked Louis if we could involve Walter and he acquiesced, albeit reluctantly. Louis wasn't the trusting kind, and he most certainly did not like involving the police in his affairs. Nevertheless, Walter, although retired, had connections with the NYPD that I no longer had, and was on better terms with serving officers than I was. Admittedly, that wasn't difficult. There were those in the department who suspected that I had blood on my hands, and would dearly have liked to call me to account for it. Cops on the street were less problematical for me, but Walter still had the respect of those higher up who might be in a position to offer assistance if it was needed.

"You'll go back to the city tonight?" I asked Louis.

He nodded. "I want to find me that G-Mack."

I hesitated before I spoke.

"I think you should wait."

Louis's head tilted slightly, and his right hand slapped lightly against the arm of his chair. He was a man of few unnecessary movements, and this pretty much qualified as an explosion of emotion.

"Why would you think that?" he said evenly.

"This is what I do," I reminded him. "You go in there all fired up with your guns blazing and everybody with even a passing concern for their own personal safety will disappear, whether they know you or not. If he gets away we'll need to tear the city apart to find him, and we'll waste valuable time doing it. We know nothing about this guy. We need to change that before we go after him. You're thinking about revenge for what he did to the woman in there. That can come later. What concerns us is her daughter. I want you to hold off."

There was a risk involved in doing this. G-Mack now knew that someone was asking questions about Alice. Assuming that Martha was right, and something bad had befallen her, then the pimp had two options: he could sit tight, plead ignorance, and tell the women under him to do the same; or he could run. I just hoped that his nerve held until we got to him. My guess was that it would: he was new, since Louis knew nothing of him, and young, which meant that he was probably arrogant enough to consider himself a playa on the street. He had managed to establish some kind of operation at the Point. He would be reluctant to abandon it until it became absolutely necessary to do so.

There was a long silence as Louis considered his options.

"How long?" he said.

I looked to Walter.

"Twenty-four hours," he said. "By then, I should have what you need."

"Then we'll move on him tomorrow night," I said.

"We?" asked Louis.

"We," I said.

He locked eyes with me.

"This is personal," he said.

"I understand."

"We need to be clear on that. You got your way of doing things, and I respect that, but your conscience got no part to play in this. You start doubting, I want you to walk away. That goes for everyone."

His eyes flicked momentarily toward Walter. I could sense that Walter was about to respond, so I reached out and touched his arm, and he relaxed slightly. Walter would not involve himself in anything that violated his own strict moral code. Even without the badge, Walter was still a cop, and a good one. He had no need to justify himself to Louis.

Nothing more was said. We were done. I told Walter to use the office phone, and he began making some calls. Louis went to wake Martha so that he could bring her back to New York with him. Angel joined me at the front door.

"Does she know about you two?" I asked.

"I've never met her before," said Angel. "Tell you the truth, I wasn't even sure that the family existed. I figured someone bred him in a cage, then released him into the wild. But I think she's smart. If she doesn't know now, she'll guess soon enough. Then we'll see."

We watched as Rachel walked two of her friends to their car. She was beautiful. I loved the way that she carried herself, her poise, her grace. I felt something tear inside me, like a weakness in a wall that slowly begins to expand, threatening the strength and stability of the whole.

"She won't like it," said Angel.

"I owe Louis," I replied.

Angel almost laughed. "You got no debt to him, or to me. Maybe you feel like you do, but we don't see it that way. You have a family now. You have a woman who loves you, and a daughter who depends on you. Don't screw it up."

"I don't intend to. I know what I have."

"Then why are you doing this?"

What could I tell him? That I wanted to do this, that I needed to do this? It was part of it, I knew. Maybe also, in some low, hidden part of myself, I wanted to force them away, to hasten what I saw as an inevitable end.

But there was one more element, one that I could not explain to Angel, or to Rachel, or even to myself. I felt it as soon as I saw the cab moving along the road, drawing slowly closer and closer to the house. I felt it as I watched the woman step onto the gravel in our drive. I felt it as she told her story, trying to hold back the tears but desperate not to show weakness in front of strangers.

She was gone. Alice was gone, and wherever she now was she would never walk through this world as she once did. I couldn't say how I knew it, any more than Martha could explain her sense that her daughter was at risk to begin with. This woman, filled with courage and love, was brought here for a reason. There was a connection, and it would not be denied. I had learned from bitter experience that the troubles of others that found their way to my door were meant for my intervention, and could not be ignored.

"I don't know," I said. "I just know that it has to be done."

Gradually, most of the guests slipped away. They seemed to take with them whatever gaiety they had brought along, leaving none behind in our house. Rachel's parents, as well as her sister, were staying the night with us. Walter and Lee were due to spend a couple of days with us too, but Martha's visit had caused the abandonment of that plan and they were already on their way home so that Walter could talk to cops in person if necessary.

I was clearing up outside when Frank Wolfe cornered me. He was taller than I, and bulkier. He'd played football in high school, and there were colleges sufficiently impressed by him to consider offering him a scholarship, but Vietnam intervened. Frank didn't even wait for the draft. He was a man who believed in duty and responsibility. Joan was already pregnant when he left, although neither of them knew at the time. His son, Curtis, was born while he was "in country," and a daughter followed two years later. Frank won some medals, but he never spoke about how he came by them. When Curtis, who had become a deputy with the county sheriff's office, was killed during a bank raid, he didn't disintegrate or descend into self-pity the way some men might have done but instead held his family close to him, binding them to him so that they would have him to lean upon, so that they would not fall. There was much that was admirable about Frank Wolfe, but we were too dissimilar to ever manage more than a few civil words to each other.

Frank had a beer in his hand, but he wasn't drunk. I had heard him talking to his wife earlier, and they had witnessed Martha's arrival and the conclave that resulted. I figured Frank had subsequently slowed down on the booze, either of his own volition or at his wife's instigation.

I picked up some paper plates and threw them into the garbage bag. Canine Walter was shadowing me, hoping to snatch any scraps that fell in his path. Frank watched me but didn't move to lend a hand.

"Everything okay, Frank?" I said.

"I was going to ask you the same thing."

There was no point in brushing him off. He hadn't become a good lawyer by lacking persistence. I finished clearing the plates from the trestle table, tied up the garbage bag, and went to work on the empty bottles with a new bag. They made a satisfying *clink* as they hit the bottom.

"I'm doing my best, Frank," I said softly. I didn't want to have this discussion with him, not now and not ever, but it was upon us.

"With respect, I don't think you are. You got duties now, responsibilities."

I smiled, despite myself. There were those two words

again. They defined Frank Wolfe. He would probably have them inscribed on his gravestone.

"I know that."

"So you got to live up to them."

He tried to emphasize his point by waggling the beer bottle at me. It diminished him, somehow, making him appear less like a concerned father and more like a garrulous drunk.

"Listen, this thing you do, it's got Rachel worried. It's always got her worried, and it's put her at risk. You don't put the people you love at risk. A man just doesn't do that."

Frank was trying his best to be reasonable with me, but he was already getting under my skin, maybe because all that he was saying was true.

"Look, there are other ways that you can use the skills you have," he said. "I'm not saying give up on it entirely. I got contacts. I do a lot of work with insurance companies, and they're always looking for good investigators. It pays well: better than what you earn now, that's for sure. I can ask around, make some calls."

I was hurling the bottles into the bag with more force now. I took a deep breath to rein myself in, and tried to drop the next one as gently as I could.

"I appreciate the offer, Frank, but I don't want to work as an insurance investigator."

Frank had run out of "reasonable," so he was forced to uncork something a little more potent. His voice rose.

"Well, you sure as hell can't keep doing what you do now. What the hell is wrong with you? Can't you see what's happening? You want the same thing to happen a—"

He stopped abruptly, but it was too late. It was out now. It lay, black and bloody, on the grass between us. I was suddenly very, very tired. The energy drained from my body, and I dropped the sack of bottles on the ground. I leaned against the table and lowered my head. There was a shard of sharp wood against the palm of my right hand. I pressed down steadily upon it, and felt skin and flesh give way beneath the pressure.

Frank shook his head. His mouth opened, then closed again without uttering a word. He was not a man given to apologies. Anyway, why should a man apologize for telling the truth? He was right. Everything that he had said was right.

And the terrible thing was that Frank and I were closer in spirit than he realized: we had both buried children, and both of us feared more than anything else a repetition of that act. Had I chosen to do so, I could have spoken at that moment. I could have told him about Jennifer, about the sight of the small white coffin disappearing beneath the first clods of earth, about organizing her clothes and her shoes so that they could be passed on to children still living, about the appalling sense of absence that followed, of the gaping holes in my being that could never be filled, of how I could not walk down a street without being reminded of her by every passing child. And Frank would have understood, because in every young man fulfilling his duty he saw his absent son, and in that brief truce some of the tension between us might have been erased forever.

But I did not speak. I was retreating from them all, and the old resentments were coming to the fore. A guilty man, confronted by the self-righteousness of others, will plead bitter innocence or find a way to turn his guilt upon his accusers.

"Go to your family, Frank," I told him. "We're done here."

And I gathered up the garbage and left him in the evening darkness.

Rachel was in the kitchen when I returned, making coffee for her parents and trying to clean up some of the mess left on the table. I started to help her. It was the first time we had been alone since we had returned from the church. Rachel's mother came in to offer help, but Rachel told her that we could take care of it. Her mother tried to insist.

"Mom, we're fine," said Rachel, and there was an edge to her voice that caused Joan to beat a hasty retreat, pausing only to give me a look that was equal parts sympathy and blame.

Rachel used the blade of a knife to begin scraping the food from a plate into the trash can. The plate had a dark blue pattern upon its rim, although it wouldn't have it for much longer if Rachel continued to scratch at it.

"So, what's going on?" she asked. She didn't look at me as she spoke.

"I could ask you the same thing."

"What does that mean?"

"You were kind of hard on Angel and Louis today, weren't you? You hardly spoke a word to them while they were here. In fact, you've hardly spoken a word to me."

"Maybe if you hadn't spent the afternoon cloistered in your office we might have found time to speak."

It was a fair criticism, although we had been in the office for less than an hour.

"I'm sorry. Something came up."

Rachel slammed the plate down on the edge of the sink. A small blue chip flew from the edge and was lost on the floor.

"What do you mean, something came up? It's your daughter's *fucking* christening!"

The voices in the living room went quiet. When the conversation picked up again, it sounded muted and strained.

I moved toward her.

"Rach—," I began.

She raised her hands and backed away.

"Don't. Just don't."

I couldn't move. My hands felt awkward and useless. I didn't know what to do with them. I settled for putting them behind my back and leaning against the wall. It was as close as I could come to a gesture of surrender without raising them above my head or exposing my neck to the blade. I didn't want to fight with Rachel. It was all too fragile. The slightest misstep, and we would be surrounded by the fragments and shards of our relationship. I felt my right hand stick to the wall. When I looked down there was blood upon it, left by the splinter cut.

"What did that woman want?" said Rachel. Her head was down, loose strands of hair falling over her cheeks and eyes. I wanted to see her face clearly. I wanted to push back her hair and touch her cheek. Like this, her features hidden, she reminded me too much of another.

"She's Louis's aunt. Her daughter has gone missing

in New York. I think she came to Louis as a last resort."

"Did he ask you for help?"

"No, I offered to help."

"What does she do, her daughter?"

"She was a street prostitute, and an addict. Her disappearance won't be a priority for the cops, so someone else will have to look for her."

Rachel ran her hands through her hair in frustration. This time she did not try to stop me as I moved to hold her. Instead, she allowed me to press her head gently to my chest.

"It will just take a couple of days," I said. "Walter has made some calls. We have a lead on her pimp. It may be that she's safe somewhere, or in hiding. Sometimes women in the life drop out for a time. You know that."

Slowly, her arms reached around my back and held me.

"Was," she whispered.

"What?"

"You said 'was.' She *was* a prostitute."

"It's just the way that I phrased it."

Her head moved against me in denial of the lie.

"No, it's not. You know, don't you? I don't understand how you can tell, but I think you just know when there's no hope. How can you carry that with you? How can you take the strain of that knowledge?"

I said nothing.

"I'm frightened," she said. "That's why I didn't talk to Angel and Louis after the christening. I'm frightened of what they represent. When we spoke about them being godfathers to Sam, before she was born, it was like, well, it was like it was a joke. Not that I didn't want them to do it, or that I didn't mean it when I agreed, but it seemed like no harm could come of it. But today, when I saw them there, I didn't want them to have anything to do with her, not in that way, and at the same time I know that each of them, without a second thought, would lay down his life to save Sam. They'd do the same for you, or for me. It's just . . . I feel that they bring . . ."

"Trouble?" I said.

"Yes," she whispered. "They don't mean to, but they do. It follows them."

Then I asked the question that I had been afraid to ask.

"And do you think that it follows me too?"

I loved her for her answer, even as another fissure appeared in all that we had.

"Yes," she said. "I think those in need find you, but with them come those who cause misery and hurt."

Her arms gripped me tighter, and her nails dug sharply into my back.

"And I love you for the fact that it pains you to turn away. I love you for wanting to help them, and I've seen the way you've been these last weeks. I've seen you after you walked away from someone you thought you could help."

She was talking about Ellis Chambers from Camden, who had approached me a week earlier about his son. Neil Chambers was involved with some men in Kansas City, and they had their hooks pretty deep in him. Ellis couldn't afford to buy him out of his trouble, so somebody was going to have to intervene on Neil's behalf. It was a muscle job, but taking it would have separated me from Sam and Rachel, and would also have involved a degree of risk. Neil Chambers's creditors were not the kind of individuals who took kindly to being told how to run their affairs, and they were not sophisticated in their methods of intimidation and punishment. In addition, Kansas City was way off my turf, and I told Ellis that he might find the men involved were more amenable to some local intervention than the involvement of a stranger. I made some inquiries, and passed on some names to him, but I could see that he was disappointed. For better or worse, I'd gained a reputation as a "go-to" guy. Ellis had expected more than a referral. Somewhere inside, I too believed that he deserved more.

"You did it for me, and for Sam," said Rachel, "but I could tell the effort that it caused you. You see, that's the thing of it: whichever way you turn, there will be pain for you. I just didn't know how much longer you could keep turning away from those who reached out to you. I guess now I know. It ended today."

"Rachel, she's family to Louis. What else could I do?"

She smiled sadly.

"If it hadn't been her, it would have been someone else. You know that."

I kissed the top of her head. She smelled of our child.

"Your dad tried to talk to me outside."

"I bet you both enjoyed that."

"It was great. We're considering going on vacation together."

I kissed her again.

"What about us?" I asked. "Are we okay?"

"I don't know," she said. "I love you, but I don't know."

With that she released me, and left me alone in the kitchen. I heard her climb the stairs, and there came the creak of the door to our bedroom, where Sam lay sleeping. I knew that she was looking down upon her, listening to her breathe, watching over her so that no harm would come to her.

That night, I heard the voice of the Other calling from beneath our window, but I did not go to the glass. And behind her words I discerned a chorus of voices, whispering and weeping. I covered my ears against them and squeezed my eyes tightly closed. In time, sleep came, and I dreamed of a gray leafless tree, its sharp branches curving inward, thick with thorns, and within the prison that they formed brown mourning doves fluttered and cried, a low whistling rising from their wings as they struggled, and blood upon their feathers where the thorns had pierced their flesh. And I slept as a new name was carved upon my heart.

4

The Spyhole Motel was an unlikely oasis, a resting place for travelers who had almost entirely despaired of ever finding respite before the Mexican border. Perhaps they had skirted Yuma, tired of lights and people, longing to see the desert stars in all their glory, and had instead found themselves facing mile upon mile of stone and sand and cactus, bordered by high mountains they could not name. Even to stop briefly by the roadside was to invite thirst and discomfort, and maybe the attentions of the Border Patrol, for the coyotes ran their illegals along these routes, and the *migras* were always on the lookout for those who might be colluding with them in the hope of making some easy money. No, it was better not to stop here, wiser to keep moving in the hope of finding comfort elsewhere, and that was what the Spyhole promised.

A sign on the highway pointed south, advising the weary of the proximity of a soft bed, cold sodas, and functioning air-conditioning. The motel was simple and unadorned, apart from a vintage illuminated sign that buzzed in the night like a great neon bug. The Spyhole consisted of fifteen rooms set in an *n* shape, with the office at the bottom of the left arm. The walls were a light yellow, although without closer examination it was difficult to say whether this was their original color or if constant exposure to the sands had resulted in their transformation to that hue, as though the desert would tolerate the motel's presence only if it could lay some claim to it by absorbing it into the landscape. It lay in a natural alcove, a gap between mountains known as the Devil's Spyhole. The mountains gave the motel a little shade, although barely steps from its office the heat of the desert winds blew through the Devil's Spyhole itself like the blast from the open door of an incinerator. A sign outside the office warned visitors not to wander from the motel's property. It was illustrated with snakes and spiders and scorpions, and a drawing of a cloud puffing superheated air toward the black stick figure of a man. The drawing might almost have been comical, were it not for the fact that blackened figures were regularly found on the sands not far from the motel: illegals, mostly, tempted by the deceptive promise of great wealth.

The motel derived as much of its custom from referrals as from those who saw its sign in passing on the highway. There was a truck stop ten miles west, Harry's Best Rest, with an all-night diner, a convenience store, showers and bathrooms, and space for up to fifty rigs. There was also a noisy cantina, frequented by specimens of human life that were barely one step up from the predatory desert creatures outside. The truck stop, with its lights and noise and promise of food and company, sometimes attracted those who had no business there, travelers who were merely tired and lost and seeking a place to rest. Harry's Best Rest was not meant for them, and its staff had learned that it was prudent to send them on their way with a suggestion that they seek some comfort at the Spyhole. Harry's Best Rest was owned by a man named Harry Dean, who occupied a role that would have been familiar to his predecessors on the border a century before. Harry walked a thin line, doing just enough to satisfy the law and keep the *migras* and Smokies from his door, which in turn usually enabled him to stay on the right side of those individuals, mired in criminality, who frequented the shadier corners of his establishment. Harry paid some people off, and was in turn paid off. He turned a blind eye to the whores who serviced the truckers in their rigs or in the little cabanas to the rear, and to the dealers who supplied the drivers with uppers and other narcotics to keep them up or bring them down as the need arose, as long as they kept their supply off the premises and safely stored amid the tangles of junk in the back of their assorted pickups and automobiles, the smaller vehicles interspersed among the huge rigs like bottom feeders following the big predators.

It was 2 A.M. on Monday, and the Best Rest had quietened down some as Harry helped Miguel, his bar manager, to clean up behind the counter and restock the beer and liquor. Technically the bar was no longer open for business, although anyone who wanted a drink at this time of night could still be served at the diner next door. Nevertheless, men continued to sit in the shadows, nursing their shots, some talking together, some alone. They were not the kind of men who could be told to leave. They would fade into the night in their own time, and of their own accord. Until then, Harry would not trouble them.

A connecting doorway led from the cantina into the diner. A sign on the diner side announced that the bar was now closed, but the main door to the cantina remained unlocked for the present. Harry heard it open and looked up to see a pair of men enter. Both were white. One was tall and in his early forties, with graying hair and some scarring to his right eye. He wore a blue shirt, a blue jacket, and jeans that were a little long at the ends, but was otherwise largely unremarkable in appearance.

The other man was almost as tall as his companion, but obscenely fat, his enormous belly hanging pendulously between his thighs like a great tongue lolling from an open mouth. His body appeared out of proportion to his legs, which were short and slightly bowed, as though they had struggled for many years to support the load they were required to bear and were now buckling under the strain. The fat man's face was perfectly round and quite pale, but his features were very delicate: green eyes enclosed by long, dark lashes; a thin, unbroken nose; and a long mouth with full, dark lips that were almost feminine. But any passing resemblance to traditional notions of facial beauty were undone by his chin, and the tumorous, distended neck in which it lost itself. It rolled over his shirt collar, purple and red, like an intimation of the gut that lay farther down. Harry was reminded of an old walrus that he had once seen in a zoo, a great beast of blubber and distended flesh on the verge of collapse. This man, by contrast, was far from the grave. Despite his bulk, he walked with a strange lightness, seemingly gliding across the peanut-shell-strewn floor of the cantina. Harry's shirt was streaked with sweat even though the AC was blasting, yet the fat man's face was entirely dry, and his white shirt and gray jacket appeared untouched by perspiration. He was balding, but his remaining hair was very black and cut short against his skull. Harry found himself mesmerized by the man's appearance, the mix of terrible ugliness and near beauty, of obscene bulk and irreconcilable grace. Then the spell was broken, and Harry spoke.

"Hey," said Harry. "We're closed."

The fat man paused, the sole of his right foot poised just above the floor. Harry could see an unbroken peanut just beneath his shoe leather.

The foot began to complete its descent. The shell started to flatten beneath the weight.

And Harry was suddenly confronted by the face of the fat man, inches from his own, staring straight at him. Then, before he could even begin to take in his presence, the fat man was to his left, then to his right, all the time whispering in a language Harry couldn't understand, the words an unintelligible mass of sibilance and occasional harsh consonants, their precise meaning lost to him but their intimation clear.

Stay out of my way. Stay out of my way or you'll be sorry.

The fat man's face was a blur, his body zipping from side to side, his voice an insistent throbbing inside Harry's head. Harry felt nauseous. He wanted it to stop. Why wasn't anyone intervening on his behalf? Where was Miguel?

Harry reached out a hand in an effort to support himself against the bar.

And the movement around him suddenly ceased.

Harry heard the peanut shell crack. The fat man was where he had previously been, fifteen or twenty feet from the bar, his colleague behind him. Both were looking at Harry, and the fat man was smiling slightly, privy to a secret that only he and Harry now shared.

Stay out of my way.

In a far corner, Harry saw a hand raised: Octavio, who took care of the whores, absorbing a cut of their income in return for protection, and passing on a little of it to Harry in turn.

This was none of Harry's business. He nodded once, and returned to cleaning off the overspill from the beer taps. He managed to complete his task, then slipped quietly into the little bathroom behind the bar, where he sat on the toilet seat for a time, his hands trembling, before he vomited violently into the sink. When he returned to the cantina, the fat man and his partner were gone. Only Octavio was waiting for him. He didn't look much better than Harry felt.

"You okay?" he asked.

Harry swallowed. He could still taste bile in his mouth.

"Better we forget, you understand?" said Octavio.

"Yeah, I get you."

Octavio gestured to the bar, pointing out the bottle of brandy on the top shelf. Harry took the bottle and poured the alcohol into a highball glass. He figured that Octavio didn't need a snifter, not this time. The Mexican put a twenty on the bar.

"You need one too," he said.

Harry poured himself a glass, keeping his hand heavy.

"There was a girl," said Octavio. "Not local. Black Mexican."

"I remember," said Harry. "She was here tonight. She's new. Figured her for one of yours."

"She won't be back," said Octavio.

Harry lifted the glass to his lips, but found that he couldn't drink. The taste of bile was returning. Vera, that was the girl's name, or the name she had given when Harry had asked. Few of these women used their real name for business. He'd spoken to her once or twice, just in passing. He'd seen her maybe three times in all, but no more than that. She'd seemed pretty nice, for a whore.

"Okay," said Harry.

"Okay," said Octavio.

And like that, the girl was gone.

There were only three rooms occupied at the Spyhole Motel. In the first room, a young couple on a road trip to Mexico were bickering, still argumentative after a long, uncomfortable journey. Soon they would descend into uneasy, prickly silence, until the boy made the first move toward reconciliation, heading out into the desert night and returning with sodas from the machine by the office. He would place one of the cans against the small of the girl's back, and she would react with a shiver. He would kiss her, and tell her that he was sorry. She would kiss him back. They would drink, and soon the heat and the arguments would appear to be forgotten.

In the next room, a man sat in his vest upon a bed, watching a Mexican game show. He had paid for his room in cash. He could have stayed in Yuma, for he had business there in the morning, but his face was known and he disliked staying in the city for longer than he had to. Instead, he sat in the remote motel and watched couples hug each other as they won prizes worth less than the money in his wallet.

The last room on this arm of the motel was taken by another solo traveler. She was young, barely into her twenties, and she was running. They called her Vera in

Harry's Best Rest, but those who were seeking her knew her as Sereta. Neither name was real, but it no longer mattered to her what she was called. She had no family now, or none that cared. In the beginning, she had sent money home to her mother in Ciudad Juárez, supplementing the meager income she gleaned from her work in one of the big *maquiladoras* on Avenida Tecnológico. Sereta and her older sister Josefina had worked there too, until that November day when everything changed for them.

When she called home Sereta would tell Lilia, her mother, that she was working as a waitress in New York. Lilia did not question her, even though she knew that her daughter, before she left for the north, had frequently been seen leaving the gated communities of the Campestre Juárez, where the wealthy Americans lived, and the only local women admitted to such places were servants and whores. Then, in November 2001, the body of Sereta's sister Josefina was one of eight found in an overgrown cotton field near the Sitio Colosio Valle mall. The bodies were badly mutilated, and the protests of the poor increased in volume, for these were not the first young women to die in this place, and there were stories told of wealthy men behind barred gates who had now added killing for pleasure to their list of recreations. Sereta's mother told her to leave and not to come back. She never mentioned the Campestre Juárez to her, and the rich men in their black cars, but she knew.

One year later, Lilia too was dead, taken by a cancer that her daughter believed was a physical manifestation of pain and grief, and now Sereta was alone. In New York, she had found a kindred spirit in Alice, but that friendship too had been sundered. Alice should have stayed with her, but the grip of the sickness was tight upon her, and she had made her own choice to remain close to the big city. Sereta, instead, had headed south. She knew these desert places and how they worked. She wanted those who were pursuing her to think that she had crossed into Mexico. Instead, she planned to skirt the border, making for the West Coast, where she hoped to disappear for a time until she could figure out her next move. She knew that what she had was valuable. After all, she had listened to a man die for it.

Sereta too was watching television, but the volume was down low. She found the glow comforting but did not wish the babble to disturb her thoughts. Money was the problem. Money was always the problem. She had been forced to run so suddenly that there was no time to plan, no time to assemble what few funds she had to her name. She had a friend bring her car to her, then drove away, putting as much space between herself and the city as possible.

She'd heard about the Best Rest in the past. It was a place where nobody asked too many questions and where a girl could make some money quickly and then move on without any further obligation, as long as she paid her cut to the right people. She took a room at the Spyhole, negotiating a pretty good deal, and already had nearly $2,000 put away after just a few days, thanks in part to a particularly generous tip from a truck driver whose sexual tastes, messy but harmless, she had indulged the night before. Soon she would move along. Maybe just one more night, though, she thought, even as, unbeknownst to her, her existence had already bound itself to the lives of those who had taken her sister.

For far to the north, the Mexican named Garcia might have smiled familiarly at the mention of Josefina's name, recalling her final moments as he busied himself with the remains of another young woman . . .

There was only one other person on the motel property. He was a slim young man of Mexican descent, and he was seated behind the reception desk in the office, reading a book. The book was entitled *The Devil's Highway,* and it told of the deaths of fourteen Mexicans who had attempted to cross the border illegally not many miles from where the motel lay. The book made the young man angry, even as he felt a sense of relief that his parents had made a good life here and that such a death was not destined to be his.

It was almost 3 A.M., and he was about to lock the door and retire to the back room for some sleep when he saw the two white men approach the office. He had not heard their car pull up, and supposed that they must have deliberately parked some way off. Already he was on his guard, for that made no sense to him. There was a gun beneath the counter, but he had never had cause even to show it. Now that most people paid by credit card, motels provided poor pickings for thieves.

One of the men was tall and dressed in blue. The heels of his cowboy boots clicked upon the tiles as he entered the office. His companion was absurdly corpulent. The clerk, whose name was Ruiz, believed that he had never before seen a man who looked quite so unhealthy, and he had seen many fat Americans in his young life. The fat man's belly hung so far between his thighs that Ruiz guessed that he must have been obliged to lift it up each time he made water. He carried in his hand a tan straw hat with a white band, and wore a light jacket over a white shirt, and tan pants. His shoes were brown and polished to a high sheen.

"How you doing tonight?" asked Ruiz.

The thin man answered.

"We're doing well. You full up?"

"Nah, when we're full we turn on the 'No Vacancies' sign out on the road to save folks a trip."

"You can do that from here?" asked the thin man. He sounded genuinely interested.

"Sure," said Ruiz. He pointed to a box upon the wall, lined with switches. Each was carefully labeled with a handwritten sticker. "I just flick a switch."

"Amazing," said the thin man.

"Fascinating," said his colleague, speaking for the first time. Unlike the other man, he did not sound interested. His voice was soft, and slightly higher in pitch than a man's voice should have been.

"So, would you like a room?" asked Ruiz. He was tired and wanted to get the two men booked in and their cards processed so that he could catch up on his sleep. He also, he realized, wanted to get them out of the office. The fat man smelled peculiar. He hadn't noticed any stench from the one in blue, but the tubby guy had an unusual body odor. He smelled earthy, and Ruiz involuntarily found himself picturing pale worms breaking through damp clods of dirt and black beetles scurrying for the shelter of stones.

"We may need more than one," replied Blue.

"Two?"

"How many rooms do you have?"

"Fifteen altogether, but three are occupied."

"Three guests."

"Four."

Ruiz stopped talking. There was something wrong here. Blue was no longer even listening. Instead, he had picked up Ruiz's book and was looking at the cover.

"Luis Urrea," he read. *"The Devil's Highway."*

He turned to his companion.

"Look," he said, displaying the book to him. "Maybe we should buy a copy."

The fat man glanced at the cover.

"I know the route," he said drily. "If you want it, just take that one and save some money."

Ruiz was about to say something when the fat man struck him in the throat, slamming him back against the wall. Ruiz experienced a sense of pain and constriction as small, delicate parts of himself were crushed by the blow. He was having trouble breathing. He tried to form words, but they would not come. He fell against the wall and a second blow came. He slid slowly to the floor. His face was turning dark as he suffocated, his windpipe entirely ruined. Ruiz began to claw at his mouth and throat. He could hear a clicking noise, like the ticking of a clock counting down his final moments. The two men were not even interested in his suffering. The fat man walked around the desk, stepping carefully over Ruiz. The dying man again caught the smell of him as he switched on the "No Vacancies" sign out on the highway. His companion, meanwhile, flicked through that night's guest registration cards.

"One couple in two," he told the fat man. "One male in three. The name sounds Mexican. One woman in twelve, registered under the name Vera Gooding."

The fat man didn't acknowledge him. He was now standing over Ruiz, watching blood and spittle trail from the corners of his mouth.

"I'll take the couple," he said. "You take the Mexican."

He squatted down beside Ruiz. It was a surprisingly graceful movement, like the dipping of a swan's head. He extended his right hand and brushed the hair from the young man's brow. There was a mark on the underside of the fat man's forearm. It looked like a twin-pronged fork, recently burned into the flesh. The fat man turned Ruiz's head from left to right.

"Do you think we should bring it back for our Mexican friend?" asked Blue. "He works well with bone."

"Too much trouble," said the fat man.

His tone was dismissive. The fat man gripped Ruiz's hair, turning his head slightly, then leaned in close to him. His mouth opened slightly, and Ruiz saw a pink tongue and teeth that tapered to blunt ends. Ruiz's eyes were bulging now, and his face was purple. He spit red fluid, and as he did so the fat man's lips touched his, his mouth closing entirely upon Ruiz's, his hand clasping the young man's face and chin, keeping his jaws apart. The Mexican tried to struggle, but he could not fight both the fat man and the end that was coming. A word flashed in his head, and he thought: *Brightwell. What is Brightwell?*

His grip upon the fat man's shoulder loosened, his legs relaxed, and the fat man drew away from him and stood.

"You have blood on your shirt," Blue told Brightwell. He sounded bored.

Danny Quinn watched his girlfriend as she carefully applied the small brush to her toenails. The polish was a mix of purple and red. It made her look as though her toes were bruised, but Danny decided to keep this opinion to himself. He was content to bask for a time in the afterglow of their lovemaking, taking in her concentration and her poise. At times like these, Danny loved Melanie deeply. He had cheated on her, and would probably cheat on her again, although he prayed each night for the strength to remain faithful. He wondered sometimes at what would happen if she found out about his other life. Danny liked women, but he distinguished between sex and lovemaking. Sex meant little to him, apart from the satiation of an urge. It was like scratching an itch: if his right hand was broken and his back was itchy, then he'd use his left to deal with it. All things being equal, he would *prefer* to use his right hand, but an itch was an itch, right? If Melanie wasn't around—and her work with the bank sometimes required her to be away from home for two or three days—then Danny would go elsewhere for his pleasure. Mostly, he told the women involved that he was single. Some of them didn't even ask. One or two had fallen for him a little, and that had created problems, but he had worked them out. Danny had even used hookers on occasion. The sex was different with them, but he did not consider sex with hookers as cheating on Melanie. There was no emotion involved at all, and Danny reasoned that without emotion there was no real betrayal of his feelings for Melanie. It was clinical, and he always practised safe sex, even with the ones who offered a little extra.

Deep down, Danny wanted to be the person that Melanie thought he was. He tried to tell himself, each time he strayed, that this would be the last. Sometimes he could go for weeks, even months, without being with another woman, but eventually he would find himself alone for a time, or in a strange city, and the urge to trawl would take him.

But he did love Melanie, and if he could have turned back the clock of his life and made his choices again—his first hooker, and the shame he felt afterward; the first time he cheated on someone, and the guilt that came with it—he believed that he would live his life differently, and that he would be a better, happier man as a result.

I will start again, he lied to himself. It was like alcoholism, or any other addiction. You had to take things one day at a time, and when you fell off the wagon, well, you just got right back up again and start counting from one.

He reached out to stroke Melanie's back, and heard a knock at the door.

Melanie Gardner was afraid that Danny was cheating on her. She didn't know why she thought it, for none of her friends had ever seen him with another woman, and she had never found any telltale signs on his clothes or in his pockets. Once, while he was sleeping, she had tried to read his e-mails, but he was scrupulous about deleting both sent and received mail, apart from those that had to do with his business. There were a lot of women in his address book, but she did not recognize any of the names. Anyway, Danny was regarded as one of the best electricians in town, and in her experience it was women who tended to make most of the business calls to Danny, probably because their husbands were too ashamed to admit that there was something around the house that they could not repair themselves.

Now, as she sat on the bed, the warmth of him gradually fading, she felt the urge to confront him. She wanted to ask him if he was seeing someone else, if he had ever been with another woman in the time that they had been together. She wanted to look in his eyes as he answered, because she believed that she would be able to tell if he was lying. She loved him. She loved him so much that she was afraid to ask, for if he lied she would know and it would break her heart, and if he told her what she feared was the truth, then that would also break her heart. The tension she had been feeling had broken through at last in a dumb argument about music earlier in the evening, and then they had made love even though Melanie did not really want to. It had allowed her to delay the confrontation, nothing more, just as painting her toenails had suddenly seemed a matter of great urgency.

Melanie painstakingly filled in the last patch of clear nail upon her little toe, then placed the brush back in the polish, turning slightly as she did so. She saw Danny reaching out for her.

She opened her mouth to speak at last, and heard a knock at the door.

Edgar Certaz thumbed idly at the remote control, flashing through the channels. There were so many that by the time he had finished flicking through them all he had forgotten if there were any of the earlier ones that merited his attention. He settled at last upon a western. He thought it very slow. Three men were waiting for a train. The train came. A man with a harmonica got off. He killed the three men. An American actor whose face was familiar to him appeared as the villain, which threw Certaz a little as he had only ever seen the American play good guys. There were few Mexicans that he could see, which was good. Certaz was tired of seeing peasants in white clutching sombreros as they appealed for help against bandits from gunmen in black, as though all Mexicans were either victims or cannibals who fed on their own.

Certaz was a middleman, an intermediary. Like the woman in the next room he too had connections with Juárez, and he and his fellow *narcotraficantes* had been responsible for many deaths in the city. His was a dangerous business, but he was paid well for his troubles. Tomorrow, he would meet two men and arrange for the delivery of $2 million worth of cocaine, for which he and his associates would receive a forty per cent commission. If the delivery proceeded without a hitch, the next consignment would be considerably larger, and his reward commensurately greater. Certaz would make all of the arrangements, but at no point would either drugs or money be in his possession. Edgar Certaz had learned to insulate himself from risk.

The Colombians still controlled the manufacture of cocaine, but it was the Mexicans who were now the biggest traffickers of the drug in the world. The Colombians had given them their start in the trade, albeit unintentionally, by paying Mexican smugglers in cocaine instead of cash. Sometimes, up to half of every shipment into the United States went to the Mexicans. Certaz was one of the original mules, and had quickly worked his way up to a position of prominence in the Juárez cartel controlled by Amado Carrillo Fuentes, nicknamed "Lord of the Skies" after he pioneered the use of jumbo jets to transport huge shipments of drugs between territories.

In November 1999, a joint raid by Mexican and U.S. law enforcement unearthed a mass grave at a desert ranch named La Campana, near Juárez. The grave contained two hundred bodies, maybe more. La Campana was once the property of Fuentes and his lieutenant, Alfonso Corral Olaguez. Carrillo had died in the summer of 1997, following an overdose of anesthesia administered in the course of plastic surgery intended to change his appearance. It was rumored that his Colombian suppliers, envious of his influence, had paid off the medics. Two months later Corral was shot and killed at the Maxfim restaurant in Juárez, leading to a bloody turf war headed by Carrillo's brother Vicente. The bodies at La Campana, stored in the narcobunkers that riddled the land, included the remains of those who had crossed Carrillo, among them members of the rival Tijuana cartel as well as unfortunate peasants who happened to be in the wrong place at the wrong time. Certaz knew this, because he had helped to put some of them there. The discovery of the bodies had increased the pressure on the Mexican dealers, forcing them to be ever more careful in their operations, and so the need for men with Certaz's expertise had grown considerably. He had survived the investigations and the recriminations, and had emerged stronger and more secure than ever before.

In the movie, a woman arrived on a train. She was expecting someone to meet her, but there was nobody waiting. She took a ride out to a homestead, where her husband now lay dead on a picnic table alongside his children.

Certaz was bored. He pressed his thumb against the remote to kill the picture, and heard a knock at the door.

Danny Quinn draped a towel around his waist and went to the door.

"Who is it?" he asked.

"Police."

It was a mistake, but Brightwell was distracted. It had been a long trip, and he was tired. The heat of the day had made him weary, and now the comparative cool of the desert night had taken him by surprise.

Danny looked at Melanie. She took her purse and headed for the bathroom, closing the door behind her. They had a little weed in a Ziploc bag, but Melanie would just flush it down the john. It was a shame to lose it, but Danny could always get more.

"You got some ID?" said Danny.

He still had not opened the door. He looked through the spy hole and saw a fat man with a round face and a weird neck holding up a badge and a laminated identification card.

"Come on," said the man. "Open up. This is just routine. We're searching for illegals. I just need to take a look inside, ask you some questions, then I'll be gone."

Danny swore, but relaxed a little. He wondered if Melanie had already flushed their stash. He hoped not. He opened the door, and smelled something unpleasant. He tried to hide his shock at the cop's appearance, but failed. Already, he knew that he had made a mistake. This was no cop.

"You alone?" asks the fat man.

"My girlfriend is in the bathroom."

"Tell her to come out."

This is all wrong, thought Danny, all wrong.

"Hey," he said. "Let me have another look at that badge."

The fat man reached into his jacket pocket. When his hand reemerged, it was not holding a wallet. Danny Quinn saw a flash of silver, and then felt the blade enter his chest. The fat man grabbed Danny's hair and pushed the blade up and to the left. He heard the girl's voice calling from the bathroom.

"Danny?" said Melanie. "Is everything okay?"

Brightwell released his grip on Danny's hair and yanked the blade free. The boy collapsed onto the floor. His body spasmed, and the fat man placed his foot upon his stomach to still him. Had he more time, Brightwell might have kissed him as he had Ruiz, but there were more pressing matters to which to attend.

From the bathroom came the noise of a toilet flushing, but it was being used to mask another sound. There was the creak of a window sliding open, and a screen being forced. Brightwell walked to the bathroom and raised his right foot, then shattered the lock with the impact.

Edgar Certaz heard the knock on the adjoining room seconds after someone commenced knocking on his own door. He then discerned a male voice identify himself as a cop claiming to be hunting illegals.

Certaz was not dumb. He knew that when the cops came hunting, they didn't do it so politely. They came hard and fast, and in force. He also knew that this motel was not on their shit list, because it was relatively expensive and well run. The sheets were clean and the towels in the bathroom were changed every day. It was also far from the main routes used by the illegals. Any Mexican who got this far was not going to check into the Spyhole Motel for a bath and a porno movie. He was going to be sitting in the back of a van headed north or west, congratulating himself and his buddies on making it across the desert.

Certaz did not reply to the knock on his door. The knock came again.

"Open up," said a voice. "This is the police."

Certaz carried a lightweight Smith & Wesson mountain gun, with a short, four-inch barrel. He did not possess a license for it. While he did not have a criminal record, he knew that if he was taken in and fingerprinted, his prints would set off alarm bells in local and federal agencies, and that he would be a very old man by the time he was released, assuming that they did not find an excuse to execute him first. So two thoughts crossed Edgar's mind. The first was that if this really was a police raid, then he was in trouble. The second thought was that, if these men were not police, then they were still trouble, but trouble that could be dealt with. He heard a muffled scream from the room next door as Brightwell dealt with Danny Quinn's girlfriend.

You want me to open up, decided Edgar, then I'll open up.

He drew the Smith & Wesson, walked to the wooden door, and began firing.

Blue bucked as the first of the shots hit him in the chest, its force diminished slightly by its passage through the door. The second took him in the right shoulder as he spun, and he grunted loudly as he hit the sand. There was no use for silence now. He drew his own Double

Eagle and fired from the ground as the door to the motel room opened.

There was nobody in the gap. Then Certaz's gun appeared, low down from the left, where the Mexican was hunched beneath the window. Blue saw the dark finger tense upon the trigger and prepared for the end.

Shots came, but not from the Mexican. Brightwell was at the window, firing down at an angle through the glass. He shot Edgar Certaz in the top of the head and the Mexican tumbled forward, even as two more bullets entered his back.

Blue rose to his feet. There was now blood on his shirt too. He swayed a little.

From the back of the motel, they heard the sound of someone running. The door to the last motel room remained closed, but they knew that their quarry was no longer inside.

"Go," said Blue.

Brightwell ran. He ran less gracefully than he walked, rocking from side to side on his stubby legs, but he was still fast. He heard a car starting, then the engine being gunned. Seconds later, a yellow Buick shot around the corner of the motel. There was a young woman behind the wheel. Brightwell fired, aiming to the right of the driver's head. The windshield was hit but the car kept coming, forcing him to throw himself to one side to avoid being struck. His next shots took out the tires and blew out the rear window. He watched with satisfaction as the Buick hit the late Edgar Certaz's truck and came to a sudden halt.

Brightwell got to his feet and approached the ruined car. The young woman inside lay dazed in the driver's seat. There was blood on her face, but otherwise she appeared uninjured.

Good, thought Brightwell.

He opened the door and pulled her from the car.

"No," Sereta whispered. "Please."

"Where is it, Sereta?"

"I don't know what—"

Brightwell punched her in the nose. It broke under the impact.

"I said, where is it?"

Sereta fell to her knees, her hands against her face. He could barely understand her when she told him that it was in her purse.

The fat man reached into the car and retrieved the purse. He began tossing the contents onto the ground until he found the small silver box. Carefully, he opened it and examined the piece of yellowed vellum within. He looked at it and, seemingly content, replaced it in the box.

"Why did you take it?" he asked. He was genuinely curious.

Sereta was crying. She said something, but it was muffled by her tears and the hands that she had cupped over her ruined nose. Brightwell leaned down.

"I can't hear you," he said.

"It was pretty," said Sereta, "and I didn't have any pretty things."

Brightwell stroked her hair almost tenderly.

Blue was approaching. He staggered a little, but remained on his feet. Sereta crawled back against the car, trying to stem the bleeding from her nose. She looked at Blue, and he seemed to shimmer. For a moment she saw a black, emaciated body, tattered wings hanging from nodes upon its back, and long, taloned fingers that clutched feebly at the air. The figure's eyes were yellow, shining in a face that was almost without features, apart from a mouth filled with small, sharp teeth. Then the shape before her was, once again, a man dying upon his feet.

"Jesus, help me," she said. "Jesus, Lord God, help me."

Brightwell kicked her hard in the side of the head, and her words ceased. He dragged her limp body to the trunk of her car, opened it, then dumped her inside before walking to his own Mercedes and returning with two plastic cans of gas.

Blue leaned against the Buick as his colleague approached. His eyes lingered for a moment on the gasoline, then shifted away.

"Don't you want her?" he said.

"I would taste her words in my mouth," said Brightwell. "Strange, though."

"What is?" asked Blue.

"That she should believe in God, and not in us."

"Perhaps it is easier to believe in God," said Blue. "God promises so much . . ."

". . . but delivers so little," finished Brightwell. "We make fewer promises, but we keep them all."

Had Sereta been able to see him, then Blue would have shimmered again before her eyes. His companion did not notice. He saw Blue as he had always seen Blue.

"I am fading," said Blue.

"I know. We were careless. *I* was careless."

"It does not matter. Perhaps I will wander for a time."

"Perhaps," said Brightwell. "In time, we will find you again."

He sprayed gasoline upon his companion, dousing his clothes, his hair, his skin, then poured the remainder upon the interior of the Buick. He tossed the empty containers onto the backseat, then stood before Blue.

"Good-bye," he said.

"Good-bye," said Blue. He was almost blinded by the gasoline, but he found the open door of the Buick and eased himself into the driver's seat. Brightwell regarded him for a moment, then took a Zippo from his pocket and watched the flame take life. He tossed the lighter into the car and walked away. He did not look back, not even when the gas tank exploded and the darkness behind him was lit by a new fire as Blue passed from this world, and was transformed.

5

Each of us lives two lives: our real life and our secret life.

In our real life, we are what we appear to be. We love our husband or our wife. We care for our children. Each morning we pick up a bag or a briefcase and we do what we must to oil the wheels of our existence. We sell bonds, we clean hotel rooms, we serve beer to the kind of men with whom we would not share our air if we had a choice in the matter. We eat our lunch in a diner, or on a bench in a park where people walk their dogs and children play in the sunlight. We feel a sentimental urge to smile at the animals because of the joy they take in the simplicity of a stroll through green grass, or at the children paddling in pools and racing through sprinklers, but still we return to our desks or our mops or our bars feeling less happy than we formerly were, unable to shake off the creeping sense that we are missing something, that there is supposed to be more than this to our lives.

Our real life — anchored by those twin weights (and here they come again), our careworn friends duty and responsibility, their edges considerably curved, the better to fit upon our shoulders — permits us our small pleasures, for which we are inordinately grateful. Come, take a walk in the countryside, the earth spongy and warm beneath your feet, but be aware always of the ticking clock, summoning you back to the cares of the city. Look, your husband has made dinner for you, lighting the candle that his mother gave you for a Christmas gift, the one that now makes the dining room smell of mull and spices although it is already mid-July. See, your wife has been reading *Cosmo* again, and in an effort to add a little spice to your waning sex life has for once gone farther than JCPenney for her lingerie, and has learned a new trick from the pages of her magazine. She had to read it twice just to understand some of the terminology, and had to rely on ancient memory to summon up a picture of the sad, semitumescent organ that she now proposes to service in this manner, so long has it been since any such matters passed between the two of you without the cover of blankets and smothered lights, the easier to fantasize about J. Lo or Brad, perhaps the girl who takes your order at the sandwich bar, or Liza's kid from two doors down, the one who is just back from college and is now transformed from a geeky little boy with railroad braces into a veritable Adonis with white, even teeth and tanned, muscular legs.

And in the darkness, one upon the other, the real life blurs at its margins, and the secret life intrudes with a rush and a moan and the flicking tongue of desire.

For in our secret life, we are truly ourselves. We look at the pretty woman in marketing, the new arrival, the one with the dress that falls open when she crosses her legs, revealing a pristine expanse of pale thigh, and in our secret life we do not see the veins about to break beneath her skin, or the birthmark shaped like an old bruise that muddies the beauty of her whiteness. She is flawless, unlike the one we have left behind that morning, thoughts of her new bedroom trick already forgotten for it will be put away as surely as will be the Christmas candle, and neither trick nor light will see use for many months to come. And so we take instead the hand of the new fantasy, unsullied by reality, and we lead her away, and she sees us as we truly are as she takes us inside her and, for an instant, we live and die within her, for she needs no magazine to teach her arcane things.

In our secret life, we are brave and strong, and know no loneliness, for others take the place of once-loved (and once-desired) partners. In our secret life, we take the other path, the one that was offered to us once but from which we shied away. We live the existence we were meant to lead, the one denied us by husbands and wives, by the demands of children, by the requirements of petty office tyrants. We become all that we were meant to be.

In our secret life, we dream of striking back. We point a gun and we pull the trigger, and it costs us nothing. There is no regret at the wound inflicted, the body slumping backward, already crumpling as the spirit leaves it. (And perhaps there is another waiting at that moment, the one who tempted us, the one who promised us that this is as it was meant to be, that this is our destiny, and he asks only this one small indulgence: that he may place his lips against those of the dying man, the fading woman, and taste the sweetness of what passes from them so that it flutters briefly like a butterfly in his mouth before he swallows, trapping it deep inside him. This is all that he asks, and who are we to deny him?)

In our secret life our fists pummel, and the face that blurs with blood beneath them is the face of everyone who has ever crossed us, every individual who has prevented us from becoming all that we might have been. And *he* is beside us as we punish the flesh, his ugliness forgiven in return for the great gift that he has given us, the freedom that he has offered. He is so convincing, this blighted man with his distended neck, his great, sagging stomach, his too short legs and his too long arms, his delicate features almost lost in his pale, puckered skin, that to gaze on him from afar is like looking at a full, clear moon as a child and believing that one can almost see the face of the man who dwells within it.

He is Brightwell, and with sugared words he has fed us the story of our past, of how he has wandered for so long, searching for those who were lost. We did not believe him at first, but he has a way of convincing us, oh yes. Those words dissolve inside us, their essence coursing through our system, their constituent elements in turn becoming part of us. We begin to remember. We look deep into those green eyes, and the truth is at last revealed.

In our secret life, we once were angels. We adored, and we were adored. And when we fell, the last great punishment was to mark us forever with all that we had lost, and to torment us with the memory of all that once was ours. For we are not like the others. All has been revealed to us, and in that revelation lies freedom.

Now we *live* our secret life.

I awoke to find myself alone in our bed. Sam's cradle was empty and silent, and the mattress was cold to the touch, as though no child had ever been laid upon it. I walked to the door and heard noises coming from the kitchen below. I pulled on a pair of sweatpants and went downstairs.

There were shadows moving in the kitchen, visible through the half-open door, and I could hear closets being opened and closed. A woman's voice spoke. Rachel, I thought: she has taken Sam downstairs to feed her, and she is talking to her as she always talks to her, sharing her thoughts and hopes with her as she does whatever she must do. I saw my hand stretch out and push the door, and the kitchen was revealed to me.

A little girl sat at the top of the kitchen table, her head slightly bowed and her long blond hair brushing the wood and the empty plate that sat before her, its blue pattern now slightly chipped. She was not moving. Something dripped from her face and fell to the plate, expanding redly upon it.

Who are you looking for?

The voice did not emerge from the girl. It seemed to be coming to me both from some distant, shadowy place and also from close by, whispering coldly in my ear.

They are back. I want them to go. I want them to let me be.

Answer me.

Not you. I loved you, and I will always love you, but you are gone.

No. We are here. Wherever you are, so will we be too.

Please, I need to put you to rest at last. Everything is coming to pieces. You are tearing me apart.

She will not stay. She will leave you.

I love her. I love her as I once loved you.

No! Don't say that. Soon she will be gone, and when

she leaves we will still be here. We will stay with you, and we will lie by you in the darkness.

A crack appeared in the wall to my right, and a fissure opened in the floor. The window shattered and fragments of glass exploded inward, each shard reflecting trees and stars and moonlight, as though the whole world were disintegrating around me.

I heard my daughter upstairs, and I ran, taking the stairs two at a time. I opened the bedroom door and Rachel was standing by the crib, Sam in her arms.

"Where were you?" I asked. "I woke up and you weren't there."

She looked at me. She was tired, and there were stains on her nightshirt.

"I had to change her. I took her into the bathroom so she wouldn't wake you."

Rachel laid Sam in her cot. Once she was happy that our daughter was comfortable and settled, she prepared to return to bed. I stood over Sam, then leaned down and kissed her lightly on the forehead.

A small drop of blood fell upon her face. I dabbed it away with my thumb, then walked to the mirror in the corner. There was a small cut below my left eye. When I touched it, it stung me sharply. I stretched the abrasion with my fingers, and explored it until I had removed the tiny fragment of glass from within. A single tear of blood wept down my cheek.

"Are you okay?" asked Rachel.

"I cut myself."

"Is it bad?"

I wiped my arm across my face, smearing the blood.

"No," I lied. "No, it's not bad at all."

* * *

I left for New York early the next morning. Rachel was sitting at the kitchen table, in the seat where the night before a young girl had sat, blood slowly pooling on the plate before her. Sam had been awake for two hours, and was now crying furiously. Usually, once she was awake and fed, she was content to simply watch the world go by. Walter was a source of particular fascination for her, his presence causing Sam's face to light up whenever he appeared. In his turn, the dog always remained close to the child. I knew that dogs sometimes became disconcerted by the arrival of a new child in a house, confused by how this might affect the pecking order. Some became actively hostile as a result, but not Walter. Although he was a young dog, he seemed to recognize some duty of protection toward the little being that had entered his territory. Even the day before, during the fuss following the christening, it had taken him time to separate himself from Sam. It was only when he was assured of the presence of Rachel's mother close by that he appeared to relax and attached himself instead to Angel and Louis.

Rachel's mother was not yet awake. While Frank had returned to work that morning, managing to avoid me entirely before leaving, Joan had offered to stay with Rachel while I was gone. Rachel had accepted the offer without question, and I was grateful to her for that. The house was well protected: prompted by events in the recent past, we had installed a system of motion sensors that alerted us to the presence of anything larger than a fox on our property, and cameras kept vigil both on the main gate and the yard, and on the marshland behind, feeding images to twin monitors in my office. The investment was considerable, but it was worth it for peace of mind.

I kissed Rachel good-bye.

"It's just for a couple of days," I said.

"I know. I understand."

"I'll call you."

"Okay."

She was holding Sam against her shoulder, trying to comfort her, but she would not be comforted. I kissed Sam too, and I felt Rachel's warmth, her breast pressed against my arm. I recalled that we had not made love since Sam was born, and the distance between us seemed even greater as a result.

Then I left them, and drove to the airport in silence.

The pimp named G-Mack sat in the darkened apartment on Coney Island Avenue that he shared with some of his women. He had a place in the Bronx, closer to the Point, but he had been using it less and less frequently of late, ever since the men came looking for his two whores. The arrival of the old black woman had spooked him even more, and so he had retreated to his private crib, venturing out to the Point only at night, and keeping a distance from the main streets whenever possible.

G-Mack wasn't too sure about the wisdom of living on Coney Island Avenue. It was once a dangerous stretch of road, even back in the nineteenth century, when gang members preyed on the tourists returning from the beaches. In the 1980s, hookers and pushers colonized the area around Foster Avenue, their presence made clearer by the bright lights of the nearby gas station. Now there were still whores and dealers, but they were a little less obvious, and they fought for sidewalk space alongside Jews and Pakistanis and Russians and people from countries of which G-Mack had never even heard.

The Pakistanis had been having a hard time of it in the aftermath of 9/11, and G-Mack had heard that a lot of them were arrested by the Feds, while others had left for Canada or gone back home entirely. Some of them had even changed their names, so it sometimes seemed like there had been a sudden influx of Pakistanis named Eddie and Steve into G-Mack's world, like the plumber he'd been forced to call a week or two back after one of the bitches managed to clog up the bowl by flushing something down there about which G-Mack didn't even want to know. The plumber used to be called Amir. That was what it said on his old card, the one G-Mack had pinned to the refrigerator door with a Sinbad magnet, but on his new card he was now Frank. Frank Shah, like that was going to fool anyone. Even the three numerals, the 786 that Amir once told him stood for "In the name of Allah," were now gone from beside his address. G-Mack didn't much care either way. Amir was a good plumber, as far as he could tell, and he wasn't about to hold a grudge against a man who could do his job, especially since he might need his services again sometime. But G-Mack didn't like the smell of the Pakistani stores, or the food that they sold in their restaurants, or the way that they dressed, either too neat or too casual. He distrusted their ambition, and their manic insistence that their kids better themselves. G-Mack suspected that good old Frank-Who-Was-Really-Amir bored the ass off his kids with his sermons on the American dream, maybe pointing to black people like G-Mack as a negative example, even if G-Mack was a better businessman than Amir would ever be and even if G-Mack's people weren't the ones who steered two jets into New York's tallest buildings. G-Mack had no personal beef with the Pakistanis who lived around him, food and clothing aside, but shit like 9/11 was everybody's business, and Frankie-Amir and his people needed to make it clear just whose side they were on.

G-Mack's place was on the top floor of a three-story brownstone with brightly painted cornices, between Avenues R and S, close to the Thayba Islamic Center. The Thayba was separated from the Keshet Jewish day care center by a kids' play group, which some people might have called progress but which bothered the hell out of G-Mack, these two opposing sides being so close to each other, although maybe not as much as the fucking Hasidim further down the avenue in their threadbare black coats, their kids all pale with their fag curls. It didn't surprise G-Mack that they always hung around in groups, because there wasn't one of them strange Jews could handle himself if it came to a fight.

He listened to two of his whores babbling in the bathroom. There were nine in his stable now, and three of them slept here in cots that he rented to them as part of their "arrangement." A couple of the others still lived with their mommas, because they had children and needed someone to take care of the kids while they were on the streets, and he had rented floor space to the rest in the place over by the Point.

G-Mack rolled a joint and watched as the youngest of the three women, the little white bitch who called herself Ellen, strolled through the kitchen in her bare feet, eating toast with peanut butter smeared untidily across it. Said she was nineteen, but he didn't believe that. Didn't care none, either. There were a lot of men liked them younger, and she was taking top dollar on the streets. G-Mack had even considered setting her up somewhere private, maybe placing an ad in the *Voice* or the *Press* and charging four or five hundred an hour for her. He'd been about to do it, too, when all the shit had broken around him and he'd been forced to watch his back. Still, he liked to take a little of her honey for himself sometimes, so it was good to have her near.

G-Mack was twenty-three, younger than most of his own women. He had started out selling weed to school kids, but he was ambitious and saw himself expanding his business to take in stockbrokers and lawyers and the hungry young white guys who frequented the bars and clubs on weekends, looking for something to give them a kick for the long nights to come. G-Mack saw himself in slick threads, driving a hooked-up car. For a long time he dreamed of owning a '71 Cutlass Supreme, with cream leather interior and chrome spokes, although the Cutlass carried bullshit eighteen-inch wheels as standard and G-Mack knew that a ride was nothing unless it was sitting on twenty-twos at the least, Lexani alloys, maybe even Jordans if he wanted to rub the other brothers' noses in it. But a man who was planning on driving a '71 Cutlass Supreme with twenty-two-inch wheels was going to have to do more than push weed on pimple-faced fifteen-year-olds. So G-Mack invested in some E, along with a little coke, and slowly the dough started coming in swift and sweet.

The problem for G-Mack was that he didn't have the backbone to enter the big time. G-Mack didn't want to go back to jail. He had served six months in Otisville on an assault beef when he was barely nineteen, and he still woke up at night screaming at the memory. G-Mack was a good-looking young brother, and they'd had a time with him those first days until he tied himself

up with the Nation of Islam, who had some big moth-
erfuckers on their side and who didn't take kindly to
those who would try to punk out one of their potential converts. G-Mack spent the rest of his six clinging
to the Nation like it was driftwood after a shipwreck,
but when he left he dropped that shit like it was damaged
goods. They came looking for him, asking him questions and shit, but G-Mack was all done with them.
Sure, there were threats, but G-Mack was braver on
the outside, and eventually the Nation cut him loose as
a bad deal. He still occasionally paid lip service to the
Nation if the need arose and he was around folks who
didn't know no better, but mostly he just liked the fact
that Minister Farrakhan didn't take shit from whites,
and that the presence of his followers in their sharp
suits and shades scared the hell out of all those middle-
class doughboys.

But if G-Mack was to raise the money to finance the
lifestyle he wanted so badly, then it meant trying to
score big, and he didn't like the idea of holding that
much supply. If he was caught in possession he was
looking at a class A felony, and that was fifteen to life
right there. Even if he got lucky, and the prosecutor
wasn't having troubles at home or suffering from
prostate problems, and allowed him to plead down to
a class B, then G-Mack would spend the rest of his
twenties behind bars, and fuck anyone who said that
you were still a young man when you got out, because
six months inside had aged G-Mack more than he liked
to think about, and he didn't believe that he could
survive five to ten years inside, didn't matter whether
it was no class B, class C, or even class fucking Z.

What finally confirmed him in the belief that the

pusher's life was not for him was a raid on his crib by a couple of real bad-ass narcs. Seemed like they'd turned someone who was even more scared of prison than G-Mack, and G-Mack's name had come up in the course of the conversation. The cops hadn't found nothing, though. G-Mack always took the same shortcut onto the streets, slipping through the burned-out shell of another three-story behind his own that in turn backed onto a vacant lot. There was an old fireplace in there, and G-Mack hid his stash inside it, behind a loose brick. The cops took him in, even though they'd got fresh air in return for their warrant. G-Mack knew they didn't have nothing on him, so he kept quiet and waited for them to let him walk. It took him three days to work up the courage to go back to his stash, and he offloaded it five minutes later for half of what it was worth on the street. Since then, he'd kept his distance from drugs, and instead found another potential source of income, because if G-Mack didn't know shit about the drug trade, he did know about pussy. He'd had his share and he'd never paid for it, at least not up front and in cash, but he knew there were men out there who would. Hell, he even knew a couple of bitches who were selling it already, but they didn't have nobody to look out for them and women like that were in a vulnerable position. They needed a man to take care of them, and it didn't take long for G-Mack to convince them that he was just the man to do it. He only had to hit one every so often, and even then he didn't have to hit her hard, and the others just fell in line behind her. Then that old pimp Free Billy had died, and some of his women had come G-Mack's way, expanding his stable still further.

Looking back, he couldn't remember why he'd taken

on the junkie whore, Alice. Most of Free Billy's other girls just used grass, maybe a little coke if a john offered it or they struck lucky and managed to hold something back from G-Mack, not that he didn't search them regularly to keep that kind of theft to a minimum. Junkies were unpredictable, and just the look of them could put the johns off. But this one, she had something, ain't nobody could deny that. She was just on the verge. The drugs had taken some of the fat off her, leaving her with a body that was just about perfect and a face that gave her the look of one of those Ethiopian bitches, the ones that the modeling agencies liked on account of their features didn't look so Negro, what with their slim noses and their coffee complexions. Plus she was close to Sereta, the Mexican with the touch of black to her, and that was one fine-looking woman there. Sereta and Alice were Free Billy's girls and they made it clear to him that they came as a pair, so G-Mack had been content to live with the arrangement.

At least Alice, or LaShan as she called herself on the streets, was smart enough to realize that johns didn't like track marks. She kept a stash of liquid vitamin E capsules among her possessions, and squeezed the contents onto her arm after she shot up to hide the evidence. He guessed she shot up in other parts of her body too, secret parts, but that was her business. All G-Mack cared about was that the marks didn't show, and that she kept herself together while she was hooking. That was one good thing about heroin users: they got the nod for fifteen, maybe twenty minutes once the drug kicked in, but thirty minutes later they were ready to go. They could almost pass for normal then, until the drug started wearing off and they got sick again, all itchy and antsy. Mostly, Alice seemed to have her habit under that kind of control, but G-Mack still figured when he took her on that the junkie didn't have more than a couple of months in her. He could see it in her eyes, the way the hunger was biting more deeply now, the way her hair was slowly turning white, but with her looks he could still get good money on her for a time.

And that was how it was, for a couple of weeks, but then she started holding back on him, and her looks began fading more rapidly than even he had expected as her addiction deepened. People sometimes forgot that the shit sold in New York was stronger than just about anywhere else: even heroin was about ten percent pure, as against three to five in places like Chicago, and G-Mack had heard of at least one junkie who arrived in the city from the sticks, scored within an hour of getting there, and was dead of an OD one hour after that again. Alice still had that great bone structure, but now it was just a little too obvious without a decent cushion of flesh over it, and her skin was growing increasingly sallow in complexion as the junk took its toll. She was willing to do just about anything for her supply, so he sent her out with the worst kinds, and she went to them smiling, didn't even ask most of them if they'd put a rubber on before she went down. She ran out of vitamin E, as it cost her money that she needed for junk, so she started injecting between her toes and fingers. Soon, G-Mack realized, he would have to cut her loose, and she'd end up living on the streets, toothless and killing herself for $10 Baggies down by the Hunts Point market.

Then the old guy had come cruising in his car, his

big-ass driver calling the women over as he slowed. He'd spotted Sereta, she'd offered him Alice as well, and then the two whores had climbed in the back with the withered old freak and headed off, once G-Mack had taken note of his plate. Didn't make no sense to be taking chances. He'd talked to the driver too, just so that they were all clear on how much this was going to cost, and so the whores couldn't lie to him about the take. The driver brought them back three hours later, and G-Mack got his money. He searched the girls' bags and found another hundred in each. He let them keep fifty of it, told them he'd look after the rest. Seemed like the old guy liked what they'd shown him, too, because he came back again a week later: same girls, same arrangement. Sereta and Alice enjoyed it because it got them off the streets and the old man treated them nice. He fed them booze and chocolates in his place in Queens, let them fool around in his big old tub, gave them a little extra (which G-Mack very occasionally let slide; after all, he wasn't no monster . . .).

It was all nice and easy, until the girls disappeared. They didn't return from the old man's like they were supposed to. G-Mack didn't worry about them until he got back to his place, and then an hour or two later he took a call from Sereta. She was crying, and he had trouble calming her down enough to understand what had happened, but gradually she managed to tell him that some men had come to the house and started arguing with the old guy. The girls were in the upstairs bathroom, fixing their hair and reapplying their makeup before heading back to the Point. The new arrivals started shouting, asking him about a silver box. They told him they weren't leaving without it, and then Luke, the old man's driver, came in, and there was more shouting, followed by what sounded like a bag bursting, except Alice and Sereta had spent enough time on the streets to know a gunshot when they heard one.

After that, the men downstairs went to work on the old man, and in the course of their efforts he died. They started tearing the house apart, downstairs first. The women heard drawers being opened, pottery breaking, glass shattering. Soon the men would make their way upstairs, and then there would be no hope, but suddenly they heard the sound of a car pulling up outside. Sereta risked a glance out of the window and saw lights flashing.

"Private security," she whispered to Alice. "They must have set off an alarm somehow."

It was one man, alone. He shined a flashlight on the front of the house, then tried the doorbell. He returned to his vehicle and spoke into the radio. Somewhere in the dark, a telephone rang. It was now the only sound in the house. After a couple of seconds, Alice and Sereta heard the noise of the back door in the kitchen opening as the men left. When they were certain that all was okay, the women followed but not before they had wiped down the bathroom and bedroom, and retrieved the tissues and used condoms from the trash.

Now they were scared, afraid that someone might come after them, but G-Mack told them to be cool. Neither of them had ever been printed by the cops, so even if any prints were found, there was no way to link them to anything unless they got into big trouble with the law. They just needed to stay calm. He told them to come back to him, but Sereta refused. G-Mack started shouting and the bitch hung up on him. That was the last he heard of her, but he figured she'd head south, back to her own people, if she was scared. She was always threatening to do that anyhow, once she had enough money saved, even if G-Mack figured it was just the empty posturing and pipe-dreaming that most of these whores went in for at some time or another.

The death of the old man—his name was Winston— and his driver made the news, big time. He wasn't real wealthy, not like Trump or one of those guys, but he was a pretty well known collector and dealer in antiques. The cops figured it for a robbery gone wrong until they found some cosmetics in the bathroom, left by the women in their panic to flee the house, and then they announced that they were looking for one, maybe two women, to help them with their inquiries. The cops came trawling the Point, after it emerged that old man Winston liked to take a ride around its streets looking for women. They asked G-Mack what he knew, once they tracked him down, but G-Mack told them he knew nothing about it. When the cops said that someone had seen G-Mack talking to Winston's driver, and maybe it was his women who were with him that night, G-Mack told them that he talked to a lot of people, and sometimes their drivers, but that didn't mean he made no deals with them. He didn't even bother denying that he was a playa. Better to give them a little truth to hide the taste of the lie. He had already warned the other whores to keep quiet about what they knew, and they did as they were told, both out of fear of him and out of concern for their friends, because G-Mack had made it clear to them that Alice and Sereta were safe only as long as the men who did the killings didn't know a thing about them.

But this wasn't any botched robbery, and the men involved tracked down G-Mack just as the police had done before them, except they weren't about to be fooled by any show of innocence. G-Mack didn't like to think about them, the fat man with the swollen neck and the smell of freshly turned earth from him, and his quiet, bored friend in blue. He didn't like to remember how they had forced him against a wall, how the fat man had placed his fingers in G-Mack's mouth, gripping his tongue when he uttered the first of the lies. G-Mack had almost puked then on the taste of him, but there was worse to come: the voices that G-Mack heard in his head, the nausea that came with them, the sense that the longer he allowed this man to touch him, the more corrupted and polluted he would become, until his insides began to rot from the contact. He admitted that they were his girls, but he hadn't heard from them since that night. They were gone, he said, but they'd seen nothing. They had been upstairs the whole time. They didn't know anything that could help the cops.

Then it had come out, and G-Mack cursed the moment he had agreed to take Sereta and her junkie bitch friend into his stable. The fat man told him that it wasn't what they knew that concerned him.

It was what they had taken.

Winston had shown Sereta the box on the second night, happy and sated from his hours of mild pleasure, while Alice was cleaning herself up. He liked displaying his collection to the lovely dark-haired girl, smarter and more alert than her friend as she was, explaining the origins of some of the objects and pointing out little details about them. Sereta guessed that apart from the sex, he just wanted someone to talk to. She didn't mind. He was a nice old man, generous and harmless. Maybe it wasn't very smart of him to be trusting a pair of women he barely knew with the secrets of his treasures, but Sereta at least could be relied upon, and she was careful to watch Alice just in case her friend might be tempted to take something in the hope of fencing it later.

The box he was holding was less interesting to her than some of the other items in his possession: the jewelry, the paintings, the tiny ivory statuettes. It was a dull silver, and very plain in appearance. Winston told her that it was very old, and very valuable to those who understood what it represented. He opened it carefully. Inside, she saw a folded piece of what looked like paper.

"Not paper," Winston corrected. "Vellum."

Taking a clean handkerchief, he removed it and unfolded it for her. She saw words, symbols, letters, the shapes of buildings, and right in the center, the edge of what looked like a wing.

"What is it?" she said.

"It's a map," he said, "or part of one."

"Where's the rest of it?"

Winston shrugged. "Who knows? Lost, perhaps. This is one of a number of pieces. The rest have been scattered for a very long time. I once hoped that I might find them all, but now I doubt that I ever will. I have lately begun to consider selling it. I have already made some enquiries. We shall see . . ."

He replaced the fragment, then closed the box and restored it to its place on a small shelf by his dressing table.

"Shouldn't it be in a vault or something?" she asked.

"Why?" said Winston. "If you were a thief, would you steal it?"

Sereta looked at the shelf. The box was lost amid the curios and little ornaments that seemed to fill every corner of Winston's house.

"I was a thief, I wouldn't even be able to find it," she said.

Winston nodded happily, then shrugged off his robe.

"Time for one more, I think," he said.

Viagra, thought Sereta. Sometimes that damn blue pill was a curse.

When the men offered him money for any information that might lead to the whereabouts of the whores, it didn't take G-Mack more than a couple of moments to think about it and accept. He figured he didn't have much choice, since the fat man had made it clear that if he tried to screw them over he would suffer for it, and someone else would be running his whores as a result. He put out some feelers, but nobody had heard from either Sereta or Alice. Sereta was the smart one, he knew. If Alice stayed close by her and did as she was told, maybe cut down on her habit and tried to get straight, they might be able to stay hidden for a long time.

And then Alice had come back. She rang the doorbell on the Island Avenue crib and asked to come up. It was late at night and only Letitia was there, because she'd come down with some kind of puking bug. Letitia was Puerto Rican, and new, but she had been warned about what to do if either Sereta or Alice made an appearance. She allowed Alice to come up, told her to lie down on one of the cots, then called G-Mack on his cell. G-Mack told her to keep Alice there, not to let her go. But when Letitia went back to the bedroom, Alice was gone, and so was Letitia's bag, with $200 in cash. When she ran down to the street, there was no sign of the thin black girl.

G-Mack went ape shit when he got back. He hit Letitia, called her every damn name he could think of, then got in his car and trawled the streets of Brooklyn, hoping to catch sight of Alice. He guessed that she'd try to score using Letitia's money, so he cruised the dealers, some of them known to him by name. He was almost at Kings Highway when at last he saw her. Her hands were cuffed and she was being placed in the back of a cop car.

He followed the car to the precinct house. He could bail her out himself, but if anyone connected her to what had happened to Winston, then G-Mack would be in a world of trouble, and he didn't want that. Instead, he called the number that the fat man had given him, and told the man who answered where Alice was. The man said they'd take care of it. A day later, Boy Blue came back and paid G-Mack some money: not as much as he'd been promised but, combined with the implicit threat of harm if he complained, enough to keep him from objecting and more than sufficient to make a considerable down payment on a ride. They told him to keep his mouth shut, and he did. He assured them that she had nobody, that no one would come asking after her. He said that he knew this for sure, swore upon it, told them he knew her from way back, that her momma was dead from the virus and her poppa was a hound who got himself killed in an argument over another woman a couple of years after his daughter was born, a daughter he'd never cared to see; one of many, if the truth be told.

He'd made it all up—accidentally touching on the truth about her father along the way—but it didn't matter. He put what they gave him for her toward the Cutlass Supreme, and it now sat on chrome Jordans, number 23, in a secure garage. G-Mack was in the life now, and he had to look the part if he was going to build up his stable, although he had driven the Cutlass only on a handful of occasions, preferring to keep it carefully garaged and visiting it occasionally like he would a favorite woman. True, the cops might come asking about Alice again once they found out that she'd skipped bail, but then again they had other things to occupy them in this big, bad city without worrying about some junkie hooker who took a skip to get away from the life.

Then the black woman had come around asking questions, and G-Mack hadn't liked the look on her face one little bit. He had grown up around women like that, and if you didn't show them you meant business right from the start, then they'd be on you like dogs. So G-Mack had hit her, because that was how he always dealt with women who got out of line with him.

Maybe she'd go away, he thought. Maybe she'd just forget about it.

He hoped so, because if she started asking questions, and convinced some other people to ask questions too, then the men who paid him might hear about it, and G-Mack didn't doubt for one minute that to safeguard themselves they would bind him, shoot him, and bury him in the trunk of his car, all twenty-three inches off the ground.

It was a strange situation in which Louis and I found ourselves. I wasn't working for him, but I was working with him. For once, I wasn't the one calling the shots, and this time what was occurring was personal to him, not to me. To salve his conscience a little—assuming, as Angel remarked, that he had a conscience to begin with—Louis was picking up the tab for whatever expenses arose. He was putting me up in the Parker Meridien, which was a lot nicer than the places in which I usually stayed. The elevators played vintage cartoons on little screens, and the TV in my room was bigger than some New York hotel beds I'd known. The room was a little minimalist, but I didn't mention that to Louis. I didn't want to seem to be carping. The hotel had a great gym, and a good Thai restaurant a couple of doors up from it. There was also a rooftop pool, with a dizzying view over Central Park.

I met Walter Cole at a coffee shop down on Second Avenue. Police cadets passed back and forth by our window, hauling black knapsacks and looking more like soldiers than cops. I tried to remember when I was like them, and found that I couldn't. It was as though some parts of my past had been closed off to me while others continued to leach into the present, like toxic runoff poisoning what might once have been fertile soil. The city had changed so much since the attacks, and the cadets, with their military appearance, now seemed more suited to its streets than I did. New Yorkers had been reminded of their own mortality, their susceptibility to harm from outside agencies, with the consequence that they, and the streets that they loved, had been altered irrevocably. I was reminded of women I had seen in the course of my work, women whose husbands had lashed out at them once and would lash out at them again. They seemed always to be braced

133

for another blow, even as they hoped that it would not come, that something might have altered in the demeanor of the one who had hurt them before.

My father once hit my mother. I was young, no more than seven or eight, and she had started a small fire in the kitchen while she was frying some pork chops for his dinner. There was a phone call for her, and she left the kitchen to take it. A friend's son had won a scholarship to some big university, a particular cause for celebration as her husband had died suddenly some years before and she had struggled to bring up their three children in the years that followed. My mother stayed on the phone just a little too long. The oil in the pan began to hiss and smoke, and the flames from the gas ring rose higher. A dish towel began to smolder, and suddenly there was smoke pouring from the kitchen. My father got there just in time to stop the curtains from igniting, and used a damp cloth to smother the oil in the pan, burning his hand slightly in the process. By this point my mother had abandoned her call and I followed her into the kitchen, where my father was running cold water over his hand.

"Oh no," she said. "I was just—"

And my father hit her. He was frightened and angry. He didn't hit her hard. It was an open-handed slap, and he tried to pull the blow as he realized what he was doing, but it was too late. He struck her on the cheek and she staggered slightly, then touched her hand gently to her skin, as though to confirm to herself that she had been hit. I looked at my father, and the blood was already leaving his face. I thought he was about to fall over, for he seemed to teeter on his feet.

"Lord, I'm sorry," he said.

He tried to go to her, but she pushed him away. She couldn't look at him. In all their years together, he had never once laid a hand upon her in anger. He rarely even raised his voice to her. Now the man she knew as her husband was suddenly gone, and a stranger revealed in his stead. At that moment, the world was no longer the place that she had once thought it to be. It was alien, and dangerous, and her vulnerability was exposed to her.

Looking back, I don't know if she ever truly forgave him. I don't believe that she did, for I don't think that any woman can ever really forgive a man who raises his hand to her, especially not one whom she loves and trusts. The love suffers a little, but the trust suffers more, and somewhere, deep inside herself, she will always be wary of another strike. The next time, she tells herself, I will leave him. I will never let myself be hit again. Mostly, though, they stay. In my father's case, there would never be a next time, but my mother was not to know that, and nothing he could ever do in the years that followed would ever convince her otherwise.

And as strangers passed by, dwarfed by the immensity of the buildings around them, I thought: What have they done to this city?

Walter tapped the tabletop with his finger.

"You still with us?" he asked.

"I was just reminiscing."

"Getting nostalgic?"

"Only for our order. By the time it arrives, inflation will have kicked in."

Somewhere in the distance I could see our waitress idly spinning a mint on the counter.

"We should have made her commit to a price before she left," said Walter. "Heads up, they're here."

Two men weaved through the tables, making their way toward us. Both wore casual jackets, one with a tie, one without. The taller of the two men was probably nudging six two, while the smaller was about my height. Short of having blue lights strapped to their heads and Crown Vic–shaped shoes, they couldn't have screamed "Cops!" any louder. Not that it mattered in this place: a few years back, two guys fresh off the boat from Puerto Rico — literally, as they hadn't been in the city more than a day or two — tried to take down the diner, home to cops since time immemorial, at around midnight, armed with a hammer and a carving knife. They got as far as "This is a—" before they were looking down the barrels of about thirty assorted weapons. A framed front page from the *Post* now hung on the wall behind the register. It showed a photograph of the two geniuses, below the block headline DUMB AND DUMBER.

Walter rose to shake hands with the two detectives, and I did the same as he introduced me. The tall one was named Mackey, the short one was Dunne. Anybody hoping to use them as proof that the Irish still dominated the NYPD was likely to be confused by the fact that Dunne was black and Mackey looked Asian, although they pretty much made the case that the Celts could charm the pants off just about any race.

"How you doin?" Dunne said to me as he sat down. I could see that he was sizing me up. I hadn't met him before, but like most of his kind who had been around for longer than a few years he knew my history. He'd probably heard the stories as well. I didn't care if he believed them or not, as long as it didn't get in the way of what we were trying to do.

Mackey seemed more interested in the waitress than he was in me. I wished him luck. If she treated her suitors like she treated her customers, then Mackey would be a very old and very frustrated man by the time he got anywhere with this woman.

"Nice pins," he said admiringly. "What's she like from the front?"

"Can't remember," said Walter. "It's been so long since we've seen her face."

Mackey and Dunne were part of the NYPD's Vice Division, and had been for the past five years. The city spent $23 million each year on prostitution control, but "control" was the operative term. Prostitution wasn't going to disappear, no matter how much money the city threw at the problem, and so it was a matter of prioritizing. Mackey and Dunne were part of the Sexual Exploitation of Children Squad, which worked all five boroughs, tackling child porn, prostitution, and child sex rings. They had their work cut out: 325,000 children were subjected to sexual exploitation every year, of whom over half were runaways or kids who had been thrown out of their home by their parents or guardians. New York acted like a magnet for them. There were over five thousand children working as prostitutes in the city at any time, and no shortage of men willing to pay for them. The squad used young-looking female cops, some, incredibly, capable of passing for thirteen or fourteen, to lure "chicken hawks," as pedophile johns liked to term themselves. Most, if caught patronizing, would avoid jail time if they had no previous history, but at least they would be mandated to register as sex offenders and could then be monitored for the rest of their lives.

The pimps were harder to catch, and their methods were becoming more sophisticated. Some of the pimps had gang affiliations, which made them even more dangerous to both the girls and the cops. Then there were those who were actively engaged in trafficking young girls across state lines. In January 2000, a sixteen-year-old Vermont girl named Christal Jones was found smothered in an apartment on Zerega Avenue in Hunts Point, one of a number of Vermont girls lured to New York in an apparently well organized Burlington-to-the-Bronx sex ring. With deaths like Christal's, suddenly $23 million didn't seem like nearly enough.

Mackey and Dunne were over on the East Side to talk to the cadets about their work, but it appeared to have done little for their confidence in the future of the force.

"All these kids want to do is catch terrorists," said Dunne. "They had their way, this city would be bought and sold ten times over while they were interrogating Muslims about their diet."

Our waitress returned from far-off places, bearing coffee and bagels.

"Sorry, boys," she said. "I got distracted."

Mackey saw an opening and rushed to take advantage of it.

"What happened, gorgeous, you catch sight of yourself in a mirror?"

The waitress, whose name was Mylene, whatever kind of name that was, favored him with the same look she might have given a mosquito that had the temerity to land on her during the height of the West Nile virus scare.

"Nope, caught sight of you and had to wait for my beating heart to be still," she said. "Thought I was gonna die, you're so good looking. Menus are on the table. I'll be back with coffee."

"Don't count on it," said Walter as she vanished.

"Think you got some sarcasm on you there," Dunne remarked to his partner.

"Yeah, it burns. Still, that lady looks like a million dollars."

Walter and I exchanged glances. If that waitress looked like a million dollars, then it was all in used bills.

The pleasantries over, Walter brought us down to business.

"You got anything for us?" he asked.

"G-Mack: real name Tyrone Baylee," said Dunne. He pretty much expectorated the name. "This guy was made to be a pimp, you catch my drift."

I knew what he meant. Men who pimp women tend to be smarter than the average criminal. Their social skills are relatively good, which enables them to handle the prostitutes in their charge. They tend to shy away from extreme violence, although most consider it their duty and their right to keep their women in place with a well-placed slap when circumstances require it. In short, they're cowards, but cowards gifted with a degree of cunning, a capacity for emotional and psychological manipulation, and sometimes a self-deluding belief that theirs is a victimless crime since they are merely providing a service to both the whores and the men who patronize them.

"He's got a prior for assault. He only served six months, but he did them in Otisville, and it wasn't a happy time for him. His name came up during a narcotics investigation a year or two back, but he was pretty low down on the food chain and a search of his place turned up nothing. Seems that experience encouraged him to find an alternative outlet for his talents. He got himself a small stable of women, but he's been trying to build it up over the last couple of months. A pimp called Free Billy died a few weeks back — they called him Free Billy on account of the fact that he claimed his rates were so low he was practically giving his whores away for nothing — and his girls were divided up by the rest of the sharks out on the Point. G-Mack had to wait his turn, and by all accounts there wasn't much left for him once the others had taken their pick."

"The girl you're asking after — Alice Temple, street name LaShan — she was one of Free Billy's," said Mackey, taking up the baton. "According to the cops who work the Point she was a good-looking woman once, but she was using, and using hard. She didn't look like she was going to last much longer, even on the Point. G-Mack's been telling people that he let her go cause she wasn't worth anything to him. Said nobody was going to pay good money for a woman looked like she might be dying of the virus. Seems she was friendly with a whore named Sereta. Black Mexican. They came as a twofer. Looks like she dropped off the map about the same time as your girl, but unlike her friend, she didn't appear again."

I leaned forward.

"What do you mean by that?"

"This Alice was picked up close by Kings Highway about a week or so ago. Possession of a controlled substance. Looked like she'd just come out to score. Beat cops found her with the needle in her arm. She didn't even have time to inject."

"She was arrested?"

"It was a quiet night, so her bail was set before the sun came up. She made it within the hour."

"Who paid it?"

"Bail bondsman named Eddie Tager. Her court date was set for the nineteenth, so she still has a couple of days left."

"Is Eddie Tager G-Mack's bondsman?"

Dunne shrugged. "He's pretty low-end, so it's possible, but most pimps tend to pay bail for their whores themselves. It's usually set low, and it allows them to get their hooks deeper into the girl. In Manhattan, first-timers usually just get compulsory health and safe-sex education, but the other boroughs don't have court-based programs to meet the needs of prostitutes, so it goes harder on them over there. The cops who spoke to G-Mack say he denied just about everything except his birth."

"Why were they interested in him?"

"Because of the murder of an antiques dealer named Winston Allen. Allen had a taste for whores from the Point, and there was a rumor that maybe two of G-Mack's girls were among them. G-Mack claimed that they had it all wrong, but the date would tie in with the disappearance of Alice and her friend. We didn't know that when she was picked up, though, and her prints didn't match the partials we got from Allen's house when she was processed."

"Anyone talk with Tager?"

"He's proving hard to find, and nobody has the time

it takes to go looking under rocks for him. Let's be straight here: if you and Walter hadn't come along asking questions, Alice Temple would be struggling for attention, even with the death of Winston Allen. Women disappear from the Point. It happens."

Something passed between Dunne and Mackey. Neither was about to put it into words, though, not without some pushing.

"Lately more than usual?"

It was a blind throw, but it hit home.

"Maybe. It's just rumors, and talk from programs like GEMS and ECPAT, but there's no pattern, which presents a problem, and the ones who are going missing are mostly homeless, or don't have anyone to report them, and it's not just women either. Basically, what we got is a spike in the Bronx figures over the past six months. It might be meaningless or it might not, but unless we start turning up bodies, it's going to stay a blip."

It didn't help us much, but it was good to know.

"So back to business," said Mackey. "We figure that maybe if we feed you this information, you'll help us by taking some of the pressure off, and maybe find out something we can use on G-Mack along the way."

"Such as?"

"He's got a young girl working for him. He keeps her pretty close, but her name is Ellen. We've tried talking to her, but we've got nothing on her to justify pulling her in, and G-Mack has his women schooled halfway to Christmas on entrapment. Juvenile Crime hasn't had any luck with her either. If you find out anything about her, maybe you'll tell us."

"We hear G-Mack called your girl a skank, a junkie

skank," said Mackey. "Thought you might like to know that, just in case you were planning on talking with him."

"I'll remember that," I said. "What's his territory?"

"His girls tend to work the lower end of Lafayette. He likes to keep an eye on them, so he usually parks on the street close by. I hear he's driving a Cutlass Supreme on big-ass tires now, seventy-one, seventy-two, maybe, like he's some kind of millionaire rapper."

"How long has he been driving the Cutlass?"

"Not long."

"Must be doing okay if he can afford a car like that."

"I guess. We didn't see no tax return, so I can't say for sure, but he seems to have come into money recently."

Mackey kept his eyes fixed on me as I spoke. I nodded once, letting him know that I understood what he was intimating: someone had paid him to keep quiet about the women.

"Does he have a place?"

"He lives over on Quimby. Couple of his women live with him. Seems he has a crib over in Brooklyn as well, down on Coney Island Ave. He moves between them."

"Weapons?"

"None of these guys are dumb enough to carry. The more established ones, they maybe keep one or two knuckle grazers that they can call on in case of trouble, but G-Mack ain't in that league yet."

The waitress returned. She looked a whole lot less happy to be coming back than she did when she came over the first time, and she hadn't exactly been ecstatic then.

Dunne and Mackey ordered a tuna on rye and a turkey club. Dunne asked for a "side of sunshine" with his tuna. You had to admire his perseverance.

"Salad or fries," said the waitress. "Sunshine is extra, and you'll have to eat it outside."

"How about fries and a smile?" said Dunne.

"How about you have an accident, then I'll smile?" She left. The world breathed easier.

"You got a death wish, man," said Mackey.

"I could die in her arms," said Dunne.

"You dying on your sorry ass right now, and you ain't even near her arms."

He sighed, and poured so much sugar into his coffee his spoon pretty much stood up straight in it.

"So, you think G-Mack knows where this woman is at?" asked Mackey.

I shrugged. "We're going to ask him that."

"You think he's going to tell you?"

I thought of Louis, and what he would do to G-Mack for hitting Martha. "Eventually," I said.

6

Jackie O was one of the old-time macks, the kind who believed that a man should dress the part. He typically wore a canary yellow suit for business, set off by a white shirt with a pink tie, and yellow and white patent leather shoes. A full-length white leather coat with yellow trim was draped across his shoulders in cold weather, and the ensemble was completed by a white fedora with a pink feather. He carried an antique black cane, topped with a silver horse's head. The head could be removed with a twist, freeing the eighteen-inch blade that was concealed inside. The cops knew that Jackie O carried a sword stick, but Jackie O was never questioned or searched. He was occasionally a good source of information, and as one of the senior figures at the Point he was accorded a modicum of respect. He kept a close eye on the women who worked for him, and tried to treat them right. He paid for their rubbers, which was more than most pimps did, and made sure each was equipped with a pen loaded with pepper spray before she hit the streets. Jackie O was also smart enough to know that wearing fine clothes and driving a nice car didn't mean that what he did had any class, but it was all that he knew how to do. He used his earnings to buy modern art, but he sometimes thought that even the most beautiful of his paintings and sculptures were sullied by the manner in which he had funded their purchase. For that reason he liked to trade up, in the hope that by doing so he might slowly erase the stain upon his collection.

Jackie O didn't entertain many visitors in his Tribeca apartment, purchased on the advice of his accountant many years before and now the most valuable possession that he had. After all, he spent most of his time surrounded by hookers and pimps, and they weren't the kind of people to appreciate the art upon his walls. Real connoisseurs of art tended not to socialize with pimps. They might avail themselves of the services offered by them, but they sure weren't going to be stopping by for wine and cheese. For that reason, Jackie O enjoyed a fleeting moment of pleasure when he looked through the spy hole in his steel door and saw Louis standing outside. Here was somebody who might appreciate his collection, he thought, until he quickly realized the probable reason for the visit. He knew that he had two choices: he could refuse to let Louis in, in which case he was likely to make the situation worse, or he could simply admit him and hope that the situation wasn't already so bad that it couldn't possibly get much worse. Neither option was particularly appealing to him, but the longer Jackie O procrastinated, the more likely he was to try the patience of his visitor.

Before opening the door, he put the safety back on the H&K that he held in his right hand, then slid it into the holster that lay taped flat beneath a small table near the door. He composed his features into as close to an expression of joy and surprise as his fear would allow, unlocked and opened the door, and got as far as the words "My man! Welcome!" before Louis's hand closed around his throat. The barrel of a Glock was

pressed hard into the hollow below Jackie O's left cheek-
bone, a hollow whose size was increased by Jackie O's
gaping mouth. Louis kicked the door shut with his heel,
then forced the pimp back into the living room before
sending him sprawling across his couch. It was two
o'clock in the afternoon, so Jackie O was still wearing
his red Japanese silk robe and a pair of lilac pajamas.
He found it hard to muster his dignity dressed as he
was, but he gave it a good try.

"Hey man, what is this?" he protested. "I invite you
into my home, and this is how you treat me. Look" —
he fingered the collar of his gown, revealing a six-inch
rip in the material — "you done tore my gown, and
this shit's silk."

"Shut up," said Louis. "You know why I'm here."

"How would I know that?"

"It wasn't a question. It was a statement. You *know.*"

Jackie O gave up the act. This man was not one with
whom to play the fool. Jackie O could recall the first
time he ever set eyes on him, almost a decade before.
Even then he had heard stories, but he had not encountered the one about whom they were told. Louis was
different in those days: there was a fire burning coldly
inside him, clear for all to see, although the ferocity of
it was slowly diminishing even then, the flames flickering confusedly in a series of crosswinds. Jackie O
figured that a man couldn't just go on killing and hurting without paying a high price for it over time. The
worst of them — the sociopaths and the psychos —
they just didn't realize it was happening, or maybe some
were just so damaged to start with that there wasn't
much room for further deterioration. Louis wasn't like
that, though, and when Jackie O first knew him the

consequences of his actions were gradually beginning to take their toll upon him.

A honey trap was being set for a man who preyed on young women, after a girl was killed by him in a country far from this one. Some very powerful people had decreed that this man was to die, and he was drowned in a bathtub in his hotel room, lured there with the promise of a girl and a guarantee that no questions would be asked if she suffered a little, for he was a man with the money to indulge his tastes. It wasn't an expensive hotel room, and the man had no possessions with him when he died, other than his wallet and his watch. He was still wearing the watch when he died. In fact, he was fully clothed when he was found, because the people who had ordered his death didn't want there to be even the slightest possibility that it might be mistaken for suicide or natural causes. His killing would serve as a warning to others of his kind.

It was Jackie O's bad luck to be coming out of a hotel room on the same floor when the killer emerged, after Jackie had set up one of his marginally more expensive women for a day's work. He didn't know the man was a killer, not then, or certainly not for sure, although he sensed something circling beneath the seemingly placid surface, like the pale ghost of a shark glimpsed moving through the deep blue depths. Their eyes locked but Jackie kept moving, making for the security of crowds and people. He didn't know where the man was going, or what he had been doing in that hotel room, and he didn't want to know. He didn't even look back until he was at the corner of the hallway, the stairs in view, and by then the man was gone. But Jackie O read the papers, and he didn't need to be a mathematician to put two and two together. At that moment he cursed his high profile among his kind, and his love of fine clothes. He knew he would be easy to find, and he was right.

So this was not the first time that the killer Louis had invaded his space; nor was it the first time that his gun had pressed itself to Jackie's flesh. On that first occasion, Jackie had been sure that he was going to die, but there had been a steadiness to his voice when he said: "You got nothing to fear from me, son. If I was younger, and I had the nerve, I might have done the same myself."

The gun had slowly disengaged itself from his face, and Louis had left him without another word, but Jackie knew that he owed him a debt for his life. In time, Jackie learned more about him, and the stories he had heard started to make sense. After some years Louis returned to him, now changed somehow, and gave Jackie O his name, and asked him to look out for a young woman with a soft Southern accent and a growing love for the needle.

And Jackie had done his best for her. He tried to encourage her to seek another path as she drifted from pimp to pimp. He helped Louis to track her on those repeated occasions when he was determined to force her to seek help. He intervened with others where necessary, reminding those who had her in their charge that she was different, that questions would be asked if she was harmed. Yet it was an unsatisfactory arrangement, and he had seen the pain in the younger man's face as this woman who was blood to him was passed from man to man, and died a little in every hand. Slowly, Jackie began to care less about her, as she started to care less about herself. Now she was gone, and her failed guardian was seeking a reckoning with those responsible.

"She was G-Mack's girl," said Jackie O. "I tried talking to him, but he don't listen to no old men. I got girls of my own to look out for. I couldn't be watching her all the time."

Louis sat down on a chair opposite the couch. The gun remained pointing at Jackie O. It made Jackie O nervous. Louis was calm. The anger had disappeared as suddenly as it had manifested itself, and that made Jackie more afraid than ever. At least anger and rage were human emotions. What he was witnessing now was a man disengaging from all such feelings as he prepared to visit harm on another.

"Now, I got a problem with what you just told me," said Louis. "First of all, you said 'was,' as in she 'was' G-Mack's girl. That's the past tense, and it has a ring of permanence about it that I don't like. Second, last I heard she was with Free Billy. You were supposed to tell me if that situation changed."

"Free Billy died," said Jackie O. "You weren't around. His girls were divided up."

"Did you take any of them?"

"One, yeah. She was Asian. I knew she'd bring in good money."

"But not Alice."

Jackie O realized his mistake.

"I had too many girls already."

"But not so many that you couldn't find room for the Asian."

"She was special, man."

Louis leaned forward slightly.

"Alice was special too. To *me*."

"Don't you think I know that? But I told you, a long time ago, that I wouldn't take her. I wasn't going to have you look in my eyes and see the man who was handing her over to others. I made that clear to you."

Louis's eyes flickered.

"You did."

"I thought she'd be okay with G-Mack, honest, man," said Jackie O. "He's starting out. He wants to make his rep. I heard nothing bad about him, so I had no reason to be concerned for her. He didn't want to hear anything from me, but that don't make him no different from any of the other young bloods."

Slowly, Jackie O was beginning to recover his courage. This wasn't right. This was his place, and he was being disrespected, and over something that wasn't his concern. Jackie O had been in the game too long to take this kind of shit, even from a man like Louis.

"Anyway, the fuck you blaming me for? She wasn't my concern. She was yours. You wanted someone to look out for her all the time, then that someone should have been you."

The words came out in such a rush that, once he had started speaking, Jackie O found himself unable to stop. The accusation now lay between the two men, and Jackie O didn't know if it was going to just disappear, or explode in his face. In the end, it did neither. Louis flinched, and Jackie O saw the guilt wash like rain across his face.

"I tried," he said softly.

Jackie O nodded and looked to the floor. He had seen the woman return to the streets after each intervention by the man before him. She had checked out of public hospitals, and virtually escaped from private clinics. Once, on the last occasion when Louis had tried to take her back, she pulled a blade on him. After that Louis had asked Jackie O to continue doing what he could for her, except there wasn't much that Jackie O could do, because this woman was sliding, and sliding fast. Maybe there were better men than Free Billy for her to be with, but Free Billy wasn't the kind of man who gave up his property easily. He'd received a warning through Jackie O about what would happen to him if he didn't do right by Alice, but it wasn't like they were man and wife and Louis was the father of the bride. This was a pimp and one of his whores we were talking about. Even with the best will in the world — and Free Billy was a long way from having any kind of goodwill — there was a limit to the amount that a pimp could, or would, do for a woman who was forced to make her money from whoring. Then Free Billy died, and Alice ended up with G-Mack. Jackie O knew that he should have taken her into his stable, but he just didn't want her, even aside from anything else he had told Louis. She was trouble, and in daylight she was soon going to look like the walking dead because of all the shit she was pouring into her system. Jackie O didn't hold with junkies in his stable. They were unpredictable, and they spread disease. Jackie O always tried to make sure that his girls practised safe sex, didn't matter how much the John offered for something extra. A woman like Alice, well, hell, there was no predicting what she might do if the need was on her. Other pimps weren't as particular as Jackie O. They didn't have any social conscience. Like he said, he'd figured she'd be okay with G-Mack, except it turned out that G-Mack wasn't smart enough to do the right thing.

Jackie O had survived for a long time in his chosen profession. He grew up on these streets, and he was a wild young man in those days. He stole, sold weed, boosted cars. There wasn't much that Jackie O wouldn't do to turn a buck, although he always drew the line at inflicting harm on his victims. He carried a gun then, but he never had call to use it. Most of the time, those he stole from never even saw his face, because he kept contact to a minimum. Now junkies busted into people's cribs while they were asleep, and when those folks woke up they usually weren't best pleased to see some wired-up brother trying to steal their DVD player, and a confrontation ensued more often than not. People got hurt when there was no necessity for it, and Jackie O didn't hold with that kind of behavior.

Jackie O entered into pimping kind of accidentally. Turned out he was a pimp without even knowing it, on account of the first woman that he fell for in a serious way. Jackie O was down on his luck when he met her, due to some no-account Negroes who had ripped him off on a supply buy that would have kept him in weed for the rest of the year. This left Jackie O with some serious cash flow problems, and he found himself out on the street once he'd used up all the favors he could call in. In the end, there was barely a couch in the neighborhood that he hadn't called his bed at some point. Then he met a woman in a basement bar and one thing led to another, the way it sometimes will between a man and a woman. She was older than he by five years, and she gave him a bed for one night, then a second, then a third. She told him she had a job that kept her out late, but it wasn't until the fourth night that he saw her getting ready for the streets and he figured out what that job might be. But he stayed with her while he waited for his situation to improve, and some nights he would accompany her as she made her way to the little warren of streets upon which she plied her trade, discreetly following her and the johns to vacant lots just to make sure that no harm came to her, in return for which she would give him ten bucks. Once, on a rainy Thursday night, he heard her cry out from the cab of a delivery truck, and he came running to find the guy had slapped her over some imagined slight. Jackie O took care of him, catching him by surprise and hitting him over the back of the head with a black-jack that he kept in his coat pocket for just such an eventuality. After that, he became her shadow, and pretty soon he became the shadow for a bunch of other women too.

Jackie O never looked back.

He tried not to think too deeply about what he did. Jackie O was a God-fearing man, and gave generously to his local church, seeing it as an investment in his future, if nothing else. He knew that what he was doing was wrong in the eyes of the Lord, but if he didn't do it, then someone else would, and that someone might not care about the women the way Jackie did. That would be his argument, if it came down to it and the good Lord was looking dubious about admitting Jackie to his eternal reward.

So Jackie O watched his women and his streets, and encouraged his peers to do likewise. It made good busi-ness sense: they weren't looking out only for their whores, but for the cops too. Jackie didn't like to see his women, half naked and dressed in high heels, trying to run from Vice in the event of a descent on the Point. If they fell in those heels, then, likely as not, they'd do themselves an injury. Given enough notice, they could just slink away into the shadows and wait for the heat to disperse.

That was how the rumors came back to Jackie, shortly after Alice and her friend had disappeared from the streets. The women started to tell of a black van, its plates beaten and obscured. It was a given on the streets that vans and SUVs were to be avoided anyway, because they were tailor-made for abduction and rape. It didn't help that his women were already a little paranoid because stories were circulating about people who had gone missing in recent months: girls and younger men, in the main, most of them homeless or junkies. Jackie O had seriously considered putting some of his women on temporary medication to calm them down, so at first he was skeptical about the mythical van. No approaches were ever made to them from the men inside, they said, and Jackie suggested that it might simply be the cops in another guise, but then Lula, one of his best girls, came to him just as she was about to take to the streets.

"You need to watch out for that black Transit," she told him. "I hear they been asking after some girls used to service some old guy out in Queens."

Jackie O always listened to Lula. She was the oldest of his whores, and she knew the streets and the other women. She was the den mother, and Jackie had learned to trust her instincts.

"You think they're cops?"

"They ain't no cops. Plates are all torn up, and they feel bad, the men inside."

"What do they look like?"

"They're white. One of them's fat, real fat. I didn't get a good look at the other."

"Uh-huh. Well, you just tell the girls to walk away if they see that van. Tell them to come to me, y'hear?"

Lula nodded and went to take up her place at the nearest corner. Jackie O did some walking that night, talking to the other pimps, but it was hard with some as they were men of low breeding, and lower intelligence.

"Yo bitch spookin you, Jackie," said one, a porcine man who liked to be called Havana Slim on account of the cigars that he smoked, didn't matter that the cigars were cheap Dominicans. "You gettin old, man. Street's no place for you now."

Jackie ignored the taunt. He had been here long before Havana, and he would be here long after Havana was gone. Eventually he found G-Mack, but G-Mack just blew Jackie O right off. Jackie O could see that he was rattled, though, and the older man began filling in the blanks for himself.

One night later, Jackie O glimpsed the black van for the first time. He had slipped down an alleyway to take a leak when he saw something gleaming behind a big Dumpster. He zipped himself up as, gradually, the lines of the van were revealed to him. The rear plate was no longer battered or obscured, and Jackie O figured there and then that they were changing the plates on a regular basis. The tires were new, and although some damage had been done to the side panels, it looked purely cosmetic, an attempt to divert attention from the van and its occupants by making it appear older and less well maintained than it really was.

Jackie reached the driver's door. The windows were smoked glass, but Jackie thought that he could see one figure, maybe two, moving inside. He knocked on the glass, but there was no response.

"Hey," said Jackie. "Open up. Maybe I can help you with somethin. You lookin for a woman?"

There was only silence.

Then Jackie O did something dumb. He tried to open the door.

Looking back, Jackie O couldn't figure out why he'd done it. At best, he was going to make whoever was inside the van seriously pissed, and at worst, he could end up with a gun in his face. At least, Jackie O thought that a gun in the face was the worst that could happen.

He grasped the handle and pulled. The door opened. A stench assailed Jackie O, as if someone had taken the bloated carcass of a dead animal buried in shallow ground and suddenly pierced its hide, releasing all the pent-up gas from within. The smell must have made Jackie nauseous, because there was no other way of explaining what he thought he saw inside the cab of the van before the door was yanked closed and the van pulled away. Even now, in the comfort of his own apartment, and with the benefit of hindsight, Jackie could only recall fragmented images.

"It was like it was filled with meat," he told Louis. "Not hanging meat, but like the inside of a body, all purple and red. It was on the panels and on the floor, and I could see blood dripping from it and pooling in places. There was a bench seat in the front, and two figures sitting on it, but they were all black, except for their faces. One was huge and fat. He was closest to me, and the smell came mostly from him. They must have been wearing masks, because their faces looked ruined."

"Ruined?" asked Louis.

"I didn't get a good look at the passenger. Hell, I didn't get much of a look at anything, but the fat one, his face was like a skull. The skin was all wrinkled and black, and the nose looked like it had been broken off, with only a piece left near his forehead. His eyes were kind of green and black, with no whites to them. I saw his teeth too, because he said something when the door opened. His teeth were long, and yellow. It must have been a mask, right? I mean, what else could it be?"

He was almost talking to himself, carrying on an argument in his head that had been going on since the night he had opened the door of the van.

"What else could it be?"

Walter and I separated after our lunch with Mackey and Dunne. They offered to meet up with us again if we needed any more help.

"No witnesses," said Mackey, and there was a sly look in his eye that I didn't like. I didn't care about what they might have heard, but I wasn't going to let someone like Mackey throw my past back in my face.

"If you have something you want to say, then say it now," I said.

Dunne stepped between us.

"Just so we're clear," he said, quietly. "You handle G-Mack how you want to, but he better be breathing and walking when you're done, and if he expires, then you be sure to have a good alibi. Are we clear on that? Otherwise we'll have to come after you."

He didn't look at Walter when he spoke. His eyes remained fixed on me. Only as he turned away did he speak directly to Walter. He said: "You better be careful too, Walter."

Walter didn't reply, and I did not react. After all, Dunne had a point.

"You don't have to come along tonight," I said, once the two cops were out of sight.

"Bullshit. I'm there. But you heard what Dunne said: they'll fall on you if something happens to this G-Mack."

"I'm not going to touch the pimp. If he had anything to do with Alice's disappearance, then we'll get it out of him, and later I'll try to bring him in so he can tell the cops what he knows. But I can only speak for myself. I can't speak for anyone else."

I saw a cab on the horizon. I flagged it and watched with satisfaction as it weaved through two lanes of traffic to get to me.

"Those guys are going to bring you down with them someday," said Walter. He wasn't smiling.

"Maybe I'm dragging them down with me," I replied. "Thanks for this, Walter. I'll be in touch."

I climbed in the cab and left him.

Far away, the Black Angel stirred.

"You made a mistake," it said. "You were supposed to check her background. You assured me that no one would come after her."

"She was just a common whore," said Brightwell. He had returned from Arizona with the weight of Blue's loss heavy upon him. He would be found again, but time was pressing and they needed all of the bodies they could muster. Now, with the death of the girls still fresh in his memory, he was being criticized for his carelessness and he did not like it. He had been alone for so long, without having to answer to anyone, and the exercise of authority chafed upon him in a way that it had not previously done. He also found the atmosphere in the sparsely furnished office oppressive. There was the great desk, ornately carved and topped with green leather, and the expensive antique lamps that shed a dim light on the walls, the wooden floor, and the worn rug upon which he now stood, but there were too many empty spaces waiting to be filled. In a way, it was a metaphor for the existence of the one before whom he now stood.

"No," said the Black Angel. "She was a most *un*common whore. There are questions being asked about her. A report has been filed."

Two great blue veins pulsed at each of Brightwell's temples, extending their reach across either side of his skull, their ambit clearly visible beneath the man's corona of dark hair. He resented the reprimand, and felt his impatience growing.

"If those you had sent to kill Winston had done their job properly and discreetly, then we would not be having this conversation," he said. "You should have consulted me."

"You were not to be found. I have no idea where you go when you disappear into the shadows."

"That's none of your concern."

The Black Angel stood, leaning its hands upon the burnished desk.

"You forget yourself, Mr. Brightwell," it said.

Brightwell's eyes glittered with new anger.

"No," he said. "I have *never* forgotten myself. I remained true. I searched, and I found. I discovered you, and I reminded you of all that you once were. It was you who forgot. I remembered. I remembered it all."

Brightwell was right. The Black Angel recalled their first encounter, the revulsion it had felt, and then, slowly, the dawning understanding and the final acceptance. The Black Angel retreated from the confrontation, and turned instead to the window. Beneath its gaze, people enjoyed the sunshine, and traffic moved slowly along the congested streets.

"Kill the pimp," said the Black Angel. "Discover all that you can about those who are asking questions."

"And then?"

The Black Angel cast Brightwell a bone.

"Use your judgment," it said. There was no point in reminding him of the necessity of attracting no further attention to themselves. They were growing closer to their goal, and furthermore, it realized that Brightwell was moving increasingly beyond its control.

If he had ever truly been under its control.

Brightwell left, but the Black Angel remained lost in remembrance. Strange the forms that we take, it thought. It walked to the gilt mirror upon the wall. Gently it touched its right hand to its face, tracing the lineaments of the skull beneath the skin. Then, slowly, it removed the contact lens from its right eye. It had been forced to wear the lens for hours today as there were people to be met and papers to be signed, and now its eye felt as though it were burning. The mark did not react well to concealment.

The Black Angel leaned closer, tugging at the skin beneath its eye. A white sheen lay across the blue of the iris, like the ruined sail of a ship at sea, or a face briefly glimpsed through parting clouds.

That night, G-Mack took to the streets with a gun tucked into the waistband of his jeans. It was a Hi-Point nine-millimeter, alloy framed and loaded up with CorBon +P ammunition for maximum stopping power. The gun had cost G-Mack very little—hell, even new, the Hi-Point retailed for about ten percent of what a similar Walther P5 would go for — and he figured that if the cops came around and he had to let it go, then he wouldn't be out of pocket by too much. He had fired the gun only a couple of times, out in the New Jersey woods, and he knew that the Hi-Point didn't respond well to the CorBon ammo. It affected the accuracy, and the recoil was just plain nasty, but G-Mack knew that if it came down to it he'd be using the Hi-Point right up close, and anyone who took one from the gun at that range was going to stay down.

He left the Cutlass Supreme in the lockup, and instead drove over to the Point in the Dodge that he used for backup. G-Mack didn't care if one of the other brothers saw him driving the old-lady car. The ones that mattered knew he had the Cutlass, could take it out anytime he damn well pleased if they needed some reminding, but the Dodge was less likely to attract attention, and it had enough under the hood to get him out of trouble quickly if the need arose. He parked up in an alleyway — the same alleyway in which Jackie O had seen fit to try to confront the occupants of the black van, although G-Mack didn't know that — then slipped out onto the streets of the Point. He kept his head down, doing the rounds of his whores from the shadows, then retreated back to the Dodge. He had instructed the young bitch, Ellen, to act as an intermediary, bringing the money from the others to him instead of forcing him to return to the streets again.

He was scared, and he wasn't ashamed to admit it. He reached beneath the driver's seat and removed a Glock

23 from its slot. The Hi-Point under his arm would do if he ran into trouble on the street, but the 23 was his baby. He'd been put onto it by a guy who got drummed out of the South Carolina State Police for corruption and now did a thriving business in firearms for the more discerning customer. The Staties down in SC had adopted the 23 sight unseen, and had never had cause to complain. Loaded up with .40-caliber S&W cartridges, it was one mean killing machine. G-Mack removed the Hi-Point from his holster and balanced both weapons in his hands. Next to the Glock, it was clear what a piece of shit the Hi-Point really was, but G-Mack wasn't too concerned. This wasn't a fashion show. This was life or death, and anyway, two guns were always better than one.

We descended on Hunts Point shortly before midnight.

In the nineteenth century, Hunts Point was home to wealthy landowning families, their numbers gradually swelled by city dwellers envious of the luxurious lifestyles available to the Point's residents. After World War I, a train line was built along Southern Boulevard, and the mansions gave way to apartments. City businesses began to relocate, attracted by the space available for development and ease of access to the tri-state region. The poor and working-class families (nearly sixty thousand residents, or two-thirds of the population, in the 1970s alone) were forced out as Hunts Point's reputation grew in business circles, leading to the opening of the produce market in 1967 and the meat market in 1974. There were recycling stores, warehouses, commercial waste depots, auto glass sellers, scrap dealers — and, of course, the big markets, to and from which the trucks trundled, sometimes providing the hookers with a little business along the way. Nearly ten thousand people still lived in the district, and to their credit they had campaigned for traffic signals, modified truck routes, new trees, and a waterfront park, slowly improving this sliver of the South Bronx to create a better home for themselves and for future generations; but they were living in an area that was a crossroads for all the garbage the city of New York could provide. There were two dozen waste transfer stations on this little peninsula alone, and half of all its putrescible garbage and most of its sewage sludge ended up there. The whole area stank in summer, and asthma was rife. Garbage clung to fences and filled the gutters, and the noise of 2 million truck trips a year provided a sound track of squealing brakes, tooting horns, and beeping reverse signals. Hunts Point was a miniature city of industry, and among the most visible of those industries was prostitution.

The streets were already crammed with cars as I arrived, and women tottered between them on absurdly high heels, most of them wearing little more than lingerie. There were all shapes, all ages, all colors. In its way, the Point was the most egalitarian of places. Some of the women shuffled like they were in the final stages of Parkinson's, jerking and shifting from one foot to the other while trying to keep their spines straight in what was known locally as the "crack dance," their pipes tucked into their bras or the waistbands of their skirts. Two girls on Lafayette were eating sandwiches provided by the Nightworks outreach initiative, which tried to provide the working girls with health care, condoms, clean needles, even food when necessary. The women's heads moved constantly, watching for pimps, johns, cops. The cops liked to swoop occasionally, backing up the paddy wagons to street corners and simply sweeping any hookers within reach into the back, or pink-slipping them for disorderly conduct or obstructing traffic, even loitering, anything to break up their business. A $250 fine was a lot for these women to pay if they didn't have a pimp to back them up, and many routinely spent thirty to sixty days in the can for nonpayment rather than hand over to the courts money that they could ill afford to lose, if the poorer ones had $250 to begin with.

I went into the Green Mill to wait for the others. The Green Mill was a legendary Hunts Point diner. It had been around for decades, and was now the main resting place for cold pimps and tired whores. It was relatively quiet when I got there, since business was good on the streets. A couple of pimps wearing Philadelphia Phillies shirts sat at one of the windows, flicking through a copy of *Rides* magazine and arguing the relative merits of assorted hookups. I took a seat near the door and waited. There was a young girl seated at one of the booths. Her hair was dark and she was dressed in a short black dress that was little more than a slip. Three times I saw older women enter the diner, give her money, then leave again. After the third had departed, the girl closed the little purse containing the money and left the diner. She was back again maybe five minutes later, and the cycle resumed.

Angel joined me shortly after the girl had returned. He had dressed down for the occasion, if such a thing were actually possible. His jeans were even more worn than usual, and his denim jacket looked like it had been stolen from the corpse of a particularly unhygienic biker.

"We have him," he said.

"Where?"

"An alley, two blocks away. He's sitting in a Dodge, listening to the radio."

"He alone?"

"Looks like it. The girl over at the window seems to be bringing him his money a couple of times an hour, but she's the only one who's been near him since ten."

"You figure he's armed?"

"I would be if I was him."

"He doesn't know we're coming."

"He knows somebody's coming. Louis talked to Jackie O."

"The old-timer?"

"Right. He just gave us the lead. He figures G-Mack made a big mistake, and he's known it since the night Martha confronted him. He's edgy."

"I'm surprised he's stayed around this long."

"Jackie O thinks he'd run if he could. He's low on funds, seeing as how he spent all his money on a fancy ride, and he has no friends."

"That's heartbreaking."

"I thought you might see it that way. Pay at the register. You leave it on the table and someone will steal it."

I paid for my coffee and followed Angel from the diner.

We intercepted the girl just as she entered the alley. The pimp's Dodge was parked around a corner in a lot behind a big brownstone, with an exit behind him onto the street and one before him that connected perpendicularly with an alley. For the moment, we were out of his sight.

"Hi," I said.

"I'm not interested tonight," she replied.

She tried to walk around me. I gripped her arm. My hand entirely enclosed it, with so much room to spare that I had to tighten my fist considerably just to hold on to her. She opened her mouth to scream and Louis's hand closed around it as we moved her into the shadows.

"Take it easy," I said. "We're not going to hurt you."

I showed her my licence, but didn't give her enough time to take in the details.

"I'm an investigator," I said. "Understand? I just need a few words."

I nodded to Louis, and he carefully removed his hand from her mouth. She didn't try to scream again, but he kept his hand close just in case.

"What's your name?"

"Ellen."

"You're one of G-Mack's girls."

"So?"

"Where are you from?"

"Aberdeen."

"You and a million other Kurt Cobain fans. Seriously, where are you from?"

"Detroit," she said, her shoulders sagging. She was probably still lying.

"How old are you?"

"I don't have to answer any of your questions."

"I know you don't. I'm just asking. You don't want to tell me, you don't have to."

"I'm nineteen."

"Bullshit," said Louis. "That's how old you'll be in 2007."

"Fuck you."

"Okay, listen to me, Ellen. G-Mack is in a lot of trouble. After tonight, he's not going to be in business anymore. I want you to take whatever money is in that purse and walk away. Go back to the Green Mill first. Our friend will stay with you to make sure you don't talk to anyone."

Ellen looked torn. I saw her tense, but Louis immediately brought his hand closer to her mouth.

"Ellen, just do it."

Walter Cole appeared beside us.

"It's okay, honey," he said. "Come on, I'll walk back with you, buy you a cup of coffee, whatever you want."

Ellen had no choice. Walter wrapped an arm around her shoulder. It looked almost protective, but he kept a tight grip on her in case she tried to run. She looked back at us.

"Don't hurt him," she said. "I got nobody else."

Walter walked her across the road. She took her old seat, and he sat beside her, so that he could hear all that she said to the other women, and could stop her if she made a break for the door.

"She's just a child," I said to Louis.

"Yeah," he said. "Save her later."

G-Mack had promised to slip Ellen ten percent of whatever the other women made if she acted as his go-between for the night, a deal to which Ellen was happy to agree because it meant that she got to spend a few hours drinking coffee and reading magazines instead of freezing her ass off in her underwear while she tried to entice sleazebags into vacant lots. But it didn't do for G-Mack to be away from his women for too long. The bitches were already ripping him off. Without his physical presence to keep them in line, he'd be lucky to come out with nickels and dimes by close of business. He knew that Ellen would also take a little extra before she handed over the cash to him, so all things considered, this wasn't going to be a profitable night for him. He didn't know how much longer he could stay in the shadows, trying to avoid a confrontation that must inevitably come unless he got together enough cash to run. He had considered selling on the Cutlass, but only for about five seconds. He loved that car. Buying it had been his dream, and disposing of it would be like admitting that he was a failure.

A figure moved in his rearview mirror. The Hi-Point was back in the waistband of his jeans, but the Glock was warm in his right hand, held low down by his thigh. He tightened his grip on it. It felt slick upon the sweat of his palm. A man stood, wavering, close to the wall. G-Mack could see that he was a no-count, dressed in tattered denims and anonymous sneakers that looked like they came from a thrift store. The man fumbled in his pants, then turned to one side and leaned his forehead against the wall, waiting for the flow to start. G-Mack relaxed his grip on the Glock.

The driver's-side window of the Dodge exploded inward, showering him with glass. He tried to raise his gun as the passenger window also disintegrated, but he received a blow to the side of the head that stunned him, and then a strong hand was upon his right arm and the muzzle of a gun much bigger than his own was pressed painfully into his temple. He caught a glimpse of a black man with close-cropped graying hair and a vaguely satanic beard. The man did not look happy to see him.

G-Mack's left hand began to drift casually toward the Hi-Point concealed beneath his jacket, but the passenger door opened and another voice said: "I wouldn't."

G-Mack didn't, and the Hi-Point was slipped from his jeans.

"Let the Glock go," said Louis.

G-Mack allowed the gun to drop to the floor of the car.

Slowly, Louis eased the gun away from G-Mack's temple and opened the car door.

"Get out," said Louis. "Keep your hands raised."

G-Mack glanced to his left, where I knelt outside the passenger door. The Hi-Point in my left hand was dwarfed by my Colt. It was Big Gun Night, but nobody had told G-Mack. He stepped carefully from the car, falling glass tinkling to the ground as he did so. Louis turned him, pushing him against the side of the car and forcing his legs apart. G-Mack felt hands upon him and saw the little man in denim who had previously seemed on the verge of taking a drunken leak. He couldn't believe that he had been fooled so easily.

Louis tapped him with the barrel of his own H&K.

"You see how dumb you are?" he said. "Now, we going to give you a chance to show how smart you are instead. Turn around, slowly."

G-Mack did as he was told. He was now facing Louis and Angel. Angel was holding G-Mack's Glock. G-Mack wasn't going to be getting it back. In fact, although G-Mack probably didn't know it, he was now as close as he had ever come to being killed.

"What do you want?" asked G-Mack.

"Information. We want to know about a woman named Alice. She's one of your girls."

"She's gone. I don't know where she's at."

Louis raked his gun across G-Mack's face. The younger man curled up, his hands cupped around his ruined nose and blood flowing freely between his fingers.

"You remember a woman?" said Louis. "Came to you a couple of nights back, asked you the same question that I just asked? You remember what you did to her?"

After a moment's pause, G-Mack nodded, his head still down and drops of blood sprinkling the pitted ground beneath his feet, falling on the weeds that had sprouted between the cracks.

"Well, I ain't even started hurting you enough for what happened to her, so if you don't answer my questions right, then you won't be walking out of this alley, do you understand?"

Louis's voice dropped until it was barely a whisper.

"The worst thing about what will happen to you is that I won't kill you," he said. "I'll leave you a cripple, with hands that won't grip, ears that won't hear, and eyes that won't see. Are we clear?"

Again, G-Mack nodded. He had no doubt that this man would carry out his threats to the letter.

"Look at me," said Louis.

G-Mack lowered his hands and raised his head. His lower jaw hung open in shock, and his teeth were red.

"What happened to the girl?"

"A guy came to me," said G-Mack. His voice was distorted by the damage to his nose. "He told me that he'd give me good money if I could trace her."

"Why did he want her?"

"She was in a house with a john, a guy named Winston, and a raid went down. The guy got killed, his driver too. Alice and another girl, Sereta, were there.

171

They ran, but Sereta took something from the house before she left. The guys who did the killing, they wanted it back."

G-Mack tried to sniff back some of the blood that had now slowed to an ooze over his lips and chin. The pain made him wince.

"She was a junkie, man," he said. He was pleading, but his voice remained monotonic, as though he himself did not believe what he was telling Louis. "She was on the long slide. She wasn't earning no more than a hundred dollars out there, and that was on a good night. I was gonna cut her loose anyway. He said nothing bad would happen to her, once she told them what they wanted to know."

"And you're telling me that you believed him?"

G-Mack stared Louis straight in the face.

"What did it matter?" he said.

For the first time in all the years that I had known him, Louis seemed about to lose control. I saw the gun rising, and his finger tightening on the trigger. I reached out my hand and stopped it before it could point at G-Mack.

"If you kill him, we learn nothing more," I said.

The gun continued its upward pressure against my hand for a couple of seconds, then stopped.

"Tell me his name," said Louis.

"He didn't give me a name," said G-Mack. "He was fat and ugly, and he smelled bad. I didn't see him but once."

"He give you a number, a place to contact him?"

"The guy with him did. Slim, dressed in blue. He came to me, after I told him where she was at. He brought me my money, told me to keep my mouth shut."

"How much?" asked Louis. "How much did you sell her out for?"

G-Mack swallowed.

"Ten G's. They promised ten more if she gave them Sereta."

I stepped away from them. If Louis wanted to kill him, then let it be done.

"She was blood to me," said Louis.

"I didn't know," said G-Mack. "I didn't know! She was a junkie. I didn't think it would matter."

Louis gripped him by the throat and forced the gun against G-Mack's chest. Louis's face contorted and a wail forced itself from somewhere deep within him, issuing forth from the place where all of his love and loyalty existed, walled off from all the evil that he had done.

"Don't," said the pimp, and now he was crying. "Please don't. I know more. I can give you more."

Louis's face was close to him now, so close that blood from G-Mack's mouth had spattered his features.

"Tell me."

"I followed the guy, after he paid me off. I wanted to know where I could find him, if I had to."

"You mean in case the cops came along, and you had to sell him out to save your skin."

"Whatever, man, whatever!"

"And?"

"Let me go," said G-Mack. "I tell you, you let me walk away."

"You got to be fuckin with me."

"Listen, man, I did wrong, but I didn't hurt her. You need to talk to someone else about what happened to her. I'll tell you where you can find them, but you got to let me walk. I'll leave town, and you'll never see me again, I swear."

"You tryin to bargain with a man got a gun pushed into your chest?"

It was Angel who intervened.

"We don't know that she's dead," he said. "There may still be a chance of finding her alive."

Louis looked to me. If Angel was playing good cop and Louis bad cop, then my role was somewhere in between. But if Louis killed G-Mack, it would go bad for me. I didn't doubt that Mackey and Dunne would come looking for me, and I would have no alibi. At the very least, it would involve some awkward questions, and might even reopen old wounds that would be better off left unexplored.

"I say listen to him," I said. "We go looking for this guy. If it turns out that our friend here is lying, then you can do what you want with him."

Louis took his time deciding, and all the while G-Mack's life hung from a thread, and he knew it. At last Louis took a step back, and lowered the gun.

"Where is he?"

"I followed him to a place off Bedford."

Louis nodded.

"Looks like you bought yourself a few more hours of life," he said.

Garcia watched the four men from his hiding place behind the Dumpster. Garcia believed all that Brightwell had told him, and was certain of the rewards that he had been promised. He now bore the brand upon his wrist, so that he might be recognized by others like him, but unlike Brightwell he was merely a foot soldier, a conscript in the great war being waged. Brightwell also bore a brand upon his wrist, but although it was far older than Garcia's it appeared never to have properly healed. In fact, when Garcia stood close to Brightwell, he could sometimes detect the smell of scorched flesh from him, if a diminution of the fat man's own stench permitted it.

Garcia did not know if the fat man's name was really Brightwell. In truth, Garcia did not care. He trusted Brightwell's judgment, and was grateful to him for finding him, for bringing him to this great city once Garcia had honed his abilities to Brightwell's satisfaction, and for giving him a place in which to work and to pursue his obsessions. Brightwell, in turn, had found in Garcia a willing convert to his convictions. Garcia had just absorbed them into his own belief system, relegating other deities where necessary, or dispensing with them entirely if they conflicted utterly with the new, compelling vision of the world — both this world, and the world below — presented to him by Brightwell.

Garcia was concerned at the wisdom of not intervening once they saw the three men approach the pimp G-Mack, but he would make no move unless Brightwell moved first. They had just been a little too late. Minutes earlier, and the pimp would have been dead by the time these strangers had found him.

As Garcia watched, two of the men took G-Mack by the arms and led him from his car. The third man seemed about to follow, then stopped. He scanned the alleyway, his gaze resting for a moment on the shadows that obscured Garcia, then moved on, his head tilting back as he took in the buildings that surrounded him, with their filthy windows and their battered fire escapes. After a minute had elapsed, he followed his companions from the alley, but he kept his back to them, retreating from the lot, his eyes scanning the dirty windows as though aware of the hostile presence concealed behind them.

Brightwell had decided to kill them. He would follow the four men, then he and Garcia would slaughter them and dispose of them. He did not fear them, even the black man who moved so quickly and had an air of lethality about him. If it were done swiftly and cleanly, then the consequences would be limited.

Brightwell was standing in the grimy hallway of an apartment block, close by the entrance to the fire escape, where a single yellowed window looked down upon the alley below. He had taken the precaution of removing the starter from the fluorescent light behind him, so that he might not be seen if for any reason the lights were switched on. He was about to turn away from the window when the white man in the dark jacket, whose back had been to Brightwell for the duration of their confrontation with G-Mack, turned and scanned the windows. As his gaze fell upon Brightwell's hiding place, Brightwell felt something constrict in his throat. He took a step closer to the window, his right hand instinctively reaching out and touching the glass, his fingertips resting against the figure of the man below. Memories surged through his brain: memories of falling, fire, despair, wrath.

Memories of betrayal.

Now the man in the alley was backing away, as though he too sensed something hostile, a presence that was both unknown yet familiar to him. His eyes continued to search the windows above, seeking any sign of movement, any indication of the source of what he sensed within himself. Then he disappeared at last from Brightwell's sight, but the fat man did not move. Instead, he closed his eyes and released a trembling breath, all thoughts of killing banished from his mind. What had so long evaded him was now unexpectedly, joyously revealed.

We have found you at last, he thought.

You are discovered.

7

As I retreated down the alleyway, I tried to put a name on what I had felt as I stared at the window. The sense of being watched was strong from the moment that we confronted G-Mack, but I was unable to detect any obvious signs of surveillance. We were surrounded by brownstones and warehouses, and any one of them could have concealed a watcher, maybe just a curious neighbor or even a whore and her john on their way to a slightly pricier assignation in a run-down apartment, pausing briefly to take in the men in the alleyway before proceeding on their way, conscious always that time was money and that the demands of the flesh were pressing.

It was only when Angel and Louis began moving G-Mack, and I had a moment to scan the windows one last time, that the prickling began at the base of my neck. I was conscious of a disturbance in the night, as though a silent explosion had occurred somewhere in the distance and the shock waves were now approaching the place in which I stood. A great force seemed to rush toward me, and I half expected to see a shimmering in the air as the circle widened, churning garbage and scattering discarded newspapers as it came. My attention focused on one particular window on the fourth floor of an old brownstone, a fire door close by leading to a rusted fire escape. The window was dark, but I thought for a moment that I saw a shifting against the glass, black momentarily giving way to gray at the center. Buried memories, both alien to me yet almost familiar, tried to emerge from my unconscious. I sensed them there, moving like worms beneath frozen earth or like parasites under the skin, desperately seeking to break through and expose themselves to the light. I heard a terrible howling, and it was as if voices were raised in rage and despair, descending from some great height, twisting and tumbling through the air, their cries distorting and fading as they fell. I was among them, jostled by the flailing of my brothers, hands striking me, nails tearing in a desperate attempt to arrest the descent. There was fear in me, and regret, but more than anything else I was filled with a dreadful sense of loss. Something indescribably precious had been taken from me, and I would never see it again.

And we were burning. We were all burning.

Then this half-remembered, half-created past, this phantasm from my mind, found itself bound up with real loss, for the pain brought back the deaths of my wife and my daughter, and the emptiness that their passing had left inside. And yet the torment that I had endured on the night that they were taken from me, and the awful, debilitating pain that followed, seemed somehow less than what I now felt in the alleyway, the footsteps of my friends slowly growing distant, the protestations of the doomed man between them fading away. There was only the howling, and the emptiness, and the figure lost behind yellowed glass, reaching out to me. Something cold touched my cheek, like the unwanted caress of a lover once cherished and now rejected. I drew back from it, and thought that my response had somehow generated a reaction in the hidden figure at the window. I sensed its surprise at my presence mutate into manifest hostility, and I thought that I had never before been in proximity to such rage. Any impulse I had to ascend to the upper floor of the building immediately disappeared. I wanted to flee, to run and hide and reinvent myself somewhere far away, to cloak myself in a new identity and lie low in the hope that they would not track me down.

They.

He.

It.

How did I know this?

And as I moved slowly away, following Angel and Louis to the busy streets beyond, a voice that was once like mine spoke words that I did not understand. It said:

You are discovered.

We have found you again.

Louis was sitting in the driver's seat of his Lexus when I reached them. Angel was in the back beside G-Mack, who sat sullen and hunched, sniffing gently through his ruined nose. Before I got in beside Louis, I took a pair of cuffs from my jacket pocket and told G-Mack to attach one cuff to his right wrist and the other to the armrest of the door. When he had done so, and his right arm was crossed awkwardly over his body, I got in the car and we drove away from the Point. Louis stole a glance at me.

"Everything okay back there?"

I looked over my shoulder at G-Mack, but he appeared lost in his own misery and hurt.

"I felt like we were being watched," I said quietly. "There was someone in one of the upper stories."

"If that's true, then there was someone on the ground as well. You think they were coming for this piece of shit in the back?"

"Maybe, but we got to him first."

"They know about us now."

"I think they knew about us already. Otherwise, why start tidying up the loose ends?"

Louis checked the rearview mirror, but the nature of the night traffic made it hard to tell if we were being followed. It didn't matter. We would have to assume that we were, and wait to see what developed.

"I think you have more to tell us," I said to G-Mack.

"My man in blue came to me, paid me, then told me not to ask no questions. That's all I know about him."

"How were they going to get to her?"

"He said it wasn't none of my business."

"You use a bail bondsman named Eddie Tager for your girls?"

"Hell, no. Most of the time, they just get pink-slipped anyways. They get themselves in some serious shit, I'm gonna have me a talk with them, see if we can work something out. I ain't no charity, givin it away to no bondsman."

"I bet you're real understanding about how they pay it back too."

"This is a business. Nobody gets nothing for free."

"So when Alice was arrested, what did you do?"

He didn't reply. I slapped him once, hard, on his wounded face.

"Answer me."

"I called the number they gave me."

"Cell phone?"

"Yeah."

"You still have the number?"

"I remember it, *bitch*."

Blood had dripped onto his lips. He spit it onto the floor of the car, then recited the number by heart. I took out my cell and entered the number, then, just to be safe, wrote it in my notebook. I guessed that it wouldn't lead to much. If they were smart, they'd have disposed of the phone as soon as they had the girl.

"Where did Alice keep her personal things?" I said.

"I let her leave some stuff at my place, makeup and shit, but she stayed with Sereta most of the time. Sereta had her a room up on Westchester. I wasn't gonna have no junkie *whore* in my crib." When he said the word "whore" he looked at Louis. We had learned all that we would from G-Mack. As for Louis, he did not respond to the pimp's goads. Instead, he pulled over to drop me at my car, and I followed them to Brooklyn.

Williamsburg, like the Point, was once home to some of the wealthiest men in the country. There were mansions here, and beer gardens, and private clubs. The Whitneys rubbed shoulders with the Vanderbilts, and lavish buildings were erected, all close enough to the sugar refineries and distilleries, the shipyards and the foundries, for the smell to reach the rich if the wind was blowing the right way.

Williamsburg's status as the playground of the wealthy changed at the beginning of the last century, with the opening of the Williamsburg Bridge. European immigrants — Poles, Russians, Lithuanians, Italians —

fled the crowded slums of the Lower East Side, taking up occupancy of the tenements and the brownstones. They were followed by the Jews, in the thirties and forties, who settled mainly in Southside, among them Satmar Hasidim from Hungary and Romania, who still congregated in the section northeast of the Brooklyn Navy Yard.

Northside was a little different. It was now trendy and bohemian, and the fact that Bedford Avenue was the first stop made by the L train from Manhattan meant that it was an easy commute, so property prices were going up. Nevertheless, the area had some way to go before it achieved true desirability for those with money in their pockets, and it was not about to abandon its old identity without a fight. The Northside Pharmacy on Bedford still took care to call itself additionally a *farmacia* and an *apteka*; Edwin's Fruit and Veg store sold Zywiec beer from Poland, advertised with a small neon sign in the window; and the meat market remained the Polska-Masarna. There were delis and beauty salons, and Mike's Northstar Hardware continued in business, but there was also a little coffee shop called Reads that sold used books and alternative magazines, and the lampposts were dotted with flyers hawking loft spaces for artists' studios.

I hung a right on Tenth at Raymund's Diner, with its wooden *Bierkeller* sign illustrated by a beer and a joint of meat. One block down, at Berry, stood a warehouse building that still bore the faint traces of its previous existence as a brewery, for this area was once the heart of New York's brewing industry. The warehouse was five stories tall and badly scarred by graffiti. A fire escape ran down the center of its eastern façade, and a banner had been strung across the top floor. It read: "If You Lived Here, You'd Be Home By Now!" Someone had crossed out the word "Home" and spray painted the word "Polish" in its place. Underneath was a telephone number. No lights burned in any of the windows. I watched Louis drive around the block once, then park on Eleventh. I pulled up behind him and walked to his car. He was leaning back on his seat, talking to G-Mack.

"You sure this is the place?" Louis asked him.

"Yeah, I'm sure."

"If you're lying, I'll hurt you again."

G-Mack tried to hold Louis's gaze, but failed.

"I know that."

Louis turned his attention to Angel and me.

"Get out, keep an eye on the place. I'm gonna dump my boy here."

There was nothing that I could say. G-Mack looked worried. He had every reason to.

"Hey, I done told you everything I know," he protested. His voice broke slightly.

Louis ignored him.

"I'm not gonna kill him," he said to me.

I nodded.

Angel got out of the car, and we faded into the shadows as Louis drove G-Mack away.

The present is very fragile, and the ground beneath our feet is thin and treacherous. Beneath it lies the maze of the past, a honeycomb network created by the strata of days and years where memories lie buried, waiting for the moment when the thin crust above cracks and what was and what is can become one again. There is life down there in the honeycomb world, and Brightwell was now alerting it to his discovery. Everything had changed for him, and new plans would have to be made. He called the most private of numbers, and saw, as the sleepy voice answered, that white mote flickering in the darkness.

"They were too quick for us," he said. "They have him, and they're moving. But something interesting has emerged. An old acquaintance has returned . . ."

Louis parked the car in the delivery bay of a Chinese food store, close by the Woodhull Medical Center, on Broadway. He tossed G-Mack the key to the cuffs, watched silently as he freed his hand, then stood back to let him step from the car.

"Lie down on your belly."

"Please, man—"

"Lie *down*."

G-Mack sank to his knees, then stretched flat on the ground.

"Spread your arms and your legs."

"I'm sorry," said G-Mack. His face was contorted with fear. "You got to believe me."

His head was turned to one side so that he could see Louis. He began to cry as the suppressor was mounted on the muzzle of the little .22 that Louis always carried as backup.

"I do believe you're sorry now. I can hear it in your voice."

"Please," said G-Mack. Blood and snot mixed on his lips. *"Please."*

"This is your last chance. Have you told us everything?"

"Yeah! I got nothing else. I swear to you, man."

"You right-handed?"

"What?"

"I said, are you right-handed?"

"Yeah."

"So I figure you hit the woman with that hand?"

"I don't—"

Louis took one look around to make sure nobody was near, then fired a single shot into the back of G-Mack's right hand. G-Mack screamed. Louis took two steps back and fired a second shot into the pimp's right ankle.

G-Mack gritted his teeth and pressed his forehead against the ground, but the pain was too much. He raised his damaged right hand and used his left to push himself up and look at his wounded foot.

"Now you can't go far if I need to find you again," said Louis. He raised the gun and leveled it at G-Mack's face. "You're a lucky man. Don't forget that. But you better pray that I find Alice alive."

He lowered the gun and walked back to the car.

"Hospital's across the street," he said, then drove away.

Apart from the fire escape, there appeared to be only one way into or out of the building, and that was a single steel door on Berry. There were no bells or buzzers, and no names of residents.

"You think he was lying?" asked Angel.

Louis had rejoined us. I didn't ask him about G-Mack.

"No," said Louis. "He wasn't lying. Open it."

Louis and I took up positions at opposite corners of

the building, watching the streets while Angel worked on the lock. It took him five minutes, which was a long time for him. "Old locks are good locks," he said, by way of explanation.

We slipped inside and pulled the door closed behind us. The first floor was an entirely open space that had once been used to house the vats, with storage space for barrels and sliding doors to admit trucks. The doors were long gone, and the entrances bricked up. To the right, beside what had once been a small office, a flight of stairs led up to the next floor. There was no elevator. The next three floors were similar to the first: largely open-plan, with no signs of habitation.

The top story was different. Someone had commenced a halfhearted division of the space into apartments, although it looked like the work had been done some time before, and then abandoned. Walls had been erected but most had no doors added, so that it was possible to see the empty areas within. There appeared to be five or six apartments planned in total, but only one seemed to be finished. The green entrance door was unmarked, and closed. I took the left side, while Angel and Louis moved to the right. I knocked twice, then drew back quickly. There was no reply. I tried again, but with the same result. We now had a couple of options, neither of which appealed to me. Either we could try to break down the door or Angel could pick the two locks and risk getting his head blown off if someone was inside and listening.

Angel made the choice. He got down on one knee, spread his little set of tools on the floor, then handed one to Louis. Simultaneously, they worked the locks, both of them trying to shield themselves as best they could by keeping as much of their bodies as possible against the wall. It seemed to take a long time, but was probably less than a minute. Eventually, both locks turned, and they pushed the door open.

To the left was a galley-style kitchen, with the remains of some fast food on the counter. There was cream in the refrigerator, with three days remaining before it expired, and a paper bag filled with pita bread, also apparently fresh. Apart from some cans of beans and franks and a couple of containers of macaroni and cheese, this was the sum total of food in the apartment. The entrance hall then led into a lounge area, consisting only of a couch, an easy chair, and a TV and VCR. Again to the left was the smaller of the apartment's two bedrooms, the single bed casually made, and with a pair of boots and one or two items of clothing visible on a chair by the window. With Angel covering me, I checked the closet, but it contained only cheap trousers and shirts.

We heard a low whistle, and followed it to where Louis stood in the doorway of a second bedroom to the right, his body blocking our view. He stepped to one side, and we saw what lay within.

It was a shrine, and its inspiration lay in a place far distant from this one, and in a past far stranger than any we could imagine.

III

But thee and me He never can destroy;
Change us He may, but not o'erwhelm; we are
Of as eternal essence, and must war
With Him if He will war with us.

Lord Byron, *Heaven and Earth: A Mystery* (1821)

8

The town of Sedlec lies some thirty miles from the city of Prague. An incurious traveler, perhaps deterred by the dull suburbs, might not even deign to stop here, instead opting to press on to the nearby, and better known, town of Kutná Hora, which has now virtually absorbed Sedlec into itself. Yet it was not always thus, for this part of the old kingdom of Bohemia was one of the medieval world's largest sources of silver. By the late thirteenth century, one third of all Europe's silver came from this district, but silver coins were being minted here as early as the tenth century. The silver lured many to this place, making it a serious rival to the economic and political supremacy of Prague. Intriguers came, and adventurers, merchants, and craftsmen. And where there was power, so too there were the representatives of the one power that stands above all. Where there was wealth, there was the church.

The first Cistercian monastery was founded in Sedlec by Miroslav of Cimburk in 1142. Its monks came from Valdsassen Abbey in the Upper Palatinate, attracted by the promise of silver ore, for Valdsassen was one of the Morimon line of monasteries associated with mining. (The Cistercians, to their credit, might charitably be said to have employed a pragmatic attitude toward wealth and its accumulation.) Clearly, God Himself was smiling upon their endeavors, for deposits of silver ore were found on the monastery's lands in the late thirteenth century, and the influence of the Cistercians grew as a result. Unfortunately, God's attentions quickly turned elsewhere, and by the end of the century the monastery had suffered the first of its numerous destructions at the hands of hostile men, a process that reached its peak in the attack of 1421, which left it in smoldering ruins, the assault that marked the first coming of the Believers.

Sedlec, Bohemia, April 21, 1421

The noise of battle had ceased. It no longer shook the monastery walls, and no more were the monks troubled by fine scatterings of gray dust that descended upon their white garb, accumulating in their tonsures so that the young looked old and the old looked older still. Distant flames still rose to the south, and the bodies of the slain were accumulating inside the nearby cemetery gates, with more being added to their number every day, but the great armies were now silent and watchful. The stench was foul, but the monks were almost used to it after all these years of dealing with the dead, for bones were forever stacked like kindling around the ossuary, piled high against the walls as graves were emptied of their occupants and new remains interred in their place in a great cycle of burial, decay, and display. When the wind blew from the east, poisonous smoke from the smelting of ore was added to the mix, and those forced to work in the open coughed until their robes were dotted with blood.

The abbot of Sedlec stood at the gate of his lodge,

in the shadow of the monastery's conventual church. He was the heir of the great Abbot Heidenreich, diplomat and adviser to kings, who had died a century earlier but who had transformed the monastery into a center of influence, power, and wealth—aided by the discovery of great deposits of silver beneath the order's lands—while never forgetting the monks' duty toward the less fortunate of God's children. Thus, a cathedral grew alongside a hospital, makeshift chapels were constructed among the mining settlements sanctioned by Heidenreich, and the monks buried great numbers of the dead without stricture or complaint. How ironic it was, thought the abbot, that in Heidenrich's successes lay the very seeds that had now grown to doom the community, for it had provided a magnet of sorts for the Catholic forces and their leader, the Holy Roman Emperor Sigismund, pretender to the Bohemian crown. His armies were camped around Kutná Hora, and the abbot's efforts to keep some distance between the monastery and the emperor's forces had proved fruitless. Sedlec's reputed wealth was a temptation to all, and he was already giving shelter to Carthusian monks from Prague whose monastery had been destroyed some years earlier during the ravages that followed the death of Wenceslas IV. Those who would loot Sedlec needed no further incentive to attack, yet Sigismund, by his presence, had now made its destruction inevitable.

It was the killing of the reformer Jan Hus that had brought these events to pass. The abbot had once met Hus, an ordained priest at the University of Prague, where he was dean of the faculty of arts and, later, rector, and had been impressed by his zeal. Nevertheless, Hus's reformist instincts were dangerous. Three different popes were making conflicting claims on the papacy: John XXIII, of the Italians, who had been forced to flee Rome and had taken refuge in Germany; Gregory XXII, of the French; and Benedict XIII, of the Spaniards. The latter pair had already been deposed once, but refused to accept their fate. In such times Hus's demands for a Bible in Czech, and his continued insistence on conducting the mass in Czech rather than Latin, inevitably led to him being branded a heretic, a charge that was exacerbated by his espousal of the beliefs of the earlier heretic John Wycliffe and his branding of the foul John XXIII as the Antichrist, a view with which the abbot, at least in his own soul, was reluctant to take issue. It was hardly a surprise, then, when Hus was excommunicated.

Summoned to the Council of Constance in 1414 by Sigismund to air his grievances, Hus was imprisoned and tried for heresy. He refused to recant, and in 1415 was taken to "The Devil's Place," the site of execution in a nearby meadow. He was stripped naked, his hands and feet were tied to a stake with wet ropes, and his neck was chained to a wooden post. Oil was dumped on his head, and kindling and straw piled up to his neck. It took half an hour for the flames to catch, and Hus eventually suffocated from the thick black smoke. His body was ripped to pieces, his bones were broken, and his heart was roasted over an open fire. His remains were then cremated, the ashes shoveled into the carcass of a steer, and the whole lot cast into the Rhine.

Hus's followers in Bohemia were outraged at his death and vowed to defend his teachings to the last drop of blood. A crusade was declared against them, and Sigismund sent an army of twenty thousand into

*Bohemia to quell the uprising, but the Hussites anni-
hilated them, led by Jan Ziska, a one-eyed knight who
turned carts into war chariots and called his men
"warriors of God." Now Sigismund was licking his
wounds and planning his next move. A peace treaty
had been agreed, sparing those who would accede to
the Hussites' Four Articles of Prague, including the
clergy's renunciation of all worldly goods and secular
authority, an article to which the abbot of Sedlec was
clearly unable to accede. Earlier that day the citizens
of Kutná Hora had marched to the Sedlec monastery,
around which were gathered the Hussite troops, to
plead for mercy and forgiveness, for it was well known
that Hus's followers in the town had been thrown alive
into the mine shafts, and the citizens feared the consequences if they did not bend the knee to the attacking
troops. The abbot listened while the two sides sang the
Te Deum in acknowledgment of their truce, and he felt
ill at the hypocrisy involved. The Hussites would not
sack Kutná Hora, for its mining and minting industries
were too valuable, but they wanted to secure it for
themselves nonetheless. All of this was mere pretense,
and the abbot knew that before long both sides would
again be at each other's throats over the great wealth
of the town.*

*The Hussites had withdrawn some distance from the
monastery, but he could still see their fires. Soon they
would come, and they would spare no one found within
its walls. He was consumed by anger and regret. He
loved the monastery. He had been party to its most
recent constructions, and the very raising of its places
of worship had in itself been as much an act of contemplation and meditation as the services carried out within*

them, its every stone imbued with spirituality, the stern asceticism of its lines a precaution against any distraction from prayer and contemplation. Its church, the greatest of its kind in the land, was patterned on a Latin cross, achieving a harmony with the natural formation of the region's river valley by featuring a central axis that oriented the choir down the river's stream rather than toward the east. Yet the conventual church was also a complex variant on the original plans drawn up by the order's propagator, Bernard of Clairvaux, and it was imbued with his love of music, which manifested itself in his faith in the mysticism of numbers based on Augustine's theory of music and its application to the proportions of buildings. Purity and balance were expressions of divine harmony, and thus the conventual Church of the Assumption of Our Lady and Saint John the Baptist was a beautiful, silent hymn to God, every column a note, every perfect arch a Te Deum.

Now this wondrous structure was at risk of total destruction, even though, in its simplicity and absence of unnecessary adornment, it symbolized the very qualities that the reformists should have prized the most. Almost without realizing he was doing so, the abbot reached into the folds of his garment and removed a stone. Embedded in it was a strange creature, unlike anything the abbot had ever seen walk, crawl, or swim, now turned to stone itself, petrified as though caught in a basilisk's stare. It resembled a snail, except its shell was larger, its spirals closer together. One of the laborers had found it while quarrying by the river, and had given it to the abbot as a gift. It was said that this place had once been covered by a great sea, now long since gone, and the abbot wondered if this little animal had *once traversed its depths before it found itself marooned as the sea retreated, and was slowly absorbed by the land. Perhaps it was a relic of the Great Flood; if so, then its twin must yet exist elsewhere on the earth, but secretly the abbot hoped that such a thing was not true. He prized it because it was unique, and he thought it both sad and beautiful in the transience of its nature. Its time had passed, just as the abbot's time was now drawing to a close.*

He feared the Hussites, but he knew too that there were others who threatened the sanctity of the monastery, and it was simply a matter of which enemy breached its gates first. Rumors had reached the abbot's ears, stories meant for him, and him alone: tales of mercenaries marked with a twin-pronged brand, their number led by a Captain with a blemished eye, his footsteps forever shadowed by a fat imp of a man, ugly and tumerous. It was unclear to which side the Captain's soldiers offered their allegiance, according to his sources, but the abbot supposed that it did not matter. Such men assumed flags of convenience to hide their true aims, and their loyalty was a fire that burned cold and fast, leaving only ash in its wake. He knew what they were seeking. Despite the beliefs of ignorant men, there was little true wealth left at Sedlec. The monastery's most famed treasure, a monstrance made from gold-plated silver, had been entrusted to the Augustinians at Klosterneuburg six years earlier. Those who sacked this place would find little in the way of ecclesiastical riches to divide among themselves.

But the Captain was not interested in such trifles.

And so the abbot had set about preparing for what was to come, even as the threat of destruction drew

*closer. Sometimes the monks heard distant orders shouted;
at other times they listened to the screaming of the
injured and the dying at the gates. Still, they did not
pause in their work. Horses were saddled, and a huge
covered cart, one of two specially constructed for the
abbot's purposes, lay waiting by the hidden entrance to
the monastery garden. Its wheels were sunk deep into
the mud, driven down by the weight of the cargo that
it carried. The horses were wide-eyed and foam-flecked,
as though aware of the nature of the burden that was
being placed upon them. It was almost time.*

"A great sentence is gone forth against thee. He shall
bind thee . . ."

*Heresy, thought the abbot, as the words came unbid-
den to him. Even possession of the Book of Enoch,
condemned as false scripture, would be enough to draw
the charge down upon his head, and thus he had taken
great pains to ensure that the work remained hidden.
Nevertheless, in its contents he had found answers to
many of the questions that had troubled him, among
them the nature of the terrible, beautiful creation
entrusted to his care, and the duty of concealment that
now lay upon him.*

"Cast him into darkness . . . Throw upon him hurled
and pointed stones, covering him with darkness; there
shall he remain forever; cover his face, that he may not
see the light. And in the great day of judgment let him
be cast into the fire."

*The abbot's lodge lay at the heart of the monastery's
concentric fortifications. The first circle, in which he
now stood, housed the conventual church, reserved for
the use of the order's initiated members, the convent
building, and the cloister gallery. On the side of the*

church's transept opposite the river lay the gate of the deceased, which led into the churchyard. It was the most important portal in the monastery, its intricate sculpture standing in sharp contrast to the starkness of the architecture surrounding it. This was the gateway between earthly life and the eternal, between this world and the next. The abbot had hoped to be carried through it one day and buried alongside his brothers. Those who had already fled upon his instructions had been requested to return when it was safe, and to seek out his remains. If the gate still stood, he was to be brought through it. If it did not, a place was still to be found for him, so that he might rest beside the ruins of the chapel that he so loved.

The second circle belonged to the initiated members, and also contained the granary and a sacred plot of land at the entrance portal to the church, used to grow grain for the baking of the host. Within the third circle was the monastery gate; a church for lay members of the order, outside worshippers, and pilgrims; living quarters and gardens; and the main cemetery. The abbot stared out upon these walls that protected the monastery, their lines clear even in the darkness, thanks to the false dawn of the fires on the hillsides. It looked like a vision of hell, he thought. The abbot did not believe that Christian men should fight over God, but more than those who killed in the name of a forgiving God he hated those who used the name of God as an excuse to extend their own power. He sometimes thought that he could almost understand the anger of the Hussites, although he kept such opinions to himself. Those who did not might quickly find themselves broken upon a wheel, or burning on a pyre for their temerity.

He heard footsteps approach, and a young novice appeared by his side. His robes were filthy from his exertions.

"All is ready," said the novice. "The servants ask if they may muffle the horses' hooves, and wrap cloth around the bridles. They are concerned that the noise will bring the soldiers down upon them."

The abbot did not answer immediately. To the younger man, it seemed that the abbot had just been offered a final possibility of escape, and was tempted to accept it. At last he sighed and, like the beasts bound to the cart, accepted his inevitable burden.

"No," he said. "Let there be no silencing of hooves, no wrapping of bridles. They must make haste, and they must create noise as they do so."

"But then they will be found, and they will be killed."

The abbot turned to his novice and laid his hand gently upon the boy's cheek.

"As God wills it, so it shall be done," he said. "Now you must go, and take as many with you as it is safe to bring."

"What about you?"

"I—"

But the abbot's words were cut off by the barking of dogs in the outer circles. The monastery had been abandoned by many of those who might otherwise have come to its defense, and now only animals roamed behind the second and third walls. The sound the dogs made was panicked, almost hysterical. Their fear was palpable, as though a wolf were about to enter into their presence, and they knew that they would die fighting it. The young novice took the abbot's arm.

"Come," he urged. "There are soldiers coming."

The abbot found that he was unable to move. His feet would not respond to the urgings of his brain, and his hands were trembling. No soldiers could make the dogs respond in such a way. That was why he had ordered their release: the dogs would smell them, and alert the monks to their approach.

Then the twin gates of the inner wall were blown apart, one flying free of its hinges and landing amid a copse of trees, the other left hanging like a sot at night's end. The fleeing dogs leaped through the gap, those that were too slow killed by arrows that shot from the shadows beyond the gate.

"Go," said the abbot. "Make sure the cart reaches the road."

With one last frightened glance at the gates, and with sorrow in his eyes, the novice fled. In his place, a pair of servants joined the abbot. They bore halberds and were very old. They had remained at the monastery as much out of their inability to flee far as out of any loyalty to the abbot.

Slowly, a group of horsemen emerged from beyond the wall and entered the inner circle. Most wore plain, formfitting breastplates, with mail at the groin, armpits, and elbows. Three had cylindrical Italian sallet helmets on their heads, their features barely distinguishable through the T-shaped frontal gap. The rest had long hair that hung about their faces, concealing them almost as well as the helmets of their fellows. From their saddles dangled human remains: scalps and hands and garlands of ears. The flanks of their horses were white with spit and foam, and the animals looked close to madness. Only one man was on foot. He was pale and fat, and his neck was swollen with some dreadful purple goiter.

On his upper body he wore a huge brigandine for armor, constructed from small metal plates riveted to a textile covering, for his build was too deformed for the fitted protection worn by his allies. There were plates made in a similar manner on his thighs and shins, but his head was bare. He was very pale, with almost feminine features and large green eyes. In his hand he grasped a woman's head, his pale fingers entwined in her hair. The abbot recognized her face, even twisted in the torments of death: an idiot who sat outside the monastery gates, begging for alms, too foolish to flee her post even in wartime. As he and his fellows drew closer, the abbot could see a crudely drawn symbol upon their saddles: a red grapnel, newly created with the blood of their victims.

And then their leader emerged from the heart of his men. He rode a black horse, a spiked half-shaffron protecting its head, and a peytral guarding its chest, all intricately carved in black and silver. He was clad entirely in black armor, apart from the hood upon his head: pauldrons extending over his chest and shoulder blades; gauntlets with long protective cuffs; and tassets to cover the vulnerable spot at the top of his cuisses, where his breastplate ended and his thigh armor began. His only weapon was a long sword, which remained in its scabbard.

The abbot began to pray silently.

"Who are they?" whispered one of the servants. "Jan's men?"

The abbot found enough spittle to moisten his mouth and to free his tongue enough to speak.

"No," he said. "Not Jan's, and not men."

From the rear of the monastery he thought he

discerned the sound of the cart moving forward, urged
on by its driver. Hooves beat a slow cadence upon grass,
then upon earth as they moved onto the road. The speed
of their timpani slowly increased as they tried to put
some distance between themselves and the monastery.

The leader of the horsemen raised his hand, and six
men split from the main party and galloped around the
chapel to cut off those who were fleeing. Six more
dismounted but remained with their leader, slowly
moving in on the abbot and his men. All bore cross-
bows, already spanned with the bolt ready to be fired.
They were smaller and lighter than any the abbot had
seen before, with a crannequin for pulling back the bow
steel that was portable enough to be worn on their belts.
They fired the bolts, and the abbot's servants fell.

The Captain dug his spurs into his horse's flanks.
The animal advanced, and the Captain's shadow fell
across the old monk. The horse stopped so close to the
abbot that moisture from its nose sprayed his face. The
Captain kept his head low, and slightly turned away
from the monk, so that his face could not be seen.

"Where is it?" he said.

His voice was cracked and hoarse from the screams
of battle.

"We have nothing of value here," said the abbot.

A sound came from beneath the folds of the Captain's
hood. It might almost have been a laugh, had a snake
found a way to convey humor in its hiss. He commenced
freeing his hands from the gauntlets.

"Your mines made you wealthy," he said. "You could
not have spent it all on trinkets. It may be that you yet
have much of value to some, but not to me. I seek one
thing only, and you know what it is."

The abbot stepped forward. With his right hand, he gripped the cross around his neck.

"It is gone," he said.

In the distance, he heard horses neighing wildly, and the impact of metal upon metal as his men fought to protect the cart and its cargo. They should have left sooner, he realized. His act of concealment might not have been revealed so quickly had they done so.

The Captain leaned over his horse's neck. The gauntlets were now gone. His fingers, revealed to the moonlight, were scoured by white scars. He raised his head and listened to the cries of the monks as they were slaughtered by his men.

"They died for nothing," he said. "Their blood is on your hands."

The abbot grasped his cross more tightly. Its edges tore his skin, and blood leaked through his fingers, as though giving substance to the Captain's words.

"Go back to hell," said the abbot.

The Captain lifted his pale hands to his hood and threw back the rough material from around his face. Dark hair surrounded his beautiful features, and his skin seemed almost to glow in the night air. He extended his right hand, and a crossbow was placed in his grasp by the grinning imp at his side. The abbot saw a white mote flicker in the blackness of the Captain's right eye, and in his final moments it was given unto him to see the face of God.

"Never," said the Captain, and the abbot heard the dull report of the crossbow at the instant the bolt penetrated his chest. He stumbled back against the doorway and slid slowly down the wall. At a signal from the Captain, his men began entering the buildings of the

inner circle, their footsteps echoing on the stone as they ran. A small group of armed servants emerged from behind the conventual church, rushing forward to engage the intruders in the confined space.

More time, the abbot thought. We need more time.

His monks and servants, what few remained, were putting up fierce resistance, preventing the Captain's soldiers from entering the church and the inner buildings.

"Just a little more time, my Lord," he prayed. "Just a little."

The Captain looked down upon the abbot, listening to his words. The abbot felt his heart slow just as the Captain's men flanked the monks on the steps and entered the chapel, ascending the walls and crawling like lizards across the stones. One moved upside down across the ceiling, then dropped down behind the defenders and impaled the rearmost man upon the end of a sword.

The abbot wept for them, even as the cool tip of a bolt touched his forehead. The Captain's lieutenant, bloated and poisonous, was now kneeling by his side, his mouth open and his head tilted, as though preparing to deliver a last kiss to a lover.

"I know what you are," the abbot whispered. "And you will never find the one that you seek."

A pale finger tightened on the trigger.

This time, the abbot did not hear the shot.

It was not until the eighteenth century that the Cistercians of Sedlec were able to commence their reconstruction in earnest, including the restoration of the Church of the Assumption, left roofless and vaultless after the Hussite

wars. Seven chapels now form a ring around its pres-
bytery, and its Baroque interiors are decorated with art,
although these interiors are hidden from the sight of
the public as its restoration continues.

And yet this stunning structure, perhaps the most
impressive of its type in the Czech Republic, is not the
most interesting aspect of Sedlec. A rotary stands near
the church, and at this rotary there is a sign that reads
"Kosnice," pointing to the right. Those who follow it
will come to a small, relatively modest house of worship
seated at the center of a muddy graveyard. This is All
Saints Church, built in 1400, revaulted in the seventeenth century, and reconstructed by the architect
Santini-Aichel in the eighteenth century, who was also
responsible for much of the restoration work on the
Chapel of the Assumption. It can be entered through
an extension added by Santini-Aichel after it was discovered that the front of the church had begun to tilt. A
staircase to the right leads up to All Saints Chapel,
where once candles were lit for the dead in the two
towerlets behind the chapel itself. Even in the winter
sunlight, there is little about All Saints that might attract
more than a casual second glance from the windows of
an air-conditioned bus. After all, there are the wonders
of Kutná Hora to be seen, with its narrow little streets,
its perfectly preserved buildings, and the great mass of
Saint Barbara's dominating all.

But All Saints is not as it might seem from the outside,
for it is in fact two structures. The first, the chapel, is
aboveground; the second, known as Jesus Christ on the
Mount of Olives, lies below. While what is above is a
monument to the prospect of a better life beyond this
one, what lies beneath is a testament to the transience

of all things mortal. It is a strange place, a buried place, and none who spend time among its wonders can ever forget it.

Legend tells that Jindrich, an abbot of Sedlec, brought back with him from the Holy Land a sack of soil that he scattered over the cemetery. It came to be regarded as an outpost of the Holy Land itself, and people from all across Europe were buried there, alongside plague victims and those who had fallen in the many conflicts waged in its surrounding fields. These bones at last became so plenteous that something had to be done with them, and in 1511 the task of disposing of them was reputedly entrusted to a half-blind monk. He arranged an accumulation of skulls into pyramids, and so began the great work that would become the ossuary at Sedlec. In the aftermath of Emperor Joseph II's reforms, the monastery was purchased by the Orlik line of the Schwarzenberg family, but development of the ossuary continued. A woodcarver named Frantisek Rint was brought in, and his imagination was allowed free rein. From the remains of forty thousand people, Rint created a monument to death.

A great chandelier of skulls hangs from the ossuary ceiling. Skulls form the base for its candleholders, each resting on pelvic arches, with a humerus clasped beneath its upper jaw. Where delicate crystals should hang, bones dangle vertically, connecting the skulls to the central support via a system of vertebrae. There are more bones here, small and large, forming the support itself and adorning the chains that anchor the skulls to the ceiling. Great lines of skulls, each clasping a bone beneath its jaw, line the arches of the ossuary at each side of the chandelier. They hang in loops, and form four narrow pyramids in the center of the floor, creating a square beneath the chandelier, each skull facing a single candle.

There are other wonders too: a monstrance made of bone, with a skull at its center where the host should be, six femurs radiating from behind, smaller bones and vertebrae interwoven with them. Bones mask the wooden support around which the monstrance has been constructed and its base is a U ending at either side in another skull. There are wreaths and vases and goblets, all made of bone; even the Schwarzenberg family coat of arms is formed of bone, with a crown of skulls and pelvises at its peak. Those bones that have not found a practical use are stored in great piles beneath stone arches.

Here, the dead sleep.

Here are treasures, seen and unseen.

Here is temptation.

And here is evil.

9

The windows in the room were covered with sheets of metal riveted to the walls, preventing any natural light from entering. There were pieces of bone on a workbench: ribs, a radius and ulna, sections of skull. A smell of urine added a sharp, unpleasant character to the stale air in the room. Beneath the bench were four or five wooden packing crates containing straw and paper. Against the far wall, to the right of the blacked-out windows, was a console table. At each end rested more skulls, all missing their lower jaw, with what appeared to be a bone from the upper arm clasped beneath the upper mandible. A hole had been made in the tops of the skulls, into which candles had been inserted. They flickered, illuminating the figure that hovered behind them.

It was black, about two feet in height, and appeared to be made from a combination of human and animal remains. The wing of a large bird had been carefully stripped of its skin and feathers, and the bones skillfully fixed in place so that the wing stood outstretched, as though the creature to which it belonged were about to take flight. The wing was fixed to a section of spine from which a small rib cage also curled. It might have belonged to a child or a monkey, but I couldn't tell. To the left of the spine there was, instead of a second wing, a skeletal arm, with all of the bones in place, right down to the tiny fingers. The arm was raised, the fingers grasping. They ended in small sharp nails. The right leg looked like the back leg of a cat or dog, judging by the angle of the joint. The left was clearly closer to that of a human, but was unfinished, the wire frame visible from the ankle down.

The fusion of animal and man was clearest, though, in the head, which was slightly out of proportion to the rest of the figure. Whoever had crafted it possessed an artistry to match his disturbed vision. A multiplicity of different creatures had been used to create it, and I had to look closely to find the lines where one ended and another began: half of a primate's jaw was carefully attached to that of a child, while the upper part of the facial area between jaws and forehead had been formed using sections of white bone and bird heads. Finally, horns emerged from the top of a human skull, one barely visible and resembling that of the nodes on the head of an immature deer, the other ramlike and curling around the back of the skull, almost touching the statue's small clavicle.

"If this guy is subletting, he's in a shitload of trouble," said Angel.

Louis was examining one of the skulls upon the workbench, his face barely inches from its empty sockets.

"They look old," I said, answering a question that had not been asked.

He nodded, then left the room. I heard him moving boxes around, searching for some clue as to the whereabouts of Alice.

I followed the smell of urine to the bathroom. The tub contained more bones, all soaking in yellow liquid.

The stink of ammonia made my eyes water. I made a cursory search of the cabinets, a handkerchief pressed to my nose and mouth, then closed the door behind me. Angel was still examining the bone statue, apparently fascinated by it. I wasn't surprised. The creation looked like it belonged in an art gallery or a museum. It was repugnant, but breathtaking in its artistry and in the fluidity with which one creature's remains flowed into the next.

"I just can't figure out what the hell this is supposed to be," he asked. "It looks like a man changing into a bird, or a bird changing into a man."

"You see a lot of birds with horns?" I said.

Angel reached out a finger to touch the protuberances on the skull, then thought better of it.

"I guess it's not a bird, then."

"I guess not."

I took a piece of newspaper from the floor and used it to lift one of the skull candlesticks from the table, then shined my mini Maglite inside. There were serial numbers of some kind etched into the bone. I examined the others and all had similar markings, except for one that was adorned with the symbol of a two-pronged fork and rested on a pelvic bone. I took one of the numbered skulls and placed it in a tea chest, then carefully added the forked skull and the statue. I took the box into the next room, where Louis was kneeling on the floor. Before him stood an open suitcase. It contained tools, among them scalpels, files and small bone saws, all carefully packed away in canvas pockets, and a pair of video cassettes. Each was labeled along the side with a long line of initials, and dates.

"He was getting ready to leave," said Louis.

"Looks like it."

He gestured at the chest in my hands.

"You found something?"

"Maybe. There are marks on these skulls. I'd like someone to take a look at them, perhaps at the statue too."

Louis removed one of the cassettes from the case, placed it in the VCR, then turned on the TV. There was nothing to be seen for a time except static, then the picture cleared. It showed an area of yellow sand and stone, across which the camera panned jerkily before coming to rest upon the partially clothed body of a young woman. She lay facedown upon the ground, and there was blood upon her back, her legs, and the once-white shorts that she wore. Her dark hair was spread across the sand like tendrils of ink in dirty water.

The young woman stirred. A male voice spoke in what sounded like Spanish.

"I think he said that she's still alive," said Louis.

A figure appeared in front of the camera. The cameraman moved slightly to get a better view. A pair of expensive black boots came into view.

"No," said another voice, in English.

The camera was pushed away, preventing it from getting a clear view of the man or the girl. It picked up a sound like a coconut cracking. Someone laughed. The cameraman recovered himself and focused once again on the girl. There was blood flowing across the sand around her head.

"*Puta.*" It was the first voice again.

Whore.

The tape went blank for a moment, then resumed. This time, the girl had yellow highlights in her dark hair, but the surroundings were similar: sand and rocks. A bug stalked across a smear of blood close by her mouth, the only part of her face that was visible beneath her hair. A hand reached out, sweeping the hair back so that the cameraman could get a better view of her, then that section ended, and a new one began, with another dead girl, this one naked on a rock.

Louis fast-forwarded the tape. I lost track of the number of women. When he was done, he inserted the second cassette and did the same. Once or twice, a girl with darker skin appeared and he stopped the image, examining it closely before moving on. All of the women were Hispanic.

"I'm going to call the cops," I told him.

"Not yet. This guy ain't gonna leave this shit here for just anyone to find. He'll come back for it, and soon. If you're right about being watched in the alley, then whoever lives here could be outside right now. I say we wait."

I thought about what I was going to say to him before I opened my mouth. Rachel, had she been present to witness it, might have considered this progress on my part.

"Louis, we don't have time to wait around. The cops can do surveillance better than we can. This guy is a link, but maybe we can pick up the chain further on. The longer we stay still, the more the chances diminish of finding Alice before something bad happens to her."

I've seen people, even experienced cops, fall into the trap of using the past tense when talking about a missing person. That's why, sometimes, it pays to work out in your head what you're planning to say before the words start spilling out of your mouth.

I gently lifted the box I was holding. "Stay here for a while longer, see what else you can find. If I can't get back here first, I'll call you and give you time to get out before I talk to the cops."

Garcia sat in his car and watched the men enter his apartment. He guessed that the pimp was smarter than he had appeared to be, because there was no other way that they could have found his base so quickly. The pimp had followed someone to Garcia, probably in an effort to gain some room for maneuver in case his betrayal of the girl rebounded on him. Garcia was furious. A day or two later and the apartment would have been empty, its occupant gone. There was much in those rooms that was valuable to Garcia. He wanted it back. Yet Brightwell's instructions had been clear: follow them and find out where they go, but don't hurt them or attempt to engage them. If they separated, he was to stay with the man in the leather jacket, the one who had lingered in the alleyway as though aware of their presence. The fat man had appeared distracted as he left Garcia, but also strangely excited. Garcia knew better than to ask him why.

Don't hurt them.

But that was before Brightwell knew where they were going. Now they were in Garcia's place, and close to what they were seeking, although they might not recognize it if they saw it. Nevertheless, if they called the police, then Garcia would become a marked man in this country just as he was back home, and he might also be at risk from the very people who were sheltering him if his exposure threatened to bring down trouble on their heads. Garcia tried to recall if there was any way of connecting

Brightwell to him through whatever remained in the apartment. He didn't believe so, but he had watched some of the cop shows on TV and sometimes it seemed like they could perform miracles using only dust and dirt. Then he considered all of his hard work in recent months, the great effort of construction for which he had been brought to the city. This too was threatened by the presence of the visitors. If they discovered it, or decided to report whatever they found in Garcia's apartment, then all would be undone. Garcia was proud of what had been built; it was worthy to stand alongside the Capuchin church in Rome, the church behind the Farnese Palace, even Sedlec itself.

Garcia took out his cell. Brightwell's number was to be called only in an emergency, but Garcia figured that this qualified. He entered the digits and waited.

"They're at my place," he said, once the fat man answered.

"What remains?"

"Tools," said Garcia. "Materials."

"Anything that I should be concerned about?"

Garcia considered his options, then made his decision.

"No," he lied.

"Then walk away."

"I will," Garcia lied again.

When I'm done.

He touched his fingers to the small relic that hung from a silver chain amid the hairs of his chest. It was a shard of bone, taken from the body of the woman for whom these men were searching, these trespassers on Garcia's sacred place. Garcia had dedicated the relic to his guardian, to Santa Muerte, and now it was imbued with her spirit, her essence.

"*Muertecita*," he whispered, as his anger grew. "*Reza por mi.*"

Sarah Yeates was one of those people you needed in your life. Apart from being smart and funny, she was also a treasure trove of esoteric information, a status that was due at least in part to her work in the library of the Museum of Natural History. She was dark haired, looked about ten years younger than her age, and had the kind of personality that scared off dumb men and forced the smart ones to think fast on their feet. I wasn't sure which category I fell into where Sarah was concerned. I hoped I was in the second group, but I sometimes suspected that I might be included by default and Sarah was just waiting for a vacancy to open up in the first group so she could file me there instead.

I called her at home. It took her a few rings to answer, and when she did her voice was foggy with sleep.

"Huh?" she said.

"Hello to you too."

"Who is this?"

"Charlie Parker. Am I calling at a bad time?"

"You are if you're trying to be funny. You do *know* what time it is, right?"

"Late."

"Yeah, which is what you'll be if you don't have a good reason for calling me."

"It's important. I need to pick your brain about something."

I heard her sigh and sink back into her pillow.

"Go on."

"I have some items that I've found in an apartment.

They're human bones. Some have been made into candlesticks. There's also a statue of some kind, constructed from human and animal remains mixed together. I found a bath of urine with bones in it, and I think they may have been 'harvested' quite recently. Pretty soon I'm going to have to call the cops and tell them what I've found, so I don't have long. You're the first person I've woken over this, but I expect to wake others before the night is through. Is there anyone in the museum, or even outside it, who might be able to tell me something I can use?"

Sarah was quiet for so long that I thought she'd fallen asleep again.

"Sarah?" I said.

"Jeez, you're impatient," she said. "Give a girl time to think."

There were noises from the other end of the line as she got out of bed, told me to hold on, then put the phone down. I waited, hearing drawers opening and closing in the background. Eventually she came back.

"I'm not going to give you the name of anyone at the museum, because I'd kind of like to keep my job. It pays my rent, you know, and enables me to keep a telephone so dipshits who don't even remember to send a Christmas card can call me in the dead of night asking for my help."

"I didn't know you were religious."

"That's not the point. I like presents."

"I'll make it up to you this year."

"You'd better. Okay, if this runs dry I'll arrange for you to talk to some people in the morning, but this is the guy you need to meet anyway. You got a pen? Right, well you also have a namesake. His name is Neddo,

Charles Neddo. He's got a place down in Cortlandt Alley. The plate beside his door says he's an antique dealer, but the front of the store is full of junk. He wouldn't make enough out of it to feed flies if it weren't for his sidelines."

"Which are?"

"He deals in what collectors term 'esoterica'. Occult stuff, mainly, but he's been known to sell artifacts that you don't generally find outside of museum basements. He keeps that merchandise in a locked room behind a curtain at the back of the store. I've been in there, once or twice, so I know what I'm talking about. I seem to recall seeing items similar to the ones you're referring to, although Neddo's equivalents would be pretty old. He's the place to start, though. He lives above the store. Go wake him up, and let me get back to sleep."

"Will he cooperate with a stranger?"

"He will if the stranger offers him something in return. Just be sure to bring along your finds. If they're interesting to him, then you'll learn something."

"Thanks, Sarah."

"Yeah, whatever. I hear you found a girlfriend. How'd that happen?"

"Good luck."

"Yours, I think, not hers. Don't forget my present."

Then she hung up.

Louis moved through the unfinished floor, framed by doorways and lit by moonlight, until he came at last to the window. The window did not look onto the street. Instead, it showed Louis the dimly lit interior of a white-tiled room. In the center of the room, over a drain in the sloped floor, a chair had been fixed. There were leather restraints on the arms and the legs.

Louis opened the door and entered the white room. A shape moved to his left, and he almost fired at it before he saw his own reflection in the two-way mirror. He knelt down by the drain. The floor, the drain, all were clean. Even the chair had been scrubbed, the grain cleansed of any trace of those who had occupied it. He smelled disinfectant and bleach. His gloved fingers touched the wood of the armrest, then gripped it tightly.

Not here, he thought. Don't let her life have ended here.

Cortlandt Alley was a monkey puzzle of fire escapes and hanging wires. Neddo's storefront was black, and the only clue to his business was a small brass plate on the brickwork with the words NEDDO ANTIQUES. A black cast iron screen protected the glass, but the interior was concealed by gray drapes that had not been moved in a very long time and the whole storefront looked like it had recently been sprayed with dust. To the left of the glass was a black steel door with an intercom beside it, inset with a camera lens. The windows above were all dark.

I had seen no trace of anyone watching the apartment building when I left. Angel covered me from the door as I went to my car, and I took the most circuitous route that I could to Manhattan. Once or twice, I thought I saw a beaten-up yellow Toyota a couple of cars behind me, but it was gone by the time I got to Cortlandt Alley.

I pressed the button on the intercom. It was answered

within seconds by a man, and he didn't sound like he'd just been woken up.

"I'm looking for Charles Neddo," I said.

"Who are you?"

"My name is Parker. I'm a private investigator."

"It's a little late to be calling, isn't it?"

"It's important."

"How important?"

The alley was empty, and I could see no one on the street. I took the statue from the bag and, carefully holding it by its plinth, displayed it before the lens.

"This important," I said.

"Show me some ID."

I juggled the statue, found my wallet, and flipped it open.

Nothing happened for a time, then the voice said: "Wait there."

He took his time. Any longer and I could have put down roots. Eventually, I heard the sound of a key in the lock, and bolts being drawn back. The door opened and a man stood before me, segmented by a series of strong security chains. He was late middle-aged, with pointed tufts of gray hair sticking up from his skull that gave him the appearance of an aging punk. His eyes were very small and round, and his mouth was set in a plump scowl. He wore a bright green robe that seemed to have trouble stretching all the way around his body. Beneath it I could see black trousers and a white shirt, wrinkled but clean.

"Your identification again, please," he said. "I want to be sure."

I handed him my license.

"Maine," he said. "There are some good stores in Maine."

"You mean L. L. Bean?"

The scowl deepened.

"I was talking about antiques. Well, I suppose you'd better come in. We can't have you standing around in the dead of night."

He partially closed the door, undid the chains, then stepped aside to let me enter. Inside, a flight of worn steps led up to what I assumed were Neddo's living quarters, while to the right a door gave access to the store itself. It was through this door that Neddo led me, past glass display cases filled with antique silver, between rows of battered chairs and scuffed tables, until we came to a small back room furnished with a telephone, a huge gray filing cabinet that looked like it belonged in a Soviet bureaucrat's office, and a desk lit by a lamp with an adjustable arm and a magnifying glass fitted halfway down its length. A curtain at the rear of the office had been pulled across almost far enough to conceal the door behind it.

Neddo sat down at the desk and removed a pair of glasses from the pocket of his dressing gown.

"Give it to me," he said.

I placed the statue on a plinth, then removed the skulls and laid them at either side of it. Neddo barely glanced at the skulls. Instead, his attention was focused on the bone sculpture. He didn't touch it directly, instead using the plinth to turn it while employing a large magnifying glass to peruse it in great detail. He did not speak throughout his examination. At last he pushed it away and removed his glasses.

"What made you think I'd be interested in this?" he said. He was trying very hard to remain poker-faced, but his hands were trembling.

"Shouldn't you have asked me that before you invited me in? The fact that I'm here in your office kind of answers your question for you."

Neddo grunted. "Let me rephrase it, then: who led you to believe that I might be interested in such an item?"

"Sarah Yeates. She works at the Museum of Natural History."

"The librarian? A bright girl. I greatly enjoyed her occasional visits."

The scowl on Neddo's face relaxed slightly, and his little eyes grew animated. Judging by his words, it was clear that Sarah didn't come around so much anymore, and from the expression on his face — one of mingled lust and regret — I was pretty sure why Sarah now kept her distance from him.

"Do you always work so late?" he said.

"I could ask you the same question."

"I don't sleep very much. I am troubled by insomnia."

He slipped on a pair of plastic gloves, and turned his attention to the skulls. I noticed that he handled them delicately, almost respectfully, as though fearing to commit some desecration on the remains. It was hard to think of anything worse than what had already been done, but then I was no expert. The pelvic bone upon which the skull rested jutted out slightly from beneath the jaw, like an ossified tongue. Neddo laid it on a piece of black velvet, and adjusted the lamp so that the skull shone.

"Where did you get these?"

"In an apartment."

"There were others like this?"

I didn't know how much to tell him. My hesitation gave me away.

"I'm guessing that there were, since you seem reluctant to answer. Never mind. Tell me, how exactly were these skulls placed when you found them?"

"I'm not sure what you mean."

"Were they arranged in a particular way? Were they resting on anything else?"

I thought about the question.

"There were four bones to one side of the statue and between the skulls, piled one on top of the other. They were curved. They looked like sections of hip. Behind it was a length of vertebrae, probably from the base of a spine."

Neddo nodded.

"It was incomplete."

"You've seen something like this before?"

Neddo lifted the skull and gazed into the empty sockets of its eyes.

"Oh yes," he said softly.

He turned to me.

"Don't you think that there's something beautiful about it, Mr. Parker? Don't you find edifying the idea that someone would take bones and use them to create a piece of art?"

"No," I said, with more force than I should have used.

Neddo looked at me over the tops of his glasses.

"And why is that?"

"I've met people before who tried to make art out of bone and blood. I didn't much care for them."

Neddo waved a hand in dismissal. "Nonsense," he said. "I don't know what manner of men you're speaking of but—"

"Faulkner," I said.

Neddo stopped talking. It was a guess, nothing more, but anyone who was interested in such matters could not help but know of the Reverend Faulkner, and perhaps also of others whom I had encountered. I needed Neddo's help, and if that meant dangling the promise of revelations before him, then I was content to do that.

"Yes," he said after a time, and now he seemed to be looking at me with renewed interest. "Yes, the Reverend Faulkner was such an individual. You met him? Wait, wait, you're the one, aren't you? You're the detective who found him? Yes, I remember now. Faulkner vanished."

"So they say."

Neddo was now rigid with excitement.

"Then you saw it? You saw the book?"

"I saw it. There was no beauty to it. He made it from skin and bone. People died for its creation."

Neddo shook his head. "Still, I would give a great deal to look upon it. Whatever you may say or feel about him, he was a part of a tradition. The book did not exist in isolation. There were others like it: not so ornate, perhaps, or so ambitious in their construction, but the raw materials remain the same, and such anthropodermic bindings are sought after items among collectors of a certain mien."

"Anthropodermic?"

"Bindings made of human skin," said Neddo, matter-of-factly. "The Library of Congress holds a copy of the *Scrutinium Scripturarum,* printed in Strasbourg some time before 1470. It was presented to the library by one Dr. Vollbehr, who noted that its wooden boards had been covered in human skin during the nineteenth century. It is claimed also that the Harvard Law Library's volume of Juan Gutierrez's *Practicarum Quaestionum Circa Leges Regias Hispaniae Liber Secundus*, from the seventeenth century, is similarly bound with the skin of one Jonas Wright, although the identity of the gentleman remains in question. Then there is the Boston Athenaeum's copy of *The Highwayman* by James Allen, or George Walton, as the scoundrel was also known. A most unusual item. Upon Allen's death, a section of his epidermis was removed and tanned to look like deerskin, then used to bind a copy of his own book, which was then presented to one John Fenno Junior, who had narrowly escaped death at Allen's hands during a robbery. That I *have* seen, although I can't vouch for any of the others. I seem to recall that it had a most unusual smell . . .

"So you see that, regardless of any feelings of disgust or animosity you may have for the Reverend Faulkner, he was by no means unique in his efforts. Unpleasant, perhaps, and probably homicidal, but an artist of sorts nevertheless. Which brings us to this item."

He placed it back upon the velvet once again.

"The person who made this was also working in a tradition: that of using human remains as ornamentation, or memento mori, if you prefer. You know what 'mem—'"

He stopped. He looked almost embarrassed.

"Of course you do. I'm sorry. Now that you've mentioned Faulkner, I recall the rest, and the other one. Terrible, just terrible."

And yet, beneath the veneer of sympathy, I could see his fascination bubble and I knew that, if he could, he would have asked me about it all: Faulkner, the book, the Traveling Man. The chance would never come his way again, and his frustration was almost palpable.

"Where was I?" he said. "Yes, bones as ornamentation . . ."

And so Neddo began to speak, and I listened and learned from him.

In medieval times, the word "church" referred not merely to the building itself, but to the area around it, including the "chimiter," or cemetery. Processions and services were sometimes held within the courtyard, or atrium, of the church, and similarly, when it came to the disposal of the bodies of the dead, people were frequently buried within the main building, against its walls, even under the rainspouts—or *sub stillicidio* as it was termed, as the rainwater was adjudged to have received the sanctity of the church while running down its roof and walls. "Cemetery" usually meant the outer church area, the *atrium* in Latin, or *aitre* in French. But the French also had another word for *aitre*: the *charnier,* or charnel house. It came to mean a particular part of the cemetery, namely the galleries along the churchyard, above which were placed ossuaries.

Thus, as Neddo explained it, a churchyard in the Middle Ages typically had four sides, of which the church itself generally formed one, with the three remaining walls decorated with arcades or porticoes in which the bodies of the dead were placed, rather like the cloisters of a monastery (which themselves served as cemeteries for the monks). Above the porticoes, the skulls and limbs of the dead would be placed once they had dried sufficiently, occasionally arranged in artistic compositions. Most of the bones came from the *fosses aux pauvres,* the great common graves of the poor in the center of the atrium. These were little more than ditches, thirty feet deep and fifteen or twenty feet across, into which the dead were cast sewn up in their shrouds, sometimes as many as fifteen hundred in a single pit covered by a thin layer of dirt, their remains easy prey for wolves and the grave robbers who supplied the anatomists. The soil was so putrefying that bodies quickly rotted, and it was said of some common graves, such as Les Innocents in Paris and Alyscamps in the Alps, that they could consume a body in as few as nine days, a quality regarded as miraculous. As one ditch filled, another, older one was opened up and emptied of its bones, which were then put to use in the ossuaries. Even the remains of the wealthy were pressed into service, although they were first buried in the church building, typically interred in the dirt beneath its flagstones. Up to the seventeenth century, it mattered little to most people where their bones ended up just as long as they remained in the vicinity of the church, so it was common to see human remains in the galleries of the charnels, or the church porch, even in small chapels specially designed for the purpose.

"Churches and crypts decorated in such a manner were thus not uncommon," concluded Neddo, "but the model for this construction is most particular, I think: Sedlec, in the Czech Republic."

His fingers traced the contours of the skull, then inserted themselves into the gap at the base of the head so that he could touch the cavity within. As I watched, his body grew tense. He stole a glance at me, but I pretended not to notice. I picked up a silver scalpel with a bone handle and proceeded to examine it, watching in the blade as Neddo turned the skull upside down and allowed the lamplight to illuminate what was inside.

While his attention was distracted, I drew aside the curtain at the back of the office.

"You have to go now," I heard him say, and his tone had changed. Interest and curiosity had been replaced by alarm.

The door behind the curtain was closed, but not locked. I opened it. From behind me I heard Neddo give a shout, but he was too late. I was already inside.

The room was tiny, barely the size of a closet, and lit by a pair of red bulbs inset into the wall. Four skulls sat in a neat line beside a sink that smelled strongly of cleaning products. There were more bones on shelves lining the room, sorted according to size and the area of the skeleton from which they had come. I saw pieces of flesh suspended in glass jars: hands, feet, lungs, a heart. Seven containers of yellowing liquid stood in a small glass cabinet, apparently specially constructed to hold them. Each held a fetus in varying stages of development, the last jar exhibiting a child that appeared fully formed to my eye.

Elsewhere there were picture frames made from femurs; an array of flutes of different sizes constructed from hollowed-out bones; even a chair built from human remains, with a red velvet cushion at its heart like a slab of raw meat. I saw crude candlesticks and crosses, and a deformed skull made monstrous by some terrible disorder of the body that had caused cauliflower-like growths to explode from the forehead.

"You must leave," said Neddo. He was panicked, although I didn't know whether it was due to the fact that I had entered his storeroom, or because of what he had felt and seen in the interior of the skull. "You shouldn't be here. There's nothing more that I can tell you."

"You haven't told me anything at all," I said.

"Take everything to the museum in the morning. Take all of it to the police, if you wish, but I can't help you any further."

I picked up one of the skulls from beside the sink.

"Put that down," said Neddo.

I turned the skull in my hand. It had a neat hole low down, close to where the vertebrae would once have connected to it. I could see similar holes in the other skulls. They were execution shots.

"You must do well when there are revivals of *Hamlet*," I said.

I let the skull rest on my palm.

"Alas, Poor Yorick. A fellow of infinite jest, as long as you understood a little Chinese."

I showed him the hole in the skull.

"China is where these skulls came from, right? There aren't too many other places where people get executed so neatly. Who do you think paid for the bullet, Mr. Neddo? Isn't that how it works in China? You get driven in a truck to a football stadium, and then someone shoots you in the head and sends the bill to your relatives? Except these poor souls probably didn't have any relatives to claim them, so some enterprising individuals took it upon themselves to sell their remains. Maybe they first harvested the liver, the kidneys, even the heart, then stripped the flesh from the bones and offered the rest to you, or someone like you. There must be a law against trading in the remains of executed prisoners, don't you think?"

Neddo took the skull from my hand and returned it to its place beside the others.

"I don't know what you're talking about," he said. It sounded hollow.

"Tell me about what I brought, or I'll inform some people of what you have here," I said. "Your life will become very difficult as a result, I guarantee it."

Neddo stepped out of the closet doorway and returned to his desk.

"You knew it was there, didn't you, the mark inside the skull?" he said.

"I felt it with my fingertips, just like you did. What is it?"

Neddo appeared to be growing smaller as I watched, deflating in his chair. Even his robe suddenly seemed to fit him less snugly.

"The numbers inside the first skull indicate that its origins were recorded," he said. "It may have come from a body donated to medical science, or from an old museum display. In any event, it was originally legitimately acquired. The second skull bears no such number, only the mark. There are others who can tell you more than I can about it. I do know that it is very inadvisable to become involved with the individuals responsible for making it. They call themselves 'Believers.'"

"Why was it marked?"

He answered my question with another.

"How old do you think that skull is, Mr. Parker?"

I drew closer to the desk. The skull looked battered and slightly yellowed.

"I don't know. Decades, maybe?"

Neddo shook his head.

"Months, perhaps even weeks. It has been artificially aged, run through dirt and sand then soaked in a preparation of urine. You can probably smell it on your fingers."

I decided not to check.

"Where did it come from?"

He shrugged. "It looks Caucasian, probably male. There are no obvious signs of injury, but that means little. It could have come from a mortuary, I suppose, or a hospital, except that, as you seem to have surmised from the additions to my storeroom, human remains are hard to acquire in this country. Most of them, apart from the ones donated to medical science, have to be purchased from elsewhere. Eastern Europe was a good source, for a time, but it is now more difficult to obtain unregistered cadavers in such countries. China, as you've gathered, is less particular, but there are problems with the provenance of such remains, and they are expensive to obtain. There are few other options, apart from the obvious."

"Such as supplying your own."

"Yes."

"Killing."

"Yes."

"Is that what that mark means?"

"I believe so."

I asked if he had a camera, and he produced a dusty Kodak instant from a drawer in his desk. I took about five photographs of the outside of the skull, and three or four of its interior, adjusting the distance each time in the hope that the mark would come out clearly in at least one of them. In the end, I got two good images, once the photographs had developed on the desk before us.

"Have you ever met any of these 'Believers'?" I said.

Neddo squirmed in his seat. "I meet a great many distinctive people in the course of my business. One might go so far as to say that some of them are sinister, even actively unpleasant. So, yes, I have met Believers."

"How do you know?"

Neddo pointed at the sleeve of his gown, about an inch above his wrist.

"They bear the grapnel mark here."

"A tattoo?"

"No," said Neddo. "They burn it into their flesh."

"Did you get any names?"

"No."

"Don't they have names?"

Neddo looked positively ill.

"Oh, they all have names, the worst of them anyway."

His words seemed familiar to me. I tried to remember where I had heard them before.

They all have names.

But Neddo had already moved on.

"Others have asked about them, though, in the relatively recent past. I was visited by an agent of the FBI, perhaps a year ago. He wanted to know if I'd received any suspicious or unusual orders relating to arcana, particularly bones or bone sculpture, or ornate vellum. I told him that all such orders were unusual, and then he threatened me in much the same way that you have just done. A raid upon my premises by government agents would have been both inconvenient and embarrassing to me, and potentially ruinous if it led to criminal charges. I told him what I told you. He was unsatisfied, but I remain in business."

"Do you remember the agent's name?"

"Bosworth. Philip Bosworth. To be honest, had he not shown me his identification, I would have taken him for an accountant, or a clerk in a law office. He looked a little fragile for an FBI man. Nevertheless, the range of his knowledge was most impressive. He returned to clarify some details on another occasion, and I confess I enjoyed the process of mutual discovery that ensued."

Once again, I was aware of an undertone to Neddo's words, an almost sexual pleasure in the exploration of such subjects and material. The "process of mutual discovery"? I just hoped that Bosworth had bought him dinner first, and that the encounters with Neddo had brought him more satisfaction than my own. Neddo was as slippery as an eel in a bucket of Vaseline, and every useful word that he spoke came wrapped in layers of obfuscation. It was clear that he knew more than he was telling, but he would answer only a direct question, and the replies came unadorned with any additional information.

"Tell me about the statue," I said.

Neddo's hands began to tremble again.

"An interesting construction. I should like more time to study it."

"You want me to leave it here? I don't think that's going to happen."

Neddo shrugged and sighed. "No matter. It is worthless, a copy of something far more ancient."

"Go on."

"It is a version of a larger bone sculpture, reputedly eight or nine feet in height. The original has been lost for a very long time, although it was created in Sedlec in the fifteenth century, crafted from bones contained in its ossuary."

"You said that the bone candleholders were also replicas of originals from Sedlec. It sounds like someone has a fixation."

"Sedlec is an unusual place, and the original bone statue is an unusual piece, assuming it exists at all and is not simply a myth. Since no one has ever seen it, its precise nature is open to speculation, but most interested parties are in agreement on its appearance. The statue you have brought with you is probably as accurate a representation as I have ever seen. I have examined only sketches and illustrations before, and a great deal of effort has gone into this piece. I should like to meet whoever is responsible for its construction."

"So would I," I said. "What was the purpose of the original? Why was it made?"

"Versions upon versions," said Neddo. "Your sculpture is a miniature of another, also made in bone. That larger bone statue, though, is itself a representation, although the model for its construction is made of silver, and thus extremely valuable. Like this one, it is a depiction of a metamorphosis. It is known as the *Black Angel*."

"A metamorphosis of what kind?"

"A transformation from man to angel, or man to demon to be more accurate, which brings us to the point upon which opinions differ. Clearly, the *Black Angel* would be a considerable boon to any private collection simply for its intrinsic value, but that is not why it has been so avidly sought. There are those who believe that the silver original is, in effect, a kind of prison, that it is not a depiction of a being transforming, but the thing itself; that a monk named Erdric confronted Immael, a fallen angel in human form, at Sedlec, and that in the course of the conflict between them Immael fell into a vat of molten silver just as his true form was in the process of being revealed. Silver is supposedly the bane of such beings, and Immael was unable to free himself from it once he had become immersed. Erdric ordered that the silver be slowly cooled, and the residue poured from the vat. What remained was the *Black Angel:* Immael's form, shrouded in silver. The monks hid it, unable to destroy what lay within but fearful of allowing the statue to fall into the hands of those who might wish to free the thing inside, or use it to draw evil men to themselves. Since then, it has remained hidden, having been moved from Sedlec shortly before the monastery's destruction in the fifteenth century. Its whereabouts were concealed in a series of coded references contained in a map. The map was then torn into fragments, and dispersed to Cistercian monasteries throughout Europe.

"Since then, myth, speculation, superstition, and perhaps even a grain of truth have all combined to create an object that has become increasingly fascinating over the space of half a millennium. The bone version of the statue was created almost contemporaneously, although why I cannot say. It was, perhaps, merely a way of reminding the community of Sedlec of what had occurred, and of the reality of evil in this world. It went missing at the same time as the silver statue, presumably to save it from the depredations of war, particularly after Sedlec was attacked and destroyed."

"The Believers, are they among those searching for it?"

"Yes, more than any others."

"You seem to know a lot about it."

"And I don't even consider myself to be an expert."

"Then who is?"

"There is an auction house in Boston, the House of

Stern, run by a woman named Claudia Stern. She specializes in the sale of arcana, and has a particular knowledge of the *Black Angel* and the myths associated with it."

"And why is that?"

"Because she claims to be in possession of one of the map fragments, and is due to auction it next week. The object is controversial. It is believed to have been uncovered by a treasure seeker named Mordant, who found it beneath a flagstone in Sedlec some weeks ago. Mordant died in the church, apparently while trying to flee with the fragment.

"Or, more precisely, I suspect, while trying to flee *from* someone."

What if?

The words had haunted Mordant for so long. He was cleverer than many of his breed, and warier too. He was constantly seeking the greater glory, the finer prize, disdaining even to trouble himself with the search for meaner rewards. Laws meant little to him: laws were for the living, and Mordant dealt exclusively with the dead. To this end, he had spent many years contemplating the mystery of Sedlec, poring again and again over myths of dark places, and of what might once have been concealed within them. As was, so yet might be.

What if?

Now he was within the ossuary itself, its alarm system overridden using a pair of clips and a length of wire, the air impossibly cold as he descended the stairs into the heart of the construct. He was surrounded by bones, by the partial remains of thousands of human beings, but this did not trouble him as much as it might have disturbed a more sensitive soul. Mordant was not a superstitious man, yet even he had to admit to a nagging sense of transgression in this place. Curiously, it was the sight of his exhalations made visible that made him uneasy, as though a presence were drawing his very life force from him, draining him slowly, breath by breath.

What if?

He walked between pyramids of skulls, beneath great traceries of vertebrae and garlands of fibulae, until he came to the small altar. He dropped a black canvas bag onto the floor. It jangled weightily when it landed. He withdrew a heavy pointed hammer from within, and set to work on the edges of a stone built into the floor, the shadow of the crucifix above falling upon him as moonlight filtered through the window behind.

What if?

He broke through the mortar, and saw that a few more taps would expose a gap large enough to accommodate the crowbar. So lost was he is in his work that he did not hear the approach from behind, and it was not until a faint musty smell came to his nostrils that he paused and turned, still on his knees. He looked up, and he was no longer alone.

What if?

Mordant raised himself slightly, almost apologetically, as though to indicate that there was a perfectly reasonable explanation for his presence in this place, and for the desecration he was committing, but as soon as he felt certain of his leverage he pushed himself forward and struck out with the flat of the hammer. He missed his target, but managed to clear himself a space through which he could see the steps. Hands grasped for him, but he was slick and fast and determined to escape. His blows were connecting now. He was almost clear. He reached the steps and ascended, his sight fixed on the door.

Mordant registered the presence to his right just a second too late. It emerged from the shadows, striking a blow that caught Mordant on the Adam's apple and pushed him back to the very edge of the stairway. For a moment, he teetered on the brink of the top step, his arms swaying in an effort to steady himself, before he fell backward, tumbling head over heels.

What if?

And Mordant's neck broke on the last step.

It was always cold in the ossuary at Sedlec, which was why the old woman had wrapped herself up warm. A ring of keys dangled from her right hand as she followed the path to Santini-Aichel's door. The care of this place had been in her family for generations, and its upkeep was supported by the books and cards sold from a small table by the door, and by the admission charge levied on those visitors who made the effort to come there. Now, as she approached, she saw that the door was ajar. There was a smear of blood upon the first of the stones within. Her hand rose to her mouth, and she halted at the periphery. Such a thing as this had never been known before: the ossuary was a sacred place, and had been left untouched for centuries.

She entered slowly, fearful of what she was about to see. A man's body lay splayed before the altar, his head tilted at an unnatural angle. One of the stones beneath the crucifix had been entirely removed, and something gleamed dully in the early morning light. The shards of one of the beautiful skull candleholders congregated at *the dead man's feet. Curiously, her first concern was not for him, but for the damage that had been caused to the ossuary. How could someone do this? Did they not realize that these were once people like them, or that there was a beauty to what had been created from their remains? She lifted a piece of the skull from the floor, rubbing it gently between her fingers, before her attention was distracted by another new addition to the ossuary.*

She reached for the small silver box by the dead man's hand. The box was unlocked. Carefully, she raised the lid. There was vellum contained within, the rolled document apparently uncorrupted. She touched it with her fingers. It felt smooth, almost slick. She lifted it out and began to unroll it. In the corner was a coat of arms: it depicted a battle-ax against the backdrop of an open book. She did not recognize it. She saw symbols, and architectural drawings, then horns, and part of an inhuman face contorted in agony. The drawing was immensely detailed, although it ended at the neck, but the old woman wanted to see no more than she had been given to witness. It was already too horrific for her eyes. She replaced the vellum in the box and rushed to get help, barely noticing that the ossuary was slightly warmer than it should have been, and that the heat was coming from the stones beneath her feet.

And in the darkness far to the west, two eyes opened suddenly in an opulent room, twin fires ignited in the night. And at the heart of one pupil, a white mote flickered with the memory of the Divine.

Neddo was almost finished.

"Sometime between the discovery of the body and its removal following the arrival of the police, the fragment, which was contained in a silver box, disappeared," he said. "Now, a similar fragment has been offered for sale through Claudia Stern. There's no way of telling if it is the Sedlec fragment, but the Cistercian order has made clear its objections to the sale. Nevertheless, it appears to be going ahead. There will be a great deal of interest, although the auction itself will be a very private affair. Collectors of such material tend to be, um, reclusive and somewhat secretive. Their fascinations can be open to misunderstanding."

I looked at the ephemera gathered in Neddo's dingy store: human remains reduced to the status of ornaments. I felt an overpowering urge to be gone from this place.

"I may have more questions for you," I said.

I took a business card from my wallet and laid it on the desk. Neddo glanced at it, but didn't pick it up.

"I'm always here," he replied. "Naturally, I'm curious to see where your inquiries lead you. Feel free to contact me, day or night."

He smiled thinly.

"In fact, night is probably best."

Garcia watched the building, growing increasingly uneasy as one hour rolled by, then another. He had tried to follow the man who was of such concern to Brightwell, but he was not yet familiar with the streets of this huge city, and had lost him within minutes. He believed that the man would return to his friends, and they were now Garcia's most pressing concern as they were still in his apartment. He had expected the police to come, but they had not. At first, it gave him hope, but now he was not so sure. They must have seen what was there. Perhaps they had even watched some of the tapes in his collection. What kind of men did not call the police in such a situation?

Garcia wanted his possessions back, and one in particular. It was important to him, but it was also the only item that could connect him, and the others, to the girl. Without it, the trail would be almost impossible to find.

A car pulled up, and the man got out and rang the bell to Garcia's building. Garcia was relieved to see that he had the large wooden box in his hands. He only hoped that whatever he had removed from the apartment was still contained within it.

Minutes later, the door opened and the Negro and his smaller companion left. Now there was only one man in the apartment, alone.

Garcia uncloaked himself from the shadows and moved toward the doorway.

I made one last search of the rooms. Louis and Angel had been through the apartment again, but I wanted to be sure that nothing had been missed. When I was done with the occupied areas, I went to the white-tiled room that Louis had discovered. Its purpose was clear. While it had been thoroughly cleaned, I wondered how much work had gone in to removing evidence from the pipes. They were probably new, since the room was a recent addition. If someone had bled into the drain, traces might remain.

Tins of paint, and old paintbrushes, their bristles now entirely hardened, stood on a trestle table by the far wall, alongside a pile of old paint-spattered sheets. I pulled at the pile, raising a little cloud of red dust. I examined the residue, then swept the sheets from the table. There was more brick dust on the wood, and on the floor below. I tested the wall with my hand, and felt brick scrape against brick. I looked more closely and saw the brickwork was not quite even around the edges of a section perhaps eighteen inches in height. Using my fingers, I gripped the exposed edge and began moving it from left to right, shifting it until I was able to pull it forward entirely. It fell to the table, still in one piece, leaving a hole exposed. I could make out a shape inside. I knelt down and shined the flashlight upon it.

It was a human skull, mounted upon a pillar of bones around which a red velvet cloth had been partially tied. A gold-sequinned scarf covered the head, leaving only the eye sockets, the nasal cavity, and the mouth exposed. At the base of the pillar finger bones had been placed in an approximation of the pattern of two hands, the bones adorned with cheap rings. Beside them, offerings had been placed: chocolate, and cigarettes, and a shot glass containing an amber liquid that smelled like whiskey.

A locket gleamed in the flashlight's beam, silver against the white of the bone pillar. I used a rag to reach out and take it in my hand, then flipped open the catch. Inside there were pictures of two women. The first I did not recognize. The second was the woman named Martha, who had come to my house in search of hope for her child.

Suddenly, there was an explosion of light and sound. Wood and stone splintered close to my right arm, shards of it striking my face and blinding me in my right eye. I killed the flashlight and dropped to the floor as a small, bulky figure was briefly silhouetted in the doorless entrance before ducking back out of sight. I heard the terrible twin clicks as another round was jacked into the shotgun's chamber and a man's voice uttering the same words over and over again. It sounded like a prayer.

"*Santa Muerte, reza por mi. Santa Muerte, reza por mi . . .*"

Faintly, just above his words, I caught the sound of footsteps on the stairs below as Angel and Louis ascended, closing the trap. The gunman noticed them too, because the volume of his prayers increased. I heard Louis's voice shout, "Don't kill him!" And then the gunman appeared again, and the shotgun roared. I was already moving when the trestle table disintegrated, one of its legs collapsing as the shooter entered the room, screaming his prayer over and over as he came, jacking, firing, jacking, firing, the noise and the dust filling the room, clouding my nose and my eyes, creating a filthy mist that obscured details, leaving only indistinct shapes. Through my blurred vision, I saw a squat, dark form. A cloud of light and metal ignited before it, and I fired.

10

The Mexican lay amid the ruins of the trestle table, the discarded sheets tangled around his feet like the remains of a shroud. One of the paint cans had opened, showering his lower body with white. Blood pumped rhythmically from the hole in his chest and into the paint, propelled by the beating of his slowly failing heart. His right hand clutched at the wall, crawling spiderlike across the brickwork as he tried to touch the skull on the altar.

"*Muertecita,*" he said once more, but now the words were whispered. "*Reza por mi.*"

Louis and Angel appeared in the doorway.

"Shit," said Louis. "I told you not to kill him."

Dust still clouded the room, and the contents of the hole in the wall were not yet visible to him. He knelt beside the dying man. His right hand clasped the Mexican's face, turning it toward him.

"Tell me," he said. "Tell me where she is."

The Mexican's eyes remained fixed upon a distant spot. His lips continued to move, repeating his mantra. He smiled, as though he had glimpsed something that was invisible to the rest of us, a rip in the fabric of existence that permitted him to see at last the reward, or the punishment, that was his and his alone. I thought I saw wonder in his gaze, and fear, even as his eyes began to lose their brightness, his eyelids drooping.

Louis slapped him hard on the cheek. He held a small photograph of Alice in his right hand. I had not seen it before. I wondered if his aunt had given it to him, or if it were his own possession, a relic of a life left behind but not forgotten.

"Where is she?" said Louis.

Garcia coughed up blood. His teeth were red as his lips tried to form the imprecation one final time, and then he shuddered and his hand fell from the brickwork and splashed in the paint as he died.

Louis lowered his head and covered his face with his hand, the picture of Alice now pressed to his skin.

"Louis," I said.

He looked up, and for a second I didn't know how to continue.

"I think I've found her."

The Emergency Service Unit was the first on the scene, responding to the "shots fired" alert from the dispatcher. Soon I was looking down the barrels of Ruger Mini-14s and H&K nine-millimeter submachine guns, trying to identify surnames and badge numbers in the confusion of lights and shouts that accompanied their arrival. The ESU cops took in the killing room, the dead Mexican, the bones arrayed in the apartment, and then, once they realized that the action was over for the evening, retreated and let their colleagues from the Nine-Six take control. I tried to answer their questions as best I could at the start, but soon lapsed into silence. It was, in part, to protect both me and my friends — I did not want to give away too much until I had a chance to compose my thoughts and get my story straight — but it was also a consequence of the image that I could not shake. I saw, over and over, Louis standing before the gap in the bricks, staring into the skeletal face of a girl that he had once known, his hands poised before her, wanting to touch all that remained but unable to do so. I watched him as he drifted back to another time and another place: a houseful of women, his days among them drawing to a close, even as another was added to their number.

I remember her. I remember her as a little baby, watching over her when the women were cooking or cleaning. I was the only man who held her, because her daddy, Deeber, was dead. I killed him. He was the first. He took my momma from me, and so I erased him from the world in retaliation. I didn't know then that my momma's sister was pregnant by him. I just knew, although there was no proof, that he had hurt my momma so badly that she had died, and that he would hurt me in the same way when his chance came. So I killed him, and his daughter grew up without a father. He was a base man with base appetites, hungers that he might have sated on her as the years went on, but she never got to see him or to understand the kind of man that he was. There were always questions for her, lingering doubts, and once she began to guess the truth of what had happened, I was far from her. I disappeared into the forest one day when she was still a child, and chose my own path. I drifted away from her, and from the others, and I did not know of what had befallen her until it was too late.

That is what I tell myself: I did not know.

Then our paths crossed in this city, and I tried to make up for my failures, but I could not. They were too grievous, and they could not be undone. And now she is dead, and I find myself wondering: Did I do this?

Did I set this in motion by quietly, calmly deciding to take the life of her father before she was born? In a sense, were we not both father to the woman she became? Do I not bear responsibility for her life, and for her death? She was blood to me, and she is gone, and I am lessened by her passing from this world.

I am sorry. I am so sorry.

And I turned away from him as he lowered his head, because I did not want to see him this way.

I spent the rest of the night, and a good part of the morning, being interviewed by the NYPD in the Nine-Six over on Meserole Avenue. As an ex-cop, even one with some unanswered questions surrounding him, my stock had some value. I told them that I was given a lead on the Mexican's apartment by a source, and had found the door to the warehouse open. I entered, saw what the apartment contained, and was about to call the police when I was attacked. In defending myself, I had killed my attacker.

Two detectives were interviewing me, a woman named Bayard and her partner, a big red-haired cop named Entwistle. They were scrupulously polite to start with, due in no small part to the fact that seated to my right was Frances Neagley. Before I arrived in New York, Louis had arranged for a nominal fee to be paid into my account by the firm of Early, Chaplin & Cohen, with whom Frances was a senior partner. Officially, I was in her employ, and therefore could claim privilege if any awkward questions were asked. Frances was tall, impeccably groomed even after my early call, and superficially charming, but she hung out in the kinds of bars where blood dried on the floor at weekends and had a reputation for stonewalling so hard that she made titanium seem pliable by comparison. She had already done a good job of simultaneously distracting and frightening most of the cops with whom she had come into contact.

"Who tipped you off on Garcia?" asked Entwistle.

"Was that his name?"

"Seems so. He's not in a position to confirm it right now."

"I'd prefer not to say."

Bayard glanced at her notes.

"It wouldn't be a pimp named Tyrone Baylee, would it, aka G-Mack?"

I didn't reply.

"The woman you were hired to find was part of his stable, right? I assume you spoke to him. I mean, it would make no sense *not* to speak to him if you were looking for her, right?"

"I spoke to a lot of people," I said.

Frances intervened. "Where are you going with this, Detective?"

"I'd just like to know when Mr. Parker here last spoke to Tyrone Baylee."

"Mr. Parker has neither confirmed nor denied that he *ever* spoke to this man, so the question is irrelevant."

"Not to Mr. Baylee," said Entwistle. He had yellowed fingers, and his voice rumbled with catarrh. "He was admitted to Woodhull early this morning with gunshot wounds to his right hand and right foot. He had to crawl to get there. Any hopes he ever had of pitching for the Yankees are pretty much gone."

I closed my eyes. Louis hadn't seen fit to mention the fact that he had visited a little retribution on G-Mack.

"I spoke to Baylee around midnight, one A.M.," I said. "He gave me the address in Williamsburg."

"Did you shoot him?"

"Did he tell you that I shot him?"

"He's all doped up. We're waiting to hear what he has to say."

"I didn't shoot him."

"You wouldn't know who did?"

"No, I wouldn't."

Again, Frances interjected.

"Detective? Can we move on?"

"Sorry, but your client, or your employee, or whatever you choose to call him, seems to be bad for the health of the people he meets."

"So," said Frances, her tone one of perfect reasonableness, "either slap a health warning on him and let him go, or charge him."

I had to admire Frances's fighting talk, but goading these cops didn't seem like a great idea with Garcia's body still cooling, G-Mack recovering from bullet wounds, and the shadow of the Brooklyn Metropolitan Detention Center looming over my future sleeping arrangements.

"Mr. Parker killed a man," said Entwistle.

"A man who was trying to kill him."

"So he says."

"Come on, Detective, we're going around in circles here. Let's be adult about this. You have a room torn up by shotgun blasts; a crumbling warehouse filled with bones, some of which may prove to be the remains of the woman Mr. Parker was hired to find; and two VCR tapes that appear to contain images of at least one woman being killed, and probably others. My client has indicated that he will cooperate with the investigation in any way that he can, and you're spending your time trying to trip him up with questions about an individual who suffered injuries subsequent to his meeting with my client. Mr. Parker is available for further questions at any time, or to answer any charges that may be pressed at a future date. So what's it going to be?"

Entwistle and Bayard exchanged a look, then excused themselves. They were gone for a long time. Frances and I sat in silence until they returned.

"You can go," said Entwistle. "For now. If it's not too much trouble, we'd appreciate it if you let us know if you plan on leaving the state."

Frances began gathering her notes.

"Oh," added Entwistle. "And try not to shoot anyone for a while, huh? See how you like it. It might even take."

Frances dropped me back at my car. She didn't ask me anything further about the events of the night before, and I didn't offer. We both seemed happier that way.

"I think you're okay," she said as we pulled up close by the warehouse. There were still cops outside, and curious onlookers kept vigil with the TV crews and assorted other reporters. "The man you killed got off three or four shots for your one, and if the bones in the warehouse are tied in to him, then nobody is going to come chasing you in connection with his death, especially if the remains you found in the wall turn out to be those of Alice. They may decide to go after you for discharging a weapon, but when it comes to PIs, that's a judgment call. We'll just have to wait and see."

I had retained a license to carry concealed in New York ever since I left the force, and it was probably the best $170 I spent every two years. The license was issued at the discretion of the commissioner, and in theory he could have denied my application for renewal, but nobody had ever raised an objection. I suppose it was a lot to ask for them to let me go around shooting the gun as well.

I thanked Frances and got out of the car.

"Tell Louis I'm sorry," she said.

I called Rachel once I was back at my hotel. She answered on the fourth ring.

"Everything okay?" I asked.

"Everything's fine," she said.

Her voice was flat.

"Is Sam all right?"

"She's good. She slept through till seven. I've just fed her. I'll put her down again for an hour or two now."

The line went quiet for about five seconds.

"How are you doing?" she said.

"There was some trouble earlier," I said. "A man died."

Again, there was only silence.

"And I think we found Alice," I said, "or something of her."

"Tell me."

She sounded suddenly weary.

"There were human remains in a tub. Bones, mostly. I found more behind a wall. Her locket was with them."

"And the man who died? Was he responsible?"

"I don't know for sure. It looks like it."

I waited for the next question, knowing that it had to come.

"Did you kill him?"

"Yes."

She sighed. I could hear Sam starting to cry. Rachel hushed her.

"I have to go," she said.

"I'll be back soon."

"It's over, right?" she said. "You know what happened to Alice, and the man who killed her is dead. What more can you do? Come home. Just—come home, okay?"

"I will. I love you, Rachel."

"I know." I thought I could hear something catch in her voice as she prepared to hang up the phone. "I know you do."

I slept until past midday, when I was awoken by the ringing of the telephone. It was Walter Cole.

"Seems like you had a busy night," he said.

"How much do you know?"

"A little. You can fill me in on the rest. There's a Starbucks over by Daffy's. I'll see you there in thirty minutes."

I made it in forty-five, and even then I was pushing it. On my way across town, I thought about what I had done, and about what Rachel had said when we spoke. In one sense, it was over. I felt certain that dental records and DNA tests, if necessary using Martha's DNA for comparison, would confirm that the remains found in Garcia's apartment were those of Alice. So Garcia was involved, and may even have been directly responsible for her death. But that didn't explain why Alice had gone missing to begin with, or why Eddie Tager had paid her bond. Then there was the antique dealer Neddo and his talk of "Believers," and the FBI agent Philip Bosworth, who appeared to be engaged in an investigation that mirrored, at least in some way, my own. Finally, I was aware of my own unease, and the sense that there was something else moving beneath the surface details of the case, weaving through the hidden, hollow caverns of the past.

My hair was still wet from a hasty shower when I sat down across from Walter at a corner table. He wasn't alone. Dunne, the detective from the coffee shop, was with him.

"Your partner know you're seeing other people?" I asked him.

"We have an open relationship. As long as he doesn't have to hear about it, he's cool. He thinks you shot G-Mack, though."

"So do the cops over at the Nine-Six. For what it's worth, I didn't pull the trigger on him."

"Hey, it's not like we really care so much. Mackey just doesn't want it coming back to haunt him, someone hears we sicced you on him."

"A couple of people pointed us in his direction. You can tell your partner he doesn't have anything to worry about."

"'Us?'" said Dunne.

Damn. I was tired.

"Walter and me."

"Right. Sure."

I didn't want to get into this with Dunne. I didn't even know why he was here.

"So," I said, "what are we doing here: testing muffins?"

Dunne looked to Walter for an ally.

"He's a hard guy to help," he said.

"He's very self-sufficient," said Walter. "It's a strong-man pose. I think it hides a conflicted sexuality."

"Walter, with all due respect, I'm not in the mood for this."

Walter raised a placating hand. "Easy. Like Dunne said, we're trying to help."

"Sereta, the other girl—it looks like they've found her too," said Dunne.

"Where?"

"Motel just outside of Yuma."

"The Spyhole killings?" I had watched some of the news reports on TV.

"Yeah. They've identified her for certain as the girl found in the trunk of the car. They kind of figured that anyway, since the car was registered to her and a section of her license survived the fire, but they were waiting for confirmation. It looks like she was still alive, and conscious, when the flames got to her. She managed to kick in the backseat before she died."

I tried to remember the details.

"Wasn't there a second body in the car?"

"Male. He's a John Doe. No ID, no wallet. They're still trying to chase him down with what they have, but it's not like they can put a picture of him on milk cartons. Maybe on BBQ charcoal come the summer, but not until then. He'd been shot in the shoulder and chest. Fatal bullet was still in him. It came from a thirty-eight, same gun as they found on the Mexican who died in one of the motel rooms. They were operating on the assumption that he might have been the target of a botched hit. Guy was tied up with some pretty bad people, and the *Federales* down in Mexico were real anxious to speak to him. Now, with this Alice thing up here, maybe there's another angle."

According to G-Mack, Alice and Sereta had been present when Winston and his assistant were killed, but they hadn't seen anything. They had taken something, though, and apparently this item was sufficiently valuable that the individuals involved were prepared to kill to get it back. They found Alice, and perhaps from her they gained some knowledge of where Sereta was hiding. I didn't like to think of how they had acquired that information.

"Your friend G-Mack will probably be released from hospital tomorrow," said Dunne. "From what I hear, he says he still doesn't know anything about what happened to his hookers, and he didn't get a look at the guy who shot him. Whoever put the bullet in his leg knew what he was doing. The ankle joint and the heel were shattered to pieces. Guy is gonna be a gimp for the rest of his life."

I thought of Alice's skull resting in the alcove in Garcia's apartment. I imagined Sereta's final minutes of life, as the heat grew in intensity, slowly roasting her before the flames took hold. By selling Alice out, G-Mack had condemned them both to death.

"That's tough," I said.

Dunne shrugged. "It's a tough world. Speaking of that, Walter says he tried to talk to Ellen, the young hooker."

I remembered the young girl in the dark clothing.

"You get anywhere with her?"

Walter shook his head.

"Hard outside, and getting harder inside. I'm going to talk to Safe Horizon about her, and I have a buddy in the Juvenile Crime Special Projects Squad. I'll keep trying."

Dunne stood and picked up his jacket.

"Look," he said to me, "if I can help you out, I will. I owe Walter, and if he wants to call in that debt for you, then I'm okay with that. But I like my job, and I plan on keeping it. I don't know who put those fucking bullets in that piece of shit, but if you happen to meet him, you tell him to take it to Jersey next time. We clear?"

"Clear," I said.

"Oh, and one last thing. They did find something else unusual in the Spyhole. The desk clerk's blood was smeared on his face, and they pulled foreign DNA from the samples. Weird thing was, it was all degraded."

"Degraded?"

"Old and debased. They think the samples might have been corrupted somehow. They contained toxins, and they're still trying to identify most of them. It's like somebody rubbed a piece of dead meat across the kid's face."

We gave him a five-minute start, then left.

"So what now?" asked Walter as we tried to avoid getting run over by a bus.

"I need to talk to some people. You think you can find out who owns that warehouse in Williamsburg?"

"Shouldn't be too hard. The Nine-Six is probably on top of it already, but I'll see what I can get from the city assessor's office."

"The cops at the Nine-Six have a name on the man I killed. I don't imagine they're going to share much information with me, so keep your ear to the ground, see what filters through."

"No problem. You planning on staying at the Meridien for another night?"

I thought of Rachel.

"Maybe one more. After that, I need to go home."

"You talk to her?"

"This morning."

"Did you tell her what happened?"

"Most of it."

"That sound you hear in the back of your mind? That's thin ice cracking. You need to be with her now. Hormones, everything gets screwed up. You know that. Even little things can seem like the end of the world, and big things, well, they just really might be the end."

I shook his hand.

"Thanks."

"For the advice?"

"No, the advice sucked. 'Thanks' is for stepping up to the plate on this one."

"Hey, once a cop," he said. "I miss it sometimes, but this helps. It reminds me of why I'm better off out of it."

My next call was to Louis. I met him at a coffee shop on Broadway, up in the Gay Nineties. He didn't look like he'd slept much, and although he was clean-shaven and his shirt was neatly pressed, he appeared uncomfortable in his clothes.

"Martha's cousin is flying up today," he said. "She's bringing dental records, medical stuff, anything she can find. Martha was staying in some shit hole in Harlem. I made her move, so they're both booked into the Pierre now."

"How is she?"

"She hasn't given up hope. Says it may not be Alice. The locket doesn't mean nothing, except that the guy took it from her."

"And you? What do you think?"

"It's her. Like you, I just knew. I felt it as soon as I saw the locket."

"The cops should have a positive ID by tomorrow, then. They'll probably release her in a day or two, once the M.E. has made his report. Will you go back with the remains?"

Louis shook his head.

"I don't think so. I won't be welcome. Anyway, there's history down there. Better to let it rest. I got other things to be doing."

"Like?"

"Like finding the ones who did this to her."

I sipped my coffee. It was already going cold. I raised the cup to the waitress, then watched quietly as she warmed it up.

"You should have told me what you did to G-Mack," I said, as soon as she was out of earshot.

"I had other things on my mind."

"Well, in future, if we're going to do this, you'll have to share your thoughts some. Two detectives over in the Nine-Six liked me a lot for the shooting. The fact that I'd left another man dead on their patch didn't help my case."

"They say how that pimp asshole is doing?"

"He was still woozy when I was at the Nine-Six, but since then he's come around. He told the cops that he didn't see a thing."

"He won't talk. He knows better than to say anything."

"That's not the point."

"Look," said Louis. "I ain't asking you to get involved in this. I didn't ask you to begin with."

I waited for him to say something more. He didn't.

"You finished?" I said.

"Yeah, I'm done." He raised his right hand in apology. "I'm sorry."

"There's nothing to be sorry for. If you shoot someone, just let me know, that's all. I want to be sure I can say I was somewhere else. Especially if, for once, I *was* somewhere else."

"The men who killed Alice are gonna find out that the pimp talked," said Louis. "The man's dead."

"Well, when they come he won't be able to run away, that's for sure."

"So what now?"

I told him about the death of Alice's friend Sereta near Yuma, and the body found in the car with her.

"He wasn't shot in the car," I said. "Mackey told me that the cops followed a blood trail from outside the room to the door of the Buick. This guy walked to the car, then he sat in the driver's seat with the door wide open while he burned alive."

"Could be someone was holding a gun on him."

"It would have to be a pretty big gun. Even then, getting shot would be a whole lot more attractive than burning. Plus he wasn't one of the guests registered. They're all accounted for."

"One of Sereta's johns?"

"If he was, he left no trace in her room. Even if that were true, what was he doing outside the Mexican's hotel room getting shot through the door?"

"So he was one of the killers?"

"It looks that way. He screws up, gets shot, then instead of taking him with them, his buddies leave him in the car and set him on fire."

"And he doesn't object."

"He doesn't even get up from his seat."

"So someone found out where Sereta was, and came looking for her."

"And killed her when she was found."

He made the connections, just as I had earlier. "Alice told them."

"Maybe. If she did, they forced it from her."

He thought about it some more. "It's hard for me to say this, but if I was Sereta, I wouldn't have told Alice more than she needed to know. Maybe general things, a safe number to contact her at, but no more. That way, if they came for Alice, there wouldn't be too much she could give away."

"So somebody down there ratted her out, probably based on whatever Alice's killers got out of her."

"Which means somebody down there knows somebody up here."

"Garcia might have been the contact. Given how close the Spyhole was to the border, the Mexican connection would make sense. It could be worth finding out some more."

"This wouldn't just be a way of getting me out of the city so you can pursue a, uh, more *diplomatic* line of inquiry?"

"That would assume that I'm cleverer than I am."

"Not cleverer, just slicker."

"Like I said, someone down there may have information that could help us. Whoever it is, he or she is unlikely to give it up easily. If I were you, I'd be looking to strike out at someone right about now. I'm just giving you a focus for your anger."

Louis raised his spoon and pointed it at me. He

managed to rustle up what might almost have been a smile.

"You been spending too long sleeping with psychologists."

"Not lately, but thanks for the thought."

Louis was right, though: I wanted him gone for a couple of days. It would save me having to keep my movements from him. I was afraid that if I gave him too much information, then he would take it upon himself to try to force answers from the people involved. I wanted the first shot at the bail bondsman. I wanted to speak to whoever had rented the warehouse space to Garcia. And I wanted to track down the FBI agent, Bosworth. After all, I thought, I could always set Louis on them later.

I went back to my hotel, but with one extra item in my trunk. I had entrusted the bone sculpture to Angel before he left the warehouse, and now Louis had returned it to me. If the cops found out that I had withheld it, I would be in serious trouble, but the sight of it had allowed me to gain access to Neddo, and I had a feeling that it would open other doors if necessary. Waving a photograph or a Crayola drawing wouldn't have quite the same impact.

Angel and Louis were due to fly down to Tucson that evening, via Houston. In the meantime, Walter got back to me with a name: the warehouse was part of an estate that had become tied up in some endless legal squabble, and the only contact the cops could find was a lawyer named David Sekula with an office on Riverside Drive. The telephone number on the banner at the warehouse went straight to an automatic answering service for a leasing company called Ambassade Realty, except Ambassade

Realty appeared to be a dead end. Its CEO was deceased, and the company was no longer in business. I took down Sekula's address and telephone number. I would call him in the morning, when I was fresh and alert.

I left three messages for Tager, the bail bondsman, but he didn't return my calls. His office was up in the Bronx, close by Yankee Stadium. Tager, too, would be tomorrow's work. Someone had asked him to post bail for Alice. If I found out who that person was, I would be one step closer to discovering those responsible for her death.

As Angel and Louis made their way to the Delta terminal at JFK, a man who might have been able to answer some of their most pressing questions passed through immigration, collected his baggage, and entered the arrivals hall.

The priest had arrived in New York on a BA flight from London. He was tall and in his late forties, with the build of a man who enjoyed his food. His unruly beard was lighter and redder than his head hair and gave him a vaguely piratical aspect, as though he had only recently ceased tying firecrackers to its ends in order to frighten his enemies. He carried a small black suitcase in one hand and a copy of that day's *Guardian* in the other.

A second man, slightly younger than the visitor, was waiting for him as the doors hissed closed behind him. He shook the priest's hand and offered to carry his case, but the offer was declined. Instead, the visitor handed the newspaper to the younger man.

"I brought you a *Guardian* and *Le Monde*," he said. "I know you like European newspapers, and they're expensive over here."

"You couldn't have brought a *Telegraph* instead?"

The younger man spoke with a faint Eastern European accent.

"It's a little conservative for my liking. I'd only be encouraging them."

His companion took the *Guardian* and examined the front page as he walked. What he saw there seemed to disappoint him.

"We're not all as liberal as you are, you know."

"I don't know what happened to you, Paul. You used to be on the side of the good guys. They'll have you buying shares in Halliburton next."

"This is no longer a country for heedless liberals, Martin. It's changed since last we were here."

"I can tell that. There was a chap back there in immigration who just stopped short of bending me over a table and poking me in the arse with his finger."

"He would be a braver man than I. Still, it's good to have you here."

They walked to the parking lot and didn't speak of the matters that concerned them until they were out of the airport.

"Any progress?" said Martin.

"Rumors, nothing more, but the auction is in a matter of days."

"It will be like putting blood in the water to see what it attracts, but fragments are no good to them. They need it all. If they're as close as we think, they'll bite."

"It's a risky business you've involved us in."

"We were involved anyway, whether we wanted it or not. Mordant's death ensured that. If he could find his way to Sedlec, then others could too. Better to retain a little control over what transpires than none at all."

"It was a guess. Mordant was lucky."

"Not that lucky," said Martin. "He broke his neck. At least it looks like it was an accident. Now, you said there were rumors."

"Two women disappeared from the Point. It seems that they were present when the collector Winston was killed. Our friends tell us that both have since been found dead: one in Brooklyn, the other in Arizona. It's reasonable to suppose that whatever they took from Winston's collection has now been secured."

The bearded priest closed his eyes briefly, and his lips moved in a silent prayer.

"More killings," he said, when he was finished. "That's too bad."

"That's not the worst of it."

"Tell me."

"There have been sightings: an obese man. He's calling himself Brightwell."

"If he has come out of hiding, it means that they believe they're close. Lord Jesus, Paul, don't you have any good news for me?"

Paul Bartek smiled. It was a grim smile, but he was still worried that the next piece of news was affording him a degree of pleasure. He would have to confess it at some point. Nevertheless, it was worth a few Hail Marys to pass it on to his colleague.

"One of their people has been killed. A Mexican. The police believe he was responsible for the death of one of the prostitutes. They think her remains are among those found in his apartment."

"Killed?"

"Shot to death."

"Somebody did the world a favor, but he'll pay for it. They won't like that. Who is he?"

"His name is Parker. He's a private detective, and it seems that he makes quite a habit of things like this."

Brightwell sat at the computer screen and waited for the printer to finish spewing out the final pages of the job. When it was done, he took the sheaf of papers and sorted through them, ordering them according to date, starting with the oldest of the cuttings. He read through the details of those first killings once again. There were pictures of the woman and child as they had been in life, but Brightwell barely glanced at them. Neither did he linger on the description of the crime, although he was aware that there was a great deal that remained unsaid in the articles. He guessed that the injuries inflicted on the man's wife and daughter were too horrific to print, or that the police had hoped at the time to hold back such details in case they encouraged copycats. No, what interested Brightwell was the information on the husband, and he marked with a yellow highlighter those parts that were particularly noteworthy. He performed a similar exercise on each of the subsequent pages, following the man's trail, re-creating the history of the preceding five years, noting with interest the way past and present intersected in his life, how some old ghosts were raised while others were laid to rest.

Parker. Such sadness, such pain, and all as penance for an offense against Him that you cannot even recall committing. Your faith was misplaced. There is no redemption, not for you. You were damned, and there is no salvation.

You were lost to us for so long, but now you are found.

11

David Sekula occupied a suite of modest offices in a nice old brownstone on Riverside. A brass plate on the wall announced his status as an attorney-at-law. I pressed the button on the intercom by the door. It gave out a reassuring two-note chime, as if to convince those who might be tempted to run away in the interim that everything would be all right in the end. Seconds later the speaker spluttered into life, and a female voice asked if she could help me. I gave her my name. She asked if I had an appointment. I confessed that I didn't. She told me Mr. Sekula wasn't available. I told her that I could sit on the steps and wait for him, maybe open a Mickey's Big Mouth to pass the time, but if I had to take a leak, then things might get messy.

I was buzzed in. A little charm goes a long way.

Sekula's secretary was spectacularly good looking, albeit in a vaguely threatening way. Her hair was long and black, and tied loosely at the back with a red ribbon. Her eyes were blue and her skin was pale enough to make the hints of red at her cheeks look like twin sunsets, while her lips would have kept a whole Freudian symposium going for a month. She wore a dark blouse that wasn't quite transparent yet still managed to hint at what appeared to be very expensive black lace lingerie. For a moment, I wondered if she was scarred in some way, because it seemed like there were irregular patterns visible on her skin where the blouse pressed against it. Her gray skirt ended just above the knee, and her stockings were thick and black. She looked like the kind of woman who would promise a man a night of ecstasy unlike anything he had ever previously imagined, but only as long as she could kill him slowly immediately afterward. The right man might even consider that a good deal. Judging by the expression on her face, I didn't think she was about to make me that kind of offer, not unless she could bypass the ecstasy part and get straight to the slow torture. I wondered if Sekula was married. If I had suggested to Rachel that I needed a secretary who looked like this woman, she would only have agreed if I signed up for temporary chemical castration beforehand, with the threat of a more permanent solution always on the horizon if I ever felt tempted to stray.

The reception area, carpeted in gray, took up the entire front room, with a black leather couch beneath the bay window and a very modern coffee table made from a single slab of black glass in front of it. There were matching easy chairs at either side of the table, and the walls were decorated, if that was the right word, with the kind of art that suggested someone suffering from severe depression had stood in front of a blank canvas for a very long time, then made a random stroke with a black paintbrush before slapping a hefty price tag on the result and entering lifelong therapy. All things considered, minimalism seemed to be the order of the day. Even the secretary's desk was untroubled by anything resembling a file or a piece of stray paper. Maybe Sekula wasn't very busy, or perhaps he just spent his days staring dreamily at his secretary.

I showed her my license. She didn't look impressed.

"I'd like a few minutes of Mr. Sekula's time."

"Mr. Sekula is busy."

I thought I could hear the low drone of one side of a telephone conversation coming from behind a pair of black doors to my right.

"Hard to imagine," I said, taking in the spotless reception area once again. "I hope he's firing his decorator in there."

"What is this about?" said the secretary. She didn't deign to use my name.

"Mr. Sekula appears to be responsible for a property in Williamsburg. I wanted to ask him about it."

"Mr. Sekula is involved with a lot of properties."

"This one is pretty distinctive. It seems to have a lot of dead people in it."

Sekula's secretary didn't even blink at the mention of what had occurred in Williamsburg.

"Mr. Sekula has been over that with the police," she said.

"Then it should all be fresh in his mind. I'll just take a seat and wait until he's done in there."

I sat down in one of the chairs. It was uncomfortable in the way that only very expensive furniture can be. After two minutes, the base of my spine was aching. After five minutes, the rest of my spine was aching too, and other parts of my body were crying out in sympathy. I was considering lying on the floor instead when the black doors opened and a man in a charcoal gray pinstripe suit stepped into the reception area. His hair was light brown and trimmed as carefully as potentially prizewinning topiary, so that not a single strand was out of place. He had the bland good looks of a part-time model, his features without a single flaw or hint of individuality that might have lent them character or distinction.

"Mr. Parker," he said. "I'm David Sekula. I'm sorry you had to wait. We're busier than we might appear."

Clearly, Sekula had heard everything that was said in the reception room. Perhaps the secretary had simply left the room-to-room intercom open. Either way, it made me curious as to whom Sekula had been talking with on the phone. It might have been nothing to do with me, in which case I would have to face the possibility that the world didn't revolve around me. I wasn't sure that I was ready to take that step yet.

I shook Sekula's hand. It was soft and dry, like an unused sponge.

"I hope you've recovered from your ordeal," he said, ushering me toward his office. "What happened in that place was terrible."

The cops had probably explained my involvement to Sekula when they interviewed him. Clearly, they'd forgotten to include his secretary in the loop, or maybe they'd tried to tell her but she couldn't understand them through their drool.

Sekula paused by his secretary's desk.

"No calls, please, Hope," he told her.

Hope? It was hard to believe.

"I understand, Mr. Sekula," she replied.

"Nice name," I told her. "It suits you."

I smiled at her. We were all friends now. Maybe they'd invite me to go away with them on a trip. We could drink, laugh, reminisce about how awkward that first encounter between us had been before we all got to know one another and realized how swell each of us truly was.

Hope didn't smile back. It looked like the trip was off.

Sekula closed the doors behind us and waved me to an upright chair in front of his desk. The chair faced the window, but the drapes were drawn so I couldn't see what lay beyond them. Compared to the reception area, his office looked like a bomb had hit it, but it was still neater than any lawyer's office I had ever been in before. There were files on the desk, but they were neatly stacked and housed in nice clean folders, each marked with a printed label. The trash can was empty, and it looked like the filing cabinets were hidden behind the false oak fronts that lined two walls, or simply didn't exist at all. The art on Sekula's walls was also a lot less disturbing than the paintings in the reception area: there was a large Picasso print of a faun playing a lute, signed no less, and a big canvas that resembled a cave drawing of horses rendered in layered oils, the horses literally carved into the paint: the past re-created in the present. It too was signed by the artist, Alison Rieder. Sekula saw me looking at it.

"Do you collect?" he said.

I wondered if he was being funny, but he seemed serious. Sekula must have paid his investigators way above the going rate.

"I don't know enough about it to collect," I said.

"But you have art on your walls?"

I frowned. I wasn't sure where this was going.

"Some, I guess."

"Good," he said. "A man should appreciate beauty, in all its forms."

He inclined his chin toward the office door, behind which lay the increasingly less enticing form of his secretary, and grinned. I was pretty certain that if he did that in front of the lady in question she'd cut off his head and stick it on a railing in Central Park.

Sekula offered me a drink from a cabinet against the wall, or coffee if I preferred. I told him I was fine as I was. He took his seat at his desk, steepled his fingers, and looked grave.

"You're unhurt after the incident?" he said. "Apart from—"

He touched his fingers to his left cheek. I had some cuts on my face from the splinters, and there was blood in my left eye.

"You should see the other guy," I said.

Sekula tried to figure out if I was joking. I didn't tell him that the image of Garcia slumped against the wall was still fresh in my mind, his blood soaking the dusty, paint-spattered sheets, his lips moving in prayer to whatever deity permitted him to collude in the killing of women yet still offered hope and succor to those who prayed to it. I didn't tell him of the metallic smell of the dying man's blood, which had infected what little food I had consumed throughout the day. I didn't tell him of the stench that rose from him as he died, or the way his eyes glazed over with his last breath.

And I did not mention the sound of that final breath, or the manner in which it was released from him: a long, slow exhalation, both reluctant and relieved. It had always seemed somehow apt that words connected with freedom and escape should be used to describe the moment when dullness replaced brightness, and life became death. To be close to another human being at that instant was enough to convince one, however briefly, that something beyond understanding passed from the body with that final sigh, that some essence began its journey from this world to another.

"I can't imagine what it must be like to kill a man," said Sekula, as though all that I had just considered had been revealed to him through my eyes.

"Why would you even want to imagine it?" I said.

He seemed to give the question some serious thought.

"I suppose there have been times when I've wanted to kill someone," he said. "It was a fleeting thing, but it was there. I thought, though, that I could never live with the consequences; not just the legal consequences, but the moral and psychological ones. Then again, I have never been placed in the situation where I was seriously forced to consider taking the life of another. Perhaps, under such circumstances, it would be within my capabilities to kill."

"Have you ever defended someone accused of a killing?"

"No. I deal mainly in business affairs, which brings us to the matter in hand. I can only tell you what I told the police. The warehouse was once a storehouse for the Rheingold brewing company. It closed in 1974, and the warehouse was sold. It was acquired by a gentleman named August Welsh, who subsequently became one of my clients. When he died, some legal difficulties arose over the disposal of his estate. Take my advice, Mr. Parker: make a will. Even if you have to write it on the back of a napkin, do it. Mr. Welsh was not so farsighted. Despite repeated entreaties on my part, he refused to commit his intentions to paper. I think he felt that making a will would in some way be an acknowledgment of the imminence of his mortality. Wills, in his view, were for people who were dying.

I tried to tell him that everyone was dying: him, me, even his children and his grandchildren. It was to no avail. He died intestate, and his children began to bicker among themselves, as is often the case in such situations. I tried to manage his estate as best I could in the interim. I ensured that his portfolio remained watertight, that any funds accruing were immediately reinvested or lodged to an independent account, and I endeavored to produce the best results from his various properties. Unfortunately, the Rheingold warehouse was not one of his better investments. Property values in the area are improving, but I could find no one who was willing to commit sufficient funds to the redevelopment of the building. I left the matter in the hands of Ambassade Realty, and largely forgot about it until this week."

"Were you aware that Ambassade went out of business?"

"I'm sure that I must have been informed, but passing on responsibility for the leasing of the building was probably not a priority at the time."

"So this man, Garcia, had signed no lease with either Ambassade or your firm."

"Not that I'm aware of."

"Yet some work had been done on the top floor of the warehouse. There was power, and water. Someone was paying the utilities."

"Ambassade, I assume."

"And now there's nobody at Ambassade left to ask."

"No, I'm afraid not. I wish I could be of more help."

"That makes two of us."

Sekula composed his features into an expression of regret. It didn't quite take, though. Like most professionals, he wasn't fond of those outside his field casting doubts upon any aspect of his business. He stood, making it clear to me that our meeting was now over.

"If I think of anything that might be of help to you, I'll try to let you know," he said. "I'll have to tell the police first, of course, but under the circumstances I would have no objection to keeping you informed as well, as long as the police confirmed that to do so would not interfere with the progress of their investigation."

I tried to interpret what Sekula had just said, and came to the conclusion that I had learned all that I was going to from him. I thanked him, and left him with my card. He walked me to the office door, shook my hand once again, then closed the door behind me. I tried one last time to chip away at his secretary's permafrost exterior by expressing my gratitude for all that she'd done, but she was impervious to insincerity. If Sekula was keeping her company at night, then I didn't envy him. Anyone sleeping with her would need to wrap up against the cold first, and maybe wear a warm hat.

My next call was to Sheridan Avenue in the Bronx, where Eddie Tager had his office. There was a lot of competition for business, and the streets east of Yankee Stadium, and near the courthouse, were lined with bondsmen. Most were at least bilingual in their advertising, and the ones that could afford neon usually made sure that the word *fianzas* was at least as conspicuous as "bail" in their windows.

There was a time when the bail industry was the preserve of pretty nasty characters. They still existed, but they were strictly minor players. Most of the bigger bail bondsmen were backed by the major insurance firms, including Hal Buncombe. According to Louis, he was the bondsman that Alice was supposed to call if she ever found herself in trouble. The fact that she hadn't called him indicated the animosity she felt for Louis, even when she was in the most desperate of situations. I met Buncombe in a little pizzeria on 161st, where he was eating the first of two slices from a paper plate. He was about to wipe his fingers on a napkin in order to shake hands, but I told him not to worry about it. I ordered a soda and a slice, and joined him at his table. Buncombe was a small wiry man in his fifties. He radiated the mixture of inner calm and absolute self-belief that is the preserve of those who have seen it all and who have learned enough from their past mistakes to ensure that they no longer repeated them too often.

"How's business?" I asked.

"It's okay," he said. "Could be better. We've taken some skips already this month, which isn't good. We figure we gave up two hundred and fifty thousand dollars to the state last year, which means we're playing catch-up from the start of this one. I'll have to stop being nice to people. In fact, I've already stopped."

He raised his right hand. I noticed that his knuckles were bruised, the skin broken in places.

"I pulled a guy off the streets earlier today. Just had a bad feeling about him. If he skipped, he'd cost us fifty thou, and I wasn't prepared to take that chance."

"I take it he objected."

"He took a couple of swings," Buncombe conceded. "We hauled him out to Rikers but they aren't taking bodies, and the judge who set bail is on the West Coast until tomorrow, so I have him in a room in back of the office. He claims he has an out-of-state asset that he can offer as collateral — a house in some crack alley in Chicago — but we can't take out-of-state or out-of-country property, so we'll just have to hold him overnight, try to get him locked up safe in the morning."

He finished his first slice, and started in on his second.

"Tough way to make money," I said.

"Not really." He shrugged. "We're good at our job, my partners and me. Like Joe Namath said, it's only bragging if you can't do it."

"What can you tell me about Eddie Tager?" I asked. "Is he good at his job too?"

"Tager's bad news. Real low-end. He's so desperate he works mostly Queens, Manhattan, and they're hard, real hard. The Bronx and Brooklyn are picnic boroughs by comparison, but beggars can't be choosers. Tager deals with small-time beefs: not just bonds, but fines too. I hear most of the hookers don't like turning to him if they're in trouble — he likes them to give up a little extra as a show of thanks, if you catch my drift — which is why I was surprised when I heard that he supplied the cut slip for Alice. She would have been warned about him."

He stopped eating, as though he had suddenly lost his appetite, and dropped the remains of the slice onto the plate before dumping it in the trash.

"I feel bad about what happened. I was trying to deal with paperwork over here, and doing what I could over the phone. Someone told me in passing that the cops had pulled Alice in on a drug trawl, but I figured I had a couple of hours and that she could just sit tight until I picked up a few more bonds to make it worth my while heading over there to check up on her. It's a pain in the ass waiting for Corrections to release one inmate. Makes more sense to build up four or five, then wait for them all to be cut loose. By the time I got over there, she was already gone. I saw the slip and figured that she decided to go with Tager. I knew she had a problem with our 'mutual friend,' so I didn't take it personally. You know, she was a mess by the end. Last time I saw her, she wasn't looking good, but she didn't deserve what happened to her. Nobody deserves that."

"Have you seen Tager lately?"

"Our paths don't cross so much anymore, but I asked around. Looks like he's gone to ground. It could be that he's running scared. Maybe it got back to him that the girl had connections, and that certain people were going to take a dim view of his involvement once she didn't reappear."

Buncombe gave me directions to Tager's office. He even offered to come along with me, but I declined. I didn't believe that I'd need help making Eddie Tager talk. Right then, words were the only currency he had with which to buy his life.

Eddie Tager was so low-rent that he lived and worked out of the back of a fire-damaged bodega that had closed for renovations sometime during Watergate and never reopened. I found the place without too much trouble, but there was no answer when I tried the bell. I went around back and tried hammering on the rear door. It came ajar slightly under the impact of my fist.

"Hello?" I said.

I opened the door wider and stepped inside. I was in the kitchen area of a small apartment. A counter separated it from a living room furnished with brown carpet, a brown couch, and a brown TV. Even the wallpaper was light brown. There were newspapers and magazines scattered around. The most recent was dated two days earlier. Straight ahead was a hallway with an open door leading into the main office. To the right was a bedroom, and beside that a small bathroom with mold growing on the shower curtain. I checked each room before ending up in the office. It wasn't exactly spotless, but there was at least an attempt at order. I went through the recent files but could find nothing relating to Alice. I sat down in Tager's chair and searched the drawers of his desk, but nothing struck me as important. I found a box containing business cards in the top drawer, but none of the names was familiar to me.

There was a small pile of mail behind the door. It was all junk and bills, including one from Tager's cell phone company. I opened it and flipped through the pages until I came to the date of Alice's arrest. Like most bondsmen, Tager used his cell phone a lot in the course of his business. On that day alone he had made thirty or forty calls, the frequency of them increasing as the night drew on. I placed the bill back in its envelope and was about to put it in my jacket pocket so that I could take a closer look at it later when I saw a dark smear on the paper. I looked at my fingers and saw blood. I wiped them on the envelope, then tried to find the source, retracing my steps until I was back at Tager's chair.

The blood was congealing on the underside and right-hand corner of the desk. There wasn't a lot of it, but when I shined my flashlight on it I thought I could see some hairs mixed in, and there were stains on the carpet. The desk was big and heavy, but when I checked the area around the legs I saw marks on the fabric where the desk had shifted slightly. If the blood was Tager's, then someone had hit the bondsman's head pretty hard against the corner of the desk, probably when he was already sprawled on the floor.

I went back to the kitchen and soaked my handkerchief under the faucet, then cleaned down every surface that I had touched. When I was done, my handkerchief was covered in pink stains. I left the same way that I had entered, once I was certain that there was nobody around. I didn't make any calls about the blood. If I did, I'd have to explain what I was doing there, and then I'd need my own bail bondsman. I didn't think Tager was coming back, though. Someone had asked him to post bail for Alice, which meant that he was complicit in the sequence of events that had led to her death. Garcia had not been acting alone, and now it looked like his confederates were taking care of the weak links in the chain. I patted the cell phone bill in my pocket. Somewhere in that list of numbers was, I hoped, another link that they might have overlooked.

It was now late, and dark. I decided that there was nothing more that I could do until the morning, when I would run the numbers from Tager's cell phone bill. I went back to my hotel room and called Rachel. Her mother answered the phone and told me that Rachel was already in bed. Sam had slept badly the night before and had spent most of the day crying until, exhausted at last, she had succumbed to rest. Rachel had fallen asleep immediately after. I told Joan not to disturb her, but to let her know that I'd called.

"She's worried about you," said Joan.

"I'm okay," I said. "Be sure to tell her that."

I promised that I'd try to return to Maine by late

the next day, then hung up the phone and ate at the Thai place beside the hotel, just because it was something to do other than sitting alone in my room with the fear that my relationship was disintegrating in my hands. I stuck to the vegetarian dishes. After my visit to Tager's office, the coppery taste of spilled blood had returned to my mouth with a vengeance.

Charles Neddo sat in his office chair, his desk scattered with illustrations, all of them taken from books written after 1870, and most depicting variations on the *Black Angel*. He had never quite understood why there were no depictions prior to that date. No, that wasn't true. Rather, the drawings and paintings became more uniform in the last quarter of the nineteenth century, less speculative and with a certain commonality to their lines, especially those originating with Bohemian artists. Depictions from earlier centuries were far more diverse, so that without a written indication of the source, imagined or otherwise, it would be impossible to tell that all were renderings of the same subject.

There was music playing in the background, a collection of Satie piano pieces. Neddo liked their air of melancholy. He removed his glasses, leaned back from his desk, and stretched. The wrinkled cuffs of his shirt rolled back on his thin arms, exposing a small mass of scar tissue above his left wrist, as though a mark of some kind had been inexpertly obscured in the relatively recent past. It was stinging slightly now, and Neddo touched his left hand gently to the scarring, the tips of his fingers following the lines of the grapnel once branded upon his skin. One could turn away, he thought, and hide oneself among worthless antiques, but the old obsessions lingered.

Otherwise, why would he have surrounded himself with bones?

He returned to the drawings, aware now of a rising sense of excitement and anticipation. The private detective's visit had revealed a great deal to him, and earlier that evening he had received another unexpected call. The two monks had been nervous and impatient, and Neddo understood that their presence in the city was a sign that events were moving quickly now, and that a resolution of sorts would soon be achieved. Neddo told them all that he knew, and then received absolution from the older one for his sins.

Satie came to an end, and the room fell into silence as Neddo put his papers away. He believed that he knew what Garcia had been creating, and why it was being built. They were close, and now, as never before, Neddo was aware of the conflict raging within himself. It had taken him many years to break free of their influence, but like an alcoholic he feared that he would never really be free of the urge to fall. He touched his left hand to the cross around his neck, and felt the scar on his wrist begin to burn.

Rachel was deep in sleep when her mother woke her. She was startled and tried to say something, but her mother's fingers pressed themselves to her lips.

"Shhh," whispered Joan. "Listen."

Rachel remained quiet and still. There was no sound for a moment, and then she heard the scuffling noises coming from the roof of the house.

"There's someone up there," said Joan.

Rachel nodded, still listening. There was something odd about the sounds. They were not quite footsteps.

Instead, it seemed to her that whoever was up there was crawling across the slates, and crawling quickly. She was reminded, unpleasantly, of the movements of a lizard. The noise came again, but this time it was echoed by a vibration against the wall behind her head. The bedroom occupied the entire width of the first floor, so that the bed rested against the wall of the house. A second heavy presence was now ascending the sheer wall toward the roof, and once again it sounded like it was moving on four legs.

Rachel got up and walked quickly to the closet. She opened it quietly, moved two shoe boxes aside, and looked at the small gun safe behind them. She resented the fact that it was even there, and had insisted that it have a five-number combination lock to prevent Sam from gaining access to it, even though it was six feet off the ground on the topmost shelf. She entered the code and heard the bolts slide. Inside were two guns. She removed the smaller of the two, the .38. She hated firearms, but in the aftermath of recent events she had reluctantly agreed to learn how to use this one. She loaded it using the speed loader, then went back to her bed and knelt down. There was a small white box on the wall, with a red button on top. She pressed it just as she heard the window shaking in the next room, as though someone were trying to open it.

"Sam!" she shouted.

The alarm began to sound, tearing apart the silence of the marshes as Rachel ran to Sam's room, Joan close behind her. She could hear the child crying, terrified by the sudden burst of noise. The door was open, and faced the window. Sam was writhing in her cot, her little hands beating against the air and her face almost purple with the force of her tears. For a fleeting instant, Rachel thought she could see something pale move against the window, and then it was gone.

"Take her," said Rachel. "Get her into the bathroom and lock the door."

Joan grabbed the child and ran from the room.

Slowly, Rachel approached the window. The gun was a little unsteady in her grip, but her finger no longer rested outside the guard and instead was gently touching the trigger. Nearer now: ten feet, five, four, three . . .

The sound of crawling again came from above her head, this time moving away from Sam's room and toward the far side of the house. The noise distracted Rachel, and she lifted her head to follow its progress, as though the intensity of her gaze could penetrate the ceiling and slates and permit her to see what was above.

When she looked back to the window there was a face there, hanging upside down in the night from the top of the glass, dark hair dangling vertically from pale features.

It was a woman.

Rachel fired, shattering the window. She kept firing, even as the sound of the presences on the roof and wall came again, growing fainter now as they fled. She could see blue light scything through the darkness, and heard Sam crying even above the noise of the alarm. And then she was crying with her daughter, howling with fear and anger, her finger still pulling the trigger over and over even as the hammer struck only the empty casings and the night air flooded the room, bringing with it the smell of saltwater and marsh grass and dead winter things.

12

F ew people would have described Sandy and Larry
    Crane as happy individuals. Even Larry's fellow VFW
members, upon whom time was inexorably taking its toll
and who now boasted a rapidly dwindling platoon of
World War II survivors among their number, tended at
best to tolerate Larry and his wife when they occasionally attended a veterans' social event. Mark Hall, the
only other member of their little band who was still alive,
often told his wife that in the aftermath of D-Day it was
really just a question of who was going to kill Larry first:
the Germans or his own side. Larry Crane could peel an
orange in his pocket and open a candy bar with so little
noise as to suggest that his time might have been better
served in a special operations unit, except that Larry was
a born coward and therefore of little use to his own unit,
never mind to an elite group of hardened soldiers forced
to operate behind enemy lines in desperate conditions.
Hell, Mark Hall could have sworn that he'd seen Larry
crouching behind better men during combat in the hope
that they would take a bullet before he did.

And sure enough, that was what happened. Larry
Crane might have been a cheap sonofabitch, and yellow
as a buttercup's ass to boot, but he was also lucky. In
the midst of carnage, the only blood he ever got on
him was other men's. Hall might not have admitted it

to anyone later, might even have been reluctant to admit it to himself, but as the war wore on he found himself sticking close to Larry Crane in the hope that some of that luck might rub off on him. He guessed that it had, because he'd lived when others had died.

It wasn't all good luck, though. He'd paid a price by becoming Larry Crane's creature, bound to him by the shared knowledge of what they had done in the Cistercian monastery at Fontfroide. Mark Hall didn't talk about that with his wife, no sir. Mark Hall didn't talk about that with anyone except his God, and then only in the ultimate secret confessional of his own mind. He hadn't set foot in church since that day, had even managed to convince their only daughter to have her wedding outdoors by offering her the most expensive hotel in Savannah as a venue. His wife assumed that he'd suffered some crisis of faith over what he'd endured during the war, and he let her believe that, supporting her assumptions by making occasional dark references to "the things I saw over in Europe." He supposed that there was even a little kernel of truth hidden beneath the shell of the lie, because he had seen some terrible things, and done some terrible things too.

God, they were only children when they went off to fight, virgins, and virgin children had no call to be holding guns and firing them at other children. When he looked at his grandchildren, and saw how cosseted and naive they were despite the pretence of knowingness that they maintained, he found it impossible to visualize them as he had once been. He recalled sitting on the bus to Camp Wolters, his momma's tears still drying on his cheek, listening while the driver told the Negroes to sit at the back because the front seats were for the white folks, didn't matter that they were all headed for the same conflict and that bullets were blind to race. The blacks didn't object, although he could see the resentment simmering in a couple of them, and their fists tightened as some of the other recruits joined in, wisecracking at them as they walked to their seats. They knew better than to respond. One word from them and the whole situation would have exploded, and Texas was tough back then. Any one of those Negroes raised a hand to a white man and they wouldn't have to worry about the Germans or the Japanese, because their own side would take care of them before they had time to break in their boots, and nobody would ever be called to answer for what befell them.

Later, he heard that some of those black men, the ones who could read and write, were told to sign up for officer candidates' school, on account of the fact that the army was organizing a division of black soldiers, the Ninety-second, to be known as the Buffalo Division after the black soldiers who fought in the Indian wars. He was with Larry Crane by then, the two of them sitting in some god-awful rain-drenched field in England when someone told them about it, and Crane started off bitching about how the niggers were getting the breaks while he was still a grunt. The invasion was imminent, and soon some of those black soldiers found their way to England too, which made Crane bitch even more. It didn't matter to him that their officers weren't allowed to enter headquarters by the front door like the white officers, or that the black troops had crossed the Atlantic without any escort because they weren't considered as valuable to the war effort. No, all Larry Crane saw was uppity Negroes, even after the beach at Omaha was secured, their unit smoking cigarettes on the walls of a captured German emplacement, and they looked down to see the black soldiers walking with sacks along the sand, filling them with the body parts of the men who had died, reduced to the level of collectors of human garbage. No, even then Larry Crane saw fit to complain, calling them cowards who weren't fit to touch the remains of better men, although it was the army that dictated that they weren't fit to fight, not then, not until men like General Davis pushed for the integration of black GIs into infantry combat units in the winter of 1944, and the Buffalo Division began fighting its way through Italy. Hall had few problems with Negro soldiers. He didn't want to bunk with them, and he sure as hell wasn't about to drink from the same bottle, but it seemed to him that they could take a bullet as well as the next man, and as long as they kept their guns pointed in the right direction he was happy to wear the same uniform as they. By comparison with Larry Crane, this made Mark Hall a bastion of liberalism, but Hall had sufficient self-knowledge to recognize that by making only a cursory effort to contradict Crane or tell him to keep his damn mouth shut he was culpable too. Time and time again, Hall tried to put distance between himself and Larry Crane, but he grew to realize that Larry was a survivor, and an uneasy bond developed between the two men until the events at Fontfroide occurred and that bond became something deeper, something unspeakable.

And so Mark Hall maintained a pretense of friendship with Larry Crane, sharing a drink with him when there was no way to avoid doing otherwise, even inviting him to that goddamned ruinous wedding, though his wife had made it clear that she didn't want either

Larry or his slovenly wife sullying her daughter's special day with their presence, and sulked for a week when he informed her that he was paying for the whole fucking day, and if she had a problem with his friends, then maybe she should have put more money into her bank account so that she could have paid for the entire wedding herself. Yeah, he'd told her all right. He was a big guy, a great guy, swearing at his wife to cover his own shame and guilt.

Hall figured that he had something on Larry Crane too: after all, they had both been there together, and both were complicit in what had occurred. He'd allowed Larry to dispose of some of what they had found, and then had accepted his share of the money gratefully. The cash had enabled Hall to buy a piece of a used car dealership, and he built upon that initial investment to make himself the auto king of northeast Georgia. That was how he was depicted in his newspaper ads and in the TV commercials: he was the Auto King, the Number One Ruler on Prices. Nobody Beats the Auto King. Nobody Can Steal His Crown When It Comes to Value.

It was an empire built on good management, low overheads, and a little blood. Just a little. In the context of all the blood spilled during the war, it was hardly more than a spot. He and Larry never spoke about what happened after that day, and Hall hoped that he would never have to speak of it again until the day he died.

Which, curiously, was kind of what happened, in the end.

Sandy Crane sat on a stool by the kitchen window, watching her husband wrestle a garden hose like he was Tarzan trying to subdue a snake. She puffed boredly on her menthol cigarette and tipped some of the ash into the sink. Her husband always hated it when she did that. He said it made the sink reek of old mints. Sandy thought the sink stank pretty bad already, and a dab of ash wasn't going to make a whole lot of difference. If he didn't have the smell of her cigarettes to whine about, she had no doubt that he would find something else. At least she got a little pleasure out of smoking, which went some way toward helping her to put up with her husband's shit, and it wasn't like those fucking cheap cartons that Larry bought for himself smelled any better.

Larry was squatting now, trying to untangle the hose, and failing. It was his own fault. She had told him often enough that if he rolled it up properly instead of throwing it half-assed into the garage, then he wouldn't have these problems, but then Larry wasn't one to take advice from anyone, least of all his wife. In a way, he spent his life trying to get out of messes that he created for himself, and she spent her life telling him that she'd told him so.

Speaking of half-assed, the cleft of Larry's buttocks was now clearly visible above the waistband of his pants. She could hardly bear to see him naked now. It pained her, the way everything about him sagged: his buttocks, his belly, his little shriveled organ, now practically hairless like his little shriveled head. Not that she was any bargain herself, but she was younger than her husband and knew how to make the best of what she had, and how to hide her deficiencies. A number of men had learned, just a little too late, how deficient Sandy Crane was once her clothes hit the floor, but they'd screwed her anyway. A lesser woman wouldn't have known whom to despise more: the men or herself. Sandy Crane didn't worry too much about it, and as in most other areas of her life, settled for despising everyone but herself equally.

She had met Larry when he was already in his fifties, and she was twenty years his junior. He hadn't been much to look at, even then, but he was in a pretty good position financially. He owned a bar and restaurant in Atlanta, but he sold up when the "faggots" started making the area their own. That was her Larry: dumber than a busload of tongueless morons, so prejudiced that he was incapable of seeing that the gays who were moving into the neighborhood were infinitely classier and wealthier than his existing clientele. He sold the business for maybe a quarter of what it was now worth, and he had seethed over it ever since. If anything, it had made him even more of a sexist, racist bigot than he ever was before, which was saying something because Larry Crane was already only a couple of holes in a pillowcase away from putting burning crosses in people's backyards.

Sometimes she wondered why she bothered staying with Larry at all, but the thought was quickly followed by the realization that snatched moments in motel rooms or in other women's bedrooms were unlikely to be translated into long-term relationships with a sound financial underpinning. At least with Larry she had a house, and a car, and a moderately comfortable lifestyle. His demands were few, and growing fewer now that his sex drive had deserted him entirely. Anyway, he was so coiled up with piss and fury at the world that it was only a matter of time before he had a stroke or a heart attack. That garden hose might yet do her a favor, if she could learn to keep her mouth shut for long enough.

She finished her cigarette, lit another from its dying

embers, then tossed the butt in the waste disposal. The newspaper lay on the table, waiting for Larry to return from his labors so that he could have something else to complain about for the rest of the day. She picked it up and flipped through it, conscious that this simple act would be enough to get her husband pissed. He liked to be the first to read the newspaper. He hated the smell of perfume and menthol upon its pages, and raged at the way she wrinkled and tore it as she read, but if she didn't look at it now, then it would be old news by the time she got to it; old news, what's more, with Larry's toilet stink upon it, since her husband seemed to concentrate best when he was sitting on the can, forcing his aged body to perform another racked, dry evacuation.

There was nothing in the newspaper. There never was. Sandy didn't know quite what she expected to find in there every time she opened it. She just knew that she was always disappointed when she was done. She turned her attention to the mail. She opened all of it, even the letters addressed to her husband. He always bitched and moaned when she did that, but most of the time he ended up passing them on to her to deal with anyway. He just liked to pretend that he still had some say in the matter. This morning, though, Sandy wasn't in the humor for his bullshit, so she just ripped into what was there in the hope that it might provide her with a little amusement. Most of it was trash, although she laid aside the coupon offers, just in case. There were bills, and offers of bum credit cards, and invitations to subscribe to magazines that would never be read. There was also one official-looking manila envelope. She opened it and read the letter within, then reread it to be sure she'd picked up all of the details. Attached to the letter were two color photocopies of pages from the catalog of an auction house in Boston.

"Holy shit," said Sandy. "Sweet holy shit."

Some ash fell onto the page from her cigarette. She brushed it off quickly. Larry's reading glasses lay on the shelf beside his vitamins and his angina medication. Sandy picked them up and gave them a quick clean with a kitchen towel. Her husband couldn't read for shit without his glasses.

Larry was still struggling with the hose when her shadow fell across him. He looked up at her.

"Get out of the light, dammit," he said, then saw what she had done to his newspaper, which, in her distracted state, she had tucked untidily under her arm.

"The hell have you done with the paper?" he said. "It ain't fit for nothin but the bottom of a birdcage now you been at it."

"Forget the damn newspaper," she said. "Read this." She handed the letter to him.

He stood up, puffing a little and tugging his pants up over his meager paunch.

"I can't read without my glasses."

She produced his glasses and watched impatiently while he examined the lenses and wiped them on the filthy edge of his shirt before putting them on.

"What is this?" he asked. "What's so important you had to turn my newspaper into an asswipe to bring it to me?"

Her finger pointed to the piece in question.

"Holy shit," said Larry.

And for the first time in over a decade, Larry and Sandy Crane enjoyed a moment of shared pleasure.

*   *   *

The Black Angel

Larry Crane had been keeping things from his wife. It had always been his way. Early in their relationship, for example, Larry hadn't bothered to mention the times that he'd cheated on her, for obvious reasons, and thereafter tended to apply to most of his dealings with Sandy the maxim that a little knowledge was a dangerous thing. But one of Larry's few remaining vices, the horses, had gotten a little out of hand, and he currently owed money to the kind of people who didn't take a long view on such matters. They had informed him of their position just two days before, when Larry made a vig payment significant enough to allow him to hold on to all ten of his digits for another couple of weeks. It was now at the point where his house was the only asset he could readily turn to cash because even disposing of the car wouldn't cover what he owed, and he didn't see how Sandy would approve of his selling their home and moving them into a doghouse in order to pay his gambling debts.

He could try turning to Mark Hall, of course, but that was a reservoir that he had well and truly tapped out a couple of years back, and only absolute desperation would bring him back to it again. In any case, Larry would be playing a dangerous game if he used the blackmail card on Old King Hall, because Hall might just call his bluff and Larry Crane had no desire to see out the remainder of his life in a jail cell. He figured Hall knew this. Old Hallie might be a lot of things, but stupid was not one of them.

And so Larry Crane had been wrestling with the garden hose, wondering if there might not be a way to turn Sandy to some use by strangling her with it, dumping the body, and claiming the insurance, when the lady in question cast her shadow upon him. Larry knew then

293

that he had about as much chance of successfully killing his wife as he had of looking after the Playboy Mansion on the days when Hugh Hefner was feeling a little under the weather. She was big and strong, and mean with it. If he even tried to lay a hand on her she'd break him like he was a swizzle stick in one of her cheap cocktails.

But as he read and reread the letter, it quickly became apparent to him that he might not have to resort to such desperate measures after all. Larry had seen something like the item described in the photocopies, but he had never suspected that it might be worth money, and now here was a story informing him that it could bring in tens of thousands of dollars, maybe more. That "could" was an important caveat, though. What was being sought was not actually in the possession of Larry Crane. Instead, it rested in the ownership of one Marcus E. Hall, the Auto King.

While the face of the Auto King remained that of Mark Hall, the old man was now little more than a figurehead. His sons, Craig and Mark Jr., had taken over the day-to-day running of the family business almost a decade ago. Jeanie, his daughter, had a twenty percent share in the company, based on the fact that it was Craig and Mark Jr. who did all the work while Jeanie just had to sit back and wait for the check to clear. Jeanie didn't see it that way, though, and had been raising quiet hell over it for the past five years. The King saw the hand of her husband, Richard, at work. Dick, as his sons liked to call him both to his face and behind his back, and always with a little added venom, was a lawyer, and if there was one species of rodent that would use the excuse of money to gnaw its way into a family's heart and consume all the goodness inside, it was a lawyer. The King suspected that as soon as he was dead, Dick would start producing pieces of paper in court and demanding a bigger share of the business backdated to the time when the Virgin Mary herself was in mourning. The King's own legal people had declared everything to be watertight and above reproach, but that was just more lawyers telling their client what they thought he wanted to hear. There would be days in court after he died, of that the King had no doubt, and his beloved dealership, and equally beloved family, would be torn apart as a result.

The King was standing outside the office of the main lot on Route 17, sipping coffee from a big cup emblazoned with a gold crown. He still liked to put in a couple of days each month, and the other salesmen didn't object because any money he earned in commission was put into a communal pot. At the end of every month, one salesman's name was drawn from a hat over beers in Artie's Shack, and all of the money went to him, or to her, for two women now worked on the King's lots, and they sold a bunch of cars to the kind of men who had wires running straight from their dicks to their wallets. The winner paid for beers and food, and so everyone was happy.

It was four in the afternoon, dead time, and since it was a weekday in the middle of the month, the King didn't expect it to pick up much before closing. While they might get a few walk-ins once the office workers finished up, the only thing most of them would have in their pockets would be their hands.

Then, right at the end of the lot, he saw a man leaning into the windshield of a 2001 Volvo V70 Turbo wagon, 2.4 auto, leather interior, AM/FM/cassette/CD player, sunroof, forty-five thousand miles. Thing had been driven like it was made of eggshells, so there wasn't a scratch on the paintwork. The King's boys had it tagged at twenty thousand, with plenty of room for maneuver. The guy was wearing a sun visor and dark glasses, but the King couldn't tell much else about him other than that he looked a little old and beat-up. The King's eyesight wasn't so good these days, but once he got his marks in focus he could tell more about them in thirty seconds than most psychologists could learn in a year of sessions.

The King put his cup down on the windowsill, straightened his tie, slipped the keys to the Volvo from the lockup box, and headed out into the lot. Someone asked him if he needed any help. There was a burst of laughter. The King knew what they were doing: looking out for him while pretending that they weren't.

"Guy is older than I am," he said. "I'm only worried that he don't die before I get him to sign the papers."

There was more laughter. The King could see that the old man at the Volvo had now opened the driver's door and slipped into the seat. That was a good sign. Getting them into the damn car was the hardest part, and once they were test driving, then guilt started to kick in. The salesman, a nice guy, was taking time out of his busy schedule to go for a ride with them. He knew a little about sport, maybe liked the same music once he'd taken a flip through the dial and found something that made the mark smile. After he'd gone to all that trouble, well, what could a decent human being do but listen to what the man had to say about this beautiful automobile? And hey, it was hot out there, right, so better to do it in the cool of the office with a cold can of soda in one hand, huh? What do you mean, talk to your wife first? She's gonna love this car: it's safe, it's clean, it's got solid resale value. You walk out of this lot without signing, and it won't be here once you're done having a conversation with the little lady that you didn't need to have to begin with, because she's going to tell you what I'm telling you: it's a steal. You get her hopes up and then bring her down here only to find out that this baby is gone and you're going to be in a worse position than you were before you started. Talk to the bank? We got a finance package right here that's better than any bank. Nah, they're just numbers: you're never gonna end up paying back that much . . .

The King reached the Volvo, leaned down, and looked in through the driver's window.

"Well, how you doin to—"

The pitch died on his lips. Larry Crane grinned up at him, all yellow teeth, unwashed hair, and dirt-encrusted wrinkles.

"Why, I'm doin fine, King, just fine."

"You lookin at buyin a car there, Larry?"

"I'm lookin, King, that's for sure, but I ain't buyin yet. Bet you could do me a favor, though, we bein old war buddies and all."

"I can cut you a deal, sure," said the King.

"Yeah," said Larry. "Bet you could cut me one, and I could cut you one right back."

He lifted one mangy buttock from the seat and broke wind loudly. The King nodded, even the false warmth he had managed to generate now fading rapidly.

"Uh-huh," he said. "Uh-huh. You ain't here to buy no car, Larry. What do you want?"

Larry Crane leaned over and opened the passenger door.

"Sit in with me, King," he said. "You can roll the windows down, the smell gets too much for you. I got a proposition to make."

The King didn't take the seat.

"You ain't gettin no money from me, Larry. I told you that before. We're all done on that score."

"I ain't askin for money. Sit in, boy. Ain't gonna cost you nothin to listen."

The King exhaled a wheezy breath. He looked over at the office, wishing he'd never left his coffee, then lowered himself into the Volvo.

"You got the keys for this piece of shit?" asked Larry.

"I got 'em."

"Then let's you and me go for a ride. We got some talkin to do."

France, 1944

The French Cistercians were used to hiding secrets. From 1164 to 1166, the monastery at Pontigny, in Burgundy, gave shelter to Thomas Becket, the English prelate exiled for opposing Henry II, until he decided to return to his diocese and was murdered for his troubles. Loc-Dieu, at Martiel in the Midi-Pyrénées, provided a refuge for the Mona Lisa during World War II, its combination of a fortress's high walls and the grandeur of a country manor rendering it most appropriate for such a lady's enforced retreat. It is true that other monasteries farther afield held treasures of their own: the Cistercians of Dulce Cor, or "Sweetheart", at Loch Kindar in Scotland, were entrusted with the embalmed heart of John, Lord Balliol,

in 1269, and of his wife, the Lady Devorgilla, who
followed him to the grave two decades later; and Zlatá
Koruna in the Czech Republic held a spine reputed to
have come from the crown of thorns placed upon the
head of Christ, purchased from King Louis himself by
Premysl Otakar II. Yet these were relics known to be
retained, and while they were guarded by the monks,
there were few concerns by the twentieth century that
an awareness of their presence might lead to the monasteries themselves being targeted.

No, it was those artifacts retained in silence, hidden
behind cellar walls or within great altars, that placed
at risk the monasteries and their inhabitants. The
knowledge of their presence was passed on from abbot
to abbot, so that few knew what lay beneath the library
at Salem in Germany, or under the ornate church paving
at Byland in Yorkshire's North Riding.

Or in Fontfroide.

There had been monks at Fontfroide since 1093,
although the first formal community, probably made
up of former hermits from the Benedictine order, was
established in 1118. The abbey of Fontfroide itself
appeared in 1148 or 1149 and quickly became a front-
line fortress in the fight against heresy. When Pope
Innocent III moved against the Manicheans, his legates
were two monks from Fontfroide, one of whom, Pierre
de Castelnau, was subsequently assassinated. A former
abbot of Fontfroide led the bloody crusade against the
Albigensians, and the monastery aligned itself staunchly
against the Catharist forces of Montsegur and Queribus
otherwise tolerated by the liberals of Aragón. It was
perhaps no surprise that Fontfroide should eventually
seize the greatest of prizes, and so the abbey was finally

rewarded for its steadfastness when its former abbot, Jacques Fournier, became Pope Benedict XII.

Fontfroide was wealthy to boot, its prosperity based upon the twenty-five farmsteads that it owned and its grazing herds of over twenty thousand cattle, but gradually the monks grew fewer and fewer, and during the French Revolution Fontfroide was turned into a hospice by the city of Narbonne. In a way, this was Fontfroide's salvation, for it led to the preservation of the abbey when so many others fell into ruin, and a Cistercian community flourished once again at the abbey from 1858 until 1901, when the state put Fontfroide up for sale and it was bought and preserved by a pair of French art lovers from the Languedoc.

But in all that time, even during periods when no monks graced its cloisters, Fontfroide remained under the close scrutiny of the Cistercians. They were there when it was a hospice, taking care of the sick and injured in the guise of laymen, and they returned to its environs when the wealthy benefactors, Gustave Fayet and his wife, Madeleine d'Andoque, purchased it to prevent it from being shipped, brick by brick, to the United States. There is a little church that lies less than a mile from Fontfroide, a far humbler offering to God than its great neighbor. It is called, in English, the Vigil Church, and from there the Cistercians kept watch over Fontfroide and its secrets. For almost five hundred years, its treasures had remained undisturbed, until World War II entered its final phase, the Germans began to retreat, and the American soldiers came.

"No," said the King. "Uh-uh. I got one of those letters too, and I threw it in the trash."

Mark Hall knew that times had changed, even if Larry Crane didn't. In those months after the war the world was still in chaos, and a man could get away with a great deal once he took even a little care about it. It wasn't like that now. He had kept a watchful eye on the newspapers, and had followed the case of the Meadors with particular interest and concern. Joe Tom Meador, while serving with the U.S. Army during World War II, had stolen manuscripts and reliquaries from a cave outside Quedlinburg in central Germany, where the city's cathedral had placed them for safekeeping during the conflict. Joe Tom mailed the treasures to his mother in May 1945, and once he returned home he took to showing them to women in return for sexual favors. Joe Tom died in 1980, and his brother Jack and sister Jane decided to sell the treasures, making a futile effort to disguise their origins along the way. The haul was valued at about $200 million, but the Meadors got only $3 million, minus legal fees, from the German government. Furthermore, by selling the items they attracted the interest of the U.S. attorney for eastern Texas, Carol Johnson, who initiated an international investigation in 1990. Six years later, a grand jury indicted Jack, Jane, and their lawyer, John Torigan, on charges of illegally conspiring to sell stolen treasures, charges that carried with them a penalty of ten years in prison and fines of up to $250,000. That they got away with paying $135,000 to the IRS was beside the point for Mark Hall. It was clear to him that the smart thing would be to take to the grave the knowledge of what he and Larry had done in France during the war, but now here was dumb and greedy Larry Crane about to draw them into a whole world of potential hurt. Hall was already troubled by the appearance of the letter. It meant that someone was making connections, and drawing conclusions from them. If they stayed quiet and refused to take the bait, then maybe Hall would be able to go to his grave without spending his children's inheritance on legal fees.

They were parked in the driveway outside the King's house. His wife was away visiting Jeanie, so theirs was the only car present. Larry laid a shaky hand on the King's arm. The King tried to shake it off, but Larry responded by turning the resting hand into a claw and gripping the King tightly.

"Just let's take a look at it, is all I'm sayin. We just need to compare it with the picture, make sure it's the same thing we're talking about. These people are offering a whole lot of money."

"I got money."

For the first time, Larry Crane's temper frayed.

"Well I sure as fuck don't," he shouted. "I got shit, King, and I'm in trouble."

"What kind of trouble can an old goat like you get into?"

"You know I always liked to gamble."

"Ah, Jesus. I knew you was the kind of fool thought he was smarter than other fools, but the only folks who should bet on horses are those who can afford to lose. Last I heard, you weren't exactly high on that list."

Crane took the insult, absorbing the blow. He wanted to lash out at the King, to beat his head against the pine-fresh dashboard of this Scandinavian piece of shit, but doing that wouldn't get him any closer to the money.

"Maybe," he said, and for a few moments Crane allowed his self-hatred, so long buried beneath his hatred of others, to shine through. "I never had your smarts, that's for sure. I married bad, and I made bad decisions in business. I ain't got no kids, and could be that's for the best. I'd've screwed them up too. I figure, all told, I got a lot of what I deserved, and then some."

He released his grip on the King's arm.

"But these men, they're gonna hurt me, King. They'll take my house, if they can get it. Hell, it's the only thing I have left that's worth anything, but they'll cause me pain along with it, and I can't handle no pain like that. All I'm askin is that you take a look at that thing you got to see if it's a match. Could be we can cut a deal with the folks that are lookin for it. It just takes a phone call. We can do this quiet, and no one will ever know. Please, King. Do this for me, and you'll never have to see me again. I know you don't like me bein around, and your wife, she'd see me burnin in the fires of hell and she wouldn't waste her sweat to cool me down, but that don't bother me none. I just want to hear what this guy has got to say, but I can't do that unless I know that we have what he's lookin for. I got my part here."

He removed a greasy brown envelope from a plastic grocery bag that lay on the backseat. Inside was a small silver box, very old and very battered.

"I never paid it much mind, until now," he explained.

Even seeing it here, in the driveway of his own house, gave the King the creeps. He didn't know why they had taken it to begin with, except that some voice in his head had told him it was strange, maybe even valuable, the first time he'd laid eyes on it. He liked to think he'd have known that, even if those men had not died trying to keep it for themselves.

303

But that was in the aftermath, when his blood was still hot; his blood, and the blood of others.

"I don't know," said the King.

"Get it," whispered Larry. "Let's put them together, just so we can see."

The King sat in silence, unmoving. He stared at his nice house, his neatly kept lawn, the window of the bedroom he shared with his wife. If I could undo just one element of my life, he thought, if I could take back just one action, it would be that one. All that has followed, all the happiness and joy, has been blighted by it. For all the pleasure I have enjoyed in life, for all of the wealth that I have amassed and all the kudos I have gained, I have never known one day of peace.

The King opened the car door and walked slowly to his house.

Private Larry Crane and Corporal Mark E. Hall were in real trouble.

Their platoon had been on patrol in the Languedoc — part of a joint effort with the British and Canadians to secure the southwest and flush out isolated Germans while the main U.S. force continued its eastward advance — and had wandered into a trap on the outskirts of Narbonne: Germans in brown-and-green camouflage uniforms, backed up by a half-track with a heavy machine gun. The uniforms had thrown the Americans. Because of equipment shortages, some units were still using an experimental two-piece camouflage uniform, the M1942, which resembled the clothing routinely worn by the Waffen SS in Normandy. Hall and Crane had already been involved in an incident earlier in the campaign,

*when their unit opened fire on a quartet of riflemen
from the Second Armored Division of the Forty-first
who had become cut off during bitter fighting with the
Second SS Panzer Division near Saint-Denis-le-Gast. Two
of the riflemen were shot before they had a chance to
identify themselves, and one of them had died of his
wounds. Lieutenant Henry had fired the fatal shot
himself, and Mark Hall sometimes wondered if that was
why he allowed the troops advancing out of the darkness crucial moments of grace before ordering his own
men to open fire. By then, it was too late. Hall had
never before seen troops move with the speed and precision of those Germans. One minute they were in front
of the Americans, the next they were dispersed among
the trees on both sides of the road, quickly and calmly
surrounding their enemies prior to annihilating them.
The two soldiers buried themselves in a ditch as gunfire
exploded around them and the trees and bushes were
turned to splinters that shot through the air like arrows
and embedded themselves in skin and clothing.*

"Germans," *said Crane, a little unnecessarily, his
face buried in the dirt.* "There ain't supposed to be no
Germans left here. What the hell are they doing in
Narbonne?"

*Killing us, thought Hall, that's what they're doing,
but Crane was right: the Germans were in retreat from
the region, but these soldiers were clearly advancing.
Hall was bleeding from the face and scalp as the fusillade continued around them. Their comrades were being
torn apart. Already only a handful were left alive, and
Hall could see the German soldiers closing in on the
survivors to wipe them out, twin lightning flashes now
gradually being revealed as the need for duplicity was*

eliminated. Hall could see that the half-track was American, a captured M15 mounted with a single thirty-seven-millimeter gun. This was no ordinary bunch of Germans. These men had a purpose.

He heard Crane whimpering. The other man was so close to him that Hall could smell his breath as Crane cowered against him in the hope that Hall's body would provide some cover. Hall knew what he was doing, and pushed the younger man hard.

"Get the fuck away from me," he said.

"We got to stick together," pleaded Crane. The sounds of gunfire were becoming less frequent now, and those that they heard were single bursts from German machine guns. Hall knew they were finishing off the wounded.

He started to crawl through the undergrowth. Seconds later, Crane followed.

Many miles and many years away from the events of that day, Larry Crane sat in an air-conditioned Volvo rubbing his fingers on the cross carved into the box. He tried to remember what the paper that it once contained had looked like. He recalled taking a look at the writing on the fragment, but it was unreadable to him and he had rejected the fragment as worthless. Although he did not know it, the words were Latin, and largely inconsequential. The real substance lay elsewhere, in tiny letters and digits carefully drawn into the top right-hand corner of the vellum, but both the King and Larry Crane had been distracted by the illustration upon the page. It looked like a design for something, a statue of some kind, but neither man had ever understood why anyone would want to make a statue like this, using what looked like pieces of bone and dried skin scavenged from both humans and animals.

But somebody wanted it, and if Larry Crane was right, they were prepared to pay handsomely for the pleasure.

The two soldiers were wandering aimlessly, desperately trying to find shelter from the strange, unseasonable cold that was settling in, and from the Germans who were now presumably combing the area for any survivors to ensure that their presence was not communicated to superior forces. This was no last-ditch assault, no futile German attempt to force back the Allied tide like the actions of some Teutonic King Canute. The SS men must have parachuted in, maybe capturing the half-track along the way, and Hall's belief that they had some seriously dark purpose for doing so was reinforced by what he had witnessed as he and Crane retreated: men in civilian clothing emerging from cover, shadowing the half-track and apparently directing the efforts of the soldiers. It made no sense to Hall, no sense at all. He could only hope that the path he and Crane were taking would lead them as far away as possible from the Germans' prize.

They made for higher ground, and at last found themselves in what appeared to be an uninhabited region of the Corbière hills. There were no houses, and no livestock. Hall figured that any animals that had once grazed had been killed for food by the Nazis.

It started to rain. Hall's feet were damp. The top brass had taken the view that the new buckled combat boots recently issued to soldiers would suffice for winter once treated with dubbin, but Hall now had conclusive evidence, if further evidence were needed, that even in the early fall this was not the case. The boots neither repelled water nor retained warmth, and as the two men trudged through the cold, damp grass Hall's toes began to hurt so badly that his eyes watered. In addition, problems with the supply chain meant that he and Crane were clad only in wool trousers and Ike jackets. Between them, they had four frag grenades, Crane's M1 (with a spare "immediate use" clip carried on his bandolier sling, for reasons Hall couldn't quite figure out since Crane had barely managed to fire off a couple of rounds during the ambush), and Hall's Browning automatic rifle. He had nine of his 13x20-round mags left, including the one in the gun, and Crane, as his designated assistant, had two more belts, giving them twenty-five mags in total. They also had four K rations, two each of Spam and sausage. It wasn't bad, but it wasn't good either, not if those Germans found their trail.

"You got any idea where we are?" asked Crane.

"Nope," said Hall. Of all the men he had to end up with after a goddamned massacre, it would have to be Larry Crane. The guy was unkillable. Hall felt like a pincushion, what with all the splinters that had entered him, but Crane didn't have a scratch on his body. Still, it was like they said: somebody was looking out for Crane, and by staying close by, a little of that protection had rubbed off on Hall as well. It was a reason to be thankful, he supposed. At least he was alive.

"It's cold," said Crane. "And wet."

"You think I haven't noticed?"

"You gonna just keep walking until you fall down?"

"I'm gonna keep walking until—"

He stopped. They were on the top of a small rise. To their right, white rocks shone in the moonlight.

Further on, a complex of buildings was silhouetted against the night sky. Hall could make out what looked like a pair of steeples, and great dark windows set into the walls.

"What is it?"

"It's a church, maybe a monastery."

"You think there are monks there?"

"Not if they have any sense."

Crane squatted on the ground, supporting himself with his rifle.

"What do you reckon?"

"We go down, take a look around. Get up."

He yanked at Crane, smearing blood on the other man's uniform. He felt stabs of pain run through his hand as some of the splinters were driven further into his flesh.

"Hey, you got blood on me," said Crane.

"Yeah, I'm sorry about that," said Hall. "Real sorry."

Sandy Crane was talking to her sister on the phone. She liked her sister's husband. He was a good-looking man. He wore nice clothes and smelled good. He also had money, and wasn't afraid to spread it around so that his wife could look her best at the golf club, or at the charity dinners that they seemed to attend every second week and about which her sister never tired of telling her. Well, Sandy would show her a thing or two once Larry got his hands on that money. Barely eight hours had elapsed since she opened the letter, but already Sandy had their windfall spent ten times over.

"Yeah," she said. "Larry looks like he might be coming into a little money. One of his investments paid off, and now we're just waiting for the check to be cut."

She paused to listen to her sister's false congratulations.

"Uh-huh," said Sandy. "Well maybe we might just come along with you to the club sometime, see about getting us one of those memberships too."

Sandy couldn't see her sister proposing the Cranes for membership in her swanky club for fear of being run out of the gates with the dogs at her heels, but it was fun to yank her chain some. She just hoped that, for once, Larry wouldn't find a way to screw things up.

Hall and Crane were a stone's throw away from the outer wall when they saw shadows cast by moving lights.

"Down!" whispered Hall.

The two soldiers hugged the wall and listened. They heard voices.

"French," said Crane. "They're speaking French."

He risked a glance over the wall, then rejoined Hall.

"Three men," he said. "No weapons that I can see."

The men were moving to the soldiers' left. Hall and Crane followed them from behind the wall, eventually making their way to the front of the main chapel, where a single door stood open. Above it was a tympanum carved with three bas-reliefs, including a brilliantly rendered crucifixion at the center, but the wall was dominated by a stained glass oculus and two windows, the traditional reference to the Trinity. Although they were not to know it, the door they were watching was rarely opened for any reason. In the past, it had been unlocked only to receive the remains of the viscounts of Navarre or other benefactors of the abbey to be buried at Fontfroide.

There were noises coming from inside the chapel.

Hall and Crane could hear stones being moved, and grunts of effort from the men within. A figure passed through the shadows to their right, keeping watch on the road that led to the monastery. His back was to the soldiers. Silently, Hall closed in on him, sliding his bayonet from his belt. When he was close enough, he slapped his hand over the man's mouth and placed the tip of the knife to his neck.

"Not a move, not a sound," he said. "Comprenez?"

The man nodded. Hall could see a white robe beneath the man's tattered greatcoat.

"You're a monk?" he whispered.

Again, the man nodded.

"How many inside? Use your fingers."

The monk lifted three fingers.

"They monks too?"

Nod.

"Okay, we're going inside, you and me."

Crane joined him.

"Monks," said Hall. He saw Crane breathe out deeply with relief, and felt a little of the same relief himself.

"We don't take any chances, though," said Hall. "You cover me."

He forced the monk down the flight of four stone steps that led to the church door. As they drew closer they could see the lights flickering within. Hall stopped at the entrance and glanced inside.

There was gold on the stone floor: chalices, coins, even swords and daggers that gleamed with gemstones set into their hilts and scabbards. As the monk had said, three men were laboring in the cold surroundings, their breath rising in great clouds, their bodies steaming with sweat. Two were naked from the waist up, forcing a

pair of crowbars into the gap between floor and stone.
The third, older than the others, stood beside them,
urging them on. He had sandals on his feet, almost
obscured by his white robes. He called a name, and
when no response came he moved toward the door.

Hall stepped into the chapel. He released his grip on
the monk and pushed him gently ahead of him. Crane
appeared beside him.

"It's okay," he said. "We're Americans."

The expression on the old monk's face didn't indicate that he thought this was okay at all, and Hall realized that the cleric was just as concerned about the
Allies as he was about any other potential threat.

"No," he said, "you should not be here. You must
go. Go!"

He spoke English with only the barest hint of an
accent. Behind him, the monks, who had briefly paused
in their efforts to shift the stone, now redoubled them.

"I don't think so," said Hall. "We're in trouble.
Germans. We lost a lot of guys."

"Germans?" said the monk. "Where?"

"Near Narbonne," said Hall. "SS."

"Then they will soon be here," said the monk.

He turned to the watcher and told him to return to
his post. Crane appeared on the verge of stopping him,
but Hall held him back and the monk was allowed to
pass.

"You want to tell us what you're doing?" Hall asked.

"Better that you do not know. Please, leave us."

There was a howl of rage and disappointment from
the laborers, and the great stone fell back into place.
One of the men sank to his knees in frustration.

"You trying to hide that stuff?"

There was a pause before the answer came.

"Yes," said the monk, and Hall knew that he was not telling the entire truth. He briefly wondered what kind of monk told lies in a church, and figured that the answer was a desperate one.

"You won't move that with just two men," said Hall. "We can help. Right?"

He looked to Crane, but the private's eyes were fixed on the treasure that lay upon the floor. Hall slapped Crane's arm hard.

"I said we can help them. You okay with that?"

Crane nodded. "Sure, sure."

He shrugged off his uniform jacket, placed his gun on the floor, and he and Hall joined the men at the stone. Now that he was up close, Hall could see that they were tonsured. They looked to their leader, waiting for him to respond to the Americans' offer.

"Bien," he said, at last. "Vite."

With four men now working instead of two, the stone began to lift more easily, but it was still immensely heavy. Twice it slipped back down into its resting place, until a last, great effort forced it up sufficiently far for it to be pushed back onto the floor. Hall rested his hands on his knees and stared into the hole they had created.

A silver hexagonal box, perhaps six inches in circumference and sealed with wax, lay in the dirt. It was plain and unadorned, apart from a simple cross carved into the top. The old monk knelt down and carefully reached in to retrieve it. He had just lifted it out when the alarm was raised by the sentinel at the door.

"Shit!" said Hall. "Trouble."

Already, the old monk was pushing the cache of gold

into the hole and urging his fellows to replace the stone as best they could, but they were exhausted and making slow progress.

"Please," said the monk. "Help them."

But Hall and Crane were making for the door. Carefully, they joined the lookout at the top of the steps.

Men, perhaps a dozen or more in total, were advancing along the road in the moonlight, their helmets shining. Behind them came the half-track, with more men following it. The two Americans took one look at each other and melted into the darkness.

The King stood on the top rung of the ladder and pulled the cord. The attic swam into light, illumination not quite reaching the farthest corners. His wife had told him again and again that they needed to install a window in the roof, or at least put in a stronger lightbulb, but Hall had never really made either a priority. They didn't come up here much anyway, and he was no longer entirely sure what most of these boxes and old suitcases contained. Cleaning it up was a chore that he was too old for now, so he had resigned himself, not with any great difficulty, to the fact that it would be up to his children to sort through this junk when he and Jan were dead and gone.

There was one box that he did know where to find. It was on a shelf with a collection of wartime memorabilia that was now merely accumulating dust but that, at one point, he had considered displaying. No, that wasn't quite true. Like most soldiers, he had taken souvenirs from the enemy — nothing macabre, nothing like the ears that some of those poor demented bastards in Vietnam had collected — but uniform hats, a Luger pistol, even a ceremonial sword that he had found in the scorched remains of a bunker on Omaha. He had picked them up without a second thought. After all, if he didn't take them, then someone else would, and they were no use now to their previous owners. In fact, when he entered that bunker he could smell the officer who was once probably the proud owner of the sword, as his charred body was still smoking in one corner. Not a good way to go, trapped in a cement bunker with liquid fire pouring through the gun slit. Not a good way to go at all. But once he returned home, his desire to be reminded of his wartime service diminished greatly, and any thoughts of display were banished, like the trophies themselves, to a dark, unused place.

Hall climbed further into the attic, keeping his head slightly bowed to prevent any painful knocks against the ceiling, and threaded his way through boxes and rolled-up rugs until he reached the shelf. The sword was still there, wrapped in brown paper and clear plastic, but he left it as it was. Behind it was a locked box. He had always kept it secured, in part because it contained the Luger and he didn't want his kids, when they were younger, to discover it and start playing with it like it was a toy. The key was kept in a nearby jar of rusty nails, just to further discourage idle hands. He poured the nails onto the floor until the key became visible, then used it to open the box. There was a trunk filled with old hardcover books nearby and he sat down upon it, resting the box upon his knee. It felt heavier than he remembered, but then it had been a long time since he had opened it, and he was older now. He wondered idly if bad memories and old sins accumulated weight, the burden of them steadily growing greater as the years went by. This box was foul memories given shape, sins endowed with bulk and form. It seemed almost to drag his head down to it, as though it were suspended from a chain around his neck.

He opened it and slowly began placing the contents on the floor beside his feet: the Luger first, then the dagger. It was silver and black, and emblazoned with a death's-head emblem. The blade, when withdrawn, showed spots of rust below the hilt and along the blade, but otherwise the steel was largely intact. He had greased it and wrapped it before storing it away, and his precautions had paid off. The plastic peeled away easily, and in the dim light the grease gave to the blade a glistening, organic quality, as though he had just removed a layer of skin and exposed the interior of a living thing.

He laid the knife beside the Luger and took out the third item. A lot of soldiers returned from the war with Iron Crosses taken from the enemy, mostly standard types but some, like the one Hall now held in his hand, adorned with an oak-leaf cluster. The officer from whom it was taken must have done something pretty special, Hall thought. He must have been trusted greatly to be sent to Narbonne, in the face of the advancing enemy, in order to seek out the monastery of Fontfroide and retrieve whatever was secured there.

Only two things remained in the box. The first item was a gold cross, four inches in height and decorated with rubies and sapphires. Hall had retained it, against his better judgment, because it was so beautiful, and perhaps also because it symbolized his own faith stored away in shame after what he had done. Now, as the time of his death inevitably approached, he realized that he had not misplaced that faith entirely. The cross had always been there, locked away in the attic with the discarded fragments of his own life and those of his wife and children. True, some were useless, and some were better forgotten, but there were items of value here too, things that should not have been set aside so readily.

He brushed his fingertips across the centerpiece of the ornament: a ruby as big as the ball of his thumb. *I kept it because it was precious*, he told himself. *I kept it because it was beautiful, and because, somewhere in my heart and my soul, I still believed. I believed in its strength, and its purity, and its goodness. I believed in what it represented.* It was always the second-to-last item in the box, always, for that way it rested upon the vellum fragment at the bottom, anchoring it in place, rendering its contents somehow less awful. *Larry Crane never understood. Larry Crane never believed in anything. But I did. I was raised in the faith, and I will die in the faith. What I did at Fontfroide was a terrible thing, and I will be punished for it when I die, yet the moment that I touched the fragment I knew it was a link to something far viler. Those Germans did not risk their lives for gold and jewels. To them, they were just trinkets and ornaments. No, they came for that piece of vellum, and if one good thing came out of that night it was the fact that they did not get it. It will not be enough to save me from damnation, though. No, Larry Crane and I will burn together for what we did that night.*

The SS men poured down the steps like channels of filthy, muddy water and pooled together in the little courtyard that lay before the church door, creating a kind of honor guard for the four civilians who stepped from the half-track to join them. From the shadows where he lay, Hall saw the old monk try to bar their way. He was pushed into the arms of the waiting soldiers and thrown against the wall. Hall heard him speak to the senior officer, the one with the dagger on his belt and the medal at his neck, who had accompanied the men in civilian clothes. The monk held out a bejeweled gold cross, offering it to the soldier. Hall couldn't understand German, but it was clear the the monk was trying to convince the officer that there was more where that came from, if he wanted it. The officer said something curt in reply, and then he and the civilians entered the church. Hall heard some shouting, and a short burst of gunfire. A voice was raised and Hall discerned some words that he did understand: an order to cease fire. He wasn't sure how long that would last. Once the Germans got whatever they had come for, they would leave nobody alive to talk about it.

Hall began working his way backward, moving through the darkness and into the woods, until he was facing the half-track. Its passenger door was open, and there was a soldier sitting at the wheel, watching what was taking place in the courtyard. Hall unsheathed his bayonet and crawled to the very edge of the road. When he was certain that he was out of sight of the other soldiers, he padded across the dirt and pulled himself into the half-track's cab, staying low all the time. The German sensed him at the last minute, because he turned and seemed about to shout a warning, but Hall's left hand shot up and caught him under the chin, forcing his mouth closed with a snap while the blade entered below the soldier's sternum and pierced his heart. The German trembled against the bayonet, and then grew still. Hall used the blade to anchor him to his seat before

*slipping out of the cab and into the back of the half-
track. He had a clear view of the soldiers on the right
of the steps, and of most of the courtyard, but there
were at least three hidden by the wall to the left. He
looked to his right and saw Crane peering at him from
a copse of bushes. For once, thought Hall, just once,
do the right thing, Larry. He signaled with his fingers,
indicating to Crane that he should go around the back
of the vehicle and through the trees so that he could
take out the Germans hidden from Hall.*

*There was a pause before Crane nodded and started
to move.*

Larry Crane was trying to light a cigarette, but the damn
cigarette lighter had been removed from the Volvo so that
smokers would not be encouraged to spoil its imitation
new car scent with tobacco smoke. He searched his pockets once again, but his own lighter wasn't there. He had
probably left it at home in his hurry to confront his old
buddy the Auto King with the prospect of easy wealth.
Now that he thought of it, the unlit cigarette in his mouth
tasted a little musty, which led him to suspect that he'd
left both cigarettes and lighter in the house and what was
now in his mouth was a relic of an old pack that had
somehow escaped his notice. He had taken the first jacket
he could lay a hand on, and it wasn't one that he usually
wore. It had leather patches on the elbows, for a start,
which made him look like some kind of New York Jew
professor, and the sleeves were too long. It caused him to
feel older and smaller than he was, and he didn't need
that. What he did need was a nicotine boost, and he'd
bet a dime that the King hadn't locked the door to his
house after he went inside. Larry figured there would be

matches in the kitchen. At worst, he could light up from the stove. Wouldn't be the first time, although he'd tried it once when he had a couple under his belt and had just about singed his eyebrows off. The right one still grew sort of rangy as a result.

Fuckin Auto King in his nice house with his fat wife, his slick sons, and that whiny daughter of his, looked like she could so with some feeding up and some holding down under a real man. The King didn't need any more money than he had already, and now he was making his old army buddy squirm on the hook while he thought about whether or not to take the bait. Well, he'd take the bait, whether it sat comfortably with him or not. Larry Crane wasn't about to let his fingers get broken just because the Auto King was having scruples after the fact. Hell, the old bastard wouldn't even have a business if it hadn't been for Larry. They'd have left that monastery poor as when they found it, and Hall's old age would have been spent scrounging nickels and clipping coupons, not as a respected pillar of the Georgia business community, living in a goddamned mansion in a nice neighborhood. You think they'd still respect you if they found out how you came by the money to buy into that first lot, huh? You bet your ass they wouldn't. They'd hang you out to dry, you and your bitch wife and all your miserable brood.

Larry was getting nicely stoked up now. It had been a while since he'd let the old blood run free, and it felt good. He wasn't going to take no shit from the Auto King, not this time, not ever again.

The cigarette moist with poisonous spit, Larry Crane strode into the King's house to light up.

*   *   *

The officer emerged from the church, flanked by the men in civilian clothing. One of them was carrying the silver box in his hands, while the others had packed the gold into a pair of sacks. Behind them came one of the monks whom Hall and Crane had helped with the shifting of the stone, his arms held behind his back by two SS soldiers. He was forced against the wall to join the abbot and the sentinel. Three monks: that meant one was already dead, and it looked like the rest were about to follow him. The oldest started to make one final plea, but the officer turned his back on him and directed three soldiers to take up position as a makeshift firing squad.

Hall got behind the thirty-seven-millimeter and saw that Crane was at last in place. He counted twelve Germans in his sights. That would leave just a handful more for Crane to deal with, assuming everything went without a hitch. Hall drew a deep breath, placed his hands on the big machine gun, and pulled the trigger.

The burst of noise was deafening in the silence of the night, and the power of the gun shook him as he fired. Centuries-old masonry fragmented as the bullets tore into the monastery, pockmarking the façade of the church and shattering part of the lintel above the door, although by the time they hit the wall they'd passed through half a dozen German soldiers, ripping them apart like they were made of paper. He glimpsed the muzzle flare from Crane's gun, but he couldn't hear its report. His ears were ringing and his eyes were full of dark marionettes in uniform, dancing to the beat of the music he was creating. He watched the side of the officer's head disappear and saw one of the civilians bucking against the wall, dead but still jerking with each shot that hit him. He raked the courtyard and steps until he was certain that everyone in his sights was dead, then stopped firing. He was drenched in sweat and rain, and his legs felt weak.

He climbed down as Crane advanced from the bushes, and the two soldiers looked upon their work. The courtyard and steps ran red, and fragments of tissue and bone seemed to sprout from the cracks like night blooms. One of the monks at the wall was dead, killed perhaps by a ricochet, guessed Hall, or a burst of gunfire from a dying German. The sacks of church ornaments lay upon the ground, some of their contents lying scattered beside them. Nearby rested the silver box. While Hall watched, the senior cleric reached for it. Hall could now see that he was bleeding from the face, injured by fragments of flying stone. The other monk, the sentinel, was already trying to replace the gold in the sacks. Neither said a word to the Americans.

"Hey," said Crane.

Hall looked at him.

"That's our gold," said Crane.

"What do you mean, 'our gold'?"

Crane gestured at the sacks with the muzzle of his gun. "We saved their lives, right? We deserve some reward." He pointed his gun at the monk.

"Leave it," said Crane.

The monk didn't even pause.

"Arrêt!" said Crane, then added, just in case: "Arrêt! Français, oui? Arrêt!"

By then the monk had refilled the sacks and was lifting one with each hand, preparing to take them away. Crane sent a burst of gunfire across his path. The monk stopped, waited for a second or two, then continued on his way.

The next shots took him in the back. He stumbled, the sacks falling to the ground once again, then found purchase against the wall of the church. He remained like that, propping himself up, until his knees buckled and he crumpled in a heap by the door.

"The hell are you doing?" said Hall. "You killed him! You killed a monk."

"It's ours," said Crane. "It's our future. I didn't survive this long to go back home poor, and I don't believe you want to go back to working on no farm."

The old monk was staring blankly at the body in the doorway.

"You know what you got to do," said Crane.

"We can walk away," said Hall.

"No. You don't think he'll tell someone what we done? He'll remember us. We'll be shot as looters, as murderers."

No, you'll be shot, thought Hall. I'm a hero. I killed SS men and saved treasure. I'll get — what? A commendation? A medal? Maybe not even that. There was nothing heroic about what I did. I turned a big gun on a bunch of Nazis. They didn't even get a shot off in response. He stared into Larry Crane's eyes and knew that no German had killed the monk with the chest wound. Even then, Larry had his plan in place.

"You kill him," said Crane.

"Or?"

The muzzle of Crane's gun hung in the air, midway between Hall and the monk. The message was clear.

"We're in this together," said Crane, "or we're not in this at all."

Later, Hall would argue to himself that he would have died had he not colluded with Crane, but deep inside he knew that this wasn't true. He could have fought back, even then. He could have tried reasoning and waited for his chance to make a move, but he didn't. In part, it was because he knew from past efforts that Larry Crane wasn't a man to be reasoned with, but there was more to his decision than that. Hall wanted more than a commendation or a medal. He wanted comfort, a start in life. Crane was right: he didn't want to return home as dirt poor as he was when he left. There was no turning back now, not since Crane had killed one, and probably two, unarmed men. It was time to choose, and in that instant Hall realized that maybe he and Larry Crane had been meant to find each other, and that they weren't so different after all. From the corner of his eye he registered the last of the monks make a move toward the church door, and he turned his BAR upon him. Hall stopped counting after five shots. When the muzzle flare had died, and the spots had disappeared from in front of his eyes, he saw the cross lying inches from the old man's outstretched fingers, droplets of blood scattered like jewels around it.

They carried the sacks and the box almost to Narbonne, and buried them in the woods behind the ruins of a farmhouse. Two hours later a convoy of green trucks entered the village, and they rejoined their comrades and fought their way across Europe, with varying degrees of valor, until the time came to be shipped home. Both elected to stay in Europe for a time, and returned to Narbonne in a jeep that was surplus to requirements, or became surplus as soon as *they paid a suitable bribe. Hall made contact with people in the antique business, who were acting in turn as middlemen for some of the less scrupulous collectors of art and relics, already picking their way through the bones of Europe's postwar culture. None of them seemed very much interested in the silver box or its contents. The vellum document was unpleasant at best, and even if worth anything would be difficult to dispose of to anyone but a very specialized collector. And so Crane and Hall had divided that item into two halves, with Crane taking the primitive silver box and Hall retaining the document fragment. Crane had tried to sell the box once, but had been offered next to nothing for it, so he decided to hold on to it as a souvenir. After all, he kind of liked the memories that went with it.*

Larry Crane found some long matches in a drawer, and lit his cigarette. He was watching the empty birdbath in the backyard when he heard the sound of footsteps descending the stairs.

"In here," he called.

Hall came into the kitchen.

"I don't remember inviting you inside," he said.

"Needed a light for my smoke," said Crane. "You got that paper?"

"No," said Hall.

"You listen here," said Crane, then stopped as Hall stepped toward him. Now the two old men were face-to-face, Crane with his back against the sink, Hall before him.

"No," said Hall. "You listen. I'm sick of you. You've been like a bad debt my whole life, a bad debt that I can never pay off. It ends here, today."

Crane blew a stream of smoke into Hall's face.

"You're forgettin somethin, boy. I know what you did back there outside that church. I saw you do it. I go down and I'll take you with me, you mark me."

He leaned in close to Hall. His breath smelled foul as he spoke. "It's over when I say it's over."

Crane's eyes suddenly bulged in their sockets. His mouth opened in a great oval of shock, the last of the cigarette smoke shooting forth through the gap. Hall's left hand extended in a familiar movement, closing Crane's mouth, while his right forced the blade of the SS dagger up under Crane's breastbone.

Hall knew what he was doing. After all, he'd done it before. Larry Crane's body sagged against him, and he smelled the old man's innards as he lost control of himself.

"Say it, Larry," whispered Hall. "Say it's over now."

There was blood, but less than Hall had expected. It didn't take him long to clean it up. He drove the Volvo around the back of his house, then wrapped Crane's body in plastic sheeting from the garage, leftover from the last round of renovations on the house. When he was certain that Crane was bundled up tight, he placed him, with a little trouble, in the trunk of the car, then went for a ride into the swamps.

13

Tucson airport was undergoing renovation, and a temporary tunnel led from the baggage claim to the car rental counters. The two men were given a Camry, which caused the smaller of the pair to complain bitterly as they made their way into the garage.

"Maybe if you lost some of that weight off your ass, then you wouldn't find it so damn pokey," said Louis. "I got a foot on you and I can fit into a Camry."

Angel stopped.

"You think I'm fat?"

"Gettin there."

"You never said nothing about it before."

"The hell you mean, I never said nothing? I been telling you ever since I met you that your problem is you got a sweet tooth. You need to go on that Atkins shit."

"I'd starve."

"I think you are missing the point. Folks in Africa starve. You go on a diet, you be like a squirrel. You just need to nap, let your body burn off what's already there."

Angel tried to give the flesh on his waist a discreet squeeze.

"How much can I squeeze and still be healthy?"

"They say an inch, like on the TV."

Angel looked at what he had clenched in his hand. "Is that across, or up?"

"Man, you even have to *ask* and you in trouble."

For the first time in many days, Angel allowed himself a smile, albeit a small one, and very short-lived. Since Martha's appearance at the house, Louis had barely eaten or slept. Angel would awake in the darkness to find their shared bed empty, the pillows and sheets long cold on his partner's side. On the first night, when they had brought Martha back to the city and transferred her to her new lodgings, he had padded softly to the bedroom door and watched in silence as Louis sat at a window, staring out over the city, scrutinizing every passing face in the hope that he might find Alice's among them. Guilt emanated from his pores, so that the room seemed almost to smell of something bitter and old. Angel knew all about Alice. He had accompanied his partner on his searches for her, initially along Eighth Avenue, when they first learned that she had arrived in the city, and later at the Point, when Giuliani's reforms really started to bite and Vice Enforcement began hitting the streets of Manhattan on a regular basis, NYPD "ghosts" mingling with the crowds below Forty-fourth, and monitoring teams waiting to pounce from unmarked vans. The Point was a little easier in the beginning: out of sight, out of mind, that was the Giuliani mantra. Once the tourists and conventioneers in Manhattan weren't tripping over too many teenage hookers if they accidentally—or purposely—strayed from Times Square, then everything was better than it was before. Over at Hunts Point, the Ninetieth Precinct only had the manpower to operate a ten-person special operation maybe once a month, usually targeted at the men who patronized and involving just one undercover female officer. True, there were occasional sweeps, but those were relatively infrequent in the beginning until "zero tolerance" began to hit home, the cops creating a virtual ticker-tape parade of summonses, which almost inevitably led to arrests, since the homeless and drug-addicted who formed the bulk of the city's street prostitutes could not afford to pay their fines, and that was a ninety-day stint in Rikers right there. The almost continual harassment of the prostitutes by the cops forced the women to stagger their beats in order to avoid being seen in the same spot two nights running. It also forced them to frequent increasingly isolated places with the johns, which left them open to rape, abduction, and murder.

It was into this sucking hole that Alice was descending, and their interventions counted for nothing. In fact, Angel could see that the woman sometimes seemed almost to take a strange pleasure in taunting Louis with her immersion in the life, even as it inexorably led to her degradation and, ultimately, to her death. In the end, all Louis could do was make sure that whatever pimp was feeding off her knew the consequences if anything happened to her, and paid her fines to ensure that she didn't do jail time. Finally, he could no longer bring himself to witness her decay, and it was perhaps unsurprising that she slipped through the net when Free Billy died, and came instead under the control of G-Mack.

And so Angel watched him that first night, not speaking for some time, until at last he said: "You tried."

"Not hard enough."

"She may still be out there, somewhere."

Louis gave a barely perceptible shake of his head.

"No. She's gone. I can feel it, like a part of me's been taken away."

"Listen to—"

"Go back to bed."

And he did, because there was nothing more that could be said. There was no point in trying to tell him that it wasn't his fault, that people made their own choices, that you couldn't save someone who didn't want to be saved, didn't matter how hard you tried. Louis would not, or could not, believe those things. This was his guilt, and Alice's path was not entirely of her own choosing. The actions of others had set her upon it, and his were among them.

But there was more that Angel could not have guessed at, small, private moments between Louis and Alice that perhaps only Martha might have understood, for they found an echo in the phone calls and the occasional cards that she herself received. Louis could remember Alice as a child, how she would play at his feet or fall asleep curled up beside him, bathed in the glow of their first TV. She cried when he left home, although she was barely old enough to comprehend what was happening, and in the years that followed, as his visits back grew fewer and fewer, she was always the first to greet him. Slowly, she recognized the changes that were coming over him, as the boy who had killed her father, believing him guilty of the murder of his own mother, matured into a man capable of taking the lives of others without exploring questions of innocence or guilt. Alice could not have put a name to these changes, or have precisely explained the nature of Louis's ongoing metamorphosis, but the coldness that was spreading through him touched something inside of her, and half-formed suspicions and fears about her father's death were given body and substance. Louis saw what was happening, and determined to put some distance between himself and his family, a decision made easier by the nature of his business and his reluctance to put those whom he loved at risk of reprisal. All of these tensions came to a head on the day that Louis left his childhood home for the last time, when Alice came to him as he sat in the shade of a cottonwood tree, the sun slowly setting behind him, his shadow spreading like dark blood across the short grass. By now, she was entering her teenage years, although she looked older than she was and her body was maturing more quickly than the bodies of her peers.

"Momma says you're leaving today," she said.

"That's right."

"The way she said it, it's like you ain't ever coming back."

"Things change. People change. This ain't no place for me now."

She pursed her lips, then raised her hand to her brow, shielding her eyes as she stared into the redness of the sun.

"I seen the way people look at you."

"What way is that?"

"Like they's scared of you. Even Momma, she looks like that, sometimes."

"She's got no call to be scared of me. You neither."

"Why are they scared?"

"I don't know."

"I heard stories."

Louis stood and tried to pass her by, but she blocked his way, her hands splayed against his midriff.

"No," she said. "You tell me. You tell me that the stories ain't true."

"I got no time for stories."

He gripped her wrists and turned her, slipping by her and heading toward the house.

"They say my daddy was a bad man. They say he got what he deserved."

She was shouting now. He heard her running after him, but he did not look back.

"They say you know what happened to him. Tell me! *Tell me!*"

And she struck him from behind with such force that he stumbled and fell to his knees. He tried to rise, and she slapped him on the cheek. He saw that she was weeping.

"Tell me," she said again, but this time her voice was soft, barely a whisper. "Tell me that it isn't true."

But he could not answer her, and he walked away and left them all. Only once, in the years of her descent, did Alice again bring up the subject of her father. It was fourteen months before her disappearance, when Louis still believed that she might yet be saved. She called him from the private clinic in Phoenicia, in the midst of the Catskills, and he drove up to see her that afternoon. He had placed her there after Jackie O called and told him that Alice was with him, that a john had hurt her badly and she had nearly overdosed in an effort to dull the pain. She was bruised and bleeding, her eyes slivers of white beneath heavy lids, her mouth agape. Louis brought her to Phoenicia the following morning, once she was straight enough to understand what was happening. The beating had shocked her, and she appeared more willing than ever before to consider intervention.

She spent six weeks isolated in Phoenicia, and then the call came.

Louis found her in the main garden, sitting on a stone bench. She had lost a little weight, and looked tired and drawn, but there was a new light in her eyes, a tiny, flickering thing that he had not seen in a long time. The slightest wind could blow it out, but it was there, for the moment. They walked together, the chill mountain air making her shiver slightly even though she was wearing a thick padded jacket. He offered her his coat, and she took it, wrapping it around her like a blanket.

"I drew you a picture," she said, after they had made a circuit of the grounds, talking of the clinic and the other patients she had encountered.

"I didn't know you liked to draw," said Louis.

"I never had the chance before. They told me it might help me. A lady comes in every day for an hour, more if she thinks you're making progress and she can spare the time. She says I have talent, but I don't believe so."

She reached into the pocket of her jacket and withdrew a sheet of white paper, folded to a quarter of its size. He opened it.

"It's our house," she said, as though fearful that her work was too poor to enable him to guess its subject matter.

"It's beautiful," he said, and it was. She had depicted the house as though seen through a mist, using chalks to dull the lines. A faint, warm light shone through the windows, and the door was slightly ajar. The foxgloves and dayflowers in the garden were smudges of pink and blue, the trilliums tiny stars of green and red. The forest beyond was a wash of tall brown trunks, like the masts of ships descending into a sea of green ferns.

"Thank you," he said.

"I called Momma," she said. "They said it was okay to call people, now that I'd been here for a time. I told her I was doing fine, but that ain't true. It's hard, you know?"

"I know."

She examined his face, her lips slightly pursed, and he was suddenly reminded of the girl who had confronted him beneath the cottonwood.

"I'm sorry," she said. "For blaming you."

"I'm sorry too."

She smiled, and for the first time since she was a young girl, she kissed him on the cheek.

"Good-bye." She began to shrug off his coat but he stopped her.

"You keep it," he said. "It's cold up here."

She drew the coat around her, then headed back into the clinic. He saw an orderly search the coat for contraband, then hand it back to her. She looked back at him, waved, and then was gone.

He did not know what happened subsequently. There were rumors of an argument with a fellow patient, and a painful, troubled session with one of the resident therapists. Whatever occurred, the next call he received from Phoenicia was to tell him that Alice was gone. He searched for her on the streets, but when she emerged after three weeks from whatever dark corner she had been inhabiting, that tiny light had been extinguished forever, and all he had left was a picture of a house that appeared to be fading even as he looked at it, and the memory of a last kiss from one who was, in her way, bonded more closely to him than any other in this world.

Now, for the first time since Martha's appearance and the discovery of the remains in Williamsburg, Louis seemed energized. Angel knew what it meant. Someone was about to suffer for what had been done to Alice, and Angel didn't care once it brought his partner some release.

They arrived at their rental.

"I hate these cars," said Angel.

"Yeah, so you said already."

"I'm just offended that she'd even think we looked like the kind of guys who'd drive a Camry."

They placed their bags on the ground and watched as a man in rental livery approached them. He had a small titanium case in his hand.

"You forgot one of your bags," he said.

"Thanks," said Louis.

"No problem. Car okay?"

"My friend here doesn't like it."

The guy knelt down, removed a penknife from his pocket, and carefully inserted the blade into the right front tire. He twisted the knife, removed it, and watched with satisfaction as the tire started to deflate.

"So go get something else," he said, then walked out of the garage and into a waiting white SUV, which immediately drove away.

"I guess he doesn't really work for a rental company," said Angel.

"You should be a detective."

"Doesn't pay enough. I'll go get us a bigger car."

Angel returned minutes later with the key to a red Mercury. Louis took the baggage and walked to the car, then popped the trunk. He glanced around before opening the titanium case. Two Glock nines were revealed, alongside eight spare clips bound with rubber bands into four sets of two. They wouldn't need any more than that, unless they decided to declare war on Mexico. He slipped the guns into the outer pockets of his coat and added the clips, then closed the trunk. He got in the car and found "Shiver" playing on an indie station. Louis liked Howe Gelb. It was good to support the local boys. He passed one of the Glocks and two of the spare clips to Angel. Both men checked the guns, then, once they were satisfied, put them away.

"You know where we're going?" said Angel.

"Yeah, I think so."

"Great. I hate reading maps."

He reached for the radio dial.

"Don't touch that dial, man, I'm warning you."

"Boring."

"Leave it."

Angel sighed. They emerged from the gloom of the garage into the greater darkness outside. The sky was dusted with stars, and a little cool desert air flowed through the vents, refreshing the men.

"It's beautiful," said Angel.

"I guess."

The smaller man took in the vista for a few seconds more, then said: "You think we could stop for doughnuts?"

It was late, and I was back at Cortlandt Alley, the taste of the Thai food still lingering in my mouth. I could hear laughter over on Lafayette as people smoked and flirted outside one of the local bars. The window of Ancient & Classic Inc. was illuminated, the men inside carefully positioning a new delivery of furniture and ornaments. A sign warned of a hollow sidewalk, and I thought that I could almost hear my footsteps echoing through the layers beneath my feet.

I made my way to Neddo's doorway. This time, he didn't bother with the chain once I'd told him who I was. He led me into the same back office and offered me some tea.

"I get it from the people run the store at the corner. It's good."

I watched as he poured it into a pair of china cups so small they looked like they belonged in a doll's house. As I held one in my hand I could see that it was very old, the interior a mass of tiny brown hairline cracks. The tea was fragrant and strong.

"I've been reading all about the killing in the newspapers," said Neddo. "Kept your name out of it, I see."

"Maybe they're concerned for my safety."

"More concerned than you are, clearly. Someone might suspect that you had a death wish, Mr. Parker."

"I'm happy to say that it's unfulfilled."

"So far. I trust that you weren't followed here. I have no desire to link my life expectancy with yours."

I had been careful, and told him so.

"Tell me about Santa Muerte, Mr. Neddo."

Neddo looked puzzled for a moment, then his face cleared.

"The Mexican who died. This is about him, isn't it?

"Tell me first, then I'll see what I can give you in return."

Neddo nodded his assent.

"She's a Mexican icon," he said. "Saint Death: the angel of the outcasts, of the lawless. Even criminals and evil men need their saints. She is adored on the first day of every month, sometimes in public, more often in secret. Old women pray to her to save their sons and nephews from crime, while the same sons and nephews pray to her for good pickings, or for help in killing their enemies. Death is the last great power, Mr. Parker. Depending upon how its scythe falls, it can offer protection or destruction. It can be an accomplice or an assassin. Through Santa Muerte, Death is given form. She is a creation of men, not of God."

Neddo rose and disappeared into the confusion of his store. He returned with a skull on a crude wooden block, wrapped in blue gauze decorated with images of the sun. It had been painted black, apart from its teeth, which were gold. Cheap earrings had been screwed into the bone, and a crude crown of painted wire sat upon its head.

"This," said Neddo, "is Santa Muerte. She is typically presented as a skeleton or a decorated skull, often surrounded by offerings or candles. She enjoys sex, but since she has no flesh she approves of the desires of others, and lives vicariously through them. She wears gaudy clothes, and rings upon her fingers. She likes neat whiskey, cigarettes, and chocolate. Instead of singing hymns to her during services, they play mariachi music. She is the 'Secret Saint'. The Virgin of Guadalupe may be the country's patron saint, but Mexico is a place where people are poor and struggling, and turn to crime either through necessity or inclination. They remain profoundly religious, yet they have to break the laws of church and state to survive, albeit a state that they regard as profoundly corrupt. Santa Muerte allows them to reconcile their needs with their beliefs. There are shrines to her in Tepito, in Tijuana, in Sonora, in Juárez, wherever poor people gather."

"It sounds like a cult."

"It *is* a cult. The Catholic Church has condemned her adoration as devil worship, and while I have a great many difficulties with that institution, it's not hard to see that in this case there is some justification for its position. Most of those who pray to her merely seek protection from harm in their own lives. There are others who require that she approve the visitation of harm upon others. The cult has grown powerful among the foulest of men: drug traffickers, people smugglers, purveyors of child prostitutes. There was a spate of killings in Sinaloa earlier this year in which more than fifty people died. Most of the bodies bore her image in tattoos, or on amulets and rings."

He reached across and brushed a little dust from beneath the empty sockets of the icon.

"And they are far from the worst," he concluded. "More tea?"

He refilled my cup.

"The man who died in the apartment had a statue like this one hidden in the wall of one room, and he called on Santa Muerte throughout the attack," I said. "I think he, and maybe others, used the room to hurt and to kill. I believe the skull came from the woman I was looking for."

Neddo glanced at the skull upon his own desk.

"I'm sorry," he said. "Had I known that, I would have been more sensitive about showing you this icon. I can remove it, if you prefer."

"You can leave it. At least I know now what it was meant to represent."

"The man you killed," said Neddo, "have they identified him?"

"His name was Homero Garcia. He had a criminal record from his youth in Mexico."

I didn't tell Neddo that the *Federales* were very interested in Garcia. The news of his death had drawn a great many telephone calls to the Nine-Six from the Mexicans, including a formal request from the Mexican ambassador that the NYPD cooperate in every way possible with Mexican law enforcement by providing them with copies of any and all material relating to the investigation into Garcia's death. Former juvenile delinquents did not usually excite such interest in diplomatic and legal circles.

"Where did he come from?"

I was reluctant to say more. I still knew little about Neddo, and his fascination with the display of human remains made me uneasy. He recognized my distrust.

"Mr. Parker, you may approve or disapprove of my interests, and of how I make my living, but mark me: I know more about these matters than almost anyone else in this city. I have a scholar's fascination. I can help you, but only if you tell me what you've learned."

It seemed that I didn't have too much choice.

"The Mexicans are more interested in him than they should be, given his record," I said. "They've provided some information about him to the police, but it's clear that they're holding back on more. Garcia was born in Tapito, but his family left there when he was an infant. He began training as a silversmith. Apparently, it was a tradition in his family. It seems he was melting down stolen items in return for a cut of the resale value, which led to his arrest. He was jailed for three years, then was released and returned to his trade. Officially, he was never in trouble again after that."

Neddo leaned forward in his chair.

"Where did he practice his craft, Mr. Parker?" he said, and there was a new urgency to his voice. "Where was he based?"

"In Juárez," I said. "He was based in Juárez."

Neddo released a long sigh of understanding.

"Women," he said. "The girl for whom you were searching was not the first. I think Homero Garcia was a professional killer of women."

Harry's Best Rest was less than busy when the Mercury, now considerably dustier than before, pulled up in the parking lot. There were still rigs scattered through the darkness, but there was nobody eating in the diner, and any lonely trucker looking for comfort from the cantina women could have enjoyed a range of choice had he arrived earlier in the evening, although the attentions of the police in the aftermath of the Spyhole killings had somewhat depleted even their numbers. The cantina was locked up for the night and only two of the women remained, slouched sleepily at the bar in the hope of picking up a ride from the man who remained with them, smoking a joint and sipping a last Tecate in the murk, the carnival lights that illuminated the bar barely touching his features.

Harry was out back, stacking beer crates, when Louis emerged from the darkness.

"You own this place?" he asked.

"Yeah," said Harry. "You looking for something?"

"Someone," Louis corrected. "Who takes care of the women around here?"

"The women around here take care of themselves," said Harry. He smiled at his own little joke, then turned to go back inside. His partners would deal with this man, once he had informed them of his presence.

Harry found his way blocked by a small man with three days' worth of stubble and a haircut that was a month past good. The guy looked like he was putting on a little weight, too. Harry didn't mention that. Harry didn't say anything, because the man at the door had a gun in his hand. It wasn't quite pointed at Harry, but the situation was a developing one, and there was no telling right now how it might end.

"A name," said Louis. "I want the name of the man who ran Sereta."

"I don't know any Sereta."

"Past tense," said Louis. "She's dead. She died at the Spyhole."

"I'm sorry to hear that," said Harry.

"You can tell her yourself, you don't give me a name."

"I don't want any trouble."

"Those your cabanas over there?" asked Louis, indicating three little huts that stood right at the edge of the parking lot.

"Yeah, sometimes a man gets tired of sleeping in his truck. He wants to, he can have clean sheets for a night."

"Or an hour."

"Whatever."

"If you don't start cooperating, I'm going to take you into one of those cabanas and I'm going to hurt you until you tell me what I need to know. If you give me his name, and you're lying to me, I'll come back, take you into one of those cabanas, and kill you. You have a third option."

"Octavio," said Harry quickly. "His name's Octavio, but he's gone. He left when the whore got killed."

"Tell me what happened."

"She'd been working for a couple of days when men came. One was a fat guy, real fat, the other was a quiet guy in blue. They knew to ask for Octavio. They spoke to him some, then left. He told me to forget them. That night, all those folks got killed up at the motel."

"Where did Octavio go?"

"I don't know. Honest, he didn't say. He was running scared."

"Who's looking after his women while he's gone?"

"His nephew."

"Describe him to me."

"Tall, for a Mexican. Thin mustache. He's wearing a green shirt, blue jeans, a white hat. He's in there now."

"What's his name?"

"Ernesto."

"Does he carry a gun?"

"Jesus, they all carry guns."

"Call him."

"What?"

"I said, 'Call him.' Tell him there's a girl out here wants to see him about work."

"Then he'll know I sold him out."

"I'll make sure he sees our guns. I'm sure he'll understand your reasons. Now call him."

Harry walked to the door.

"Ernesto," he shouted. "Girl out here says she'd like to talk to you about some work."

"Send her in," said a man's voice.

"She won't come in. Says she's frightened."

The man swore. They heard his footsteps approach.

The door was opened and a young Mexican stepped into the light. He looked sleepy, and the faint smell of pot hung about him.

"Stuff will ruin your health," said Louis as he slipped behind the Mexican's back and removed a silver Colt from the young man's belt, his own gun touching the nape of Ernesto's neck. "Although not as fast as a bullet will. Let's take a walk."

Louis turned to Harry.

"He won't be coming back. You tell anyone what happened here, and we'll be talking again. You're a busy man. You have a lot of things to forget now."

With that, they took Ernesto away. They drove for five miles until they found a dirt road, then headed into the darkness until they could no longer see the traffic on the highway. After a time, Ernesto told them what they wanted to know.

They drove on, coming at last to a shabby trailer that sat behind an unfinished house on unfenced land. The man named Octavio heard them coming and tried to run, but Louis shot him in the leg. Octavio tumbled down a sandy slope and came to rest in a dried-out water hole. He was told to get rid of the gun in his hand, or die where he lay.

Octavio threw away the gun and watched as the twin shadows descended on him.

"The very worst," said Neddo, "are in Juárez."

The tea had grown cold. The image of Santa Muerte still stood between us, listening without hearing, watching blindly.

Juárez: now I understood.

One and a half million people lived in Juárez, most of

them in indescribable poverty made all the more difficult for being endured in the shadow of El Paso's wealth. Here were smugglers of drugs and people. Here were prostitutes barely into puberty, and others who would never live long enough to see puberty. Here were the *maquiladoras,* the huge electrical assembly plants that provided microwaves and hair dryers to the First World, the prices kept down by paying the workers $10 a day and denying them legal protection or union representation. Outside the perimeter fences stretched row upon row of crate houses, the *colonias populares* without sanitation, running water, electricity, or paved roads, home to the men and women who labored in the *maquiladoras*, the more fortunate of whom were picked up each morning by the red-and-green buses once used to ferry American children to and from school, while the rest were forced to endure the perilous early morning walk through Sitio Colosio Valle or some similarly malodorous area. Beyond their homes lay the municipal dumps, where the scavengers made more than the factory workers. Here were the brothels of Mariscal, and the shooting galleries of Ugarte Street, where young men and women injected themselves with Mexican tar, a cheap heroin derivative from Sinaloa, leaving a trail of bloodied needles in their wake. Here were eight hundred gangs, each roaming the streets of the city with relative impunity, their members beyond a law that was powerless to act against them, or more properly too corrupt to care, for the *Federales* and the FBI no longer informed the local police in Juárez of operations on their turf, in the certain knowledge that to do so would be to forewarn their targets.

But that was not the worst of Juárez: in the last decade, over three hundred young women had been raped and murdered in the city, some *putas*, some *faciles*, but most simply hardworking, poor, and vulnerable girls. Usually it was the scavengers that found them, lying mutilated among the garbage, but the authorities in Chihuahua continued to turn a blind eye to the killings, even as the bodies continued to turn up with numbing regularity. Recently, the *Federales* had been drafted in to investigate, using accusations of organ-trafficking, a federal crime, as their excuse to intervene, but the organ-trafficking angle was largely a smokescreen. By far the most prevalent theories, bolstered by fear and paranoia, were the predations of wealthy men, and the actions of religious cults, among them Santa Muerte.

Only one man had ever been convicted for any of the killings: the Egyptian Abdel Latif Sharif, allegedly linked to the slayings of up to twenty women. Even in jail, investigators claimed, Sharif continued his killings, paying members of Los Rebeldes, one of the city's gangs, to murder women on his behalf. Each gang member who participated was reputedly paid 1,000 pesos. When the members of Los Rebeldes were jailed, Sharif was said to have recruited instead a quartet of bus drivers, who killed a further twenty women. Their reward: $1,200 per month, to be divided between them and a fifth man, as long as they killed at least four girls each month. Most of the charges against Sharif were dropped in 1999. Sharif was just one man, and even with his alleged associates could not have accounted for all of the victims. There were others operating, and they continued to kill even while Sharif was in jail.

"There is a place called Anapra," said Neddo. "It is a slum, a shanty. Twenty-five thousand people live there in the shadow of Mount Christo Rey. Do you know

what lies at the top of the mountain? A statue of Jesus."
He laughed hollowly. "Is it any wonder that people turn
away from God and look instead to a skeletal deity? It
was from Anapra that Sharif was said to have stolen
many of his victims, and now others have taken it upon
themselves to prey upon Anapra's women, or on those
of Mariscal. More and more, the bodies are being found
with images of Santa Muerte upon them. Some have
been mutilated after death, deprived of limbs, heads. If
one is to believe the rumors, those responsible have
learned from the mistakes of their predecessors. They
are careful. They have protection. It's said that they are
wealthy, and that they enjoy their sport. It may be true.
It may not."

"There were tapes in Garcia's apartment," I said.
"They showed women, dead and dying."

Neddo had the decency to look troubled.

"Yet he was here, in New York," said Neddo.
"Perhaps he had outlived his usefulness and fled. Maybe
he planned to use the tapes to blackmail the wrong
people, or to secure his safety. It may even be that such
a man would take pleasure from revisiting his crimes
by viewing them over and over. Whatever the reason
for his coming north, he does appear to provide a
human link between Santa Muerte and the killings in
Juárez. It's not surprising that the Mexican authorities
are interested in him, just as I am."

"Aside from the connection to Santa Muerte, why
would this be of concern to you?" I asked.

"Juárez has a small ossuary," said Neddo, "a chapel
decorated with the remains of the dead. It is not particularly notable, and no great skill was applied to its
initial creation. For a long time it was allowed to fall

347

into decay, but in recent years someone has devoted a great deal of time and effort to its restoration. I have visited it. Objects have been expertly repaired. There have even been new additions to its furnishings: sconces, candlesticks, a monstrance, all of far superior quality to the originals. The man responsible apparently claimed only to have used remains left to the ossuary for such a purpose, but I have my doubts. It was not possible to make a close examination of the work that had been done — the priest responsible for its upkeep was both secretive and fearful — but I believe that some of the bones were artificially aged, much like the skull that you brought to me that first evening. I asked to meet the man responsible, but he had already left Juárez. I heard later that the *Federales* were seeking him. It was said that they were under instructions to capture him alive, and not to kill him. That was a year ago.

"Across from the ossuary, the same individual had created a shrine to Santa Muerte: a very beautiful, very ornate shrine. If Homero Garcia came from Juárez, and was a devotee of Santa Muerte, then it's possible that he and the restorer of the ossuary were one and the same. After all, a man capable of intricate work with silver might well be capable of similar work with other materials, including bone."

He sat back in his chair. Once again, his fascination with the details was clear, just as it had been when he spoke about the preacher Faulkner and his book of skin and bones.

Perhaps Garcia had come to New York of his own volition, and without the assistance of others, but I doubted it. Someone had discovered his talents, found him the warehouse in Williamsburg, and given him a space in which to work. He had been brought north for his skill, out of reach of the *Federales,* and perhaps also away from those for whom he sourced, and disposed of, women. I thought again of the winged figure constructed from pieces of birds and animals and men. I remembered the empty crates, the discarded shards of bone that lay upon the worktable like the remnants of a craftsman's labors. Whatever Garcia had been commissioned to create, his work was nearing completion when I killed him.

I looked at Neddo, but he was lost in the contemplation of Santa Muerte.

And even after all that he had told me, I wondered what it was that he was keeping from me.

My cell phone rang as I was nearing the hotel. It was Louis. He gave me the number of a pay phone and told me to call him back in turn from a landline. I called from the street, using my AT&T calling card to reach the number. I could hear traffic in the background, and people singing on the street.

"What have you got?" I said.

"The pimp running Sereta was called Octavio. He went to ground after she was killed, but we found his nephew, and through him we found Octavio. We hurt him. A lot. He told us he was going back to Mexico, to Juárez, where he came from. Hey, you still there?"

I had almost dropped the phone. This was the second mention of Juárez in less than an hour. I began joining the dots. Garcia may have known of Octavio from Juárez. Sereta fled New York and entered Octavio's ambit. When Alice was found, she probably told them what she knew of her friend's whereabouts. Garcia put out some feelers, and Octavio got back to him. Then two men were dispatched to find Sereta and retrieve what was in her possession.

"Yeah," I said. "I'll explain when you get back. Where's Octavio now?"

"He's dead."

I took a deep breath but said nothing.

"Octavio had a contact in New York," Louis continued. "He was to call him if anyone came asking about Sereta. It's a lawyer. His name is Sekula."

In Scarborough, Rachel sat on the edge of our bed, cradling Sam, who had at last fallen asleep. There was a patrol car outside the house, and the Scarborough cops had boarded up the shattered window. Rachel's mother was beside her daughter, her hands clasped between her thighs.

"Call him, Rachel," said Joan.

Rachel shook her head, but she was not responding to her mother.

"It can't go on," said Joan. "It just can't go on like this."

But Rachel just held her daughter close and said nothing.

14

Walter Cole got back to me the next morning. I was still asleep when he called. I had faxed him the list of the numbers called from Eddie Tager's cell phone and asked him to see what he could do with them. If he had no luck, there were others I could turn to, this time outside the law. I just thought Walter could get the information more quickly than I could.

"You know that tampering with mail is a federal crime?" he said.

"I didn't tamper. I mistakenly assumed that it was addressed to me."

"Well, that's good enough for me. Anyone can make a mistake. I have to tell you, though: I'm running out of favors I can call in. I think this is it."

"You've done enough, and more. Don't sweat it."

"You want me to fax this to you?"

"Later. For now, just read me the names. Take them from around one A.M. on the date I marked. That's about the time Alice was picked up on the streets." Someone must have contacted Tager to tell him to bail Alice, and I was hoping that he had called that person back once he was done.

He read me the list of names, but I didn't recognize any of them. Most of them were men. Two were women.

"Give me the women's names again."

"Gale Friedman and Hope Zahn."

"The second one, was that a business or personal number?"

"It's a cell. The bills go to a box number on the Upper West Side, registered with a private company named Robson Realty. Robson was part of the Ambassade group, the same one that was looking after the apartment development in Williamsburg. Seems like Tager called her twice: once at four-oh-four A.M., and once at four-thirty-five A.M. There were no more calls from his cell until the next afternoon, and her number doesn't show up again."

Hope Zahn. I pictured Sekula in his pristine ante-room, asking his coldly beautiful secretary not to disturb him—*No calls, please, Hope*—while he sized me up. Sekula's days were numbered.

"Is that any help?" asked Walter.

"You just confirmed something for me. Can you fax that info to my room?"

I had a personal fax machine on the desk in the corner. I gave him the number again.

"I also checked the cell phone number that G-Mack gave us," said Walter. "It's a ghost. If it ever existed, there's no record of it now."

"I guessed that would be the case. It doesn't matter."

"So, what now?"

"I have to go home. After that, it all depends."

"On what?"

"The kindness of strangers, I guess. Or maybe kindness isn't the right word . . ."

I headed out for coffee and called Sekula's office along the way. A woman answered the phone, but I could tell that it wasn't Sekula's usual secretary. This girl was so chirpy she belonged in an aviary.

"Hello, could I speak to Hope Zahn, please?"

"Uh, I'm afraid she's out of the office for a few days. Could I take a message?"

"How about Mr. Sekula?"

"He's unavailable too."

"When do you expect them back?"

"I'm sorry," said the secretary, "but may I ask who's calling?"

I decided to rattle their cage a little.

"Tell Hope that Eddie Tager called. It's in connection with Alice Temple."

At the very least, if Zahn or Sekula checked back with the office it would give them something to think about.

"Does she have your number?"

"She'd like to think so," I said, then thanked her for her time and hung up.

Sandy Crane was a little concerned about her husband, which meant that the week was turning into a real collection of firsts for her: the first promise of money in a while; the first mutual joy she and her husband had experienced since Larry had finally succumbed to senescence; and now concern for her husband's well-being, albeit tinged by a considerable degree of self-interest. He hadn't yet returned from his visit to his old war buddy, but he occasionally spent nights away from home so it wasn't entirely out of the ordinary. Usually, though, his absences coincided with horse races in Florida, and rarely now did he embark upon a journey with the sense of purpose he had shown the day before. Sandy knew that her husband liked to gamble. It worried her some, but so long as he kept it within reason she wasn't going to raise a fuss. If she started complaining about his spending, then he might in turn decide to curb her excesses, and Sandy had few enough luxuries in her life as things stood.

Sandy wouldn't have put it past the old fart to try to cut her out of the deal entirely, but her fears were allayed slightly by the knowledge that Larry needed her. He was aged and weak, and he had no friends. Even if that stuck-up sonofabitch Hall agreed to play ball, Larry would need her by his side to make sure that he wasn't taken for a ride. She was still a little surprised that Larry hadn't called the night before to let her know how things were going, but he was like that. Perhaps he'd found a bar where he could bitch and moan for the night or, if Hall had agreed to play ball, where he could get himself a mild drunk on to celebrate. Even now, he was probably sleeping it off in a motel room between trips to the john to empty his bladder. Larry would be back, one way or another.

Sandy sipped a double vodka—another first, this time of day—and thought some more about what she might do with the money: new clothes, for a start, and a car that didn't smell of old man stink. She also liked the idea of a younger guy, one with a firm body and a motor that purred instead of sputtering like the failing engines of the men who currently serviced her occasional needs. She wouldn't object to paying by the hour for him, either. That way, there was nothing he could refuse to do for her.

The doorbell rang, and she spilled a little of her vodka in her rush to rise from her chair. Larry had a key, so it couldn't be Larry. But suppose something had happened to him? Maybe that bastard Hall had allowed his conscience to get the better of him and had confessed all to the cops. If that was the case, then Sandy Crane would plead dumber than the special kids in the little bus that passed by her house every morning, the strange, spooky people inside waving at her like they thought she gave a rat's ass about them when they really just creeped her out worse than snakes and spiders.

A man and a woman stood at the door. They were well dressed: the man in a gray suit, the woman in a blue jacket and skirt. Even Sandy had to admit that the woman was a looker: long dark hair, pale features, tight body. The man carried a briefcase in his hand, and the woman a brown leather satchel over her right shoulder.

"Mrs. Crane?" said the man. "My name is Sekula. I'm an attorney from New York. This is my assistant, Miss Zahn. Your husband contacted our firm yesterday. He said he had an item in which we might be interested."

Sandy didn't know whether to curse her husband's name or applaud his foresight. It depended on how things worked out for them, she supposed. The old fool was so anxious to ensure a sale that he'd contacted the people who'd sent the letter before he even had his hands on both the box and the paper it had once contained. She could almost picture him, a sly grin on his face as he convinced himself that he was playing these big city folk like they were violins, except he wasn't that smart. He'd given too much away, or raised their expectations so high that they were now at her door. Sandy wondered if he'd told them about Mark Hall, but immediately decided that he hadn't.

If they knew about Hall, then they would be standing on his doorstep, not her own.

"My husband isn't here right now," she said. "I'm expecting him back any moment."

The smile on Sekula's face didn't falter.

"Perhaps you wouldn't mind if we waited for him. We really are anxious to secure the item as soon as possible, and with the minimum of fuss and attention."

Sandy shifted uneasily on her feet.

"I don't know," she said. "I'm sure you people are okay and all, but I don't really like letting strangers into my house."

The smile seemingly etched on Sekula's face was starting to creep her out like the smiles of the kids on the bus. There was something blank about it. Even shit-for-brains Hall managed to inject a little humanity into his hammy grins when he was trying to sell some deadbeat an automobile.

"I understand," said Sekula. "I wonder if this might convince you of our good intentions?"

He leaned his briefcase against the wall, snapped the locks, and opened it so that Sandy could see the contents: a small stack of dead presidents lined up like little Mount Rushmores in green.

"Just a token of our goodwill," said Sekula.

Sandy felt herself grow moist.

"I think I can make an exception," she said. "Just this once."

The funny thing about it was that Sekula didn't want to harm the woman. That was how they had remained hidden for so long, when others had been hunted down. They did not hurt people unless it was absolutely necessary, or they had not until Sekula's investigations had added a degree of urgency to their quest. The subsequent recruitment by Brightwell of the odious Garcia had marked the beginning of the next phase, and an escalation in violence.

Sekula was a longtime Believer. He was recruited to the cause shortly after his graduation from law school. The recruitment had been subtle, and gradual, drawing on his already prodigious legal skills to track suspicious sales and to ascertain ownership and origins wherever necessary, gradually progressing to more detailed explorations of the shadowy, secret lives that so many people concealed from those around them. He viewed this as a fascinating endeavor, even as he came to understand that he was being used to target the individuals for their exploitation rather than to assist in any prosecution, public or private. The information gathered by Sekula was utilized against them, and his employers amassed influence, knowledge and wealth as a consequence, but Sekula quickly discovered that he was untroubled by this realization. He was a lawyer, after all, and had he entered the arena of criminal law he would surely have found himself defending what most ordinary people would regard as the indefensible. By comparison, the work in which he was engaged was initially morally compromised in only the faintest of ways. He had grown wealthy as a result, wealthier than most of his peers who worked twice as hard as he, and he had gained other rewards too, Hope Zahn among them. He had been directed to employ her, and he had done so willingly. Since then, she had proved invaluable to him, personally, professionally, and, it had to be admitted, sexually. If Sekula had a weakness, it was women, but Miss Zahn fed his every sexual appetite, and some others that he didn't even know were there until she discovered them for him.

And when, after a number of years, Sekula was informed of the true nature of their quest, he could barely work up the energy to be even slightly surprised. He wondered, sometimes, if this was an indication of the extent to which he had been corrupted, or if it was always in his nature, and his employers had recognized it long before he himself had. In fact, it had been Sekula's idea to target the veterans, inspired by his discovery of the details of a sale conducted through an intermediary in Switzerland shortly after the end of the Second World War. The sale had passed unnoticed amid the flurry of deals in the aftermath of the war, when looted items changed hands at a frightening rate, their previous owners, in many cases, reduced to a coating of ash on the trees of eastern Europe. It was only when Sekula gained copies of the records of the auction house from a disgruntled employee aware of the lawyer's willingness to pay moderately well for such information that the entry was revealed to him. Sekula was grateful to the Swiss for their scrupulous attention to detail, which meant that even deals of dubious origin were all recorded and accounted for. In many ways, he reflected, the Swiss had more in common with the Nazis in their desire to document their wrongdoings than they might like to admit.

The entry was straightforward, detailing the sale of a fourteenth-century jeweled monstrance to a private collector based in Helsinki. Included was a careful description of the item, sufficient to indicate to Sekula that it was part of the trove stolen from Fontfroide; the final sale price agreed; the house's commission; and the balance to be forwarded to the seller. The nominal seller was a private dealer named Jacques Gaud, based in Paris. Sekula carefully followed the paper trail back to Gaud, then pounced. Gaud's family had since built up their grandfather's business and now enjoyed a considerable reputation in the trade. Sekula, by examining the records of the Swiss auction house, had found at least a dozen further transactions instigated by Gaud that could charitably be described as suspicious. He cross-checked the items in question against his own list of treasures looted or "disappeared" during the war, and came up with enough evidence to brand Gaud as a profiteer from the misery of others, and to effectively destroy the reputation of his descendants' business as well as placing them at risk of ruinous criminal and civil actions. Following discreet approaches, and assurances from Sekula that the information he had obtained would go no further, the house of Gaud et Frères discreetly released to him copies of all the paperwork relating to the sale of the Fontfroide treasures.

It was here that the trail ran out, for the payment made through Gaud to the actual seller (following a deduction by Gaud for his assistance that was excessive to the point of extortion) was in the form of cash. The only clue that the current owners of the business were able to offer as to the identity of the men in question was that Gaud had indicated they were American soldiers. This was hardly surprising to Sekula, as the Allies were just as capable of looting as the Nazis, but he was aware of the twin massacres at Narbonne and Fontfroide. It was possible that survivors of the former might in turn have been involved in the latter, although the Americans were not present in the area in significant numbers by that phase of the war. Nevertheless, Sekula had identified a possible connection between the killing of a platoon of American GIs by SS raiders and the raiders' deaths, in turn, at Fontfroide. Through contacts in the Veterans Administration and the VFW, he discovered the identities of the surviving soldiers based in the region at the time, as well as the addresses of those others who had lost relatives in the encounter. He then sent out over a thousand letters seeking general information on wartime souvenirs that might be of interest to collectors, and a handful containing more specific information relating to the missing Fontfroide trove. If he was wrong, then there was always the chance that the letters might still elicit some useful information. If he was right, they would serve to cover his tracks. The target-specific letters detailed the rewards to be gained for the sale of unusual items relating to the Second World War, including material not itself directly related to the conflict, with a particular emphasis on manuscripts. It contained repeated assurances that all responses would be handled in the strictest confidence. The real bait was the entry from the auction catalog issued by the House of Stern, with its photograph of a battered silver box. Sekula could only hope that whoever had taken it had held on to both the box and its contents.

Then, late the previous morning, a man had called and described to Sekula what could only be a fragment of the map and the box in which it was contained. The caller was old, and tried to retain his anonymity, but he had given himself away from the moment that he used his home phone to dial New York. Now here they were, one day later, seated with an ugly drunk in polyester pants spotted with spilled vodka, watching as she got progressively more intoxicated.

"He'll be home soon," she repeatedly reassured the visitors, slurring her words. "I can't imagine where he's gotten to."

Sandy asked them to show her the money again, and Sekula obliged. She ran a podgy finger over the faces on the notes, and giggled to herself.

"Wait until he sees all this," she said. "The old fart will shit himself."

"Perhaps, while we're waiting, we might take a look at the item," Sekula suggested.

Sandy tapped her nose with the side of her finger.

"All in good time," she said. "Larry will get it for you, even if he has to beat it out of the old fuck."

Sekula felt Miss Zahn tense beside him. For the first time, his unthreatening façade began to fragment.

"Do you mean that the item is not actually your husband's to sell?" he asked, carefully.

Sandy Crane tried to retrieve her mistake, but it was too late.

"No, it's his to sell, but you see there's this other fella and, well, he has a say in it too. But he'll agree. Larry will make him agree."

"Who is he, Mrs. Crane?" said Sekula.

Sandy shook her head. If she told him, he'd go away and talk to Hall himself, and he'd take all that lovely money with him. She'd said too much already. It was time to clam up.

"He'll be back soon," she said firmly. "Believe me, it's all taken care of."

Sekula stood. It should have been easy. The money would have been handed over, the manuscript would have come into their possession, and they would have simply left. If Brightwell subsequently decided to kill the seller, then that was his call to make. He should have guessed that it would never be so simple.

Sekula wasn't good at this part. That was why Miss Zahn was with him. Miss Zahn was very good at it, very good indeed. She was already on her feet, removing her jacket and unbuttoning her blouse while Sandy Crane watched, her mouth hanging open and vague expressions of incomprehension falling dully from her tongue. It was only when Miss Zahn undid the last button and slipped the blouse from her body that the Crane woman at last began to understand.

Sekula thought the tattoos upon his lover's body were fascinating, even if he found it almost impossible to imagine the pain that their creation must have caused her. Apart from her face and hands, her skin was entirely obscured by the illustrations, the monstrous, distorted faces blending into one another so it was almost impossible to identify individual beings among them. Yet it was the eyes that were the most disturbing aspect, even for Sekula. There were so many of them, large and small, encompassing every imaginable color, like oval wounds upon her body. Now, as she advanced toward Sandy Crane, they seemed to alter, the pupils expanding and contracting, the eyes rotating in their sockets, exploring this new unfamiliar place, with the drunken woman now cowering before them.

But it was probably no more than a trick of the light.

Sekula stepped into the hallway and closed the door behind him. He went into the dining room across the hall and sat down in an armchair. It gave him a clear view of the driveway and the street beyond. He tried to find a magazine to read, but all he could see were copies of the *Reader's Digest* and some supermarket tabloids. He heard Mrs. Crane say something in the room beyond, and then her voice became muffled. Seconds later, Sekula grimaced as she started screaming against the gag.

The FBI's New York field division had moved location so often in its history that it should have been staffed by Gypsies. In 1910, when it first opened, it was located in the old post office building, a site now occupied by City Hall Park. Since then, it had opened up shop at various points on Park Row; in the Subtreasury Building at Wall and Nassau; at Grand Central Terminal; in the U.S. Courthouse at Foley Square; on Broadway; and in the former Lincoln Warehouse at East Sixty-ninth, before finally making a home at the Jacob Javits Federal Building, down near Foley Square again.

I called the FBI shortly before eleven and asked to be put through to Special Agent Philip Bosworth, the man who had visited Neddo to inquire about his knowledge of Sedlec and the Believers. I got bounced around before ending up with the OSM's department, or what used to be the chief clerk's office before everybody got a shiny new title. The office service manager and his staff were responsible for non-investigative matters. A man who identified himself as Grantley asked me my name and business. I gave him my license number and told him I was trying to get in touch with Special Agent Bosworth regarding a missing person investigation.

"Special Agent Bosworth is no longer with this office," said Grantley.

"Well, can you tell me where I can find him?"

"No."

"Can I give you my number and maybe you could pass it on to him?"

"No."

"Can you help me in any way at all?"

"I don't think so."

I thanked him. I wasn't sure for what, but it seemed the polite thing to do.

Edgar Ross was still one of the special agents in charge at the New York division. Unlike SACs in most of the other field offices, the SAC wasn't the final authority in New York. Ross answered to the assistant director in charge, a pretty good guy named Wilmots, but Ross still had a whole little family of assistant SACs under his command and was therefore the most influential law enforcement official I knew. Our paths had crossed during the pursuit of the man who had killed Susan and Jennifer, and I think Ross felt he owed me a little slack as a result of what had occurred. I even suspected that he had a grudging affection for me, but maybe that was the result of my watching too many TV cop shows in which gruff lieutenants secretly harbored homoerotic fantasies about the mavericks under their command. I didn't think Ross's feelings about me went quite that far, but then he was a difficult man to read sometimes. One never knew.

I called his office shortly after I was done with Grantley. I gave my name to Ross's secretary and waited. When she came back on the line, she told me that Ross wasn't available but said she'd pass on the fact that I'd called. I thought about holding my breath while I waited for him to call back, but figured that I'd have blacked out long before that ever happened. From the brief delay in our exchange, though, I gathered that Ross was around but had tightened up since last we spoke. I was anxious to get back to Rachel and Sam, but I wanted to accumulate all the information that I could before I left the city. I felt I had no option but to take an expensive cab ride down to Federal Plaza.

The area was a peculiar clash of cultures: on the east side of Broadway there were the big federal buildings, surrounded by concrete barricades and adorned with weird rusting pieces of modern sculpture. On the other side, directly facing the might of the FBI, were storefronts that advertised cheap watches and caps while doing a profitable sideline in assisting with immigration applications, and discount clothing stores that offered suits for $59.99. I grabbed a coffee at a Dunkin' Donuts, then settled down to wait for Ross. He was, if nothing else, a man of routine. He'd confessed as much to me, the last time we'd met. I knew that he liked to eat most days at Stark's Veranda, at the corner of Broadway and Thomas, a government hangout that had been around since the end of the nineteenth century, and I just hoped that he hadn't suddenly taken to lunching at his desk. By the time he eventually emerged from his office I'd been waiting two hours and my coffee was long since finished, but I felt a touch of satisfaction at my investigative skills when he headed for the Veranda, quickly followed by the pain of rejection when I saw the expression on his face as I fell into step beside him.

"No," he said. "Get lost."

"You don't write, you don't call," I said. "We're losing touch. What we have now just isn't the same as it used to be."

"I don't want to be in touch with you. I want you to leave me alone."

"Buy me lunch?"

"No. No! What part of 'leave me alone' don't you understand?"

He stopped at the crosswalk. It was a mistake. He should have taken his chances with the traffic.

"I'm trying to trace one of your agents," I said.

"Look, I'm not your personal go-to guy at the Bureau," said Ross. "I'm a busy man. There are terrorists out there, drug dealers, mobsters. They all require my attention. They take up a lot of my time. The rest, I save for people I like: my family, my friends, and basically anyone who isn't you."

He scowled at the oncoming traffic. He might even have been tempted to draw his gun and wave it around threateningly in order to cross.

"Come on, I know you secretly like me," I said. "You've probably got my name written on your pencil case. The agent's name is Philip Bosworth. The OSM's office told me he was no longer with the division. I'd just like to get in touch with him."

I had to give him credit for trying to shake me off. I took my eye off him for just a second, and instantly he was skipping through oncoming traffic like a government-funded Frogger. I caught up with him, though.

"I was hoping you'd be killed," he said, but secretly I knew he was impressed.

"You pretend you're such a tough guy," I said, "but I know you're all warm and fuzzy inside. Look, I just need to ask Bosworth some questions, that's all."

"Why? Why is he important to you?"

"The thing in Williamsburg, the human remains in

the warehouse? He may know something about the background of the people involved."

"People? I heard there was one guy. He got shot. You shot him. You shoot a lot of people. You ought to stop."

We were at the entrance to the Veranda. If I tried to follow Ross inside, the staff would have my ass on the sidewalk faster than you could say "deadbeat". I could see him balancing the wisdom of stepping inside and trying to forget about me against the possibility that I might know something useful—that, and the likelihood that I would still be outside when he was done, and then the whole thing would just start over again.

"Somebody set him up there, gave him a place to live and work," I said. "He didn't do it alone."

"The cops said you were investigating a missing person case."

"How'd you know that?"

"We get bulletins. I had someone call the Nine-Six when your name came up."

"See, I knew you cared."

"Caring is relative. Who was the girl they found?"

"Alice Temple. Friend of a friend."

"You don't have too many friends, and I have my suspicions about some of the ones you do have. You keep bad company."

"Do I have to listen to the lecture before you help me?"

"You see, *that's* why things are always so difficult with you. You don't know when to stop. I've never met a guy who was so keen on mixing it up."

"Bosworth," I said. "Philip Bosworth."

"I'll see what I can do. Someone will get back to

you, maybe. Don't call me, okay? Just don't call me."

The Veranda's door opened, and we stepped aside to let a gaggle of old women leave. As the last of them departed, Ross slipped inside the restaurant. I was left holding the door.

I counted to five, waiting until just before he got out of sight.

"So," I shouted, "I'll call you, right?"

Mark Hall couldn't stop vomiting. Ever since he'd come home, his stomach had bubbled with acid, until eventually it just rebelled and began spewing out its contents. He had barely slept the night before, and now his head and body ached dully. He was just thankful that his wife was away; otherwise, she'd have been fussing over him, insisting that a doctor should be called. Instead, he was free to slump on the bathroom floor, his cheek flat against the cool of the toilet bowl, waiting for the next spasm to hit. He didn't know how long he'd been there. All he knew was that whenever he thought of what he'd done to Larry, the smell of Crane's last breath came back to him, like Larry's ghost was breathing upon him from the beyond, and a fresh bout of puking would immediately commence.

It was strange. He had hated Crane for so long. Every time Hall saw him, it was as though he were watching an imp grinning at him from beyond the grave, a reminder of the judgment he must inevitably face for his sins. He had long hoped that Crane would simply crawl off and die, but as in wartime, Larry Crane had proved to be a tenacious survivor.

Mark Hall had killed his share of men during the war: some of them from far away, distant figures falling in the echo of a rifle shot, others up close and personal, so that their blood had spattered his face and stained his uniform. None of those deaths had troubled him after the first, as the naive boy who had taken the bus to basic training was transformed into a man capable of ending the life of another. It was a just war, and had he not killed them, then they would surely have despatched him. But he had believed his days of killing to be far behind him, and he had never envisioned himself taking a knife to an unarmed old man, even one as odious as Larry Crane. The shock of it, and the disgust that it engendered, had sucked the energy from him, and nothing could ever be the same again.

Hall heard the doorbell ring, but he didn't get up to answer it. He couldn't. He was too weak to stand, and too ashamed to face anyone even if he could. He stayed on the floor, his eyes closed. He must have dozed off, because the next thing he remembered, the bathroom door was opening, and he was looking at two pairs of feet: a woman's and a man's. His eyes followed the woman's legs over her skirt to her hands. Hall thought that he could see blood on them. He wondered if his own hands looked the same way to her.

"Who are you?" he said. He could barely speak. His voice sounded like the slow sweepings of a yard brush over dusty ground.

"We've come to talk about Larry Crane," said Sekula. Hall tried to raise his head to look, but it hurt him to move.

"I haven't seen him," said Hall.

Sekula squatted before the old man. He had a clean, scrubbed face and good teeth. Hall didn't like him one bit.

"What are you, police?" said Hall. "If you're cops, show me some ID."

"Why would you think we are police, Mr. Hall? Is there something you'd like to share with us? Have you been a bad boy?"

Hall dry-retched, the memory of Larry Crane's death smell coming back to him.

"Mr. Hall, we're in kind of a hurry," said Sekula. "I think you know what we've come for."

Dumb, greedy Larry Crane. Even in death he had found a way to ruin Mark Hall.

"It's gone," said Hall. "He took it with him."

"Where?"

"I don't know."

"I don't believe you."

"To hell with you. Get out of my house."

Sekula rose and nodded to Miss Zahn. This time, he stayed in the room, just to make sure that she understood the urgency of the situation. It didn't take long. The old man started talking as soon as the needle approached his eye, but Miss Zahn inserted it anyway, just to be sure that he wasn't lying. By that time, Sekula had looked away. The stink of vomit was already getting to him.

When she was done, they took Hall, now blind in his left eye, and bundled him into the car, then drove him to where he had dumped the body of Larry Crane in a muddy hollow beside a filthy swamp. The box was cradled against Crane's chest, where Hall had placed it before leaving his old war buddy to rot. After all, he figured that if Crane wanted it so badly, he should take it with him wherever he was going.

Carefully, Sekula removed the box from the old man's

grasp, and opened it. The fragment was inside, and undamaged. The box had been well designed, capable of protecting its contents from water, from snow, from anything that might damage the information it held.

"It's intact," said Sekula to the woman. "We're so close now."

Mark Hall, the Auto King, sat on the dirt in his old man pants, his left hand cupped to his ruined eye. When Miss Zahn took him by the hand and led him to the water, he did not struggle, not even when she forced him to kneel and held his head beneath the surface until he drowned. When he grew still, they dragged him to the hollow and laid him beside his former comrade, uniting the two old men in death as they had been united, however unwillingly, in life.

15

Walter Cole called me as I was driving from the city.

"I've got more news," he said. "The M.E. has confirmed the identity of the remains found in Garcia's apartment. It's Alice. Toxicology tests also revealed the presence of DMT, dimethyltryptamine, in a small section of tissue that was found still adhering to the base of her skull."

"I've never heard of it. What does it do?"

"Apparently it's a hallucinogenic drug, but it has very particular symptoms. It causes feelings of paranoia, and makes users hallucinate alien intelligences, or monsters. Sometimes it makes them think that they're traveling through time, or onto other planes of existence. Want to hear something else that's interesting? They found traces of DMT in Garcia's body too. The M.E. thinks it might have been administered through the food in his kitchen, but they're still running tests."

It was possible that Alice had been given the drug in order to make her more cooperative, allowing her captors to masquerade as her saviors once the effects of the drug began to wear off. But Garcia had been fed DMT too, perhaps as a means of keeping him under some form of control by ensuring that he remained in a state of near-constant fear. The dosage wouldn't have to be high: just enough to keep him on edge, so that his paranoia could be manipulated if required.

"I've got something else for you, too," said Walter. "The building in Williamsburg had a basement. The entrance was hidden behind a false wall. It seems we now know what Garcia was doing with the bones."

It was the NYPD's Forensic Investigation Division that found the basement. They had taken their time, going through the building floor by floor, working from the top down, checking the plans for the building against what they saw around them, noting what was recent and what was old. The cops who broke down the wall found a new steel door in the floor, nearly forty square feet and secured with heavy-duty locks and bolts. It took them an hour to get it open, backed up by the same Emergency Service Unit that had responded on the night Garcia died. When the door was open, the ESU descended a set of temporary wooden stairs into the darkness.

The space beneath was of the same dimensions as the main steel door, and some twelve feet deep. Garcia had been hard at work in the hidden space. Garlands of sharpened bone hung from the corners of the basement, meeting in a cluster of skulls at each corner. The walls had been concreted and inset with pieces of blackened bone to the halfway mark, sections of jawbones, femurs, finger bones, and rib jutting out as though discovered in the course of some ongoing archaeological dig. Four towers of candleholders created from marble and bone stood in a square at the center of the room, the candles held in skull-and-bone arrangements similar to those I had discovered in Garcia's apartment, with four chains of bones linking them, as though sealing off access to some as yet unknown addition to the ossuary. There was also a small alcove two or three feet in height, empty but clearly also awaiting the arrival of another element of display, perhaps the small bone sculpture that now rested in the trunk of my car.

The M.E.'s office was going to have a difficult task identifying the remains, but I knew where they could start: with a list of dead or missing women from the region of Juárez, Mexico, and the unfortunates who had disappeared from the streets of New York since Garcia's arrival in the city.

I drove north. I made good time once I cleared the boroughs, and arrived in Boston shortly before 5 P.M. The House of Stern was situated in a side street almost within the shadow of the Fleet Center. It was an unusual location for such a business, audibly close to a strip of bars that included the local outpost of Hooters. The windows were smoked glass, with the company's name written in discreet gold lettering across the bottom. To the right was a wood door, painted black, with an ornate gold knocker in the shape of a gaping mouth, and a gold mailbox filigreed with dragons chasing their tails. In a slightly less adult neighborhood, the door of House of Stern would have been a compulsory stop for Halloween trick-or-treaters.

I pressed the doorbell and waited. The door was opened by a young woman with bright red hair and purple nail polish that was chipped at the ends.

"I'm afraid we're closed," she said. "We open to the public from ten until four, Monday to Friday."

"I'm not a customer," I said. "My name's Charlie Parker. I'm a private investigator. I'd like to see Claudia Stern."

"Is she expecting you?"

"No, but I think she'll want to see me. Perhaps you might show her this."

I handed over the box in my arms. The young woman looked at it a little dubiously, carefully removing the layers of newspaper so that she could see what was inside. She revealed a section of the bone statue, considered it silently for a moment, then opened the door wider to admit me. She told me to take a seat in a small reception area, then vanished through a half-open green door.

The room in which I sat was relatively unadorned, and a little down-at-the-heels. The carpet was worn and frayed and the wallpaper was wearing thin at the corners, heavily marked by the passage of people and the bumps and scrapes it had received during the movement of awkward objects. Two desks stood to my right, covered in papers and topped by a pair of sleeping computers. To my left were four packing crates from which piles of curly wood shavings poked like unruly clown hair. A series of lithographs hung on the wall behind them, depicting scenes of angelic conflict. I walked over to take a closer look at them. They were reminiscent of the work of Gustave Doré, the illustrator of the *Divine Comedy,* but the lithographs appeared to be based on some other work unfamiliar to me.

"The angelic conflict," said a female voice from behind me, "and the fall of the rebel host. They date from the early nineteenth century, commissioned by Dr. Richard Laurence, professor of Hebrew at Oxford, to illustrate his first English translation of the Book of Enoch, in 1821, then abandoned and left unused following a disagreement with the artist. These are among the only extant copies. The rest were all destroyed."

I turned to face a small, attractive woman in her early fifties, dressed in black slacks and a white sweater smudged here and there with dark marks. Her hair was almost entirely gray, with the faintest hint of gold at the temples. Her face was relatively unlined, the skin tight and the neck bearing only the slightest trace of wrinkles. If my estimate of her age was correct, she was wearing her years well.

"Ms. Stern?"

She shook my hand. "Claudia. I'm pleased to make your acquaintance, Mr. Parker."

I returned my attention to the illustrations.

"Out of curiosity, why were the remaining drawings destroyed?"

"The artist was a Catholic named Knowles, who worked regularly for publishers in London and Oxford. He was quite accomplished, although somewhat derivative of others in his style. Knowles was unaware of the controversial nature of Enoch when he agreed to undertake the commission, and it was only when the subject of his work came up during discussions with his local parish priest that he was alerted to the history of the scripture in question. Do you know anything of the biblical apocrypha, Mr. Parker?"

"Nothing worth sharing," I replied. That wasn't entirely true. I had come across the Book of Enoch before, although I had never seen the actual text. The Traveling Man, the killer who had taken my wife and daughter, had made reference to it. It was just one of a number of obscure sources that had helped to fuel his fantasies.

She smiled, revealing white teeth that were yellowing slightly at the edges and the gums.

"Then perhaps I can enlighten you, and you can in turn enlighten me about the object with which you introduced yourself to my assistant. The Book of Enoch was part of the accepted biblical canon for about five hundred years, and fragments of it were found among the Dead Sea Scrolls. Laurence's translation was based upon sources dating from the second century B.C., but the book itself may be older still. Most of what we know, or think we know, of the fall of the angels comes from Enoch, and it may have been that Jesus Christ himself was familiar with the work, for there are clear echoes of Enoch in some of the later gospels. It subsequently fell out of favor with theologians, largely because of its theories on the nature of angels."

"Like how many can dance on the head of a pin?"

"In a way," said Ms. Stern. "While there was at least some acceptance that the origins of evil on earth lay in the fall of the angels, their nature provoked disagreement. Were they corporeal? If so, what of their appetites? According to Enoch, the great sin of the dark angels was not pride, but lust: their desire to copulate with women, the most beautiful aspect of God's greatest creation, humanity. This led to disobedience, and a rebellion against God, and they were cast out of heaven as punishment. Such speculations found little favor with the church authorities, and Enoch was denounced and removed from the canon, with some even going so far as to declare it heretical in nature. Its contents were largely forgotten until 1773, when a Scottish explorer named James Bruce traveled to Ethiopia and secured three copies of the book that had been preserved by the church in that country. Fifty years later, Laurence produced his translation, and thus Enoch was revealed to the English-speaking world for the first time in over a millennium."

"But without Knowles's illustrations."

"He was concerned about the controversy that might arise following its publication, and apparently his parish priest told him that he would refuse him the sacraments if he contributed to the work. Knowles notified Dr. Laurence of his decision, Laurence traveled to London to discuss the matter with him, and in the course of their discussions a heated argument arose. Knowles began casting his illustrations into the fire, the originals as well as the proof copies. Laurence snatched what he could salvage from the artist's desk and fled. To be honest, the illustrations are not particularly valuable in themselves, but I am fond of the story of their creation and decided to hold on to them, despite occasional requests that they be offered for sale. In a way, they symbolize what this house has always set out to do: to ensure that ignorance and fear do not contribute to the destruction of arcane art, and that all such pieces find their way to those who would most appreciate them. Now, if you'd like to come through, we can discuss your own piece."

I followed her through the green door and down a corridor that led to a workshop area. Here, the secretary with the red hair was checking the condition of some leather-bound books in one corner, while in another a middle-aged man with receding brown hair worked on a painting illuminated by a series of lamps.

"You've come along at an interesting time," said Claudia Stern. "We're preparing for an auction, the centerpiece of which is an item with links to Sedlec, a quality that it shares with your own statue. But then, I imagine that you knew that already, given your presence here. Might I ask who recommended that you bring the bone sculpture to me?"

"A man named Charles Neddo. He's a dealer in New York."

"I know of Mr. Neddo. He is a gifted amateur. He occasionally comes up with some unusual objects, but he has never learned to distinguish between what is valuable and what should be discarded and forgotten."

"He spoke highly of you."

"I'm not surprised. Frankly, Mr. Parker, this house is expert in such matters, a reputation painstakingly acquired over the last decade. Before we came on the scene, arcane artifacts were the preserve of backstreet merchants, grubby men in dark basements. Occasionally, one of the established names would sell 'dark material,' as it was sometimes known, but none of them really specialized in the area. Stern is unique, and it is rarely that a seller of arcana fails to consult us first before putting an item up for auction. Similarly, a great many individuals approach us on both a formal and informal basis with queries relating to collections, manuscripts, even human remains."

She moved to a table, upon which stood the statue found in Garcia's apartment, now carefully positioned on a rotatable wheel. Her finger flipped the button on a desk lamp, casting white light upon the bones.

"Which brings us to this fellow. I assume Mr. Neddo told you something of the image's origins?"

"He seemed to think that it was a representation of a demon trapped in silver sometime in the fifteenth century. He called it the *Black Angel*."

"Immael," said Ms. Stern. "One of the more interesting figures in demonic mythology. It's rare to find a naming so recent."

"A naming?"

"According to Enoch, two hundred angels rebelled, and they were cast down initially on a mountain called Armon, or Hermon: *herem,* in Hebrew, means a curse. Some, of course, descended farther, and founded hell, but others remained on earth. Enoch gives the names of nineteen, I think. Immael is not among them, although that of his twin, Ashmael, is included in certain versions. In fact, the first record of Immael derives from manuscripts written in Sedlec after 1421, the year in which the *Black Angel* is reputed to have been created, all of which has contributed to its mythology."

She slowly turned the wheel, examining the sculpture from every possible angle.

"Where did you say you found this?"

"I didn't."

She lowered her chin and peered at me over the tops of her half-glasses.

"No, you didn't, did you? I should like to know, before I go any farther."

"The original owner, who was also probably the artist responsible, is dead. He was a Mexican named Garcia. Neddo believed that he was also behind the restoration of an ossuary in Juárez, and the creation of a shrine to a Mexican figurehead called Santa Muerte."

"How did the late Mr. Garcia meet his end?"

"You don't read the papers?"

"Not if I can help it."

"He was shot."

"Most unfortunate. He appeared to have considerable talent, if he made this. It really is very beautiful. My guess is that the human bones used are not old. I see little evidence of wear. The majority are from children, probably chosen for reasons of scale. There are also some canine and avian bones, and the nails on the ends of its limbs appear to be cat claws. It's most remarkable, but probably unsalable. Questions would be asked about the provenance of the child bones. There is the strong possibility that they may be linked to the commission of a crime. Anyone trying either to buy or sell it without involving the authorities would leave him- or herself open to charges of obstructing the course of justice, at the very least."

"I wasn't trying to sell it. The man who made this was involved in the killing of at least two young women in the United States, and perhaps many more in Mexico. Someone arranged for him to come north to New York. I want to find out who that might have been."

"So where does the statue fit in, and why bring it to me?"

"I thought it might pique your interest and allow me to ask you some questions."

"Which it did."

"I've been holding one question back: tell me about the Believers."

Ms. Stern killed the light. The gesture allowed her a moment to compose her features, and to hide partially the expression of alarm that briefly transformed her features.

"I'm not sure that I understand."

"I found a symbol carved inside a skull in Garcia's apartment. It was a grapnel. According to Neddo, it's used by a group of some kind, a cult, to identify its members and to mark some of its victims. The Believers have an interest in the history of Sedlec and in the recovery of the original statue of the *Black Angel*, assuming it even exists. You're about to auction off a fragment of a vellum map that is supposed to contain clues to the location of the statue. I would imagine that would be enough to attract the attention of these people."

I thought Ms. Stern was going to spit on the ground, so obvious was her distaste at the subject I had raised.

"The Believers, as they term themselves, are freaks. As I'm sure Mr. Neddo informed you, we sometimes deal with strange individuals in the course of our work, but most of them are harmless. They are collectors, and can be forgiven their enthusiasms, as they would never hurt another human being. The Believers are another matter. If the rumors are to be credited, and they are only rumors, they have existed for centuries, and their formation was a direct result of the confrontation in Bohemia between Erdric and Immael. Their numbers are small, and they keep a very low profile. The sole reason for their existence is to reunite the Black Angels."

"Angels? Neddo only told me about one statue."

"Not a statue," said Ms. Stern, "but a being."

She led me to where the man with receding hair was working upon the restoration of the painting. It was a large canvas, about ten feet by eight, and depicted a battleground. Fires burned on distant hills, and great armies moved through ruined houses and scorched fields. The detail was intricate, each figure beautifully and carefully painted, although it was difficult to tell if what I was seeing was the battle itself or its aftermath. There appeared to be pockets of fighting continuing in sections of the painting, but most of the central area consisted of courtiers surrounding a regal figure. Some distance from him, a one-eyed man rallied troops to himself.

The work had been placed upon an easel and surrounded by lights, almost like a patient in an operating theater. Upon the shelves around it stood microscopes, lenses, scalpels, magnifying glasses, and jars of assorted chemicals. While I watched, the restorer took a thin wooden stick and scored it with a penknife, then pushed it into cotton and rotated it to create a cotton bud of the required thickness. When he was satisfied with his creation, he dipped it into a jar of liquid and began carefully applying it to the surface of the painting.

"That's acetone mixed with white spirit," said Ms. Stern. "It's used to clean away unwanted layers of varnish, tobacco, and fire smoke, the effects of pollution and oxidization. One has to be careful to find the correct chemical balance for every painting, because the requirements of each one will be quite unique. The intention is to achieve a strength sufficient to remove dirt and varnish, even paint added by later artists or restorers, without burning through to the original layers beneath. This has been, and continues to be, a particularly painstaking restoration, as the anonymous artist used a mixture of techniques."

She pointed to two or three areas in the work where the paint appeared exceptionally thick.

"Here, he has used oil-free paints, giving his pigment an unusual consistency, as you can see. The impasto—the thicker areas of paint—have accumulated layers of dust in the grooves, which we've had to remove with a combination of acetone and scalpel work."

Again her hands danced across the work, almost but not quite touching the surface.

"There is also a great deal of craquelure, this web effect where the old pigments have dried and degraded over time. Now, let me show you something."

She found a smaller painting, depicting a solemn-looking man in ermine and a black hat. Across the room, her secretary abandoned her work and moved over to join us. Apparently, Miss Stern's master classes were worth attending.

"In case you were wondering, this is the alchemist Dr. Dee," she explained. "We are due to offer this for sale at our auction, alongside the painting upon which James is currently working. Now, let me adjust the lighting."

She turned off the large lights surrounding the paintings, using a central switch. For a moment we were in semidarkness, until our corner of the room was suddenly illuminated by an ultraviolet glow. Our teeth and eyes now shone purple, but the greatest change was visible upon the two paintings. The smaller work, the depiction of the alchemist Dee, was spattered with specks and dots, as though the entire work had been attacked by a demented student of Jackson Pollock. The larger painting, though, was almost entirely clear of such marks, apart from a thin half-moon in one corner where the restorer was still working.

"The dots on the portrait of Dee are called 'overpaint,' and they show the areas where previous restorers have retouched or filled in damaged areas," said Miss Stern. "If one were to perform the same experiment in almost any great gallery in the world, one would witness the same effect on most of the works present. The preservation of great works of art is a constant process, and it has always been so."

Miss Stern lit the main lights once again.

"Do you know what a 'sleeper' is, Mr. Parker? In our business, it is an object whose value is unrecognized by an auction house, and that subsequently passes into the hands of a buyer who realizes its true nature. This battlefield painting is just such a sleeper: it was discovered in a provincial auction house in Somerset, England, and bought for the equivalent of one thousand dollars. It's clear that the sleeper has not been restored at any point in its existence, although it appears to have been kept in relatively good condition, apart from the inevitable effects of natural aging. Yet there was one large area of concealment in the bottom right-hand corner, noticeable once the overpaint was revealed by the ultraviolet light. Originally, sections of this work had been crudely worked upon to conceal some of the detail it contained. It was uncovered relatively easily. What you are seeing here is the second stage of the restoration. Take a step back and look at that area with a new eye."

The bottom right-hand corner showed the bodies of monks, all of them wearing white, hanging from the wall of a monastery. Human bones were stacked in pyramids beneath their feet, and one of the monks had an arrow in the center of his forehead. A grapnel had been painted upon the front of each monk's robes in what appeared to be blood. A group of mounted soldiers was riding away from them, led by a tall armored figure with a white mote in his right eye. Human heads dangled from their saddles, and their horses wore spikes upon their foreheads.

If the bearded figure was their leader, it was to one of his men that one's eye was immediately drawn. He was not riding a horse, but instead walked alongside his captain, bearing a bloodied sword in his right hand. He was a fat imp, gross and deformed, with a great goiter or tumor at his neck. He wore a tunic of leather plates that failed to conceal the enormity of his belly, and his legs seemed almost to be collapsing under the great burden of his bulk. There was blood around his mouth, where he had fed upon the dead. In his left hand he held aloft a banner bearing the symbol of the grapnel.

"Why was this hidden?" I asked.

"This is the aftermath of the sacking of the monastery at Sedlec," said Miss Stern. "The killing of the monks during a period of truce was first blamed upon Jan Ziska and his Hussites, but this painting may be closer to the truth. It seems to suggest that the killings were the work of mercenaries, operating in the confusion of the aftermath and led by these two men. Later documentary evidence, including the testimony of eyewitnesses, supports the artist's version of events."

She spread the index and middle fingers of her right hand to indicate the bearded rider and the grotesque figure cavorting beside him. "This one"—she indicated the fat man—"has no name. Their leader was known simply as 'the Captain,' but if one is to believe the myths surrounding Sedlec, he was really Ashmael, the original Black Angel. According to the old stories, after the banishment from heaven, Ashmael was shunned by the company of the fallen because his eyes were marked by their last glimpse of God. In his loneliness, Ashmael tore himself in two so that he would have company in his wanderings, and he gave the name Immael to his twin. Eventually, they grew weary and descended into the depths of the earth near Sedlec, where they slept until the mines were dug. Then they awoke, and found the world above at war, so they began fomenting conflict, playing one side off against the other, until at last Immael was confronted and cast down into molten silver. Ashmael immediately commenced searching for him, but when he reached the monastery the statue had already been spirited away, so he avenged himself on the monks and continued his quest, a quest which, according to the tenets of the Believers, goes on to this day. So now you know, Mr. Parker. The Believers exist to reunite two halves of a fallen angel. It is a wonderful story, and now I plan to sell it in return for twenty percent of the purchase price. In the end, I am the only person who will profit from the story of the Black Angels."

I was home before midnight. The house was silent. I went upstairs and found Rachel asleep. I didn't wake her. Instead, I was about to check up on Sam when Rachel's mother appeared at the door and, putting a finger to her lips to hush me, indicated that I should follow her downstairs.

"Would you like coffee?" she asked.

"Coffee would be good."

She heated some water and retrieved the ground beans from the freezer. I didn't speak as she went about preparing the coffee. I sensed that it wasn't my place to begin whatever conversation we were about to have.

Joan placed a cup of coffee in front of me and cradled her own in her hands.

"We had a problem," she said. She didn't look at me as she spoke.

"What kind of problem?"

"Someone tried to get into the house through Sam's window."

"A burglar?"

"We don't know. The police seem to think so, but Rachel and I, we're not so sure."

"Why?"

"They didn't set the motion sensors off. The sensors weren't disabled either, so we can't figure out how they got to the house. And this is going to sound crazy, I know, but it seemed as if they were crawling up the exterior. We heard one of them moving on the outside wall behind Rachel's bed. There was another on the roof, and when Rachel went into Sam's room, she says she saw a woman's face at the window, but it was upside down. She shot at it and—"

"She *what*?"

"I'd taken Sam out of the room, and Rachel had set off the panic button. She had a gun, and she shot the window out. We had it replaced today."

I hid my face in my hands for a few moments, saying nothing. I felt something touch my fingers, and then Joan took my hand in hers.

"Listen to me," she said. "I know that sometimes it might seem like Frank and I are hard on you, and I know you and Frank don't get along too well, but you have to understand that we love Rachel, and we love Sam. We know that you love them too, and that Rachel cares about you, and loves you more deeply than she's ever loved any other man in her life. But the feelings she has for you are costing her a great deal. They've put her life at risk in the past, and they're bringing her pain now."

Something caught in my throat when I tried to speak. I took a sip of coffee to try to dislodge it, but it would not be moved.

"I know Rachel has told you about Curtis," said Joan.

"Yes," I said. "He sounded like he was a good man."

Joan smiled at the description.

"Curtis was pretty wild when he was a teenager," said Joan, "and wilder still when he was in his twenties. He had a girlfriend, Justine, and, boy, he drove her crazy. She was much gentler than he was, and though he always looked out for her, I think he kind of frightened her some, and she left him for a time. He couldn't understand why, and I had to sit him down and explain to him that it was okay to cut loose a little, that young men did those kinds of things, but at some point you had to start behaving like an adult, and rein in the young part. It didn't mean that you had to spend the rest of your life in a suit and tie, never raising your voice or stepping out of line, but you had to recognize that the rewards a relationship brought came at a price. The cost was a whole lot less than what you got in return, but it was a sacrifice nonetheless. If he wasn't prepared to make that sacrifice by growing up, then he had to just let her go and accept that she wasn't for him. He decided that he wanted to be with her. It took some time, but he changed. He was still the same boy at heart, of course, and that wild streak never left him, but he kept it in check, the way you might train a horse so you could harness its power and channel its energy. Eventually, he became a policeman, and he was good at what he did. Those people who killed him made the world a poorer place by taking him from it, and they broke so many hearts, just so many.

"I never thought I'd be having that conversation again with a man, and I understand that the circumstances are not the same. I know all that you've gone through, and I can imagine some of your pain. But you have to choose between the life you're being offered here, with a woman and a child, maybe a second marriage and more children to come, and this other life that you lead. If something happens to you because of it, then Rachel will have lost two men that she loved to violence; but if something happens to her or to Sam as a consequence of what you do, then everyone who loves Rachel and Sam will be torn apart, and you worst of all, because I don't believe that you could survive that loss a second time. Nobody could.

"You're a good man, and I understand that you're driven to try to make things right for people who can't help themselves, for those who've been hurt, or even killed. There's something noble in that, but I don't think you're concerned with nobility. It's sacrifice, but not the right kind. You're trying to make up for things that can never be undone, and you blame yourself for allowing them to occur even though it wasn't in your power to stop them. But at some point you're going to have to stop blaming yourself. You're going to have to stop trying to change the past. All of that is gone, hard as it may be to accept. What you have now is new hope. Don't let it slip away, and don't let it be taken from you."

Joan rose and emptied the remains of her coffee into the sink, then placed the mug in the dishwasher.

"I think Rachel and Sam are going to come stay with

us for a little while," she said. "You need time to finish whatever it is you're doing, and to think. I'm not trying to come between you. None of us are. I wouldn't be having this conversation with you if that was the case. But she's frightened and unhappy, and that's not even taking into account the aftermath of the birth and all the confused feelings that brings with it. She needs to be around other people for a little while, people who'll be there for her round the clock."

"I understand," I said.

Joan placed her hand on my shoulder, then kissed me gently on the forehead.

"My daughter loves you, and I respect her judgment more than that of anyone else that I know. She sees something in you. I can see it too. You need to remember that. If you forget it, then it's all lost."

The Black Angel walked in the moonlight, through tourists and residents, past stores and galleries, scenting coffee and gasoline on the air, distant bells tolling the coming of the hour. It examined the faces of the crowds, always seeking those that it might recognize, watching for eyes that lingered a second too long upon its face and form. It had left Brightwell in the office, lost among shadows and old things, and now replayed their conversation in its head. It smiled faintly as it did so, and lovers smiled too, believing that they saw in the expression of the passing stranger the remembrance of a recent kiss, and a parting embrace. That was the angel's secret: it could cloak the vilest of feelings in the most beautiful of colors, for otherwise no one would choose to follow its path.

Brightwell had not been smiling when earlier they had met.

"It is him," said Brightwell.

"You are jumping at shadows," the Black Angel replied.

Brightwell withdrew a sheaf of copied papers from the folds of his coat and placed them before the angel. He watched as its hand flicked through them, taking in snatches of headlines and stories, and with each page that it read its interest grew, until at last it was crouched over the desk, its shadow falling upon words and pictures, its fingers lingering upon names and places from cases now solved or buried: Charon, Pudd, Charleston, Faulkner, Eagle Lake, Kittim.

Kittim.

"It could be coincidence," said the angel softly, but it was said without conviction, less a statement than a step in an ongoing process of reasoning.

"So many?" said Brightwell. "I don't believe that. He has been haunting our footsteps."

"It's not possible. There is no way that he can know his own nature."

"We know *our* nature," said Brightwell.

The angel stared intently into Brightwell's eyes and saw anger, and curiosity, and the desire for revenge.

And fear? Yes, perhaps just a little.

"It was a mistake to go to the house," said the angel.

"I thought we could use the child to draw him to us."

The Black Angel stared at Brightwell. No, it thought, you wanted the child for more than that. Your urge to inflict pain has always been your undoing.

"You don't listen," it said to him. "I've warned you about drawing attention to us, especially at so delicate a juncture."

Brightwell appeared about to protest, but the angel

stood and removed its coat from the antique coat stand by its desk.

"I need to go out for a while. Stay here. Rest. I'll return soon."

And so the angel now walked the streets, like a slick of oil trailing through the tide of humanity, that smile darting occasionally across its face, never lingering for more than a second or two, and never quite reaching its eyes. Once an hour had gone by, it returned to its office, where Brightwell sat patiently in a corner, far from the light.

"Confront him if you wish, if it will confirm or disprove what you believe."

"Hurt him?" said Brightwell.

"If you have to."

There was no need to ask the last question, the one that remained unspoken. There would be no killing, for to kill him would be to release him, and he might never be found again.

Sam lay awake in her crib. She didn't look at me as I approached. Instead, her gaze was fixed raptly on something above and beyond the bars. Her tiny hands made grabbing motions, and she seemed to be smiling. I had seen her like that before, when Rachel or I stood over her, either talking to her or offering her some bauble or toy. I moved closer, and felt a coldness in the air around her. Still Sam didn't look at me. Instead, she gave what sounded like a little giggle of amusement.

I reached across the crib, my fingers outstretched. For the briefest of moments, I thought that I felt a substance brush against my fingers, like gossamer or silk. Then it was gone, and the coldness with it. Immediately, Sam began to cry. I took her in my arms and held her, but she wouldn't stop. There was movement behind me, and Rachel appeared at my side.

"I'll take her," she said, her arms reaching for Sam, and irritation in her voice.

"It's okay. I can hold her."

"I *said* I'll take her," she snapped, and it was more than annoyance now. I had been called to scenes of domestic arguments as a cop and had seen mothers latch on to their children in the same way, anxious to protect them from any threat of violence, even as their husbands or partners attempted to make up for whatever they had done or had threatened to do, once the police were present. I had seen the look in those women's eyes. It was the same as the one that I now saw in Rachel's. I handed the baby to her without a word.

"Why did you have to wake her?" said Rachel, holding Sam against her and stroking her gently on the back. "It took me hours to get her down."

I found my voice.

"She was awake. I just went over to look at her and—"

"It doesn't matter. It's done."

She turned her back to me, and I left them both and undressed in the bathroom, then took a long shower. When I was done, I went downstairs and found a pair of sweatpants and a T-shirt, then headed into my office and rousted Walter from the couch. I'd make a bed there for the night. Sam had stopped crying, and there was no sound from upstairs for a time, until at last I heard Rachel's soft footfalls on the stairs. She had put on a dressing gown over her nightshirt. Her feet were bare. She leaned against the door, watching me. I couldn't say anything at first. When I tried to speak there was again that tickling in my throat. I wanted to shout at her, and I wanted to hold her. I wanted to tell her that I was sorry, that everything would be all right, and I wanted her to say the same to me, even if neither of us was telling the entire truth.

"I was just tired," she said. "I was surprised to see you back."

Despite all that Joan had said, I still wanted more.

"You acted like you thought I was going to drop her, or hurt her," I said. "It's not the first time, either."

"No, it's not that," she said. She moved toward me. "I know you'd never do anything to harm her."

Rachel tried to touch my hair, and to my shame, I pulled away. She started to cry, and the sight of her tears was shocking to me.

"I don't know what it is," she said. "I don't know what's wrong. It's — you weren't here, and someone came. Some*thing* came, and I was frightened. Do you understand? I'm *scared*, and I hate being scared. I'm better than that, but you make me feel this way."

Now it was out. Her voice was raised as her face contorted into an expression of utter hurt and rage and grief.

"You make me feel this way for Sam, for myself, for you. You go away when we need you to be here, and you put yourself in harm's way for — for what? For strangers, for people you've never met? I'm *here*. Sam is *here*. This is your life now. You're a father, you're my lover. I love you — God Jesus, I do love you, I love you so much — but you can't keep doing this to me and to us. You have to choose, because I can't go through another year like this one. Do you know what I've done?

Do you know what your work has made me do? I have blood on my hands. I can *smell* it on my fingers. I look out of the window and I can see the place where I spilled it. Every day I glimpse those trees, and I remember what happened there. It all comes back to me. I killed a man to protect our daughter, and last night I would have done it again. I took his life out there in the marshes, and I was glad. I hit him, and I hit him again, and I wanted to keep hitting him. I wanted to tear him to pieces, and for him to feel every second of it, every last bit of pain. I saw the blood rise in the water, and I watched him drown, and I was happy when he died. I knew what he wanted to do to me and to my baby, and I fucking wasn't going to let that happen. I fucking hated him, and I hated you for making me do what I did, for putting me in that place. I hated you."

Slowly, she slid to the floor. Her mouth was wide open, her lower lip curled in upon itself, tears falling and falling and falling, misery without end.

"I *hated* you," she repeated. "Do you understand? I can't do this. I can't hate you."

And then the words ceased and there were only sounds without meaning. I heard Sam crying, but I couldn't go to her. All that I could do was reach out to Rachel, whispering and kissing as I tried to quell the pain, until at last we lay upon the floor together, her fingers on my back and her mouth against my neck as we tried to hold on to all that we were losing by binding ourselves to each other.

We slept together that night. In the morning she packed some things, put the baby in the child seat of Joan's car, and prepared to leave.

"We'll talk," I said, as she stood by the car.

"Yes."

I kissed her on the mouth. She put her arms around me, and her fingers touched the back of my neck. They lingered there, and then were gone, but the scent of her remained, even after the car had disappeared, even after the rain came, even after sunlight faded and darkness rose and the stars scattered the night sky like sequins fallen from the gown of a woman half imagined, half recalled.

And through the emptiness of the house a cold crept, and as I fell into sleep a voice whispered:

I told you she would leave. Only we remain.

A touch like gossamer fell upon my skin, and Rachel's perfume was lost in the stink of earth and blood.

And in New York, the young prostitute named Ellen woke from her place beside G-Mack and felt a hand upon her mouth. She tried to struggle, until she felt the cool of the gun metal against her cheek.

"Close your eyes," said a man's voice, and she thought that she recognized it from somewhere. "Close your eyes and be still."

She did as she was told. The hand remained over her mouth, but the gun was moved away from her. Beside her, she heard G-Mack start to wake. The painkillers made him drowsy, but they usually wore off during the night, forcing him to take some more.

"Huh?" said G-Mack.

She heard five words spoken, and then there was a sound like a book being dropped upon the floor. Something warm sprayed her face. The hand was removed from her mouth.

"Keep your eyes closed," said the voice.

She kept her eyes squeezed shut until she was certain that the man was gone. When she opened them again, there was a hole in G-Mack's forehead and the pillows were red with his blood.

16

Without Rachel and Sam around, I fell into a black place. I don't recall much of the twenty-four hours that followed their departure. I slept, I ate little, and I didn't answer the phone. I thought about drinking, but I was already so consumed by self-loathing that I was unable to lower myself further. Messages were left, but none that mattered, and after a time I just stopped listening to them. I tried to watch some television, even flicked through the newspaper, but nothing could hold my attention. I pushed thoughts of Alice, of Louis, of Martha far from me. I wanted no part of them.

And as the hours crept slowly by a pain grew inside me, like an ulcer bleeding into my system. I lay fetally upon the couch, my knees drawn into my chest, and spasmed as the hurt ebbed and flowed. I thought that I heard noises from upstairs, the footsteps of a mother and a child, but when I went to look there was nobody there. A towel had fallen from the clothes dryer, the door of which now stood open, and I could not recall if it was I who had left it that way. I thought about calling Rachel every second minute, but I did not lift the phone. I knew that nothing would come of it if I did. What could I say to her? What promises could I make without doubting, even as I spoke the words, that I would be able to keep them?

Again and again, Joan's words came back to me. I had lost so much once; such a loss would be unendurable a second time. In the new and unwelcome quiet of the house, I felt time slipping once more, so that past and present blurred, the dams that I had tried so hard to erect between what once was and what yet might be weakening still further, spilling agonizing memories into my new life, mocking the hope that old ghosts could ever be laid to rest.

It was the silence that brought them, the sense of existences briefly halted. Rachel still had clothes in the closets and cosmetics on her dressing table. Her shampoo hung in the shower stall, and there was a strand of her long, red hair lying like a question mark on the floor beneath the sink. I could smell her on the pillow, and the shape of her head was clear on the cushions of the couch by our bedroom window, where she liked to lie and read. I found a white ribbon beneath our bed, and an earring that had slipped behind the radiator. An unwashed coffee cup bore a trace of her lipstick, and there was a candy bar in the refrigerator, half eaten.

Sam's little crib still stood in the center of her room, for Joan had retained the one used by her own children and it was easier to simply retrieve that from her attic rather than disassemble Sam's own crib and transport it to Vermont. I think, perhaps, that Rachel was also reluctant to remove the crib from our house, knowing the pain it would cause me with its unavoidable implications of permanence. Some of Sam's toys and clothes lay on the floor by the wall. I picked them up and put the dirty bibs and tops into the laundry basket. I would wash them later. I touched the place where she slept. I caught her baby smell on my fingers. She smelled as Jennifer once did.

And I remembered: all of these things I did before, when blood lay drying in the cracks on the kitchen floor. There was discarded clothing upon a bed, and a doll on a child's chair. There was a cup on a table, half filled with coffee, and a glass bearing traces of milk. There were cosmetics and brushes and hair and lipstick and lives ended in the middle of tasks half-done, so that for a moment it seemed as though they must surely return, that they had merely slipped away for a few moments and would come back eventually to finish their nighttime drinks, to place the doll on the shelf where it belonged, to resume their lives and permit me to share that place with them, to love me and to die with me and not leave me alone to grieve for them, until at last I grieved so long and so hard that something returned, phantasms conjured up by my pain, two entities that were almost my wife and child.

Almost.

Now I was in another house, and again there were reminders of lives around me, of tasks left unfinished and words left unsaid, except that these existences were continuing elsewhere. There was no blood on the floor, not yet. There was no finality here, merely a pause for breath, a reconsideration. They could go on, perhaps not in this place, but somewhere far away, somewhere safe and secure.

Fading light, falling rain, and night descending like soot upon the earth. Voices half heard, and touches in the darkness. Blood in my nose, and dirt in my hair.

We remain.

Always, we remain.

I awoke to the sound of the telephone. I waited for the machine to pick up the message. A man's voice spoke, vaguely familiar but nobody I could place. I let the cassette roll on.

Later, after I had showered and dressed, I walked Walter as far as Ferry Beach and let him play in the surf. Outside the Scarborough Fire Department, men were cleaning down the engines with hoses, the winter sunlight occasionally breaking through the clouds and causing the droplets to sparkle like jewels before they disintegrated upon the ground. In the early days of the fire department, steel locomotive wheels were used to summon the volunteers, and there was still one outside Engine 3's station over at Pleasant Hill. Then, in the late 1940s, Elizabeth Libby and her daughter, Shirley, took over the emergency dispatch service, operating out of the store on Black Point Road where they lived and worked. They would activate their Gamewell alarm system when a call came in, which in turn set off air horns at the station houses. The two women were on duty twenty-four hours a day, seven days a week, and in their first eleven years in charge of the service they went away together only twice.

One of my earliest memories of Scarborough was of watching old Clayton Urquhart presenting a plaque to Elizabeth Libby for long service in 1971. My grandfather was a volunteer member of the fire department, helping out when the need arose, and my grandmother was one of the women who worked the mobile canteen that provided food and drink to the firefighters when they were tackling big blazes, or fires of long duration, so they were both there for the presentation. Elizabeth Libby, who used to give me candy when we visited her, wore winged glasses and had a white flower pinned to her dress. She dabbed happily at her eyes with a white lace handkerchief as people she'd known all her life said nice things about her in public.

I tied Walter to the cemetery gate and walked to the place where my grandfather and grandmother were interred. She had died long before he, and I had few lasting memories of her apart from that occasion when Elizabeth Libby received her plaque. I had buried my grandfather myself, taking a spade after the mourners had gone and slowly covering the pine casket in which he lay. It was a warm day, and I laid my jacket upon a headstone. I think I talked to him while I worked, but I don't remember what I said. I probably spoke to him as I had always done, for men are ever boys with their grandfathers. He was a sheriff's deputy once, but a bad case poisoned him, taking hold of his conscience and tormenting it so that he knew no rest from the thoughts that pursued him. In the end, it would be left to me finally to close the circle and help to bring an end to the demon that had taunted my grandfather. I wondered if he left those agonies behind him when he died, or if they followed him into the next world. Did peace come to him with his last breath, finally silencing the voices that had haunted him for so long, or did it come later, when a boy that he had once danced upon his knee fell upon the snow and watched as an old horror bled away to nothing?

I pulled a weed from beside his headstone. It came away easily, as such plants will. My grandfather taught me how to distinguish the weeds from the plants: good flowers have deep roots, and the bad ones dwell in shallow soil. When he told me things, I did not forget them. I filed them away, in part because I knew that he might ask me about them at some future date, and I wanted to be able to answer him correctly.

"You have old eyes," he used to tell me. "You should have an old man's knowledge to match them."

But he slowly began to grow frail, and his memory started to fail him, the Alzheimer's stealing him away, little by little, relentlessly thieving all that was valuable to him, slowly disassembling the old man's memory. And so it was left to me to remind him of all that he had once told me, and I became the teacher to my grandfather.

Good flowers have deep roots, and bad ones dwell in shallow soil.

Shortly before he died, the disease gave him a temporary release, and things that had seemed lost forever returned to him. He remembered his wife, and their marriage, and the daughter they had together. He recalled weddings and divorces, baptisms and funerals, the names of colleagues who had gone before him into the last great night that glows faintly with the light of a promised dawn. Words and memories rushed from him in a great torrent, and he lived his life over again in a matter of hours. Then it was all gone, and not a single moment of his past remained, as though that flood had scoured away the final traces of him, leaving an empty dwelling with opaque windows, reflecting all but revealing nothing, for there was nothing left to reveal.

But in those last minutes of lucidity, he took my hand, and his eyes burned more brightly than they had ever done before. We were alone. His day was drawing to a close, and the sun was setting upon him.

"Your father," he said. "You're not like him, you know. All families have their burdens to bear, their troubled souls. My mother, she was a sad woman, and my father could never make her happy. It wasn't his fault, and it wasn't hers. She was just the way that she was, and people didn't understand it then. It was a sickness, and it took her in the end, like cancer took your mother. Your father, he had something of that sickness in him too, that sadness. I think maybe that was part of what attracted your mother to him: it spoke to something inside of her, even if she didn't always want to hear what it said."

I tried to remember my father, but as the years passed after his death it grew harder and harder to picture him. When I tried to visualize him, there was always a shadow across his face, or his features were distorted and unclear. He was a policeman, and he shot himself with his own gun. They said that he did it because he couldn't live with himself. They told me that he killed a girl and a boy, after the boy seemed about to pull a weapon on him. They couldn't explain why the girl had also died. I guess there was no explanation, or none that could suffice.

"I never got to ask him why he did what he did, but I might have understood it a little," said my grandfather. "You see, I have some of that sadness too, and so do you. I've fought it all my life. I wasn't going to let it take me the way that it took my mother, and you're not going to let it take you either."

He gripped my hand tighter. A look of confusion passed across his face. He stopped talking and narrowed his eyes, trying desperately to remember what it was that he wanted to say.

"The sadness," I said. "You were talking about the sadness."

His face relaxed. I saw a single tear break from his right eye and slip gently down his cheek.

"It's different in you," he said. "It's harsher, and some of it comes from outside, from another place. We didn't pass it on to you. You brought it with you. It's part of you, part of your nature. It's old and—"

He gritted his teeth, and his body shook as he fought for those last minutes of clarity.

"They have *names*."

The words were forced out, spit from his system, ejected like tumors from within.

"They have names," he repeated, and his voice was different now, harsh and filled with a desperate hatred. For an instant he was transformed, and he was no longer my grandfather but another being, one that had taken hold of his ailing, fading spirit and briefly reenergized it in order to communicate with a world it could not otherwise reach. "All of them, they have names, and they're here. They've always been here. They love hurt and pain and misery, and they're always searching, always looking.

"And they'll find you, because it's in you as well. You have to *fight* it. You can't be like them, because they'll want you. They've always wanted you."

He had somehow raised himself from his bed, but now he fell back, exhausted. He released his grip, leaving the imprint of his fingers on my skin.

"They have names," he whispered, the disease surging forward like ink clouding clear water and turning it to black, claiming all of his memories for its own.

I dropped Walter back at the house and played my unheard messages for the first time. The walk had cleared my head, and the time spent tending to the grave had brought me a little peace, even as it had reminded me of why Neddo's words about the names of the Believers had seemed familiar to me. It might also have been the fact that I had come to a kind of decision, and there was no point in agonizing any longer.

None of the messages came from Rachel. One or two contained offers of work. I deleted them. The third was from Assistant SAC Ross's secretary in New York. I called her back, and she told me that Ross was out of the office, but promised to contact him in order to let him know that I'd called. Ross got back to me before I had time to make a sandwich. It sounded like he was in a restaurant or a bar. I could hear dishes banging behind him, the tinkling of china against crystal, and people talking and laughing as they ate.

"What was the big hurry with Bosworth, if it was going to take you half a day to call back?" he asked.

"I've been distracted," I said. "Sorry."

The apology seemed to throw Ross.

"I'd ask if you were doing okay," he said, "but I wouldn't want you to start thinking that I cared."

"It's okay. I'd just view it as a moment of weakness."

"So, you still interested in this thing?"

It took me a while to reply.

"Yes," I said. "I'm still interested."

"Bosworth wasn't my responsibility. He wasn't a field agent, so he fell under the remit of one of my colleagues."

"Which one?"

"Mr. 'That Doesn't Concern You.' Don't push it. It doesn't matter. Under the circumstances, I might have dealt with Bosworth the same way that he did. They put him through the process."

"The process" was the name given to the Feds' unofficial method for dealing with agents who stepped out of line. In serious cases, like whistleblowing, efforts were first made to discredit the agent involved. Fellow agents would be given access to the personnel file for the individual involved. Colleagues would be questioned about the agent's habits. If the agent had gone public with something, potentially damaging personal information might in turn be leaked to the press. The FBI had a policy of not firing whistleblowers, as there was a danger that by doing so the Bureau might lend credence to the individual's accusations. Hounding a recalcitrant agent, and smearing his or her name, was far more effective.

"What did he do?" I asked Ross.

"Bosworth was a computer guy, specializing in codes and cryptography. I can't tell you much more than that, partly because I'd have to kill you if I did, but mostly because I can't explain it to you anyway, since I don't understand it. It seems he was doing a little personal work on the side, something to do with maps and manuscripts. It earned him a reprimand from OPR"—the Office of Professional Responsibility was in charge of investigating allegations of misconduct within the FBI—"but it didn't go to a disciplinary hearing. That was about a year ago. Anyway, Bosworth took some leave after that, and next thing he popped up in Europe, in a French jail. He was arrested for desecrating a church."

"A church?"

"Technically, a monastery: Sept-Fons Abbey. He was caught digging up the floor of a vault in the dead of night. The legate in Paris got involved, and managed to keep Bosworth's background out of the papers. He was suspended with pay when he returned, and ordered to seek professional help, but he wasn't monitored. He came back to work in the same week that an interview with an 'unnamed FBI agent' appeared in some UFO magazine alleging that the Bureau was preventing a proper investigation of cult activities in the United States. It was clearly Bosworth again, burbling some nonsense about linked crypts and codified map references. The Bureau decided that it wanted him gone, so he was put through the process. His security clearance was downgraded, then pretty much removed entirely, apart from allowing him to switch on his computer and play with Google. He was shifted to duties beneath his abilities, given a desk beside a men's room in the basement, and virtually cut off from contact with his colleagues, but he still wouldn't break."

"And?"

"In the end, he was given the option of a 'fitness for duty' examination at the Pearl Heights Center in Colorado."

Fitness for duty examinations were the kiss of death for an agent's career. If the agent refused to submit to one, he or she was automatically fired. If the agent submitted, then a diagnosis of mental instability was frequently the outcome, decided long before the agent even arrived at the testing center. The evaluations were carried out in medical facilities with special contracts to examine federal employees, and usually stretched over three or four days. Subjects were kept isolated, apart from their interactions with medical personnel, and required to answer up to six hundred yes-or-no questions. If they weren't already crazy when they went in, the process was designed to make them crazy by the time they left.

"Did he take the test?"

"He traveled to Colorado, but he never made it to the center. He was automatically dismissed."

"So where is he now?"

"Officially, I have no idea. Unofficially, he's in New York. It seems that his parents have money, and they own an apartment up on First and Seventieth in a place called the Woodrow. Bosworth lives there, as far as anyone can tell, but he's probably a basket case. We haven't been in contact with him since his dismissal. So now you know, right?"

"I know not to join the FBI and then start dismantling churches."

"I don't even like you walking by the building, so recruitment is hardly a concern for you. This stuff didn't come for free. If Bosworth is tied in with this thing in Williamsburg, then I want a heads-up."

"That's fair."

"Fair? You don't know from fair. Just remember: I want to be informed first if Bosworth smells bad on this."

I promised to get back to him if I found out anything he should know. It seemed to satisfy him. He didn't say good-bye before he hung up, but he didn't say anything hurtful either.

The most recent call was from a man named Matheson. Matheson was a former client of mine. Last year, I'd looked into a case involving the house in which his daughter had died. I couldn't say that it had ended well, but Matheson had been satisfied with the outcome.

His message said that someone was making inquiries about me, and had approached him for a recommendation, or so they claimed. The visitor, a man named Alexis Murnos, said he was calling on behalf of his employer, who wished to remain anonymous for the present. Matheson had a highly developed sense of suspicion, and he gave Murnos as little to go on as possible. All he could get out of Murnos, who declined to leave a contact number, was that his employer was wealthy and appreciated discretion. Matheson asked me to call him back when I got the message.

"I wasn't aware that you'd added discretion to your list of accomplishments," Matheson said, once his secretary had put me through to him. "That's what made me suspicious."

"And he gave you nothing?"

"Zilch. I suggested that he contact you himself, if he had any concerns. He told me that he would, but then said that he'd appreciate it if I kept his visit strictly between the two of us. Naturally, I called you as soon as he left."

I thanked Matheson for the warning, and he told me to let him know if there was anything more that he could do. As soon as we were done, I called the offices of the *Press Herald* and left a message there for Phil Isaacson, the paper's art critic, once they'd confirmed that he was due in later that day. It was a long shot, but Phil's expertise extended from architecture to law and beyond, and I wanted to talk to him about House of Stern and the auction that was due to take place there. That reminded me that I had not yet heard back from Angel or Louis. It was a situation that was unlikely to last very much longer.

I decided to drive into Portland to kill some time until I heard from Phil Isaacson. Maybe tomorrow I would leave Walter with my neighbors and return to New York, in the hope that I might be able to get in touch with former special agent Bosworth. I set the alarm system in the house, and left Walter half-asleep in his basket. I knew that as soon as I was gone he would make a beeline for the couch in my office, but I didn't care. I was grateful to have him around, and his hairs on the furniture seemed like a small return for the company.

"They all have names."

My grandfather's words came back to me as I drove, now echoing not only Neddo but also Claudia Stern.

"Two hundred angels rebelled . . . Enoch gives the names of nineteen."

Names. There was a Christian bookstore in South Portland. I was pretty certain that they'd have a section on the apocrypha. It was time to take a look at Enoch.

The car, a red 5 Series BMW, picked me up at Route I and stayed with me when I left the highway for Maine Mall Road. I pulled into the parking lot in front of Panera Bread and waited, but the car, with two men inside, headed on by. I gave them five minutes, then moved out of the lot, keeping an eye on my rearview mirror as I drove. I saw the BMW parked over by the Dunkin' Donuts but it didn't try to follow me this time. Instead, after making a couple of loops of the area, I spotted its replacement. This time the BMW was blue, and it had only one man in the front, but it was clear that I was the object of his attentions. I almost felt resentful. Twin BMWs: these guys were being hired by the hour, and being paid cheap. Part of me was tempted to confront them, but I wasn't sure that I'd be able to control my temper, which meant there was a good chance that things could end badly. Instead I made a call. Jackie Garner answered on the first ring.

"Hey, Jackie," I said. "Want to break some heads?"

*   *   *

I sat in my car outside Tim Horton's doughnut shop. The blue BMW was in the Maine Mall's lot, across the street, while its red sibling waited in the parking lot of the Sheraton. One at each side of the road. It was still amateurish, but it showed promise.

My cell phone rang.

"How you doing, Jackie?"

"I'm at the Best Buy."

I looked up. I could see Jackie's van idling in the fire lane.

"It's a blue BMW, Mass. plates, maybe three rows in. He'll move when I move."

"Where's the other car?"

"Over by the Sheraton. It's a red BMW. Two men."

Jackie seemed confused.

"They're using the same badge?"

"Same model, just a different color."

"Dumb."

"Kind of."

"What are you going to do?"

"Let them come, I guess. We'll deal with them. Why?"

I got the sense that Jackie had an alternative solution.

"Well," he said, "you see, I brought some friends. Do you want this done quietly?"

"Jackie, if I wanted it done quietly, would I have called you?"

"That's what I thought."

"So who did you bring along?"

He tried to avoid the question, but I pinned him down.

"Jackie, tell me: who did you bring?"

"The Fulcis." He sounded vaguely apologetic.

Dear God: the Fulci brothers. They were mooks for

hire, twin barrels of muscle and flab with more chips on their shoulders than all the employees of the Frito company put together. Even the "for hire" part was misleading. If the situation offered sufficient scope for mayhem, the Fulcis would happily offer their services for free. Tony Fulci, the elder of the two brothers, held the record for being the most expensive prisoner ever to have been jailed in Washington State, calculated on a length-of-stay basis. Tony did some time there at the end of the nineties, when a lot of prisons were hiring out their inmates to large corporations to do telesales and call-center work. Tony was given a job phoning people on behalf of a new ISP named FastWire, asking its rivals' customers to consider switching service from their current provider to the new kid on the block. The sum total of Tony Fulci's only conversation with a customer went pretty much as follows:

Tony (reading slowly from an idiot card): *I am calling on behalf of FastWire Comm—*
Customer: *I'm not interested.*
Tony: *Hey, let me finish.*
Customer: *I told you: I'm not interested.*
Tony: *Listen, what are you, stupid? This is a good deal.*
Customer: *I told you, I don't want it.*
Tony: *Don't you hang up that phone. You hang up that phone and you're a dead man.*
Customer: *You can't talk to me like that.*
Tony: *Hey, fuck you! I know who you are, I know where you live, and when I get out of here in five months and three days, I'm gonna look you up, and then I'm gonna tear*

you limb from limb. Now, you want this
piece-of-shit deal, or not?

FastWire quickly abandoned its plans to extend the use of prisoners as callers, but not quickly enough to prevent it from being sued. Tony cost Washington's prisons $7 million in lost contracts once the FastWire story got around, or $1.16 million for every month Tony was incarcerated. And Tony was the calm one in the family. All things considered, the Fulcis made the Mongol hordes look restrained.

"You couldn't have found anyone more psychotic?"

"Maybe, but they would have cost more."

There was no way out of it. I told him I'd head toward Deering Avenue and try to draw the solo tail away, with Jackie following. The Fulcis could intercept the other guys wherever they chose.

"Give me two minutes," said Jackie. "I just gotta tell the Fulcis. Man, they're juiced. You don't know what this means to them, getting to do some real detective work. Tony just wished you could have given him a little more notice. He would've come off his meds."

The Fulcis didn't have to go far to take the red BMW. They simply blocked it off in the Sheraton's lot by parking their truck behind it. The Fulcis drove a customized Dodge 4X4 inspired by the monster-truck DVDs that they watched when they weren't making other people's lives more interesting in a Chinese way.

The BMW's doors opened. The driver was a clean-shaven, middle-aged man in a cheapish gray suit that made him look like an executive for a company that was struggling to make ends meet. He weighed maybe

150, or roughly half a Fulci. His companion was bigger and swarthier, possibly bringing their combined weight up to a Fulci and a quarter, or a Fulci and a half if Tony was abusing his diet pills. The Fulcis' Dodge had smoked glass windows, so the guy in the suit could almost have been forgiven for what he said next.

"Hey," he said, "get that fucking tin can out of the way. We're in a hurry here."

Nothing happened for about fifteen seconds, while the Fulcis' primitive, semimedicated brains tried to equate the words they'd heard spoken with their own vision of their beloved truck. Eventually, the door on the driver's side opened, and a very large, very irate Tony Fulci jumped gracelessly from the cab to the ground. He wore a polyester golf shirt, elastic-waisted pants from a big-man store, and steel-toed work boots. His belly bulged under his shirt, the sleeves of which stopped above his enormous biceps, the material insufficiently Lycraed to make the stretch demanded of it by his pumped arms. Twin arcs of muscle reached from his shoulders to just below his ears, their symmetry undisturbed by the intrusion of a neck, giving him the appearance of a man who had recently been force-fed a very large coat hanger.

His brother Paulie joined him. He made Tony look a little on the dainty side.

"Jesus Christ," said the BMW's driver.

"Why?" said Tony. "Does he drive a fucking tin can as well?"

Then the Fulcis went to work.

The blue BMW stayed with me all the way to Deering Avenue, hanging back two or three cars but always keeping me in sight. Jackie Garner was right behind him all the way. I had picked the route because it was guaranteed to confuse anyone who wasn't a native, and the fact that he was still within the Portland city limits, instead of being led into open country, would make the tail less likely to believe that he had been spotted and was about to be confronted. I reached the point where Deering becomes one-way, just before the intersection with Forest, forcing all traffic heading out of town to make a right. I brought the tail with me as I turned, then went left on to Forest, left again back on to Deering, and took a hard right to Revere. The BMW had no choice but to stick with me all the way or risk being dumped, so that when I braked suddenly he had to do the same. When Jackie shot in behind him he realized what was happening. There was no other option for the BMW except to try to use the bread company's lot to buy himself some space and time. He pulled in fast and we came at him in a V, trapping him against the wall.

I kept my gun tight against my body as I approached. I didn't want to scare anyone who might happen by. The driver kept his wrists on the wheel, his fingers slightly raised. He wore a baggy blue suit with a matching tie. The wire of his cell phone earpiece was clipped to the lapel of his jacket. He was probably having trouble raising his buddies.

I nodded to Jackie. He had a little snub-nose Browning in his right hand. He kept it fixed on the driver as he opened the door.

"Get out," I said. "Do it slowly."

The driver did as he was told. He was tall and balding, with black hair that was just a little too long to look good.

"I'm not armed," he said.

Jackie pushed him against my car and frisked him anyway. He came up with a wallet, and a .38 from an ankle holster.

"What's this?" said Jackie. "Soap?"

"You shouldn't tell lies," I said. "They'll turn your tongue black."

Jackie tossed me the wallet. Inside was a Massachusetts driver's license, identifying the man before us as one Alexis Murnos. There were also some business cards in his name for a company named Dresden Enterprises, with offices in the Prudential in Boston. Murnos was the head of corporate security.

"I hear you've been asking questions about me, Mr. Murnos. It would have been a lot easier to approach me directly."

Murnos didn't reply.

"Find out about his friends," I told Jackie.

Jackie stepped back to make a call on his cell. Most of it consisted of "uh-huh's" and "yeahs," apart from one worrying interjection of "Jesus, it broke that easy? Guy must have brittle bones."

"The Fulcis have them in the bed of their truck," he told me when he was done. "They're rent-a-cops from some security agency in Saugus. Tony says he thinks they'll stop bleeding soon."

If Murnos was troubled by the news, he didn't show it. I had a feeling that Murnos was probably better at his job than the other two jokers, but somebody had asked him to do too much too quickly, and with limited resources. It seemed like time to prick his professional pride.

"You're not very good at this, Mr. Murnos," I said.

"Corporate security at Dresden Enterprises must leave a little something to be desired."

"We don't even know what Dresden Enterprises is," said Jackie. "He could be responsible for guarding chickens."

Murnos sucked air in through his teeth. He had reddened slightly.

"So," I said, "are you going to tell me what this is about, maybe over a cup of coffee, or do you want us to take you to meet your friends? It sounds like they're going to need a ride home, eventually, and maybe some medical attention. I'll have to leave you with the gentlemen who are currently looking after them, but it'll only be for a day or two until I find out more about the company you're working for. That will mean paying a visit to Dresden Enterprises, possibly with a couple of people in tow, which could be very professionally embarrassing for you."

Murnos considered his options. They were kind of limited.

"I guess coffee sounds good," he said, finally.

"See?" I said to Jackie. "That was easy."

"You got a way with people," said Jackie. "We didn't even have to hit him."

He sounded mildly disappointed.

It transpired that Murnos was actually empowered to tell me a certain amount, and to deal with me directly. He just preferred to sneak around until he was certain of all the angles. In fact, he admitted that he had amassed a considerable quantity of information on me without ever leaving his office, and he had partly guessed that Matheson would contact me. If the worse came to the worst, as it just had, he would then get a chance to see what I did when my feathers were ruffled.

"My colleagues aren't really bleeding in the back of a truck, are they?" he asked. We were sitting at a table in Big Sky. It smelled good in there. Behind the counter, the kids who did the baking were cleaning down baking trays and freshening the coffee.

I exchanged a guilty look with Jackie. He was eating an apple scone, his second.

"I'm pretty certain that they are," I said.

"The guys that took care of them, they ain't too particular about these things," said Jackie. "Plus one of your people said something insensitive about their truck."

I was grateful to Jackie for all that he'd done, but it was time to get him out of the way. I asked him to find the Fulcis and make sure they didn't inflict any further damage on anyone. He bought them a bag of scones and went on his way.

"You have interesting friends," said Murnos, once Jackie was gone.

"Believe me, you haven't even met the most entertaining ones. If you have anything to share with me, then now's the time."

Murnos sipped his coffee.

"I work for Mr. Joachim Stuckler. He is the CEO of Dresden Enterprises. Mr. Stuckler is a venture capitalist specializing in software and multimedia."

"So he's wealthy?"

"Yes, I think that would be a fair comment."

"If he's wealthy, why does he hire cheap labor?"

"That was my fault. I needed men to help me, and I'd used those two before. I didn't expect them to be beaten for their trouble. Neither did I expect to be cornered in a parking lot and relieved of my weapon by someone who then offered to buy me coffee and a scone."

"It's been one of those days for you."

"Yes, it has. Mr. Stuckler is also a collector of note. He has the wealth to indulge his tastes."

"What does he collect?"

"Art, antiques. Arcane material."

I could see where this was leading.

"Such as little silver boxes from the fifteenth century?"

Murnos shrugged. "He is aware that you were the one who found the remains in the apartment. He believes that your case may impinge upon something of interest to him. He would like to meet you to discuss the matter further. If you were free, he would appreciate a few hours of your time. Naturally, he will pay you for your trouble."

"Naturally, except I'm not really in the mood for a trip to Boston."

Murnos shrugged again.

"You were looking for a woman," he said matter-of-factly. "Mr. Stuckler may be able to provide you with some information on those responsible for her disappearance."

I glanced over at the kids behind the counter. I wanted to hit Murnos. I wanted to beat him until he told me all that he knew. He saw that desire in my face.

"Believe me, Mr. Parker, my knowledge of this affair is limited, but I do know that Mr. Stuckler had nothing to do with whatever happened to the woman. He merely learned that you were the one who killed Homero

Garcia and discovered human remains in his apartment. He is also aware of the opening of the chamber in the basement of the building. I made some inquiries on his behalf, and discovered that your interest lay in the woman. Mr. Stuckler is happy to share whatever insights he may have with you."

"And in return?"

"You may be able to fill some gaps in his own knowledge. If you cannot, then Mr. Stuckler is still willing to talk with you, and to tell you whatever he feels may be of help to you. It is a win-win situation for you, Mr. Parker."

Murnos recognized that I had no choice, but he had the decency not to gloat. I agreed to meet with his employer over the next couple of days. Murnos confirmed the arrangement in a cell phone conversation with one of Stuckler's assistants, then asked me if it was okay if he left. I thought it was nice of him to ask, until I realized that he was only looking for his gun back. I accompanied him outside, emptied the bullets down a drain, and handed the gun to him.

"You should get another gun," I said. "That one isn't much use to you on your ankle."

Murnos's right hand flexed, and I was suddenly looking down the barrel of a Smith & Wesson Sigma .380, four inches tall and a pound in weight.

"I *have* another gun," he said. "It looks like I'm not the only one who hires cheap."

He kept the muzzle trained on me for just a second longer than necessary before allowing it to disappear back into the folds of his coat. He smiled at me, then got into his car and drove away.

Murnos was right. Jackie Garner was a lunkhead,

but not as big a lunkhead as the guy who employed him.

I drove back toward Scarborough, stopping off first at the Bible store. The woman behind the counter was happy to help me, and seemed only slightly disappointed when I didn't add some little silver angel statues or a "My Guardian Angel Says You're Too Close" bumper sticker to my purchase of two books on the apocrypha.

"We sell a lot of those," she told me. "There's a heap of folks who think that the Catholic Church has been hiding something all these years."

"What could they be hiding?" I asked, despite myself.

"I don't know," she said, speaking slowly as she would to an idiot child, "because it's *hidden*."

I left her to it. I sat in my car and flicked through the first of the books, but there wasn't much that was of use to me. The second was better, as it contained the entire Book of Enoch. The names of the fallen angels appeared in chapter 7, and as Claudia Stern had said, Ashmael's was among them. I glanced quickly through the rest of the book, much of which seemed fairly allegorical in nature, apart from the early descriptions of the angels' banishment and fall. According to Enoch, they were not subject to death, even after they fell, and nor would they ever be forgiven for all that they had done. Instead, the fallen angels set about teaching men to make swords and shields, and lecturing them on astronomy and the movements of the stars, "so that the world became altered . . . And men, being destroyed, cried out." There were also some details about the Greek theologian Origen, who was anathematized for suggesting that the angels who fell were those "in whom the divine love had grown cold" and that they were then "hidden in gross bodies such as ours, and have been called men."

I saw again the painting in Claudia Stern's work-shop; the figure of the Captain; the bloody grapnel on the dead monks' robes; and the grossest figure of all—the fat, distorted creature marching by his leader's side, all bloodied and grinning with the joy of killing.

I picked up a sandwich at Amato's on Route I and filled up on gas before heading east for home. At the pump beside me, two men, one bearded and overweight, the other younger and trimmer, were consulting a map in their grimy black Peugeot. The bearded man was wear-ing a gray hand-knitted sweater. A clerical collar was visible at his neck. They didn't pay me any attention, and I didn't offer them any help.

As I drew near my house, I saw a car parked in front of the driveway. It wasn't quite blocking me, but it would be difficult to go around it without slowing down. A man was leaning against the hood, and the weight of his body had forced the front of the car down so far that the fender was on the verge of nuzzling the ground. He was taller than I by five or six inches, and massively, obesely overweight, shaped like a great egg, with a huge wad of fat at his belly that hung down over his groin and lapped at his thighs. His legs were very short, so short that his arms appeared longer than they. His hands, far from being flabby and awkward, were slim and almost delicate, although the wrists were heavy and swollen. Taken together, the various parts of his body appeared to have been inexpertly assembled from a variety of donors, as though a young Baron Frankenstein had been let loose in his toy box with the leftovers from a massacre at Weight Watchers. He wore plain black shoes on small feet, and tan trousers that had been altered at the legs to fit, the ends folded inside and inexpertly stitched, making it possible to judge the extent of the alterations by the circle of holes halfway up his shins. The swelling at his stomach was too big, or too uncomfortable, to encompass, so the waistband of the trousers ran underneath it, thereby allowing it to hang free beneath his billowing white shirt. The shirt was buttoned right to the neck, constricting it to such an extent that the circle of flab concealing the collar was a violent reddish purple in color, like the terrible discoloration that occurs in a corpse when the blood has gathered at the extremities. I could see no hint of a jacket under his brown camel-hair overcoat. There were buttons missing from the front, possibly after some futile and ultimately doomed attempt to close it. His head balanced finely on the layered fats of his neck, narrowing from a very round skull to a small, distinctly weak chin, an inverted sparrow's egg atop the larger ostrich egg of his body. His features should have been lost in jowls and flab, sunken into them like a child's drawing of the man in the moon. Instead, they retained their definition, losing themselves only as they drew nearer his neck. His eyes were closer to gray than green, as though capable only of a monochrome version of human sight, and no lines extended from them. He had long eyelashes, and a thin nose that flared slightly at the end, exposing his nostrils. His mouth was small and feminine, with something almost sensual about the curvature of the lips. He had small ears with very pronounced lobes. His head was closely shaved but his hair was very dark, so that it was easy to discern the imprint of the faded widow's peak above his forehead. His resemblance to the foul creature in the painting at Claudia Stern's auction house was startling. This man was fatter, perhaps, and his features more worn, but it was still as though the figure with the bloodied mouth had detached himself from the canvas and assumed a new existence in this world.

I stopped my Mustang a short distance from him. I preferred not to draw up alongside him. He didn't move as I stepped from my car. His hands remained clasped below his chest, resting upon the first swelling of his belly.

"Can I help you?" I said.

He thought about the question.

"Perhaps," he said.

His washed-out eyes regarded me. He did not blink. I felt a further slight glimmer of recognition, this time more personal, as when one hears a song playing on the radio, one that dates from one's earliest childhood and is recalled only on the faintest of levels.

"I don't usually conduct business at my home," I said.

"You don't have an office," he replied. "You make yourself difficult to find, for an investigator. One might almost suspect that you didn't want to be traced."

He moved away from his car. He was strangely grace-ful, seeming almost to skate across the ground rather than to walk. His hands remained clasped on his belly until he was only a couple of feet away from me, then his right hand extended toward me.

"Let me introduce myself," he said. "My name is Brightwell. I believe we have matters to discuss."

As his hand moved through the air, the sleeve of his coat dangled loosely, and I glimpsed the beginnings of a mark upon his arm, like twin arrowheads recently burned into the flesh. Immediately I backed away, and my hand moved for the gun beneath my jacket, but he was faster than I, so fast that I barely saw him move. One moment there was space between us, the next there was none, and he was pressed hard against me, his left hand digging into my right forearm, the nails tearing through the fabric of my coat and into my skin, drawing blood from the flesh. His face touched mine, his nose brushing against my cheek, his lips an inch from my mouth. Sweat dropped from his brow and fell upon my lips before slowly dripping onto my tongue. I tried to spit it away but it congealed inside, coating my teeth and adhering to the roof of my mouth like gum, its force so strong that it snapped my mouth closed, causing me to bite the tip of my tongue. His own lips parted, and I saw that his teeth came to slightly blunted points, as though they had gnawed too long on bone.

"Found," he said, and I smelled his breath. It smelled of sweet wine and broken bread.

I felt myself falling, tumbling through space, overcome by shame and sorrow and a sense of loss that would never end, a denial of all that I loved that would stay with me through all eternity. I was aflame, screaming and howling, beating at the fires with my fists, but they would not be extinguished. My whole being was alive with burning. The heat coursed through my veins. It animated my muscles. It gave form to my speech and light to my eyes. I twisted in the air and saw, far below, the waters of a great ocean. I glimpsed my own burning shape reflected in them, and others beside me.

This world was dark, but we would bring light to it.

Found.

And so we fell like stars, and at the moment of impact I wrapped the tattered remnants of charred black wings around me, and the fires went out at last.

I was being dragged somewhere by the collar of my jacket. I didn't want to go. I had trouble keeping my eyes open, so that the world drifted between darkness and half-light. I heard myself speaking, muttering the same words over and over.

"Forgive me. Forgive me. Forgive me."

I was almost at Brightwell's car. It was a big blue Mercedes, but the backseat had been removed to enable him to push back the driver's seat and give him room to move. The car stank of meat. I tried to fight him but I was weak and disoriented. I felt drunk, and the taste of sweet wine was upon my tongue. He opened the trunk, and it was filled with burning flesh. My eyes closed for the last time.

And a voice called my name.

"Charlie," it said. "How have you been? I hope we're not interrupting."

I opened my eyes.

I was still standing at the open door of my Mustang. Brightwell had moved a few steps from his car, but had not yet reached me. To my right was the black Peugeot, and the bearded man with the clerical collar had jumped from the car and was now pumping my hand furiously.

"It's been a long time. We had some trouble finding this place, let me tell you. I never thought that a city boy like you would end up out in the boonies. You remember Paul?"

The younger man stepped around the hood of the

Peugeot. He was careful not to turn his back on the huge figure watching us from a short distance away. Brightwell seemed uncertain of how to proceed, then turned around, got in his car, and drove in the direction of Black Point. I tried to make out the license plate, but my brain was unable to make sense of the numbers.

"Who are you?" I said.

"Friends," said the bearded priest.

I looked down at my right hand. There was blood dripping from my fingers. I rolled up my sleeve and saw five deep puncture wounds upon my arm.

I stared at the road ahead, but the Mercedes was gone from sight.

The priest handed me a handkerchief to stem the bleeding.

"On the other hand," he said, "that was definitely *not* a friend."

IV

I tell them there is no forgiveness,
and yet there is always forgiveness.

Michael Collins (1890–1922)

17

We sat around the kitchen table while the marshes prepared to flood, waiting for the coming of the tides that would bring with them death and regeneration. Already the air felt different; there was a stillness to nature, a watchfulness, as though every living thing that depended on the marshes for its existence was attuned to its rhythms and knew instinctively what was about to occur.

I cleaned out the cuts on my arm, although I could not quite trace the chain of events that led to my receiving them. I still had a sense of vertigo, a dizziness that left me feeling uncertain on my feet, and I could not rinse the taste of sweet wine from my mouth.

I offered my visitors coffee, but they expressed a preference for tea. Rachel had left some herbal tea behind the instant coffee. It smelled a little like someone had taken a leak in a rosebush. The bearded cleric, who introduced himself as Martin Reid, winced slightly when he tasted it, but he persevered. Clearly, those years spent following his vocation had endowed him with a degree of inner strength.

"How did you find me?" I asked.

"It wasn't too hard to connect you to the events in Brooklyn," he said. "You make quite an impression wherever you go. We learned a little more about you from Mr. Neddo in New York."

Neddo's involvement with these men was a surprise. I had to confess that Neddo now unconditionally gave me the creeps. I couldn't deny that he had an extensive knowledge of certain matters, but the pleasure that he derived from it was troubling. Being around him was like keeping company with a semi-reformed addict whose ambition to stay clean was not as urgent as his love for the narcotic.

"I think Mr. Neddo may be morally suspect," I said. "You may become tainted by association."

"We are all flawed in our own way."

"Maybe, but my closet isn't filled with Chinese skulls fresh from the executioner's gun."

Reid conceded the point.

"Admittedly, I try not to delve too deeply into his acquisitions. He is, nevertheless, a useful source of information, and you have reason to be grateful to him for informing us of your visit to him, and of the path that your investigation is following. The gentleman on the road didn't look best pleased by our intrusion into his business. If we hadn't arrived when we did, it could have turned very ugly. Or in his case, uglier."

"He certainly isn't a looker," I conceded.

Reid gave up on his tea. "That's terrible," he said. "I'll still be tasting that on the day I die."

I apologized once again.

"The man on the road told me that his name was Brightwell," I said. "I think you know a little more than that about him."

The younger priest, who had introduced himself as Paul Bartek, looked to his colleague. They were both Cistercian monks, based in Europe but staying for the present in a monastery in Spencer. Reid had a Scottish accent, but Bartek's was harder to identify: there were traces of French and American English, as well as something more exotic.

"Tell me what happened on the road," said Reid. "What did you feel?"

I tried to recall the sensations I had experienced. The memory seemed to intensify my nausea, but I persevered.

"One minute he seemed to be leaning against his car, and the next he was right in my face," I said. "I could taste his breath. It tasted like wine. Then he was gripping my arm and dragging me toward his car. He made those cuts on my arm. The trunk opened, and it looked like a wound. It was made of flesh and blood, and it stank."

Reid and Bartek exchanged a look.

"What?" I said.

"We could see both of you as we approached," said Bartek. "He never moved. He didn't touch you."

I displayed the cuts for them.

"Yet I have these."

"That you do," said Reid. "There's no denying it. Did he say anything to you?"

"He said that I was hard to track down, and that we had matters to discuss."

"Anything else?"

I remembered the sensation of falling, of burning. I did not want to share it with these men because it brought with it a sense of great shame and regret, but something told me that they were trustworthy, even good, and that they were ready to provide answers to some of the questions that I had.

"There was a sense of vertigo, of descending from a

great height. I was burning, and there were others burning around me. I heard him speak as he was dragging me to the car, or as I thought he was."

"What did he say?"

"'Found.' He said I was found."

If Reid was surprised by this, then he kept it hidden well. Bartek didn't have his friend's poker features. He looked shocked.

"Is this man a Believer?" I asked.

"Why would you say that?" said Reid.

"He had a mark on his arm. It looked like a grapnel. Neddo told me that they marked themselves."

"But do you even know what a Believer is?" said Reid. There was something skeptical, almost patronizing, in his tone that I didn't care for.

I kept my voice low and even. It took a lot of effort.

"I don't like it when someone assumes my ignorance, and by implication dangles the promise of enlightenment in front of me," I said. "I don't even care for it when people tease dogs with treats, so don't overstep the mark here. I know what they're looking for, and I know what they're capable of doing to get it."

I stood and retrieved the book that I had bought in South Portland. I threw it to Reid, and he caught it awkwardly with both hands, splaying the pages. I spit a volley of words at him as he examined its pages.

"Sedlec. Enoch. Dark angels in corporeal form. An apartment with human remains yellowing in a piss-filled bath. A basement decorated with human bones, waiting for the arrival of a silver statue with a demon trapped inside it. A man who sits placidly in a burning car while his body turns to ash. And a young woman's skull, trimmed with gold, left in an alcove after she'd been murdered in a purpose-built tiled room. Are we any clearer now, Father or Brother, or whatever it is you like to be called?"

Reid had the decency to look apologetic, but I was already regretting my outburst in front of these strangers, not merely out of shame at my own loss of temper, but because I didn't want to give anything away in my anger.

"I'm sorry," said Reid. "I'm not used to dealing with private detectives. I always tend to assume that nobody knows anything, and to be honest, I'm rarely surprised."

I sat down once again at the table, and waited for him to continue.

"The Believers, or those who lead them, are convinced that they are fallen angels, banished from heaven, reborn over and over in the form of men. They feel that they are incapable of being destroyed. If they are killed, then they roam in noncorporeal form until they find another suitable host. It may take years, decades even, before they do so, but then the process begins again. If they are not killed, then they believe that they age infinitely more slowly than human beings. Ultimately, they are immortal. That is what they believe."

"And what do you believe?"

"I don't believe that they're angels, fallen or otherwise, if that's what you're asking. I used to work in psychiatric hospitals, Mr. Parker. A popular delusion among patients was that they were Napoleon Bonaparte. I'm sure that there was a good reason why they favored Bonaparte over, say, Hitler, or General Patton, but I never really cared enough to find out what that might be. It was enough to know that a forty-year-old gentleman from Pakistan who weighed two hundred pounds in his bare feet was, in all probability, not Napoleon Bonaparte; but the fact that I didn't believe he was whom he claimed to be made no difference to him. Similarly, it doesn't matter whether we go along with the convictions of the Believers or not. They believe, and they convince other weaker souls to go along with that belief. They appear particularly adept at the power of suggestion, at planting false memories in fertile ground, but they and the people with whom they surround themselves are no still less dangerous for being deluded."

But there was more to them than that. The circumstances of Alice's death provided clear evidence that these individuals were infinitely more unpleasant, and more powerful, than even Reid was prepared to acknowledge, at least here, and to me. There was also the matter of the DMT, the drug found in Alice's remains and in Garcia's body. It wasn't just force of will that bound people to them.

"What did he mean by telling me that I was 'found'?"

"I don't know."

"I don't believe you."

"That's your prerogative."

I let it go.

"What do you know about a company called Dresden Enterprises?"

It was Reid's turn to be surprised.

"I know a little. It's owned by a man named Joachim Stuckler. He's a collector."

"I'm supposed to meet him in Boston."

"He contacted you?"

"He sent one of his flying monkeys to make the arrangements. In fact, he sent three flying monkeys, but two won't be taking to the air again anytime soon. They tried to play clever too, incidentally."

Reid looked uneasy at the implied threat.

"I'd remind you that we are also stronger than we appear, and that just because we wear collars doesn't mean we won't try to defend ourselves."

"The men who stomped Stuckler's envoys are named Tony and Paulie Fulci," I said. "I don't think they're good Catholics, despite their heritage. In fact, I don't think they're good anythings, but they take a certain pride in their work. Psychotics are funny that way. I have no qualms about setting the Fulcis on you, assuming that I don't decide to make your lives difficult myself, or hand you on to someone who makes the Fulcis look like missionary workers.

"I don't know what you think is going on here, but let me explain it for you. The young woman who was killed was called Alice Temple. She was the cousin of one of my closest friends, but 'cousin' doesn't explain the obligation he feels toward her, just as 'friend' doesn't communicate the magnitude of my debt to him. We're looking for the men responsible, and we will find them. You may not care much for my threats. You may not even be troubled by the possibility of being stomped by six hundred pounds of misplaced Italian American pride. But let me tell you something: my friend Louis is infinitely less tolerant than I am, and anyone who gets in his way, or holds back information, is playing with fire, and will get badly burned.

"You seem to be looking at this like it's some kind of intellectual game with information as the forfeit, but there are lives involved, and right now I don't have time to trade with you. Either help me now or get out and accept any consequences that arise when we come looking for you again."

Bartek looked at the floor.

"I know all about you, Mr. Parker," said Reid, haltingly at first. "I know what happened to your wife and your daughter. I've read about the men and women whom you've hunted down. I also suspect that, unknowingly, you've come close to these Believers before, for you've certainly destroyed some who shared their delusions. You couldn't make the connection, and for some reason neither could they, not until recently. Perhaps it is to do with the difference between good and evil: good is selfless, while evil is always self-interested. Good will attract good to itself, and those involved will unite toward a common goal. Evil, in turn, draws evil men, but they will never truly act as one. They will always be distrustful, always jealous. Ultimately, they seek power for themselves alone, and for that reason they will always fall apart at the end."

He smiled a little sheepishly. "I'm sorry, I have a tendency to wax philosophical. It is a consequence of dealing with such matters. Anyway, I know too that you have a partner now, and a little girl. I don't see any trace of them here. There are dirty dishes in your sink, and I see in your eyes that you're troubled by things that have nothing to do with this case."

"That's none of your business," I said.

"Oh, but it is. You're vulnerable, Mr. Parker, and you're angry, and they'll exploit that. They'll use it to get at you. I don't doubt for one moment that you're prepared to hurt people who frustrate you or who get in your way. Right now, I don't think you'd even need much of an excuse to do it, but believe me when I say that we were being cautious in our answers for good reason. Maybe you're right, though. Maybe the time has come to be honest with each other. So let me begin.

"Stuckler has two faces, and two collections. One he displays to the public, and the other is entirely private. The public collection consists of paintings, sculpture, antiques, all with ironclad provenance, and above reproach in both taste and source. The second collection betrays his origins. Stuckler's father was a major in Der Führer Regiment of the Second SS Panzer Division. He was a veteran of the Russian front, and he was one of those who later carved a bloody trail through France in 1944. He was at Tulle when they hanged ninety-nine civilians from lampposts as reprisals for attacks on German forces by the Maquis, and he had gasoline on his hands after the slaughter and burning of over six hundred civilians at Oradour-sur-Glane. Mathias Stuckler followed orders, apparently without question, just as might be expected of one of the army's elite.

"His other role was as a treasure seeker for the Nazis. Stuckler had a background in art history. He was a cultured man, but as with a great many cultured men, his taste for beautiful things coexisted with a barbarous nature. He helped to loot the Hapsburg royal family's treasures from Vienna in 1938, including what some fool believed was the spear of Longinus, and he was a favorite of Himmler's. Himmler had a particular passion for the occult; after all, this was a man who sent expeditions to Tibet to seek the origins of the Aryan race, and who used slave labor to renovate Wewelsburg castle to resemble Camelot, complete with round table. Personally, I don't think Stuckler believed a word of it, but it gave him an excuse to loot and to acquire treasures for his own gratification and reward, which he set aside carefully as the opportunity arose.

"After the war, those treasures found their way to his son, and that is what we believe forms the bulk of the private collection. If the rumors are true, some of Goering's art collection has also since found its way to Joachim Stuckler's vaults. Goering attempted to send a trainload of stolen art to safety from his hunting lodge in Bavaria toward the end of the war, but the train was abandoned and the collection disappeared. A painting by François Boucher, stolen from a Paris gallery in 1943 and known to be part of Goering's trove, was quietly repatriated last year, and Stuckler was reputed to have been the source. It seems that he made inquiries about selling it, and its provenance was discovered. To avoid embarrassment, he handed it back to the French, claiming that he himself had purchased it some years earlier under a misapprehension. Stuckler has always denied the existence of a secret cache, and claims that if his father did manage to assemble such a trove of looted items — and he has publicly stated his belief that this is a lie — then its whereabouts died with his father."

"What happened to his father?"

"Mathias Stuckler was killed in 1944 during an incident at the French Cistercian monastery of Fontfroide in the Corbière Hills. The circumstances have never been fully explained, but a party of SS soldiers, a number of civilian liaisons from the University of Nuremberg, and four Cistercian monks were shot to death during a confrontation in the monastery courtyard. Stuckler was doing his master's bidding, but something unexpected occurred. In any event, the treasure at Fontfroide was denied him."

"And what was the treasure?"

"Ostensibly a valuable fourteenth-century gold crucifix, various gold coins, a quantity of gemstones, two gold chalices, and a small jeweled monstrance."

"It doesn't sound like the kind of haul that would drag the SS up a mountain in the face of an advancing enemy."

"The gold was a decoy. The real treasure lay in a nondescript silver box. It was a fragment of a coded map, one of a number placed in similar boxes during the fifteenth century and then dispersed. The knowledge contained within them has since been lost to us, which might have been for the best if the boxes too had been irretrievably lost."

"Careless of you to mislay your own statue," I said.

Reid flinched slightly, but otherwise gave no indication that my awareness of the Black Angel and the story of its creation was perhaps greater than he had anticipated.

"It wasn't an item that the order was anxious to display," said Reid. "From the beginning, there were those who said that it should be destroyed utterly."

"Why wasn't it?"

"Because, if one believes the myth of its creation, they feared that any attempt to destroy it would release what lay within. Those were more credulous times, I hasten to add. Instead, it was hidden, and the knowledge of its whereabouts dispersed to trusted abbots in the form of vellum fragments. Each fragment contains a great deal of ancillary information—illustrations, dimensions of rooms, partial accounts of the creation of the statue you mentioned—and a numerical reference alongside a single letter: either *D* or *S*, for 'dexter' or 'sinister,' right or left. They are units of measurement, all taken from a single starting point. Combined together, they are supposed to give the precise location of a vault. Stuckler was trying to assemble the map when he died, as many others before him had tried to do. The Fontfroide fragment disappeared following the attack, and has not been seen since.

"You know that the statue is rumored to lie buried in the vault. That's what Stuckler was attempting to recover, and that's what the Believers are also trying to locate. Recent developments have given their search a new impetus. A fragment of the map was found earlier this year at Sedlec, in the Czech Republic, but has since disappeared: stolen, we assume. We believe that a second went missing from a house in Brooklyn some weeks back."

"Winston's house."

"Which is how you came to be involved, for we now know that two women were present in the house when the killings occurred, and were subsequently hunted down in the belief that they were in possession of the fragment."

"That's two pieces, excluding Fontfroide."

"Three more pieces, one from Bohemia, one from Italy, and another from England, have been missing for centuries. The contents of the Italian section have long been common knowledge, but the rest are almost certainly in the wrong hands. Yesterday, we received information that a fragment, possibly the missing piece from Fontfroide, may have been acquired in Georgia.

Two veterans of World War Two were found dead in a swamp. It's not clear how they died, but both were survivors of an attack by SS soldiers near Fontfroide, the same SS soldiers who were subsequently killed at the monastery."

"Was Stuckler responsible for the deaths of the veterans?"

"He may have been, although it would be out of character for him. We believe that he has at least one fragment, and possibly more. He is certainly driven in his quest."

I couldn't see Murnos colluding in the deaths of two old men. He didn't seem like the type.

"Is Stuckler a Believer?"

"We have no evidence to suggest that he is, but they keep themselves well hidden. It is entirely possible that Stuckler is one of them, or he may even be a renegade, one who has chosen to take his chances against his fellows."

"So it could be that he's competing with them for possession of this map?"

"A fragment is due to be auctioned this week at an obscure auction house in Boston run by a woman named Claudia Stern. It is our understanding that this is the Sedlec fragment, although we cannot prove it. The map and the box went missing from Sedlec before a proper examination could be made, and their authenticity verified. We have investigated the possibility of taking legal action to stop the sale until its provenance can be determined, but we have been instructed that any such attempt would fail. We have no proof that it was taken from Sedlec, or that the Cistercian order has any claim to its ownership. Soon, all the pieces will be available for examination; and then they will go hunting for the statue."

I watched them leave as the evening grew dark and quiet. I hadn't learned as much as I had hoped, but neither had they. We were still circling one another, wary of giving too much away. I had not mentioned Sekula to Reid and Bartek, but Angel and Louis had taken on the task of checking out his office once they returned to New York. If they found out anything more, then they would tell me.

I closed the door and called Rachel on her cell. My call went straight to her message system. I thought about trying her parents' number, but I didn't want to have to deal with Frank or Joan. Instead, I walked Walter along the marshes, but when we came to a copse of trees at the farthest extreme of the woods he would go no further, and grew agitated until we turned back to the house. The moon was already visible in the sky, and it was reflected in the waters of the little pond, like the face of a drowned man hanging in its depths.

Reid and Bartek drove toward 1–95. They did not speak until they were heading south on the interstate.

"Why didn't you tell him?" asked Bartek.

"I told him enough, maybe too much."

"You lied to him. You said that you didn't know what it meant to be 'found.'"

"These people are deluded."

"Brightwell isn't like the rest. He's different. How can it be otherwise, the way he keeps reappearing, unchanged?"

"Let them believe what they want to believe, Brightwell

included. There's no point in worrying him more than he is. The man already looks weighed down by his burdens. Why should we add to them?"

Bartek stared out the window. Great mounds of earth had been torn up for the widening of the highway. Trees lay fallen, waiting to be cut up and transported. The outlines of digging equipment were visible against the darkening sky, like beasts frozen in the midst of some great conflict.

No, he thought. It's more than a delusion. It's not merely the statue that they've been seeking.

He spoke carefully. Reid had a temper, and he didn't want him sulking in the driver's seat for the rest of the journey.

"He will have to be told, regardless of any other problems he may have," he said. "They'll come back, because of who they believe he is. And they'll hurt him."

Ahead of them, the Kennebunk exit was approaching. Bartek could see the parking lot of the rest stop, and the lights of the fast food outlets. They were in the fast lane, a big rig on their inside.

"Bugger," said Reid. "I knew I shouldn't have brought you along."

He floored the accelerator, cut in front of the truck, and made the exit. Seconds later they were heading back the way that they had come.

Walter was already barking by the time their car pulled up. He had learned to respond to the warning noises from the motion sensor at the gate. Now that Rachel was gone, I had opened the gun safe and placed one gun in the hall stand and another in the kitchen. The third, the Smith 10, I tried to keep close to hand wherever I was. I watched the big priest come to the door. The younger one stayed by the car watching the road.

"Lose your way?" I said as I opened the door.

"A long time ago," said Reid. "Is there somewhere we can go to eat? I'm starving."

I took them to the Great Lost Bear. I liked the Bear. It was unpretentious and inexpensive, and I didn't want to be stiffed on a pricey meal by a pair of monks. We ordered hot wings, and burgers and fries. Reid seemed impressed by the selection of beers and went for some British import that looked like it had been bottled in the time of Shakespeare.

"So where were you stricken by remorse at your dishonesty?" I asked.

Reid shot Bartek a poisonous look.

"The voice of my bloody conscience started up somewhere beside a Burger King," he said.

"It wasn't quite the road to Damascus," said Bartek, "but then you're no Saint Paul, apart from a shared bad temper."

"As you seem aware, I wasn't entirely forthcoming about certain matters," said Reid. "My young colleague here appears to feel that we should make clear the risks that you're facing, and what Brightwell meant by your being 'found.' I stand by what I said earlier: they're deluded, and they want others to share their delusions. They can believe what they want to believe, and you don't have to go along with it, but I now accept that those beliefs can still be a threat to you.

"It goes back to the apocrypha, and the fall of the angels. God forces the rebels from heaven, and they burn in their descent. They are banished to hell, but some choose instead to wander the nascent earth, consumed by hatred of God and, eventually, the growing hordes of humanity that they see around them. They identify what they believe to be the flaw in God's creation: God has given man free will, and so he is open to evil as well as good. So the war against God continues on earth, waged through men. I suppose you could term it guerrilla warfare, in a way.

"But not all of the angels turned their backs on God. According to Enoch, there was one who repented and believed that he could still be forgiven. The others tried to hunt him down, but he hid himself among men. The salvation he sought never came, but he continued to believe in the possibility that it might be offered to him if he made reparation for all that he had done. He did not lose faith. After all, his offense was great, and his punishment had to be great in return. He was prepared to endure whatever was visited upon him in the hope of his ultimate salvation. So our friends, these Believers, are of the opinion that this last angel is still out there, somewhere, and they hate him almost as much as they hate God himself."

Found.

"They want to kill him?"

"According to their tenets, he can't be killed. If they kill him, they lose him again. He wanders, finds a new form, and the search has to start over."

"So what are their options?"

"To corrupt him, to make him despair so that he joins their ranks again; or they can imprison him forever, lock him up somewhere so that he weakens and wastes away, yet can never enjoy the release of death. He will endure an eternity of slow, living decay. An appalling thought, if nothing else."

"You see," said Bartek, "God is merciful. That is what I believe, that is what Martin believes, and that is what, according to Enoch, the solitary angel believed. God would even have forgiven Judas Iscariot, had he asked for his forgiveness. Judas wasn't damned for betraying Christ. He was damned for despairing, for rejecting the possibility that he might be forgiven for what he had done."

"I always thought Judas got a raw deal," said Reid. "Christ had to die to redeem us, and a lot of people played a part in getting Him to that point. You could argue that Judas's role was preordained, and that, in the aftermath, no man could have been expected to bear the burden of killing God without despairing. You might have thought that there would have been a little room for maneuver in God's great scheme for Judas."

I sipped at an alcohol-free beer. It didn't taste great, but I wasn't about to blame the beer for that.

"You're telling me that they think I might be this angel they've been seeking."

"Yes," said Reid. "Enoch is very allegorical, as you've surely learned by now, and there are places where the allegory bleeds into the more straightforward aspects. Enoch's creator meant the repentant angel to symbolize the hope of forgiveness that we all should hold within us, even those who have sinned most grievously. The Believers have chosen to interpret it literally, and in you they think they've found their lost penitent. They're not certain, though. That's why Brightwell tried to get close to you."

"I didn't tell you when we first met, but I think I've seen someone who looked like Brightwell before," I said.

"Where?"

"In a painting from the fifteenth century. It was in Claudia Stern's workshop. It's going to be auctioned this week, along with the box from Sedlec."

I expected Reid to scoff at my mention of a similarity to Brightwell, but he didn't.

"There's a lot that is interesting about Mr. Brightwell. If nothing else, he—or ancestors who looked startlingly like him—has been around for a long, long time."

He nodded to his companion, and Bartek began spreading upon the table pictures and photographs from a file by his feet. We were right at the rear of the Bear, and the waitress had been told that we were okay for the present, so we would be left undisturbed. I drew the first picture toward me with my finger. It was a black-and-white photograph of a group of men, most of them in Nazi uniforms. Interspersed with them were civilians. There were about twelve men in all, and they were seated outdoors at a long wooden table littered with empty wine bottles and the remains of food.

"The man at the back, on the left, is Mathias Stuckler," said Bartek. "The other men in uniform are members of the Special SS group. The civilians are members of the Ahnenerbe, the Ancestral Heritage Research and Teaching Society, incorporated into the SS in 1940. Effectively, it was Himmler's own research institute, and it was far from benign in its methods: Berger, its race expert, saw the potential for experimentation in the concentration camps as early as 1943. He spent eight days at Auschwitz that year, selecting over a hundred prisoners to measure and assess, then had them all gassed and shipped to the anatomy department at Strasbourg.

"All Ahnenerbe staff held SS rank. These are the men

who died at Fontfroide. This photograph was taken only a few days before they were killed. By this point, many of Stuckler's comrades from Der Führer Regiment had died trying to halt the Allied advance after D-Day. The soldiers with him in this picture were all that remained of his most loyal cadre. The rest ended up in Hungary and Austria, fighting alongside the flotsam of the Third Reich until the last day of the war. They were committed, albeit to the wrong cause."

There was nothing very distinctive about any of the figures in the group, although Stuckler was taller and bulkier than the rest, and a little younger. His features, though, were harsh, and the light in his eyes was long spent. I was about to lay the photograph to one side when Bartek stopped me.

"Look beyond them, to the people behind."

I examined the background. There were military men at some of the other tables, sometimes accompanied by women but more often surrounded by others of their kind. In one corner, a man sat drinking alone, a half-empty glass of wine before him. He was discreetly looking at the SS group while the photograph was being taken, so his face was partially visible.

It was Brightwell. He was marginally slimmer, and with slightly more hair, but his tumorous neck and the slightly feminine tilt to his features dispelled any doubts as to his identity.

"But this photograph was taken nearly sixty years ago," I said. "It must have been doctored."

Reid looked dubious. "It's always possible, but we think it's authentic. And even if this one is not, there are others about which there can be no doubt."

I drew the rest of the images nearer to me. Most were

black-and-white, some sepia-tinted. Many were dated, the oldest being from 1891. Frequently they depicted churches or monasteries, often with groups of pilgrims in front of them. In each photograph the specter of a man lurked, a strange, obese figure with full lips and pale, almost luminous skin.

In addition to the photographs, there was a high-quality copy of a painting, similar to the one Claudia Stern had shown to me, possibly even by the same artist. Once again, it depicted a group of men on horseback, surrounded by the clamor and violence of war. There were flames on the horizon, and all around them men were fighting and dying, their sufferings depicted in intricate and striking detail. The men on horseback were rendered distinctive by the marking on their saddles: a red grapnel. They were led by a man with long dark hair. He was dressed in a cloak, beneath which his armor could be seen. The artist had painted his eyes slightly out of scale, so that they were too large for his head. One had a white cast to it, as though the paint had been scratched to reveal the blank canvas beneath. To his right, the figure of Brightwell held a banner marked with a red grapnel in his hand. His right held the severed head of a woman by its hair

"This is like the painting that I saw," I said. "It's smaller, and the horsemen in this one are the focus, and not just an element, but it's very similar."

"This painting depicts a military action at Sedlec," said Bartek. "Sedlec is now part of the Czech Republic, and we know that, as the myth has it, this was the site of the confrontation between Immael and the monk Erdric. After some discussion, it was decided that it was too dangerous to keep the statue at Sedlec, and that it should be hidden. The fragments of vellum were dispersed, in each case entrusted only to the abbot of the monastery in question, who would share this knowledge with just one other of his community. The abbot of Sedlec was the only member of the order who knew where each box had been sent, and once they had been distributed he sent the statue on its journey to its new hiding place.

"Unfortunately, while the statue was in the process of being moved, Sedlec was attacked by the men in the painting. The abbot had succeeded in hiding the *Black Angel,* but the knowledge of its whereabouts was lost, because only he knew the monasteries to which the map fragments had been entrusted, and the abbots in question were sworn to secrecy under threat of excommunication and perpetual damnation."

"So the statue remains lost, if it ever existed?" I said.

"The boxes exist," said Reid. "We know that each contains a fragment of some kind of map. True, it may all be a great ruse, an elaborate joke on the part of the abbot of Sedlec. But if it is a joke, then he was killed for it, and a great many others have died for it since."

"Why not just let them look for it?" I said. "If it exists, they can have it. If it doesn't, they've wasted their time."

"It exists," said Reid simply. "That much, in the end, I do believe. It is its nature that I dispute, not its existence. It is a magnet for evil, but evil is reflected in it, not contained within. All of this"— he indicated the material on the table with a sweep of his hand—" is incidental. I have no explanation as to how Brightwell, or someone who resembles him to an extraordinary degree, came to be in these images. Perhaps he is part of a line, and these are all his ancestors. Whatever is the case, the Believers have killed for centuries, and now is the time to put a stop to them. They've grown careless, largely because circumstances have forced their hand. For the first time, they think they are growing close to securing all of the fragments. If we watch them, the order can identify them, and take steps against them."

"What kind of steps?"

"If we find evidence linking them to crimes, we can hand that information over to the authorities and have them tried."

"And if you don't find evidence?"

"Then it will be enough to make their identities known, and there will be others who will do what we cannot do."

"Kill them?"

Reid shrugged.

"Imprison them, perhaps, or worse. It's not for me to say."

"I thought you said they couldn't be killed."

"I said that *they* are convinced that they can't be destroyed. It's not the same thing."

I closed my eyes. This was madness.

"Now you know what we know," said Reid. "All we can ask is that you share with us any knowledge that might help us against these people. If you meet with Stuckler, I would be interested to hear from you what he had to say. Similarly, if you succeed in finding the FBI agent, Bosworth, you should tell us. In all of this, he remains an unknown."

I had told them about Bosworth on the journey into Portland. It seemed that they were already aware of him. After all, he had tried to tear apart one of their churches. Still, they did not know where he was, and I decided not to tell them that he was in New York.

"And finally, Mr. Parker, I want you to be careful," said Reid. "There is a controlling intelligence at work here, and it's not Brightwell."

He tapped his finger against the copy of the painting, allowing it to rest above the head of the armored captain with the white mark on his eye.

"Somewhere there is one who believes that he is the reincarnation of the Captain, which means that he suffers from the greatest delusion of all. In his mind, he is Ashmael, driven to seek his twin. For the present, Brightwell is curious about you, but his priority is to find the statue. Once that is secure, he will turn his attention back to you, and I don't think that will be a positive development."

Reid leaned across the table and gripped my shoulder with his left hand. His right reached into his shirt and removed from it a black-and-silver cross that hung around his neck.

"Remember, though: no matter what may happen, the answer to all things is here."

With that, he removed the cross and handed it to me. After a moment's hesitation, I took it.

I returned to my house alone. Reid and Bartek had offered to accompany me, and even to stay with me, but I politely declined. Maybe it was misplaced pride, but I didn't feel comfortable with the possibility that I needed two monks to watch my back. It seemed like a slippery slope that would eventually lead to nuns accompanying me to the gym, and the priests from Saint Maximilian's running my bathwater.

There was a car parked in my driveway when I pulled

in, and my front door was open. Walter was lying on the porch mat, happily gnawing on a marrowbone. Angel appeared behind him. Walter looked up, wagged his tail, then returned to his supper.

"I don't remember leaving the door open," I said.

"We like to think that your door is always open to us, and if it isn't, we can always open it with a pick. Plus, we know your alarm codes. We left a message on your cell."

I checked my phone. I hadn't heard it ring, but there were two messages waiting.

"I got distracted," I said.

"With what?"

"It's a long story," I said.

I listened to my messages as I walked. The first was from Angel. The second was from Ellis Chambers, the man I had turned away when he came to me about his son, the man I had advised to seek help elsewhere. His words deteriorated into sobs before he could finish telling me all that he wanted to say, but what I heard was enough.

The body of his son Neil had been found in a ditch outside Olathe, Kansas. The men to whom he owed money had finally lost their patience with him.

18

Few people now remember the name of Sam Lichtman. Lichtman was a New York cabdriver who, on March 18, 1941, was driving his yellow cab along Seventh Avenue near Times Square when he ran over a guy who suddenly stepped out in front of him at an intersection. According to the dead man's passport, his name was Don Julio López Lido, a Spaniard. In the confusion, nobody noticed that Don Julio had been talking to another man at the intersection before he made his fatal attempt to cross and that, as a curious crowd gathered in the wake of the accident, this second man picked up a brown leather briefcase lying near the body and disappeared.

The NYPD duly arrived, and discovered that Don Julio was staying in a Manhattan hotel. When the cops went to his room, they found maps, notes, and a great deal of material related to military aviation. FBI agents were called in, and as they dug deeper into the mystery of the dead Spaniard, they discovered that he was actually one Ulrich von der Osten, a captain in Nazi military intelligence, and the brains behind the main German spy network in the United States. The man who had fled the scene of the accident was Kurt Frederick Ludwig, von der Osten's assistant, and together the two men had managed to recruit eight accomplices who were passing details of military strength, shipping schedules, and industrial production back to Berlin, including the departure and arrival times of ships using New York Harbor and the numbers of Flying Fortresses being sent to England. The reports were written in invisible ink and mailed to pseudonymous recipients at fictitious foreign addresses. Letters to one "Manuel Alonzo," for example, were meant for Heinrich Himmler himself. Ludwig was subsequently arrested, he and his associates were tried in federal court in Manhattan, and they each received a sentence of up to twenty years for their troubles. Sam Lichtman, with one surge of gas, had managed to cripple the entire Nazi intelligence network in the United States.

My father told me Lichtman's story when I was a boy, and I never forgot it. I guessed that Lichtman was a Jewish name, and it seemed somehow apt that it should have been a Jew who knocked down a Nazi on Seventh Avenue in 1941, when so many of his fellows were already on cattle trains heading east. It was a small blow for his people, inadvertently struck by a man who then faded into folk memory.

Louis hadn't heard the story of Sam Lichtman, and he didn't appear very impressed with it when I told it to him. He listened without comment while I went through the events of the last couple of days, culminating in the visit from the two monks and the encounter with Brightwell on the road. When I mentioned the fat man, and Reid's interpretation of the words he had spoken to me on the road, something changed in Louis's demeanor. He seemed almost to retreat from me, withdrawing further into himself, and he avoided looking at me directly.

"And you think this might be the same guy who was

watching us when we took G-Mack?" said Angel. He was aware of the tension between Louis and me, and let me know with a slight movement of his eyes in his partner's direction that we could talk about it in private later.

"The feelings he aroused were the same," I said. "I can't explain it any other way."

"He sounds like one of the men who came looking for Sereta," said Angel. "Octavio didn't have a name for him, but there can't be too many guys like that walking the streets."

I thought of the painting in Claudia Stern's workshop, and the pictures and photographs that Reid and Bartek had shown me at the Great Lost Bear. I arranged the images in my mind in order of antiquity, progressing from paint strokes to sepia, then on to the man seated behind Stuckler's group, before finally recalling the figure of Brightwell himself, somehow reaching for me without moving, his nails cutting me without a hand being laid upon me. Each time he got a little older, his flesh a little more corrupted, that terrible, painful extrusion on his neck a little larger and more obvious. No, there could not be many such men on this earth. There could not ever have been many such men.

"So what now?" said Angel. "Sekula's dropped off the planet, and he was our best lead."

Angel and Louis had paid a visit to Sekula's building earlier in the week, and had gone through his apartment and his office. They had found virtually nothing in the office: insignificant files relating to a number of properties in the tri-state area, some fairly straightforward corporate material, and a folder marked with the name Ambassade Realty that contained just a single letter, dated two years earlier, acknowledging that Ambassade was now responsible for the maintenance and potential leasing of three warehouse buildings, including the one in Williamsburg. The apartment above the office wasn't much more revealing. There were clothes and toiletries, both male and female, which made it seem more and more likely that Sekula and the improbably named Hope were an item; some suitably anonymous books and magazines that suggested he and his mate bought all of their reading material at airports; and a kitchen filled with drearily healthy foodstuffs, along with a refrigerator entirely devoid of food of any kind, apart from long-life milk. According to Angel, it looked like someone had cherry-picked and then removed anything that might have been remotely interesting about Sekula's life and work in order to create the impression that here was one of the single most boring individuals ever to have passed a bar exam.

Louis returned the following day, and questioned the secretary who had so chirpily answered the phone to me. If she was under the impression that he was a cop when she answered his questions, then that was clearly some kind of misunderstanding on her side and nothing to do with any vagueness on Louis's part. She was simply a caretaker, hired from a temp agency and required to do nothing more than answer the phone, read her book, and file her nails. She hadn't seen Sekula or his secretary since the day she'd been hired, and the only means of communication she had for him was through an answering service. She said that some other policemen had called in to the office, following the discovery of the basement room in Williamsburg, but she could tell them nothing more than she had told

Louis. She did believe, though, that someone had visited the office after hours; she thought that some items might have been moved from the secretary's desk and the shelves behind it. It was also her final day, because the agency had called to say that she was being transferred to another job and should simply activate the answering machine before she left that evening.

"We still have Bosworth, and Stuckler," I said. "Plus, the auction is due to take place this week, and if Reid and Neddo are right, that map fragment is going to make some people break cover."

Louis stood abruptly and left the room. I looked to Angel for an explanation.

"It's a lot of things," he said. "He hasn't slept much, hasn't eaten. Yesterday they released Alice's remains for burial, and Martha took her home. He told her that he'd keep looking for the men who killed her, but she said it was too late. She said that if he thought he was doing all this for Alice, then he was lying to himself. She wasn't about to give him a dispensation to hurt someone just so he could feel better about his life. He blames himself for what happened."

"Does he blame me too?"

Angel shrugged.

"I don't think its that simple. This man, Brightwell, he knows something about you. Somehow, there's a connection between you and the man behind Alice's death, and Louis doesn't want to hear that, not now. He just needs time to work it out in his own way, that's all."

Angel took a beer from the cooler. He offered me one. I shook my head.

"It's quiet here," he said. "Have you spoken to her?"

"Briefly."

"How are they?"

"They're doing okay."

"When are they coming back?"

"After all this is over, maybe."

"Maybe?"

"You heard me."

Angel stopped drinking and poured the remainder of his beer down the sink.

"Yeah," he said quietly. "I heard."

And then he left me alone in the kitchen.

Joachim Stuckler lived in a white two-story house on an acre of waterfront property just outside Nahant, down in Essex County. The land was high-walled and protected by an electronic gate. The grounds were neatly tended, and mature shrubs masked the walls on the inside. From the front, the main house looked like an above-average dwelling, albeit one that had been decorated by drunken Greeks nostalgic for their homeland—the façade boasted more pillars than the Acropolis—but as I passed through the gate and followed the driveway I caught a glimpse of the back of the house and saw that it had been extended considerably. Large picture windows gleamed smokily in the sunlight, and a sleek white cruiser rested at a wooden jetty. The lapse of taste in decoration aside, Stuckler seemed to be doing okay financially.

The front door was already open when I pulled up in front of the house, and Murnos was waiting for me. I could tell from his expression that he wasn't one hundred percent behind his boss's decision to invite me over, but I got that a lot. I'd learned not to take it personally.

"Are you armed, Mr. Parker?" Murnos asked.

I tried to look sheepish.

"Just a little."

"We'll take care of it for you."

I handed over the Smith 10. Murnos then produced a circular wand from a drawer and wiped it over me. It beeped briefly at my watch and belt. Murnos checked to make sure I wasn't concealing anything potentially lethal in either, then led me to a living room, where a short, stocky man in a navy pinstripe suit set off by a raging pink tie stood posed by an ornate sideboard, just a few decades too late for *Life* magazine's celebrity photographers to immortalize him in glorious black-and-white. His hair was dark gray, and brushed backward from his forehead. His skin was lightly tanned and he had very white teeth. The watch on his wrist could have paid my mortgage for a year. The furnishings in the room and the art upon the walls could probably have covered the rest of Scarborough's mortgages for a year. Well, maybe not out on Prouts Neck, but most of the folk on Prouts Neck didn't need too much help with their bills.

He rose and stretched out a hand. It was a very clean hand. I felt kind of bad about shaking it, in case he was just being polite and secretly hoped that I wasn't going to sully him with any form of contact.

"Joachim Stuckler," he said. "I'm pleased to make your acquaintance. Alexis has told me all about you. His trip to Maine proved quite expensive. I will have to compensate the men who were hurt."

"You could have just called."

"I have to be—"

Stuckler paused, poised like a man in an orchard searching for a particularly ripe apple, then plucked the word from the air with a delicate hand gesture.

"—*cautious*," he concluded. "As I'm sure you're aware by now, there are dangerous men about."

I wondered if Stuckler, despite his posturing and vague effeminacy, was one of them. He invited me to take a seat, then offered me tea.

"You can have coffee, if you prefer. It's just a habit of mine to take midmorning tea."

"Tea is fine."

Murnos picked up the receiver of an old black telephone and dialed an extension. Seconds later a flunky arrived carrying a tray. He carefully set out a big china pot and two matching cups, along with a sugar bowl, milk, and a small plate of lemon slices. A second plate contained a selection of pastries. They looked crumbly and hard to eat. The cups were very delicate, and lined with gold. Stuckler poured a little tea into a cup, then allowed it to flow more freely once he was content with the color. When both cups were filled, he asked me how I preferred to take my tea.

"Black is fine," I said.

Stuckler winced slightly, but otherwise he hid his displeasure manfully.

We sipped our tea. It was all very pleasant. We just needed some dim bulb called Algy to wander in wearing tennis whites and carrying a racket and we could have been in a drawing room comedy, except that Stuckler was considerably more interesting than he appeared. Another call to Ross, this time answered a little more quickly than before, had given me some background on the neat, grinning little man before me. According to Ross's contact in the IWG — the Interagency Working Group, created in 1998 to delve into, among other things, the records relating to Nazi and Japanese war crimes in order to assess evidence of cooperation between U.S. organizations and individuals of questionable background from the former regimes — Stuckler's mother, Maria, had traveled to the United States with her only son shortly after the end of the war. The INS tried to have a great many of these people deported, but the preference in the CIA and, in particular, in Hoover's FBI was to keep them in the States so they could report back on Communist sympathizers within their own communities. The U.S. government wasn't too particular about whom it welcomed in those days: five associates of Adolf Eichmann, each of whom had played a part in the "Final Solution," worked for the CIA, and efforts were made to recruit at least a further two dozen war criminals and collaborators.

Maria Stuckler bargained her way to the States with the promise of documents relating to German Communists secured by her husband during his dealings with Himmler. She was a clever woman, delivering enough material to keep the Americans keen and, with each disclosure, getting a little closer to her ultimate goal of U.S. citizenship for her son and herself. Her citizenship application was personally approved by Hoover after she handed over the last of her store of documents, which related to various left-wing Jews who had fled Germany before the start of the war and had since found gainful employment in the United States. The IWG concluded that some of Maria Stuckler's information proved crucial in the early days of the McCarthy hearings, which made her something of a heroine in Hoover's eyes. Her "favored person" status enabled her to set up the antiques business that her son subsequently inherited, and to import objects of interest from Europe with little or no interference from U.S. Customs. The old woman was still alive, apparently. She lived in a nursing home in Rhode Island, and all of her faculties were fully intact at the age of eighty-five.

Now here I was, taking tea with her son in a room furnished and paid for with the spoils of war, if Reid was right in his assessment of Stuckler's private collection, and secured by an ambitious woman's slow process of betrayal over more than a decade. I wondered if it ever bothered Stuckler. Ross's contact had said that Stuckler was a generous contributor to a great many good causes, including a number of Jewish charities, although some had declined his largesse once the identity of the prospective donor became known. It might have been genuine pangs of conscience that led to his donations. It might also merely have been good public relations, a means of deflecting attention away from his business and his collections.

I realized that I had developed a sudden, deep-seated dislike for Stuckler, and I didn't even know him.

"I'm grateful to you for taking the time to come here," he said. He had no trace of an accent, German or otherwise. His tone was entirely neutral, contributing to the sense of an image that had been carefully cultivated to give away as little as possible about the origins and true nature of the man who lay behind it.

"With respect," I said, "I came here because your employee indicated that you might have some information. I can take tea at home."

Despite the calculated insult, Stuckler continued to radiate goodwill, as though he took great pleasure in the suspicion that everyone who came to his house secretly disliked him, and their jibes were merely honey on his bread.

"Of course, of course. I think perhaps I can help you. Before we begin, though, I am curious about the death of Mr. Garcia, in which I understand you played a significant part. I should like to know what you saw in his apartment."

I didn't know where this was leading, but I understood that Stuckler was used to bargaining. He had probably learned the skill from his mother, and applied it every day in his business dealings. I wasn't going to get anything out of him unless I gave him at least as much in return.

"There were bone sculptures, ornate candlesticks made from human remains, some other half-completed efforts, and a representation of a Mexican deity, Santa Muerte, made from a female skull."

Stuckler didn't seem interested in Santa Muerte. Instead he made me elaborate on what I had seen, questioning me about small details of construction and presentation. He then gestured to Murnos, who took a book from a side table and brought it to his employer. It was a black coffee table volume, with the words *Memento Mori* in red along the spine. On the cover was a photograph of a piece that might have come from Garcia's apartment: a skull resting upon a curved bone that jutted out like a white tongue from beneath the ruined jaw, which was missing five or six of its front teeth. Below the skull was a column of five or six similar curved bones.

Stuckler saw me looking.

"Each is a human sacrum," he said. "One can tell from the five fused vertebrae."

He flicked through fifty or sixty pages of text in a number of languages, including German and English, until he came to a series of photographs. He handed the volume to me.

"Please, take a look at these photographs and tell me if anything is familiar."

I leafed through them. All were in black-and-white, with a faint sepia tint. The first depicted a church of some kind, with three spires set in a triangular pattern. It was surrounded by bare trees, and an old stone wall separated at regular intervals by columns topped with carved skulls. The rest of the pictures showed ornate arrangements of skulls and bones beneath vaulted ceilings: great pyramids and crosses; garlands of bones and white chain; candlesticks and candelabras; and finally, another view of the church, this time taken from the rear, and in daylight. The surrounding walls were thick with ivy, but the monochrome textures of the photograph gave it the appearance of a swarm of insects, as though bees were massing along the walls.

"What is this place?" I said. Once again, there was something obscene about the photographs, about this reduction of human beings to a series of adornments to a church.

"First you have to answer my question," said Stuckler. He wagged a finger at me in reproach. I considered breaking it. I looked at Murnos. He didn't need telepathy to know what I was thinking. From the expression on his face, I imagined that a lot of people, maybe Murnos included, had thought about hurting Joachim Stuckler.

I ignored the finger and pointed instead to one small photograph of an anchor-shaped arrangement of bones set in an alcove beside a cracked wall. Seven humerus bones formed a stellate pattern with a skull at their center, supported in turn by what might have been portions of sternum or scapula, then a vertical column of more humerus bones, which met at last a semicircle of vertebrae curving upward on either side and ending in a pair of skulls.

"There was something similar to this in Garcia's apartment," I said.

"Is that what you showed to Mr. Neddo?"

I didn't answer. Stuckler snorted impatiently.

"Come, come, Mr. Parker. As I told you, I know a great deal about you and your work. I am aware that you consulted Neddo. It was natural that you should do so: after all, he is an acknowledged expert in his field. He is also, I might add, a Believer. Well, in his defense, perhaps 'was a Believer' might be more accurate. He has since turned his back on them, although I suspect that he retains a faith in some of their more obscure tenets."

This was news to me. Assuming Stuckler was telling the truth, Neddo had kept his connection to the Believers well hidden. It raised further questions about his loyalties. He had spoken to Reid and Bartek, and I could only hope that they knew of his background, but I wondered if Neddo had told Brightwell about me as well.

"What do you know about them?" I asked.

"That they are secretive and organized; that they believe in the existence of angelic, or demonic, beings; and that they are looking for the same item that I am seeking."

"The *Black Angel.*"

For the first time, Stuckler actually looked impressed. If I was a little more insecure, I might have blushed happily in the light of his approval.

"Yes, the *Black Angel,* although my desire for it is different from theirs. My father died seeking it. Perhaps you are aware of my background? Yes, I rather suspect that you are. I don't believe you are the kind of man who fails to equip himself with information before meeting a stranger. My father was a member of the SS, and part of the Ahnenerbe, Reichsführer Himmler's delvers into the occult. Most of it was nonsense, of course, but the *Black Angel* was different: it was real, or at least one could say with reasonable certainty that a silver statue of a being in the process of transformation from human to demonic existed. Such an artifact would be an adornment to any collection, regardless of its value. But Himmler, like the Believers, was of the opinion that it was more than a mere statue. He knew the tale of its creation. Such a story had a natural appeal for him. He began seeking the pieces of the map that contained the location of the statue, and it was for this reason that my father and his men were dispatched to the monastery at Fontfroide, after Himmler discovered that one of the boxes containing a map fragment was reputed to be hidden there. The Ahnenerbe boasted prodigious researchers, capable of unearthing the most obscure references. It was a dangerous errand, undertaken beneath the noses of the Allied forces, and it led to my father's death. The box disappeared, and so far, I have been unable to trace it."

He jabbed a finger at the book.

"In answer to your earlier question, this is Sedlec,

where the *Black Angel* came into being. That is why Garcia was working on his bone sculptures: he was commissioned to create a version of the ossuary at Sedlec, an environment worthy of holding the *Black Angel* until its secrets could be unlocked. You think such a thing to be strange?"

There was a new light in his eyes. Stuckler was a fanatic, just like Brightwell and the Believers. His veneer of sophisticated give-and-take was falling away, and to my benefit. On the subject of his particular obsession, Stuckler could not contain himself.

"Why are you so certain that it exists?" I said.

"Because I have seen it replicated," said Stuckler. "You have too, in a way."

He stood suddenly.

"Come, please."

Murnos started to object, but Stuckler silenced him with a raised hand.

"Don't worry, Alexis. Everything is coming to its natural conclusion."

I followed Stuckler through the house until we came to a doorway beneath the main stairs. Murnos stayed behind me all the way, even as Stuckler unlocked the door and we descended into the cellars of the house. They were expansive, and lined with stone. Most of the area was given over to a wine collection, which must have stretched to a thousand bottles, all carefully stored, with a thermostat on the wall monitoring the temperature. We passed through the racks of bottles until we came to a second door, this time made of metal and accessed using a keypad and a retinal scanner. Murnos opened this door, then stepped aside to allow Stuckler and me to enter.

We were in a square stone room. Glassed alcoves

around the walls contained what were clearly Stuckler's most treasured items: there were three icons, the gold upon them still intact, the colors rich and vibrant; there were gold chalices and ornate crosses; there were paintings, and small sculptures of men that might have been Roman or Greek.

But the room was dominated by a statue, perhaps eight feet in height, and constructed entirely from human bones. I had seen a similar piece of sculpture before, except on a much smaller scale, in Garcia's apartment.

It was the *Black Angel*. A single great skeletal wing was unfurled, its spines the slightly curved bones of the radius and ulna. Its arms were made from femurs and fibulae to achieve the sense of scale, its great jointed legs an ornate arrangement of carefully fused bones, the barest hint of the joins visible between them. Its head was made up of fragments of many skulls, each carefully cut and fused to create the whole. Ribs and vertebrae had been used to construct the horn that rose from its head and curved down to its great collarbone. It rested on a granite pedestal, its clawed toes hanging slightly over the edge and gripping the stone. In its presence, I felt a terrible sense of fear and disgust. The pictures of the bone adornments at Sedlec had unsettled me, but at least there might have been some purpose to them, some recognition of the passage of all mortal things. Yet this was something without merit: human beings reduced to constituent parts in the creation of an image of profound evil.

"Extraordinary, don't you think?" said Stuckler. I could not guess at how often he had stood here before it, but judging from the tone of his voice, his awe at this possession never faded.

"It's one word for it," I replied. "Where did it come from?"

"My father discovered it in the monastery at Morimondo in Lombardy, during the search for clues about the Fontfroide fragment. It was the first sign that he was close to the map. There was some damage to it, as you can see."

Stuckler pointed out fragmented bones, a crudely repaired fissure in the spine, missing fingers.

"My father's guess was that it had been transported from Sedlec, probably some time after the initial dispersal of the map fragments, and had eventually found its way to Italy. A double bluff, perhaps, to direct attention away from the original. He ordered it to be concealed. He had a number of locations for such things, and nobody dared to question his instructions on these matters. It was to have been a gift for the Reichsführer, but my father was killed before he could arrange for its transportation. Instead, it passed to my mother after the war, along with some of the other items accumulated by my father."

"But surely anyone could have made this?" I said.

"No," said Stuckler, with absolute conviction. "Only someone who had examined the original could have created it. The detail is perfect."

"How do you know, if you've never seen the model for it?"

Stuckler strode across to one of the alcoves, and carefully opened the glass cover. I followed him over. He activated a light inside. It revealed two small silver boxes, now open, with a simple cross carved into the lid of each. Beside them, carefully protected between thin layers of glass, were two pieces of vellum, each perhaps a foot square. I saw sections of a drawing, depicting a wall and window, with a series of symbols around the edge: a Sacred Heart entangled with thorns, a beehive, a pelican. There was also a series of dots on each, probably representing numbers, and the corners of what might have been shields or coats of arms. Almost immediately, I saw the combination of roman numerals and a single letter that Reid had described.

One manuscript was dominated by the drawing of a great leg, curving backward, and the clawed toes at its feet. It was almost identical to that of the statue behind us. I could detect the faintest trace of lettering concealed in the leg, but I could not read any of the letters. The second manuscript showed one-half of a skull: again, it was identical to the skull on Stuckler's bone statue.

"You see?" said Stuckler. "These fragments have been separated for centuries, ever since the creation of the map. Only someone who had seen the drawing could have constructed a representation of the *Black Angel,* but only someone who had seen the *original* could have done so in such detail. The drawing is relatively crude, the actuality much less so. You asked me why I believe it exists: this is why."

I turned my back on Stuckler and his statue. Murnos was watching me without expression.

"So you have two of the fragments," I said. "And you'll bid at auction for a third."

"I will bid, as you suggest. Once the auction is complete, I will make contact with the other bidders in order to see who among them is also in possession of pieces of the map. Nobody knows of the existence of this cellar and its contents, apart from Alexis and I.

You are the first outsider to have the privilege of seeing it, and only because of the imminence of the auction. I am a wealthy man, Mr. Parker. I will establish contacts. Deals will be struck, and I will acquire sufficient knowledge to make an accurate determination of the *Black Angel*'s resting place."

"And the Believers? You think you can buy them out?"

"Don't be fooled by the ease with which you dealt with the hired help in Maine, Mr. Parker. You were not regarded as a real danger. We can take care of them, if necessary, but I would prefer to reach an accommodation agreeable to both sides."

I doubted if that would happen. From what I had learned so far, Stuckler's reasons for seeking the *Black Angel* were very different from those of Brightwell and his kind. To Stuckler, it was merely another treasure to be stored away in his cave, albeit one with links to his own dead father. The *Black Angel* would stand alongside the bone sculpture, one darkly mirroring the other, and he would adore them both in his neat, obsessive way. But Brightwell, and the individual to whom he answered, believed that there was something hidden beneath the silver, a living being. Stuckler wanted the statue to remain intact and unexamined. Brightwell wanted to explore what lay within.

"Have you encountered a man named Brightwell?" I said.

Stuckler looked at me blankly.

"Should I have?" he asked.

I couldn't tell if he was hiding his knowledge of Brightwell, or genuinely didn't know of his existence. I wondered how recently Brightwell had emerged from the shadows, impelled by his belief that the Believers' long search was nearing an end, and if that was the reason why Stuckler professed to be unaware of him. Despite Stuckler's faintly comical bearing, he was clearly skilled in his business of choice, and had somehow managed to conduct his own search for the map fragments while avoiding the attentions of Brightwell's kind. It was a situation that was about to change.

"I think you'll be hearing from him, once he discovers that you share a common goal," I said.

"I look forward to meeting him, then," said Stuckler, and there was the hint of a smile upon his face.

"It's time for me to go," I said, but Stuckler was no longer listening. Instead, Murnos led me out, leaving his employer lost in contemplation of the ruined bodies of human beings, now fused together in a dark tribute to old, undying evil.

19

I met Phil Isaacson for dinner in the Old Port, shortly after returning from my meeting with Stuckler. It was becoming ever clearer that the following day's auction would be a turning point: it would draw those who wanted to possess the Sedlec box, including the Believers, and it would bring Stuckler into conflict with them if he succeeded in acquiring the item. I wanted to be present at the auction, but when I called Claudia Stern she wasn't available. Instead, I was told that entry to the auction was strictly by invitation only, and that it was far too late to be added to the list of invitees. I left a message for Claudia, asking her to call me, but I didn't expect to hear back from her. I didn't imagine that her clients would be pleased if she allowed a private investigator into their midst, an investigator, moreover, who was interested in the eventual destination of one of the more unusual pieces to have come on the market in recent years. But if there was one person who could be relied upon to find a way into the House of Stern, and who might know enough about the bidders to be of assistance, it was Phil Isaacson.

Natasha's used to be on Cumberland Avenue, close by Bintliff's, and its move to the Old Port was one of the few recent developments in the life of the city of which I was totally in favor. Its new surroundings were more comfortable, and if anything the food had improved, which was quite an achievement given that Natasha's was excellent to begin with. When I arrived, Phil was already seated at a table close by the banquette that ran along the length of the main dining room. As usual, he looked like the dictionary definition of dapper: he was a small, white-bearded man, dressed in a tweed jacket and tan pants, with a red bow tie neatly knotted against his white shirt. His main profession was the law, and he remained a partner in his Cumberland-based practice, but he was also the art critic of the *Portland Press Herald*. I had no problem with the newspaper, but it was still a surprise to find an art critic of Phil Isaacson's quality hiding among its pages. He liked to claim that they'd simply forgotten that he wrote for them, and sometimes it wasn't hard to imagine someone in the news editor's office picking up the paper, reading Phil's column, and exclaiming: "Wait a second, we have an *art critic*?"

I'd first met Phil at an exhibition over at the June Fitzpatrick Gallery on Park Street, where June was showing work by a Cumberland artist named Sara Crisp, who used found items—leaves, animal bones, snakeskin—to create works of stunning beauty, setting the fragments of flora and fauna against complex geometric patterns. I figured it was something to do with order in nature, and Phil seemed to generally agree with me. At least, I think he agreed with me. Phil's vocabulary was considerably more advanced than mine where the art world was concerned. I ended up buying one of the pieces: a cross made from eggshells mounted in wax, set against a red backdrop of interlocking circles.

"Well, well," said Phil, when I reached the table. "I was beginning to think you'd found someone more interesting with whom to spend your evening."

"Believe me, I did try," I said. "Looks like all the interesting people have better things to do tonight."

A waitress deposited a glass of Californian Zin on the table. I told her to bring the bottle, and ordered a selection of Oriental appetizers for two to go with it. Phil and I swapped some local gossip while we waited for the food to arrive, and he gave me tips on some artists that I might want to check out if I ever won the state lottery. The restaurant began to fill up around us, and I waited until everyone at the nearby tables appeared suitably caught up in one another's company before I broached the main subject of the evening.

"So, what can you tell me about Claudia Stern and her clients?" I asked, as Phil finished off the last prawn from the appetizer tray.

Phil laid the remains of the prawn on the side of his plate and patted his lips delicately with his napkin.

"I don't tend to cover her auctions in my column. To begin with, I wouldn't want to put people off their breakfasts by detailing the kind of items with which she sometimes deals, and secondly, I'm not convinced of the value of writing about invitation-only auctions. Besides, why would you be interested in anything she has to offer? Is this to do with a case?"

"Kind of. You could say it has a personal element to it."

Phil sat back in his chair and stroked his beard.

"Well, let's see. It's not an old house. It was founded only ten years ago and specializes in what might be termed 'esoteric' items. Claudia Stern has a degree in anthropology from Harvard, but she has a core of experts upon whom she calls when the need to authenticate items arises. Her area of interest is simultaneously wide and very specialized. We're talking about manuscripts, some human remains rendered into approximations of art, and various ephemera linked to biblical apocrypha."

"She mentioned human remains to me when I met her, but she didn't elaborate," I said.

"Well, it's not something most of us would discuss with strangers," said Phil. "Until recently—say, five or six years ago—Stern did a small but lively trade in certain aboriginal items: skulls, mainly, but sometimes more ornate pieces. Now that kind of dealing is frowned upon, and governments and tribes aren't slow to seek recovery of any such remains that are presented for auction. There are fewer difficulties with European bone sculptures, as long as they're suitably old, and the auction house made the papers some years ago when it auctioned skeletal remains from a number of Polish and Hungarian ossuaries. The bones had been used to make a pair of matching candelabra, as I recall."

"Any idea who might have purchased them?"

Phil shook his head.

"Stern is low-key to the point of secretive. It caters to a very particular type of collector, none of whom has ever, to my knowledge, complained about the way Claudia Stern conducts her business affairs. All items are scrupulously checked to ensure their authenticity."

"She never sold anyone a broomstick that didn't fly."

"Apparently not."

The waitress removed the remains of the appetizers. A few minutes later our main courses arrived: lobster for Phil, steak for me.

"I see you still don't eat seafood," he remarked.

"I think that some creatures were created ugly to discourage people from eating them."

"Or dating them," said Phil.

"There is that."

He set about tearing apart his lobster. I tried not to watch.

"So, do you want to tell me why Claudia Stern should have come to your attention?" he asked. "Strictly between ourselves, I should add."

"There's a sale taking place there tomorrow."

"The Sedlec trove," said Phil. "I've heard rumors."

One of Phil's areas of interest was the aesthetics of cemeteries, so it wasn't surprising that he was aware of Sedlec. Sometimes, the breadth of his knowledge was almost worrying.

"You know anything about it?"

"I hear that the fragment of vellum at the center of the auction contains drawings of some kind, and that in itself it's worth relatively little, apart from a certain curiosity value. I know that Claudia Stern has presented only a tiny portion of the vellum for authentication, with the remainder supposedly being kept under lock and key until a buyer is found. I also know that there has been a lot of secrecy maintained and care taken for such a minor item."

"I can tell you a little more," I said.

And I did. By the time I was done, Phil's lobster lay half-consumed on his plate. I had barely touched my beef. The waitress looked quite pained when she came to check up on us.

"Is everything okay?" she asked.

Phil's face lit up with a smile so perfect only an expert could have spotted that it was false.

"Everything was divine, but I don't have the appetite I once had," he explained.

I let her take my plate as well, and the smile faded slowly from Phil's face.

"Do you believe that this statue is real?" he said.

"I think that something was hidden, a long time ago," I replied. "Too many individuals are concerned about it for it to be a complete myth. As for its exact nature, I can't say, but it's safe to assume that it's valuable enough to kill for. How much do you know about collectors of this type of material?"

"I know some of them by name, others by reputation. Those in the business occasionally share gossip with me."

"Could you get a pair of invitations to the auction?"

"I think I could. It would mean calling in some favors, but you just told me that you believe Claudia Stern would probably prefer if you didn't attend."

"I'm hoping that she'll be sufficiently distracted by all that's happening to allow me to get a foot in the door with you by my side. If we arrive close to the auction, I'm banking on the hope that it will be easier to let us stay than to throw us out and risk disrupting the affair. Anyway, I do lots of things that people would prefer I didn't do. I'd be out of a job if I didn't."

Phil finished his wine.

"I knew this free meal would end up costing me dearly," he said.

"Come on," I said. "I know you're interested. And if anyone kills you, just think of the obituary you'll get in the *Press Herald*. You'll be immortalized."

"That is not reassuring," said Phil. "I was hoping that immortality would come to me through *not* dying."

"You may yet be the first," I told him.

"And what are your chances?"
"Slim," I said. "And declining."

Brightwell was hungry. He had fought the urges for so long, but lately they had become too strong for him. He recalled the death of the woman, Alice Temple, in the old warehouse, and the sound of his bare feet slapping on the tiles as he approached her. Temple: her name was somehow appropriate in light of the desecration that had been visited on her body. It was strange to Brightwell, the way in which he was able to stand outside himself and watch what occurred, as though his mortal form were engaged in certain pursuits while its guiding consciousness was otherwise occupied.

Brightwell opened his mouth and sucked in a deep breath of oily air. His fists clenched and unclenched, whitening his knuckles beneath his skin. He shuddered, recalling the fury with which he had torn the woman apart. That was where the separation occurred, the division of Self and Notself, one part seeking only to rend and tear while the other stood aside, calm yet watchful, waiting for the moment, the final moment. This was Brightwell's gift, the reason for his being: even with his eyes closed, or locked in complete darkness, he could sense the coming of the last breath . . .

The spasming was increasing in frequency now. His mouth was very dry. Temple, Alice Temple. He loved that name, loved the taste of her as his mouth found hers, blood and spit and sweat intermingled upon her lips, her consciousness seeping away, her strength failing. Now Brightwell was with her once again, his ensanguined fingers clutching at her head, his lips locked against her lips, the redness of her: red within, red without. She was dying, and to anyone else, from a doctor to a layman, there would be only the sight of a body deflating, the life leaving it at last as it slumped, naked, in the battered chair.

But life was not the only element departing at that moment, and Brightwell was waiting for it as it left her. He felt it as a rushing sensation in his mouth, like a sweet breeze ascending through a scarlet tunnel, like a gentle fall making way for harsh winter, like sunset and night, presence and absence, light and not-light. And then it was within him, locked inside, trapped between worlds in the ancient, dark prison that was Brightwell.

Brightwell, the guiding angel, the guardian of memories. Brightwell, the searcher, the identifier.

Brightwell's breathing grew faster. He could feel them within him, tormented and questing.

Brightwell, capable of bending the will of others to his own, of convincing the lost and forgotten that the truth of their natures lay in his words.

He needed another. The taste was on him. Deep inside him, a crescendo grew, a great chorus of voices crying out for release.

He did not regret all that had followed from her death. True, it had brought them unwanted attention. She was not alone in the world after all. There were those who cared about her, and who would not let her passing go unexamined, but the intersection of her life's path with that of Brightwell was no coincidence. Brightwell was very old, and with great age came great patience. He had always retained his faith, his certainty that each life taken would bring him closer and closer to the one who had betrayed him, who had betrayed them all for the possibility of a redemption always destined to be denied him. He had kept himself well hidden, submerging the truth of his being, burying it beneath a pretence of normality even as the three worlds—this world, the world above, and the great honeycomb world below—did all in their power to demonstrate to him that normality had no place in his existence.

Brightwell had plans for him, oh yes. Brightwell would find a cold, dark place, with chains upon the walls, and there he would bind him, and watch him through a hole in the brickwork as he wasted away, hour upon hour, day upon day, year upon year, century after century, teetering on the brink of death yet never falling finally into the abyss.

And if Brightwell were wrong about his nature—and Brightwell was rarely wrong, even in the smallest of things—then it would still be a long, lingering, agonizing death for the man who had threatened to stand in the way of the revelation that they sought, and the recovery of the one that had been lost to them for so long.

The preparations were all in place. Tomorrow they would find out what they needed to know. There was nothing more that could be done, so Brightwell allowed himself a small indulgence. Later that night, he came across a young man in the shadow of the park, and he drew him to himself with promises of money and food and strange, carnal delights. And in time, Brightwell was upon him, his hands buried deep within the boy's body, his long nails slicing organs and gently crushing veins, controling the intricate piece of machinery that was the human form, slowly bringing the boy to the climax that Brightwell sought, until at last they were locked together, lip to lip, and the surging sweetness filled Brightwell as another voice was added to the great choir of souls within.

20

Martin Reid called me first thing the next morning, leading Angel to question if he was actually in league with the very people he was supposed to be working against, since only someone involved with the devil would call at 6:30 A.M.

"Will you be attending today's event?" he asked.

"I hope so. What about you?"

He grunted.

"I'm a little too well known to mingle unnoticed in such company. Anyway, I had a fraught telephone conversation with our Miss Stern yesterday, during which I stressed once again my unhappiness with her determination to continue with the sale, despite doubts about the provenance and ownership of the box. We'll have somebody there to keep an eye on what transpires, but it won't be me."

Not for the first time, it struck me that there was something wrong with the way in which Reid was dealing with the sale of the Sedlec fragment. The Catholic Church was not short of lawyers, especially in the Commonwealth of Massachusetts, as anyone who had dealt with the archdiocese in the course of the recent abuse scandals could attest. If it were determined to stop the auction from going ahead, Claudia Stern's business would have been crawling with oleaginous men and women in expensive suits and polished shoes.

"By the way," he said. "I hear you were asking questions about us."

I had checked up on both Reid and Bartek after my meeting with them. It took me a while to find anyone who was prepared to admit that they had ever set foot in a church, let alone taken holy orders, but eventually their identities were confirmed to me through Saint Joseph's Abbey in Spencer, Massachusetts, where both men were staying. Reid was officially based at San Bernardo alle Terme in Rome, and was apparently responsible for instructing visiting clerics and nuns about the way of life of Saint Benedict, the saint most closely associated with the rules governing the order, through contemplation of places in which he spent crucial parts of his life: Norica, Subiaco, and Monte Cassino. Bartek worked out of the new monastery of Our Lady of Novy Dvur in the Czech Republic, the first monastery to be built in the Czech Republic since the fall of Communism, which was still under construction. He had previously lived in the community at Sept-Fons Abbey in France, to which he and a number of other young Czech men had fled in the early 1990s to escape religious persecution in their own country, but had also worked extensively in the United States, mainly at the Abbey of the Genesee in upstate New York. Sept-Fons, I remembered, was the monastery that Bosworth, the elusive FBI agent, had desecrated.

Still, Bartek's story sounded plausible enough, but Reid didn't strike me as the type who was content to sit at the front of a tour bus muttering platitudes through a microphone. Interestingly, the monk who explained all this to me — having first cleared it with the head of the order in the United States and, presumably, with Reid and Bartek themselves — told me that the two monks actually represented two distinct orders. Bartek was a Trappist, a group deriving its name from the Abbey of Our Lady of La Trappe in France and formed after a split in the order between those who subscribed to strict observance of silence, austerity, and simple vestments, and those like Reid, who preferred a little more laxity in their duties and lifestyles. This latter group was known as the Sacred Order of Cîteaux, or the Cistercians of the Common Observance. I also couldn't help but feel that there was a certain amount of respect, bordering on awe, in the way the monk spoke about the two men.

"I was curious," I told Reid. "And I also had only your word that you were actually a monk."

"So what did you learn?" He sounded amused.

"Nothing that you didn't give them permission to tell me," I said. "Apparently, you're a tour guide."

"Is that what they said?" said Reid. "Well, well. They also serve who only stand and wait at the bus door for latecomers. It's important that history is not forgotten. That's why I gave you the cross. I hope you're wearing it. It's very old."

As it happened, I had attached the cross to my key ring. I already wore a cross: a simple Byzantine pilgrim's cross, over one thousand years old, that my grandfather had given me as a gift when I graduated high school. I didn't think that I needed to wear another.

"I keep it close," I assured him.

"Good. If anything ever happens to me, you can give that a rub and I'll be in touch from the next world."

"I'm not sure I find that reassuring," I said. "Like a great many things about you."

"Such as?"

It sounded unlikely, but I could come to no other conclusion.

"I think you want this auction to go ahead. I don't think you and your order made more than cosmetic efforts to stop it. For some reason, it's in your interests that whatever is contained in that last fragment is revealed."

There was only silence from the other end of the line. Reid might almost have abandoned the phone, were it not for the soft susurration of his breathing.

"And what reason would that be?" he asked, and there was no longer any trace of amusement. Instead, he sounded wary. No, not wary, exactly: he wanted me to figure out the answer, but he wasn't about to give it to me. Despite all my threats of the combined wrath of Louis and the Fulcis being unleashed upon him, Reid was going to play the game his way, right until the end.

"Maybe you'd like to see the *Black Angel* too," I said. "Your order lost it, and now it wants it back."

Reid tut-tutted, and now the smiling mask was restored.

"Close," said Reid, "but no cigar for you, Mr. Parker. Look after that cross, now, and give my love to Claudia Stern."

He hung up, and I never spoke to him again.

I met Phil Isaacson at Fanueil Hall, and from there we walked to the auction house. It was clear that Claudia Stern had taken certain precautions for the sale of the map fragment. A sign announced that the house was closed for a private sale, and that all inquiries would be dealt with by phone. I rang the bell, and the door was opened by a big man in a dark suit who looked like the only thing he had ever bid on was the option of striking the first blow.

"This is a private event, gentlemen. Invitation only."

Phil removed the invitations from his pocket. I didn't know how he had acquired them. They were printed on stiff card, and embossed in gold with the word "Stern" and the date and time of the auction. The doorman examined them, then looked at both of us closely to make sure that we weren't about to produce crosses and holy water and start sprinkling the place. Once he was satisfied, he stepped aside to let us through.

"Not quite Fort Knox," I said.

"Still, more than one would usually encounter. I have to confess, I am rather looking forward to this."

Phil registered at the desk and was handed a bidding paddle. A young woman in black offered us refreshments from a tray. In fact, there were a lot of people in black present. It looked like the launch of a new Cure album, or the reception after a Goth wedding. We both opted for orange juice, then took the stairs up to the auction room. As I had hoped, there were still people milling about, and we were lost in the throng. I was surprised at the size of the crowd, but even more surprised at the fact that most of them seemed relatively normal, apart from their monochromatic dress sense, although there were a few who looked like they might spend a little too much time alone in the dark pursuing unpleasant activities, including one particularly nasty specimen with pointed nails and a black ponytail who was only one step away from wearing a T-shirt announcing that he suckled at Satan's nipple.

"Maybe Jimmy Page will be here," I said. "I should have brought along my copy of *Led Zep IV*."

"Jimmy who?" said Phil. I couldn't tell if he was kidding.

"Led Zeppelin. A popular beat combo, Your Honor."

We took a seat at the back. I kept my head down and looked through Phil's copy of the catalog. Most of the lots were books, some of them very old. There was an old facsimile of the *Ars Moriendi,* a kind of how-to guide for those hoping to avoid damnation after death, printed by the Englishman Caxton sometime after 1490, consisting of eleven block-book woodcuts depicting the deathbed temptation of a dying man. Claudia Stern clearly knew how to put together an impressive and enlightening sales package: from the couple of paragraphs describing the lot, I learned that the term "shriven" meant to be absolved of one's sins; that, therefore, to be given "short shrift" meant being allowed little time to confess before death; and that a "good death" did not necessarily preclude a violent end. I also learned from a book of saints that Saint Denis, the apostle of Gaul and patron of France, was decapitated by his tormentors, but subsequently picked up his head and went for a walk with it, which said a lot for Saint Denis's willingness to be a good sport and put on a show for the crowd.

Some of the lots appeared to be linked to one another. Lot 12 was a copy of the *Malleus Maleficarum,* the *Hammer of Witches,* that dated from the early sixteenth century and was said to have belonged to one Johann Geiler von Kaisersberg, a fire-and-brimstone cathedral preacher in Strasbourg, while a copy of his sermons from 1516 was Lot 13. Geiler's sermons were illustrated by a witch engraving by Hans Baldung, who studied under Dürer, and Lot 14 consisted of a series of erotic prints by Baldung, featuring an old man—representing

Death—fondling a young woman, apparently a theme to which Baldung returned repeatedly in his career.

There were also statues, icons, paintings—including the piece that I had witnessed being restored in the workshop, now listed only as "Kutná Hora, 15th century, artist unknown"—and a number of bone sculptures. Most of them were on display, but they bore no resemblance to those that I had seen in Stuckler's book or in Garcia's apartment. They were cruder, and less finely crafted. I was becoming quite the connoisseur of bone work.

People began to take their seats as one o'clock approached. I saw no sign of Stuckler or Murnos, but eight women were seated at a table by the auctioneer's podium, each with a telephone now pressed to her ear.

"It's unlikely that any serious bids will come from the floor for the more esoteric items," said Phil. "The buyers won't want their identities to become known, partly because of the value of some, but mostly because such interests still remain open to misinterpretation."

"You mean people will think they're freaks?"

"Yes."

"But they are freaks."

"Yes."

"As long as we're agreed on that."

Still, I guessed that Stuckler had someone on the floor watching the other bidders. He would not want to be entirely cut off from what happened during the auction. There would be others too. Somewhere among the crowd were those who called themselves Believers. I had warned Phil about them, although I believed that he at least was in no danger from them.

Claudia Stern appeared from a side door, accompanied by an older man in a dandruff-flecked black suit.

She took her place at the podium, and the man stood beside her at a high table, a huge ledger open before him in which to take down the details of the successful bidders and their bids. Ms. Stern rapped the podium with her gavel to quiet the crowd, then welcomed us to the auction. There was some preamble about payment and collection, and then the auction began. The first lot was an item familiar to me by reputation: an 1821 copy of Richard Laurence's translation of the Book of Enoch, twinned with a copy of Byron's verse drama *Heaven and Earth: A Mystery* dating from the same year. It aroused some mildly competitive bidding, and went to an anonymous telephone bidder. Geiler's copy of the *Malleus Maleficarum* went to a tiny elderly woman in a pink suit, who looked grimly satisfied with her purchase.

"I guess the rest of the coven should be pleased," said Phil.

"Know thine enemy."

"Exactly."

After five or six more items, none of which created any great stir, the twin brother of the door ape emerged from the office. He was wearing white gloves, and holding a silver box adorned with a cross. It was almost identical to the ones I had seen in Stuckler's treasury, but appeared in marginally better condition once its image was displayed on a screen beside Ms. Stern. There were fewer dents that I could see, and the soft metal was barely scratched.

"Now," said Ms. Stern. "We come to what I feel will be, for many, the prize lot of this auction. Lot Twenty, a fifteenth-century box in Bohemian silver, cross inlay, containing a fragment of vellum. Those of you with a particular interest in this lot were given ample opportunity to examine a small section of the fragment, and to obtain independent verification of its age where necessary. No further questions or objections will be entertained, and the sale is final."

A casual visitor might have wondered what all the fuss was about, given the relatively low-key introduction, but there was a definite heightening of tension in the room, and a brief flurry of whispers. I saw the women at the phones poised, pens in hand.

"I will open the bidding at five thousand dollars," said Ms. Stern.

There were no takers. She smiled indulgently.

"I know that there is interest in this room, and money to go with it. Nevertheless, I'll permit a slow start. Who will give me two thousand dollars?"

The satanist with the long nails raised his paddle, and we were off. The bids quickly climbed in increments of $500, passing the original $5,000 starting point and moving up to $10,000, then $16,000. Eventually, around the $20,000 mark, the bids from the floor dried up, and Ms. Stern turned most of her attention to the telephones, where, in a series of nods, the bidding rose to $50,000, then $75,000, and eventually reached the $100,000 mark. The bids continued to climb, finally passing $200,000, until, at $235,000, there was a pause.

"Any further bids?" asked Ms. Stern.

Nobody moved.

"I'm holding at two hundred and thirty-five thousand dollars."

She waited, then rapped the gavel sharply.

"Sold for two hundred and thirty-five thousand dollars."

The silence was broken, and the buzz of conversation resumed. Already people were drifting toward the door, now that the main business of the afternoon was concluded. Ms. Stern, sensing the same, handed the gavel over to one of her assistants, and the sale resumed with considerably less excitement than before. Ms. Stern exchanged a few words with the young woman who had taken the telephone bid, then moved quickly toward the door of her office. Phil and I stood to leave, and she glanced down as we did so, her face briefly wrinkling in puzzlement as though she were trying to remember where she had seen me before. Her gaze moved on. She nodded at Phil, and he smiled in return.

"She likes you," I said.

"I have that white-bearded charm that disarms women."

"Maybe they just don't see you as threatening."

"Which makes me all the more dangerous."

"You have a rich inner life, Phil. That's the polite way of putting it."

We were at the first landing when Ms. Stern appeared from a doorway below. She waited for us to descend to her.

"Philip, it's good to see you again."

She turned a pale cheek for him to kiss, then extended a hand toward me.

"Mr. Parker. I wasn't aware that you were on the list. I feared that your presence at this auction might make bidders uneasy, were they to become aware of the nature of your profession."

"I just came to keep an eye on Phil, in case he got carried away by the excitement and bid on a skull."

She invited us to join her for a drink. We followed

her through a door marked "Private" and into a room
cozily furnished with overstuffed couches and leather
chairs. Catalogs for past and forthcoming auctions were
piled neatly on two sideboards and fanned across an
ornate coffee table. Ms. Stern opened a lavishly stocked
bar cabinet and invited us to make our selection. I had
an alcohol-free Beck's just to be polite. Phil opted for
red wine.

"Actually, I was rather surprised you didn't make a
bid yourself, Mr. Parker," she said. "After all, you were
the one who came to me with that interesting bone
sculpture."

"I'm not a collector, Ms. Stern."

"No, I don't suppose you would be. In fact, you
appear to be a rather harsh judge of collectors, as testi-
fied to by the late Mr. Garcia's end. Have you discovered anything more about him?"

"A little."

"Anything you'd like to share?"

Her expression was one of vague superiority, capped
with a wry grin. Whatever I had to tell her about Garcia,
she figured she knew already.

"He kept videos of dead and dying women. I think
he played an active role in their creation."

A ripple passed across Ms. Stern's face, and the angle
of her grin was reduced slightly.

"And you believe that his presence in New York was
linked to the Sedlec box auctioned today," she said.
"Otherwise, why would you be here?"

"I'd like to know who bought it," I said.

"A lot of people would like to know that."

She readjusted her sights and aimed her charm at
Phil. Its veneer was thin. I got the impression that she

was displeased both by his presence and by the fact that he had not come alone. Phil, I think, sensed it too.

"All of this is, of course, off the record," she said.

"I'm not here in my journalistic capacity," said Phil.

"You know you're always welcome here, in any capacity," she replied, but she made it sound like a lie. "It's just that in this case, discretion was, and is, required."

She sipped her wine. A thin trickle dripped down the glass. It stained her chin slightly, but she didn't appear to notice.

"This was a very delicate sale, Mr. Parker. The value of the lot was directly proportionate to the degree of secrecy surrounding its contents. If the contents of the fragment were revealed before the sale — if, for example, we had permitted potential bidders to examine the entire vellum in detail, instead of just a portion — then it would have sold for far less than it did today. The majority of bidders in the room were merely curiosity seekers, faintly hoping to gain for themselves a link to an obscure occult myth. The real money was far from here. A total of six individuals went to the trouble of lodging deposits with us in order to be permitted to examine a cutting from the vellum, none of whom were in the auction room today. Not one person was allowed to view even one of the symbols or drawings depicted upon it."

"Apart from you."

"I looked at it, as did two of my staff, but frankly it was meaningless to me. Even were I able to interpret it, I would still have required the other fragments to place it in context. Our concern was that someone already in possession of additional drawings might view our fragment and add its contents to what he or she knew."

"Are you aware of its provenance?" I said. "I understand that it was in dispute."

"You're referring to the fact that it was believed to have been stolen from Sedlec itself? There is no proof that this was the same box. The item came to us from a trusted European source. We believed that it was real, and so too did those who bid upon it today."

"And you'll keep the winning bid secret?"

"As best we can. Such things have a habit of filtering out eventually, but we have no wish to make the buyer a target for unscrupulous men. Our reputation rests upon preserving the anonymity of our clients, particularly given the nature of some of the items that pass through this house."

"So you're aware that the buyer may be at risk?"

"Or it may be that others are now at risk from the buyer," she replied.

She was watching me carefully.

"Was the buyer a Believer? Is that what you're telling me?"

Ms. Stern laughed, exposing her slightly stained teeth.

"I'm telling you nothing, Mr. Parker, merely pointing out that there is more than one conclusion to be drawn. All I can say for certain is that I will be a great deal happier once the box has left my possession. Thankfully, it is small enough to be passed to the buyer without attracting undue attention. We will be done with it by close of business."

"What about you, Ms. Stern?" I said. "Do you think you might be at risk? After all, you've seen it."

She drained a little more of her wine, then stood. We rose with her. Our time here was at an end.

"I have been in this profession for a long time," she

said. "In truth, I have seen some very strange items in the course of my dealings, and I have met some equally strange individuals. None of them has ever threatened me, and none ever will. I am well protected."

I wasn't about to doubt her. Everything about the House of Stern made me uneasy. It was like a trading post at the junction of two worlds.

"Are you a Believer, Ms. Stern?"

She put her glass down, then slowly rolled up each sleeve of her blouse in turn. Her arms were unmarked. All trace of good humor left her during the performance of the act.

"I believe in a great many things, Mr. Parker, some with very good reason. One of those things is good manners, of which you appear to have none. In future, Philip, I'd be grateful if you would check with me before you bring guests to my auctions. I can only hope that your taste in companions is the only faculty that appears to have deserted you since last we met, or else your newspaper will have to look elsewhere for its art criticism."

Ms. Stern opened the door and waited for us to leave. Phil looked embarrassed. When he said good-bye to her she didn't reply, but she spoke to me as I followed Phil from the room.

"You should have stayed in Maine, Mr. Parker," she said quietly. "You should have kept your head down and lived a quiet life, then you would not have come to anyone's attention."

"You'll forgive me for not trembling," I said. "I've met people like the Believers before.

"No," she replied, "you have not."

Then she closed the door in my face.

* * *

I walked Phil to his car.

"Sorry if I made life awkward for you," I said as he closed his door and rolled down the window.

"I never liked her anyway," he said, "and her wine was corked. Tell me, though: does everybody react as badly to you as she did?"

I reflected on the question.

"Actually," I said, as I left him, "that was pretty good for me."

Angel and Louis were waiting for me nearby. They were eating oversized wraps and drinking bottled water in Louis's Lexus. Angel, I noticed, had half the world's napkin production laid over his legs, his feet, the parts of the seat not covered by his body, and the floor itself. It was a slight case of overkill, although some stray bean sprouts and a couple of blobs of sauce had hit the napkins already, so it paid to be cautious.

"He must really love you if he's letting you eat in his car," I said, as I climbed in the back to talk to them. Louis acknowledged me with a nod, but there was still something unspoken between us. I was not about to broach the subject. He would do so, in his own time.

"Yeah, it's only taken, like, a decade," said Angel. "For the first five years, he wouldn't even let me *sit* in his car. We've come a long way."

Louis was carefully wiping his fingers and face.

"You got sauce on your tie," I said.

He froze, then lifted the silk in his fingers.

"Mother—," he began, before turning on Angel. "That's your damn fault. You wanted to eat, so you made *me* want to eat. Damn."

"I think you should shoot him," I said, helpfully.

"I got some spare napkins, you want them," said Angel.

Louis snatched some from Angel's lap, sprinkled water on them, and tried to work on the stain, swearing all the time.

"If his enemies found out about his Achilles' heel, we could be in real trouble," I said to Angel.

"Yeah, they wouldn't even need guns, just soy sauce. Maybe satay if they were really playing rough."

Louis continued to swear at both of us and at the stain, all at once. It was quite a trick. It was also good to see a flash of his old self.

"It sold," I said, getting down to business. "Two hundred and thirty-five thousand dollars."

"What's the house's cut?" asked Angel.

"Phil reckoned fifteen percent of the purchase price."

Angel looked impressed. "Not bad. Did she tell you who the buyer was?"

"She wouldn't even tell me the identity of the seller. Reid figures the box was stolen from Sedlec just hours after the discovery of the damage to the church, then made its way to the auction house through a series of intermediaries. It's possible that the House of Stern itself was the final purchaser, in which case Ms. Stern made quite a killing today. As for the buyer, Stuckler wanted it badly. He's obsessed, and he almost certainly had the money to fund his obsession. He told me that he was prepared to pay whatever it took. Under the circumstances, he probably regarded two thirty-five as a bargain."

"So now what happens?"

"Stuckler gets his fragment delivered to him and tries to combine it with whatever material he already has, in an effort to locate the *Angel*. I don't think he's one of the Believers, so they'll make a move on him once he reveals himself as the purchaser. Maybe they'll offer to buy the information, in which case they'll be rebuffed, or he'll try to strike a deal with them. It could be that they'll simply take the direct approach. Stuckler's house is pretty secure, though, and he has men with him. Murnos is probably good at his job, but I still think they're underestimating the people with whom they're dealing."

"I guess we'll just have to wait and see how it works out," Louis said.

"Probably badly for Stuckler," I said.

Louis looked pained.

"I was talking about my tie . . ."

Brightwell sat in an easy chair, his eyes closed, his fingers rhythmically extending and relaxing as though from the force of the blood being pumped through his body. He rarely slept, but he found that such moments of quiet served to replenish his energies. He even dreamed, in a sense, replaying moments from his long life, reliving old history, ancient enmities. Lately, he had been remembering Sedlec, and the death of the Captain. A party of Hussite stragglers had intercepted them as they made their way toward Prague, and a stray arrow had found its mark in the Captain. While the others killed the attackers, Brightwell, himself injured, had clawed his way across the ground, the grass already damp from the Captain's wound. He had brushed the hair away from his leader's eyes, exposing the white mote that seemed always to be changing its form at the periphery while the core remained ever constant, so that looking at it was like peering at the sun through a glass. There were those who hated to see it, this reminder of all that had been lost, but Brightwell did not hesitate to look upon it when the opportunity arose. It fueled his own resentment, and gave him an added impetus to act against the Divine.

The Captain was struggling to breathe. When he tried to speak, blood bubbled up from his throat. Already, Brightwell could sense the separation beginning, spirit disengaging itself from host as it prepared to wander in the darkness between worlds.

"I will remember," whispered Brightwell. "I will never stop searching. I will keep myself alive. When the time comes for us to be reunited, with one touch I will impart all that I have learned, and remind you of all that you will have forgotten, and of what you are."

The Captain shuddered. Brightwell clasped the Captain's right hand and lowered his face to that of his beloved, and amid the stink of blood and bile he felt the body give up its struggle. Brightwell rose, and released the Captain's hand. The statue was gone, but he had learned of the abbot's map from a young monk named Karel Brabe before he died. Somewhere, the boxes were already being stored in secret places, and Karel Brabe's soul now dwelt in the prison of Brightwell's form.

But Brabe had told Brightwell something else before he died, in the hope of ending the pain that Brightwell was inflicting upon him.

"You make a poor martyr," Brightwell had whispered to the young man. Brabe was still only a boy, and Brightwell knew great lore about the body's capacities. His fingers had torn deep wounds in the young novice, and his nails were tearing at secret red places. As they snipped at veins and punctured organs, blood and words spilled from the boy in twin torrents: the flawed nature of the fragments; a statue of bone, itself concealing a secret, a twin for the obscene relic they were seeking.

The search had taken so long, so long . . .

Brightwell opened his eyes. The Black Angel stood before him.

"It is nearly over," said the angel.

"We don't know for certain that he has it."

"He has given himself away."

"And Parker?"

"After we have found my twin."

Brightwell lowered his eyes.

"It is him," he said.

"I am inclined to agree," said the Black Angel.

"If he is killed, I will lose him again."

"And you will find him again. After all, you found me."

Some of the strength seemed to leave Brightwell. His shoulders sagged, and for a moment he looked old and worn.

"This body is betraying me," he said. "I do not have the strength for another search."

The Black Angel touched his face with the tenderness of a lover. It stroked his pitted skin, the swollen flesh at his neck, his soft, dry lips.

"If you must pass from this world, then it will be my duty in turn to seek you out," it said. "And remember, I will not be alone. This time, there will be two of us to search for you."

21

That night, I spoke to Rachel for the first time since she'd left. Frank and Joan were at a local charity fund-raiser, and Rachel and Sam were alone in the house. I could hear music playing in the background: "Overcome by Happiness" by the Pernice Brothers, kings of the deceptively titled song.

Rachel sounded frantically upbeat, in the demented way common to those who are on heavy medication or who are trying desperately to keep themselves together in the face of imminent collapse. She didn't ask me about the case, but chose instead to tell me what Sam had done that day, and talk of how Frank and Joan were spoiling her. She inquired about the dog, then held the receiver to Sam's ear, and I thought I heard the child respond to my voice. I told her that I loved her, and that I missed her. I told her that I wanted her always to be safe and happy, and I was sorry for the things that I had done to make her feel otherwise. I told her that even if I wasn't around, even if we couldn't be together, I was thinking of her, and I would never, ever forget how important she was to me.

And I knew Rachel was listening too, and in this way I told her all the things that I could not say to her.

* * *

The dog woke me. He wasn't barking, merely whining softly, his tail held low while he wagged it nervously, as he did when he was trying to make amends for doing something wrong. He cocked his head as he heard some noise that was inaudible to me, and glanced at the window, his mouth forming strange sounds that I had never heard from him before.

The room was filled with flickering light, and now there was a crackling sound in the distance. I smelled smoke, and saw the light of the flames eclipsed by the drapes on the window. I left my bed and pulled the drapes apart.

The marshes were on fire. Already, the engines from the Scarborough fire department were converging on the conflagration, and I could see one of my neighbors on the bridge that crossed the muddy land below my house, perhaps trying to find the source of the blaze, fearful that someone might be hurt. The flames followed paths determined by the channels and were reflected in the still, dark surface of the waters, so that they appeared both to rise into the air and to ignite the depths. I saw birds swooping against the redness, panicked and lost in the night sky. The thin branches of a bare tree had caught fire, but the fire engines had now almost come to a halt, and hoses would soon be trained upon the tree, so perhaps it might yet be saved. The damp of winter meant that the blaze would be easily contained, but the burned grass would still be visible to all for months to come, a charred reminder of the vulnerability of this place.

Then the man on the bridge turned toward my house. The flames lit his face, and I saw that it was Brightwell. He stood unmoving, silhouetted by fire, his gaze fixed upon the window at which I stood. The headlights of the fire trucks seemed to touch him briefly, for he was suddenly luminous in his pallor, his skin puckered and diseased as he turned away from the approaching engines and descended into the inferno.

I made the call early the next morning, while Louis and Angel ate breakfast and tossed pieces of bagel for Walter to catch. They too had seen the figure on the bridge, and if anything, his appearance had deepened the sense of unease that now colored all of my relations with Louis. Angel seemed to be acting as a buffer between us, so that when he was present a casual observer might almost have judged that everything between us was normal, or as normal as it had ever been, which wasn't very normal at all.

The Scarborough firemen had also witnessed Brightwell's descent into the burning marsh, but they had searched in vain for any sign of him. It was assumed that he had doubled back under the bridge and fled, for the fire was being blamed upon him. That much, at least, was true: Brightwell had set the fire, as a sign that he had not forgotten me.

The smell of smoke and burned grass hung heavily in the air as I listened to the phone ringing on the other end of the line, and then a young woman answered.

"Can I speak to Rabbi Epstein, please?" I asked.

"May I tell him who's calling?"

"Tell him it's Parker."

I heard the phone being put down. There were young children shouting in the background, accompanied by a timpani of silverware on bowls. Then the sound was drowned out by the closing of a door, and an old man's voice came on the phone.

"It's been some time," said Epstein. "I thought you'd forgotten me. Actually, I rather hoped that you'd forgotten me."

Epstein's son had been killed by Faulkner and his brood. I had facilitated his revenge on the old preacher. He owed me, and he knew it.

"I need to talk to your guest," I said.

"I don't think that's a good idea."

"Why is that?"

"It risks drawing attention. Even I don't visit him unless it's absolutely necessary."

"How is he?"

"As well as can be expected, under the circumstances. He does not say a great deal."

"I'll need to see him anyway."

"May I ask why?"

"I think I may have encountered an old friend of his. A *very* old friend."

Louis and I took an early afternoon flight down to New York, the journey passing in near silence. Angel opted to stay at the house and look after Walter. There was no sign in Portland or New York of Brightwell, or of anyone else who might have been watching us. We took a cab to the Lower East Side in heavy rain, the traffic snarled up and the streets thronged with glistening commuters heartily weary of the long winter, but the rain began to ease as we crossed Houston Street, and by the time we neared our destination the sun was spilling through holes in the clouds, creating great diagonal columns of light that held their form until they disintegrated on the roofs and walls of the buildings.

Epstein was waiting for me in the Orensanz Center,

the old synagogue on the Lower East Side where I had first met him after the death of his son. As usual, there were a couple of young men around him who clearly had not been brought along for their conversational skills.

"So here we are again," said Epstein. He looked the same as he always did: small, gray-bearded, and slightly saddened, as though, despite his best efforts at optimism, the world had somehow already contrived to disappoint him that day.

"You seem to like meeting people here," I said.

"It's public, yet private when necessary, and more secure than it appears. You look tired."

"I'm having a difficult week."

"You're having a difficult life. If I were a Buddhist, I might wonder what sins you had committed in your previous incarnations to justify the problems you appear to be encountering in this one."

The room in which we stood was suffused with a soft orange glow, the sunlight falling heavily through the great window that dominated the empty synagogue, lent added weight and substance by some hidden element that had joined with it in its passage through the glass. The noise of traffic was muted, and even our footsteps on the dusty floor sounded distant and muffled as we walked toward the light. Louis remained by the door, flanked by Epstein's minders.

"So tell me," said Epstein. "What has happened to bring you here?"

I thought of all that Reid and Bartek had told me. I recalled Brightwell, the feel of his hands upon me as this wretched being reached out to me and tried to draw me to himself, and the look on his face before he gave himself to the flames. That sickening feeling of vertigo returned, and my skin prickled with the memory of an old burning.

And I remembered the preacher, Faulkner, trapped in his prison cell, his children dead and his hateful crusade at an end. I saw again his hands reaching out for me through the bars, felt the heat radiating from his aged, wiry body, and heard once more the words that he spoke to me before spitting his foul poison into my mouth

What you have faced until now is as nothing compared to what is approaching . . . The things that are coming for you are not even human.

I could not tell how it came to be, but Faulkner had a knowledge of hidden things. Reid had suggested that perhaps Faulkner, the Traveling Man, the child killer Adelaide Modine, the arachnoid torturer Pudd, maybe even Caleb Kyle — the bogeyman who had haunted my grandfather's life — were all linked, even if some of them were unaware of the ties that bound them to one another. Theirs was a human evil, a product of their own flawed natures. Faulty genetics might have played a part in what they became, or childhood abuse. Tiny blood vessels in the brain corrupting, or little neurons misfiring, could have contributed to their debased natures. But free will also played a part, for I did not doubt that a time came for most of those men and women when they stood over another human being and held a life in the palms of their hands, a fragile thing glowing hesitantly, beating furiously its claim upon the world, and made a decision to snuff it out, to ignore the cries and the whimpers and the slow, descending cadence of the final breaths, until at last the blood stopped pumping and instead flowed slowly from the wounds, pooling around them and reflecting their faces in its deep, sticky redness. It was there that true evil lay, in the moment between thought and action, between intent and commission, when for a fleeting instant there was still the possibility that one might turn away and refuse to appease the dark, gaping desire within. Perhaps it was in this instant that human wretchedness encountered something worse, something deeper and older that was both familiar in the resonance that it found within our souls, yet alien in its nature and in its antiquity, an evil that predated our own and dwarfed it with its magnitude. There are as many forms of evil in the world as there are men to commit them, and its gradations are near infinite, but it may be that, in truth, it all draws from the same deep well, and there are beings that have supped from it for far longer than any of us could ever imagine.

"A woman told me of a book, a part of the biblical apocrypha," I said. "I read it. It spoke of the corporeality of angels, of the possibility that they could take upon themselves a human form, and dwell in it, hidden and unseen."

Epstein was so silent and still that I could no longer hear him breathe, and the slow rise and fall of his chest appeared to have ceased entirely.

"The Book of Enoch," he said, after a time. "You know, the great rabbi Simeon ben Jochai, in the years following the crucifixion of Jesus Christ, cursed those who believed in its contents. It was judged to be a later misinterpretation of Genesis because of correspondences between the two texts, although some scholars have suggested that Enoch is actually the earlier work, and is therefore the more definitive account. But then, the apocryphal works—both the deuterocanonical books, such as Judith, Tobit, and Baruch, that follow the Old Testament, and the excised later gospels, like those of

Thomas and Bartholemew—are a minefield for scholars. Enoch is probably more difficult than most. It is a genuinely unsettling piece of writing, with profound implications for the nature of evil in the world. It is hardly surprising that both Christians and Jews found it easier to suppress it than to try to examine its contents in the light of what they already believed, and thereby attempt to reconcile the two views. Would it have been so difficult for them to see the rebellion of the angels as being linked to the creation of man? That the pride of the angels was wounded by being forced to acknowledge the wonder of this new being? That they perhaps also envied its physicality, and the pleasure it could take in its appetites, most of all in the joy that it found by joining with the body of another? They lusted, they rebelled, and they fell. Some descended into the pit, and others found a place here, and at last took upon themselves the form that they had so long desired. An interesting speculation, don't you think?"

"But what if there are those who believe it, who are convinced that they are these creatures?"

"Is that why you want to see Kittim again?"

"I think," I said slowly, "that I have become a beacon for foul things, and the worst of them are now closer than they have ever been before. My life is being torn asunder. Once, I could have turned away, and they might have passed me by, but it's too late for that now. I want to see the one you have, to confirm to myself that I am not insane and that such things can and do exist."

"Perhaps they do exist," said Epstein, "and maybe Kittim is the proof, but we have encountered resistance from him. He very quickly built up a tolerance to the drugs. Even sodium pentothal no longer has any significant effect. Under its influence, he merely rants, but we have given him a strong dose in anticipation of your visit, and it may allow you a few minutes of clarity from him."

"Do we have far to go?" I asked.

"Go?" said Epstein. "Go where?"

It took me a moment to understand.

"He's *here*?"

It was little more than a glorified cell, accessed through a utility closet in the basement. The closet was encased in metal, and the back wall doubled as a door, accessed by both a key and an electronic combination. It swung inward to reveal a soundproofed room, divided in two by steel mesh. Cameras kept a constant vigil on the area behind the wire, which was furnished with a bed, a sofa, and a small table and chair. There were no books that I could see. A TV had been fixed to the far corner of the wall, on the other side of the barrier and as far away from the cell as possible. There was a remote control device for it on the floor beside the sofa.

A figure lay on the bed, wearing only a pair of gray shorts. His limbs were like bare branches, with every muscle visible to the eye. He looked emaciated, thinner than any man that I had ever seen before. His face was turned to the wall, and his knees were drawn up to his chest. He was almost bald, apart from a few stray strands of hair that clung to his purple, flaking skull. The texture of his skin reminded me of Brightwell, and the swelling that afflicted him. They were both beings in the process of slow decay.

"My God," I said. "What happened to him?"

"He refused to eat," said Epstein. "We tried to force-feed him, but it was too difficult. Eventually, we came to the conclusion that he was trying to kill himself, and, well, we were prepared to see him die. Except he didn't die: he merely grows a little weaker with every week that goes by. He sometimes takes water, but nothing more. Mostly, he sleeps."

"How long has this been going on?"

"Months."

The man on the bed stirred, then turned over so that he was facing us. His skin had contracted on his face, so that the hollows in the bone were clearly visible. He reminded me of a concentration camp inmate, except that his catlike eyes betrayed no hint of weakness or inner decay. Instead they glittered emptily, like cheap jewels.

Kittim.

He had emerged in South Carolina as an enforcer for a racist named Roger Bowen, and a link between the preacher Faulkner and the men who would have freed him if they could, but Bowen had underestimated his employee and had failed to understand the true balance of power in their relationship. Bowen was little more than Kittim's puppet, and Kittim was older and more corrupt than Bowen could ever have imagined. His name hinted at his nature, for the *kittim* were said to be a host of dark angels who waged war against men and God. Whatever dwelt within Kittim was ancient and hostile, and worked for its own ends.

Kittim reached for a plastic beaker of water, and drank from it, the liquid spilling onto the pillow and sheets. He raised himself up until he was seated on the edge of the bed. He stayed like that for a time, as though building up the strength that he needed, then stood. He wavered slightly, and seemed about to fall, but instead shuffled across the cell toward the wire. His bony fingers reached out and gripped the strands as he forced his face against the mesh. He was so thin that, for an instant, I almost thought he might try to press his face between them. His eyes shifted first to Louis, then to me.

"Come to gloat?" he said. His voice was very soft, but betrayed no hint of his body's decay.

"You don't look so good," said Louis. "But then, you never looked good."

"I see you still bring your monkey with you wherever you go. Perhaps you could train him to walk behind you holding an umbrella."

"Still the same old joker," I said. "You know, you're never going to make friends that way. That's why you're down here, away from all the other children."

"I am surprised to see you alive," he said. "Surprised, yet grateful."

"Grateful? Why would you be grateful"

"I was hoping," said Kittim, "that you might kill me."

"Why?" I replied. "So you can . . . *wander*?"

Kittim's head tilted slightly, and he looked at me with new interest. Beside me, Epstein was watching us both carefully.

"Perhaps," he said. "What would you know of it?"

"I know a little. I was hoping you could help me to learn more."

Kittim shook his head.

"I don't think so."

I shrugged.

"Then we've nothing more to say. I would have thought that you'd be glad of a little stimulation, though. It must get lonely down here, and dull. Still, at least you have a TV. *Ricki* will be coming on soon, and then after that you can watch your stories."

Kittim stepped away from the wire, and sat down once again on his bed.

"I want to leave here," he said.

"That's not going to happen."

"I want to die."

"Then why haven't you tried to kill yourself?"

"They watch me."

"That's not answering the question."

Kittim extended his arms and turned his hands so that the palms faced upward. He looked at his wrists for a long time, as though contemplating the wounds that he might inflict upon them, were he able.

"I don't think you can kill yourself," I said. "I don't think that choice is open to you. You can't end your own existence, even temporarily. Isn't that what you believe?"

Kittim didn't reply. I persisted.

"I can tell you things," I said.

"What things?"

"I can tell you of a statue made of silver, hidden in a vault. I can tell you of twin angels, one lost, one searching. Don't you want to hear?"

Kittim did not look up as he spoke.

"Yes," he whispered. "Tell me."

"An exchange," I said. "First, who is Brightwell?"

Kittim thought for a moment.

"Brightwell is . . . not like me. He is older, more cautious, more patient. He *wants*."

"What does he want?"

"Revenge."

"Against whom?"

"Everyone. Everything."

"Is he alone?"

"No. He serves a higher power. It is incomplete, and seeks its other half. You know this."

"Where is it?"

"Hidden. It had forgotten what it was, but Brightwell found it and awoke what lay within. Now, like all of us, it cloaks itself, and it searches."

"And what will happen when it finds its twin?"

"It will hunt, and it will kill."

"And what will Brightwell get, in return for helping it?"

"Power. Victims."

Kittim lifted his gaze from the floor and looked unblinkingly at me.

"And you."

"How can you know that?"

"I am aware of him. He thinks that you are like us, but that you fell away. Only one did not follow. Brightwell believes that he has found that one in you."

"And what do you believe?"

"I do not care. I wanted only to explore you."

He lifted his right hand and stretched his fingers, twisting them in the air as though it were flesh and blood through which his nails were slowly tearing.

"Now tell me," he said, "what do you know of these things?"

"They call themselves Believers. Some are just ambitious men, and some are convinced that they are more than that. They're looking for the statue, and they're near to finding it. They are assembling fragments of a map, and soon they will have all the information that they need. They even built a shrine here in New York, in readiness to receive it."

Kittim took another sip of water.

"So they are close," he said. "After all this time."

He did not seem overjoyed at the news. As I watched him, the truth of Reid's words became clearer to me: evil is self-interested, and ultimately without unity. Whatever his true nature, Kittim had no desire to share his pleasures with others. He was a renegade.

"I have one more question," I said.

"One more."

"What does Brightwell do with the dying?"

"He touches his mouth to their lips."

"Why?"

I thought I detected a note of what might have been envy in Kittim's voice as he answered.

"Souls," said Kittim. "Brightwell is a repository of souls."

He lowered his head and lay down once more on his bed, then closed his eyes and turned his face to the wall.

The Woodrow was a nondescript place. There was no doorman in green livery and white gloves to guard its residents' privacy, and its atrium was furnished with the kind of hard-wearing green vinyl chairs beloved of struggling dentists everywhere. The outer doors were unsecured, but the inner doors were locked. To their right was an intercom and three lines of bells, each with a faded nameplate beside it. Philip Bosworth's name was not among those listed, although a number of the plates were blank.

"Maybe Ross's information was wrong," said Louis.

"It's the FBI, not the CIA," I said. "Anyway, whatever else I can say about him, Ross doesn't screw around when it comes to information. Bosworth is here, somewhere."

I tried each of the anonymous bells in turn. One was answered by a woman who appeared to be very old, very bad-tempered, and very, very deaf. The second was answered by someone who could have been her older, deafer, and even more cantankerous brother. The third bell rang in the apartment of a young woman who might well have been a hooker, judging by the confusion about an "appointment" that followed.

"Ross said the apartment was owned by Bosworth's folks," suggested Louis. "Maybe he has a different last name."

"Maybe," I conceded.

I ran my finger down the lines of bells, stopping halfway down the third row.

"But maybe not."

The name on the bell was Rint, just like that of the man responsible for the reconstruction of the Sedlec ossuary in the nineteenth century. It was the kind of joke that could come only from someone who had once tried to dig up the floor of a French monastery.

I rang the bell. Seconds later, a wary voice emerged from the speaker box.

"Hello?"

"My name is Charlie Parker. I'm a private investigator. I'm looking for Philip Bosworth."

"There's nobody here by that name."

"Assistant SAC Ross told me how to find you. If you're concerned, call him first."

I heard what might have been a snicker, and then the connection was terminated.

"That went well," said Louis.

"At least we know where he is."

We stood outside the closed doors. Nobody came in and no one went out. After five minutes went by, I tried the Rint bell again, and the same voice answered.

"Still here," I said.

"What do you want?"

"To talk about Sedlec. To talk about the Believers."

I waited. The door buzzed open.

"Come on up."

We entered the lobby. There was a blue semicircular fitting on the ceiling above us, concealing the cameras that watched the entrance and the lobby. Two elevators, their doors painted gunmetal gray, stood before us. There was a key slot in the wall between them, so that only residents could access them. As we approached, the elevator on the left opened. The top half of the interior was mirrored, with gold trim. The bottom half was upholstered in old yet well-maintained red velvet. We stepped inside, the doors closed, and the elevator rose without either of us touching a button. Clearly, the Woodrow was a more sophisticated residence than it appeared from outside.

The elevator stopped on the top floor, and the doors opened onto a small, windowless, carpeted area. Across from us was a set of double wood doors leading to the penthouse apartment. There was another blue surveillance bubble mounted on the ceiling above.

The apartment doors opened. The man who faced us wore blue chinos and a light blue Ralph Lauren shirt, and there were tassels on his tan penny loafers. The shirt was buttoned wrongly, though, and the trousers were pressed and without a single wrinkle, indicating that he had just dressed himself in a hurry from his closet.

"Mr. Bosworth?"

He nodded. I put his age at about forty, but his hair was graying, his features were newly lined with pain, and one of his blue eyes was paler than the other. As he stepped aside to admit us he shuffled slightly, as though suffering from pins and needles in one or both feet. He held the handle of the door with his left hand, while his right remained fixed in the pocket of his chinos. He did not offer to shake my hand, or Louis's. Instead, he simply closed the door behind us and walked slowly to an easy chair, holding on to its armrest with his left hand as he lowered himself down. His right hand still did not leave his pocket.

The room in which we now stood was impressively modern, with a pretty good view of the river through a row of five long windows. The carpet was white, and the seating areas furnished entirely with black leather. There was a wide-screen TV and a DVD player in a console against one wall, and a series of black bookcases stretched from floor to ceiling. Most of the shelves were empty, apart from a few pieces of pottery and antique statuary that were lost in their minimalist surroundings. A large smoked-glass dining table stood to my left, surrounded by ten chairs. It looked like it had never been used. Beyond it, I could see a pristine kitchen, every surface gleaming. To the left was a hallway, presumably leading to the bedrooms and bathroom beyond. It was like a show apartment, or one that was on the point of being vacated by its current owner.

Bosworth was waiting for us to speak. He was clearly a sick man. His right leg had already spasmed once since we had arrived, causing him some distress, and there was a tremor in his left arm.

"Thank you for seeing us," I said. "This is my colleague Louis."

Bosworth's eyes flicked between us. He licked at his

lips, then reached for a plastic tumbler of water on the small glass table beside him, carefully ensuring that he had it firmly in his grip before he raised it to his mouth. He sipped awkwardly from a plastic straw, then returned the tumbler to his table.

"I spoke to Ross's secretary," he said, once he had drained the last of the water. "She confirmed your story. Otherwise, you would not be here now, and you would instead be under the supervision of this building's security guards while you waited for the police to arrive."

"I don't blame you for being cautious."

"That's very magnanimous of you, I'm sure."

He snickered again, but the laughter was directed less at me than at himself and his debilitated condition, a kind of double bluff that failed to convince anyone in the room.

"Sit," he said, gesturing to the leather sofa on the other side of the coffee table. "It's been some time since I've had the pleasure of company, other than that of doctors and nurses, or concerned members of my own family."

"May I ask what you're suffering from?"

I already had some idea: the tremors, the paralysis, the spasms were all symptoms of MS.

"Disseminated sclerosis," he said. "Late onset. It was diagnosed last year, and has progressed steadily from the first. In fact, my doctors say the speed of my degeneration is quite alarming. The vision in my right eye was the first obvious symptom, but since then I have endured the loss of postural sense in my right arm, weakness in both of my legs, vertigo, tremors, sphincter retention, and impotence. Quite a cocktail of miseries, don't you think? As a result, I have decided to leave my apartment and abandon myself permanently to the care of others."

"I'm sorry."

"It's interesting," said Bosworth, seemingly ignoring me completely. "Only this morning, I was considering the source of my condition: a metabolic upset, an allergic reaction on the part of my nervous system, or an infection from some outside agent? I feel it is a *malevolent* illness. I sometimes picture it in my head as a white, creeping thing extending tendrils through my body, implanted within to paralyze and ultimately kill me. I wonder if perhaps I unwittingly exposed myself to some agent, and it responded by colonizing my system. But that is the stuff of madness, is it not? SAC Ross would be pleased to hear it, I think. He could pass it on to his superiors, reassuring them that they were right to end my career in the manner in which they did."

"They said that you desecrated a church."

"Excavated, not desecrated. I needed to confirm a suspicion."

"And what was the result?"

"I was proved right."

"What was the suspicion?"

Bosworth raised his left hand and waved it gently from side to side in a slow, deliberate movement, perhaps to distinguish the gesture from the tremors that continuously shook the limb.

"You first. After all, you came to me."

Once again, I was drawn into the game of feeding information to another without exposing too much of what I knew, or what I thought might be true. I had not forgotten Reid's warning from the night at the Great Lost Bear: that somewhere there was one who believed that a Black Angel dwelt within him, and so I did not mention the involvement of Reid and Bartek, or the approaches made to me by Stuckler. Instead, I told Bosworth about Alice, and Garcia, and the discoveries made in the Williamsburg building. I revealed most of what I knew about the map fragments, and Sedlec, and the Believers. I talked of the auction, and the painting in Claudia Stern's workshop, and the Book of Enoch.

And I spoke of Brightwell.

"All very interesting," he said, when I had finished. "You've learned a lot in a short time." He rose painfully from his chair and went to a drawer at the base of one of his bookshelves. He opened it, retrieved what was inside, and placed it on the table between us.

It was part of a map, drawn in red and blue inks upon thin yellowed paper, and mounted on a piece of protective board. In the top right-hand corner was a black foot with taloned toes. The margins were filled with microscopic writing, and a series of symbols. It was similar in content to the fragments I had seen in Stuckler's treasury.

"It's a copy," said Bosworth, "not an original."

"Where did this come from?"

"San Galgano, in Italy," said Bosworth, as he resumed his seat. "The monastery at San Galgano was one of the places to which a fragment was sent. It's no more than a beautiful ruin now, but in its time, its façade was noted for the purity of its lines, and it was said that its monks were consulted during the construction of the Siena cathedral. Nevertheless, it was subject to repeated attacks by Florentine mercenaries, its revenues were plundered by its own abbots, and the Renaissance in Italy led to a falling off in the number of those willing to answer the monastic call. By 1550, there were only five monks left there. By 1600, there was only one, and he lived as a hermit. When he died, the San Galgano fragment was found among his possessions. Its provenance was not understood initially, and it was retained as a relic of a holy man's life. Inevitably, rumors of its existence spread, and an order came from Rome that it should be entrusted to the care of the Vatican immediately, but by that time a copy had already been made. Subsequently, further duplicates were created, so the San Galgano section of the map is in the possession of any number of individuals by now. The original was lost on the journey to Rome. The monks transporting it were attacked, and it was said that rather than allow it to be seized along with their money and possessions, they burned it in a fit of panic. And so, all that remain are copies such as this one. This, then, is the only piece of the Sedlec map to which many people have enjoyed access, and the only clue that existed for many years as to the nature of the directions to the statue's location.

"The original creator of the map invented a simple, but perfectly adequate, means of ensuring that the location contained within it remained unknowable without all the parts of the document. Most of the writing and symbols are merely decorative, and the drawing of the church refers simply to Bernard's concept of how such places of worship should look. It is an idealized church, and nothing more. The real meat, as you're no doubt aware, is here."

Bosworth pointed to a combination of Roman numerals and a single letter, *d*, in one corner.

"It's simple. Like any treasure map worth its salt, it's based around distances from a set point. But without all of the distances involved, it's useless, and even with all of them to hand, you still need to know the location of the central reference point. All the boxes, all of the fragments, are ultimately meaningless unless you have knowledge of the basic location itself. In that sense, the map might be regarded as a clever piece of sleight of hand. After all, if people were busy searching for what they believed to be crucial clues, then they would be less likely to try to find the thing itself. Each fragment does, however, offer one piece of useful information. Look again at the copy, particularly at the imp in the center."

I stared at the document, and at the small demonic character Bosworth was pointing at. Now that I looked more closely, I could see from its skull that it was a very crude version of the bone statue that Stuckler had shown to me, barely more than a stick drawing. There was lettering visible around it, forming a circle that enclosed the figure.

"*Quantum in me est*," said Bosworth. "As much as in me lies."

"I don't understand. It's just a drawing of the *Black Angel*."

"No, it's not." Bosworth practically seethed at my inability to make the connections that he had made. "See here, and here." The trembling index finger of his left hand brushed the page. "These are human bones."

Bosworth was right. It was not a stick figure, but a bone figure. More care had been taken with the illustration than first appeared.

"The whole illustration consists of human bones: bones from the ossuary at Sedlec. This is a depiction of the re-creation of the *Black Angel*. It is the *bone statue* that conceals the actual location of the vault, but most of those who have sought the *Angel*, wrong-footed by their obsession with the fragments and dismissive of this fragment because of its relative ubiquity, have been unable to acknowledge that possibility, and those who have correctly interpreted its message have kept the knowledge to themselves, while widening their search to include the replica. But I made the connection, and if this man Brightwell is clever enough, then he has made it too. The statue has been missing since the last century, although it was rumored to be in Italy before World War Two broke out. Since then, there has been no trace of it. The Believers are not looking merely for the fragments, but for those who *possess* the fragments, in the hope that they may also have in their possession the bone sculpture. That is why Garcia re-created it in his apartment. It is not just a symbol: it is the key to the thing itself."

I tried to take in all that he had said.

"Why are you telling us this?" said Louis. It was the first time he had spoken since we entered Bosworth's apartment.

"Because I want it found," said Bosworth. "I want to know that it is in the world, but I can no longer find it for myself. I have money. If you find it, I will have it brought to me, and I'll pay you well for your trouble."

"You never explained why you dug up the floor of the monastery at Sept-Fons," I said.

"There should have been a fragment there," said Bosworth. "I traced its path. It took me five years of hunting rumors and half-truths, but I did it. Like so many treasures, it was moved for its own protection during the Second World War. It went to Switzerland, but was returned to France once it was safe to do so. It should have been beneath the floor, but it was not. Someone had taken it away again, and I know where it went."

I waited.

"It went to the Czech Republic, to the newly founded monastery at Novy Dvur, perhaps as a gift, a token of their respect for the efforts of the Czech monks to keep the faith under the Communists. That has always been the great flaw in the Cistercians' stewardship of the fragments over the last six hundred years: their willingness to entrust them to one another, to expose them briefly to the light. That is why the fragments have slowly come into the possession of others. The Sedlec fragment auctioned yesterday is, I believe, the fragment transported from Sept-Fons to the Czech Republic. It did not belong in Sedlec. Sedlec has not existed as a Cistercian community for nearly two centuries."

"So someone put it there." I said.

"Someone wanted it to be found," Bosworth said. "Someone wants to draw attention to Sedlec."

"Why?"

"Because Sedlec is not merely an ossuary. Sedlec is a trap."

Then Bosworth played his final card. He opened the second folder, revealing copies of ornate drawings, each depicting the *Black Angel* from different angles.

"You know of Rint?" he asked.

"You used his name as a pseudonym. That's how we found your bell. He was the man who redesigned the ossuary in the nineteenth century."

"I bought these in Prague. They were part of a case of documents linked to Rint and his work, owned by one of Rint's descendants, whom I found living in near penury. I paid him well for the papers, much more than they were worth, in the hope that they would provide more conclusive proof than they ultimately did. Rint created these drawings of the *Black Angel*, and according to the seller, there were once many more than this, but they were lost or destroyed. These drawings were Rint's obsession. He was a haunted man. Later, others copied them, and they became popular among specialized collectors with an interest in the myth, but Rint made the originals. The question was, how did Rint come to create such detailed drawings? Were they entirely products of his own imagination, or did he see something during his restoration that allowed him to base his illustrations upon it? I believe that the latter is the case, for Rint was clearly greatly troubled in later life, and perhaps the bone sculpture still rests in Sedlec. My illness prevents me from investigating further, which is why I am sharing this knowledge with you."

Bosworth must have seen the expression on my face change. How could he have failed to do so? It was all clear now. Rint had not glimpsed the bone sculpture, because the bone sculpture had long been lost. According to Stuckler, it spent two centuries in Italy, hidden from sight until his father discovered it. No, Rint saw the original, the *Black Angel* rendered in silver. He saw it in Sedlec when he was restoring the ossuary. Bosworth was right: the map was a kind of ruse, because the *Black Angel* had never left Sedlec. All those centuries, it had remained hidden there, and at last both Stuckler and the Believers were confident that all the information they needed to recover it was within their grasp.

And I knew also why Martin Reid had given me the small silver cross. I rubbed my fingers across it, where it rested alongside my keys. My thumb traced its lines, and the letters etched on its rear in a cruciform shape.

S

L E C

D

"What is it?" said Bosworth.

"We have to go," I said.

Bosworth stood and tried to stop me, but his weak legs and wasted arm made him no match for me.

"You know!" he said. "You know where it is! Tell me!"

He tried to raise himself, but we were already making for the door.

"Tell me!" screamed Bosworth, forcing himself up. I saw him stumbling toward me, his face contorted, but by then the elevator doors were closing. I caught a last glimpse of him, then we were descending. I got to the lobby just as a pair of uniformed men emerged from the doorway to the right of the elevator bank. Inside I could see TV monitors and telephones. They stopped as soon as they saw Louis. More precisely, they stopped as soon as they saw Louis's gun.

"Down," he said.

They hit the ground.

I went past him and opened the door. He backed out, and we were on the street, running fast, melting into the crowd as the last minutes ticked away and the Believers commenced the slaughter of their enemies.

22

They first appeared as shadows on the wall, drifting with the night clouds, following the moonlight. Then shadow became form: black-garbed raiders, their eyes distended and their features hidden by the night-vision goggles that they wore. All were armed, and as they scaled the walls, their weapons hung down from their backs, the combination of mutated eyes and slim, stingerlike black barrels making them seem more insect than man.

A boat waited offshore, sitting silently upon the waters, alert for the signal to approach if required, and a blue Mercedes stood beneath a copse of trees, its sole occupant pale and corpulent, his green eyes unencumbered by artificial lenses. Brightwell had no need for them: his eyes had long been comfortable with darkness.

The raiders descended into the garden, then separated. Two moved toward the house, the others to the gate, but at a prearranged signal all stopped and surveyed the dwelling. Seconds ticked by, but still they did not move. They were four black sentinels, like the burned remains of dead trees enviously regarding the slow coming of spring.

Inside the house, Murnos sat before a bank of TV monitors. He was reading a book, and the figures surrounding the property might have been interested to see that it was a concordance to Enoch. Its contents fueled the beliefs of those who threatened his employer, and Murnos felt compelled to learn more about them in order to understand his enemy.

"They shall be called upon earth evil spirits, and on earth shall be their habitation."

Murnos had grown increasingly uneasy with Stuckler's grand obsession, and recent events had done nothing to assuage his concerns. The purchase of the latest fragment at auction was a mistake: it would draw attention to what was already in Stuckler's possession, and Murnos did not share his employer's belief that an agreement could be reached with those others who were also seeking the silver statue.

"Evil spirits shall they be upon earth, and the spirits of the wicked shall they be called."

Beside him, a second man watched the screens, his gaze flicking carefully across each one. There was a single window in the room, overlooking the garden. Murnos had warned Stuckler about it in the past. In Murnos's opinion, the room was unsuited to its primary purpose. He believed that a security room should be virtually impregnable, capable of being used as a panic room if necessary, but Stuckler was a man of many contradictions. He wanted men around him, and he desired the impression of security, but Murnos did not think that Stuckler really considered himself to be at risk. He was his mother's creature in every way, the knowledge of his father's strength and the nature of his sacrifice instilled in him from an early age, so that it verged on the sacrilegious for him to indulge in fear, or doubt, or even concern for others. Murnos hated the old woman's occasional visits. Stuckler would send a limousine for her, and she would arrive with her private nurse, wrapped in blankets even in the height of summer, her eyes shaded by sunglasses all year round, an old crone who persisted in living while taking no joy in any aspect of the world around her, not even in her son, for Murnos could see her contempt for Stuckler, could hear it in her every utterance as she looked upon this prissy little man, softened by indulgence, his weaknesses redeemed only by his willingness to please her and his hero worship of a dead father so intense that occasionally the hatred and envy that underpinned it would bubble through, contorting him with rage and transforming him utterly.

"No food shall they eat, and they shall be thirsty; they shall be concealed, and shall rise up against the sons of men . . ."

He looked at Burke, his coworker. Burke was good. Stuckler had initially baulked at paying him what he asked, but Murnos had insisted that Burke was worth it. The others, too, had all been approved by Murnos, even if they were not quite in Burke's league.

And still Murnos believed that they were not enough.

A light began to flicker rhythmically on a panel on the wall, accompanied by an insistent beeping.

"The gate!" said Burke. "Someone's opening the gate."

It wasn't possible. The gate could be opened only from within, or by one of the three control devices contained in the cars, and all of the vehicles were on the property. Murnos checked the monitors and thought for an instant he saw a figure beside the gate, and another leaving a copse of trees.

". . . for they come forth during the days of slaughter and destruction."

And then the screens went dead.

Murnos was already on his feet when the window beside them was blown apart. Burke took the brunt of the first fusillade, shielding Murnos for valuable seconds and enabling him to get to the door. He scrambled through as bullets pinged off metal and pockmarked the plaster on the walls. Stuckler was upstairs in his room, but the noise had woken him from his sleep. Murnos could already hear him shouting as he entered the main hallway. Somewhere in the house, another window shattered. A small man with a gun appeared from the kitchen, barely more than a shadow in the gloom, and Murnos fired at him, forcing him back. He kept firing as he made for the stairs. There was a Gothic-style window on the landing, and Murnos saw a shape pass across it, ascending the outside wall toward the second floor. He tried to shout a warning as he heard more shots, but he stumbled on the stairs and the words were lost in an instant of shock. Murnos gripped the banister to lift himself up, and his hands slid wetly upon the wood. There was blood on his fingers. He looked down at his shirt and saw the stain spreading across it, and with it came the pain. He raised his gun, seeking a target, and felt a second impact at his thigh. His back arched in agony, his head striking hard against the stairs and his eyes briefly squeezing shut as he tried to control the huffing. When he opened them again there was a woman staring at him from above, the shape of her clear even beneath her dark clothing, her eyes blue and hateful. She had a gun in her hand.

Instinctively, Murnos closed his eyes again as death came.

Brightwell drove to the front of the house and entered the grounds. He followed Miss Zahn down to the cellar, through the racks of wine, and into the treasury that now lay open to him. Above him loomed the great black statue of bone. Stuckler was kneeling before it, dressed in blue silk pajamas. There was some blood in his hair, but he was otherwise unhurt.

Three pieces of vellum were handed to Brightwell, taken by his raiders from the shattered display case. He handed them over to Miss Zahn, but his gaze was fixed upon the statue. His head came almost to the level of its rib cage, the scapulae fused to the sternum at the front and to each other at the back, like an armored plate. He drew back his hand and punched hard against the mass of bone. The sternum cracked under the impact.

"No!" said Stuckler. "What are you doing?"

Brightwell struck again. Stuckler tried to stand, but Miss Zahn forced him to stay down.

"You'll destroy it," said Stuckler. "It's beautiful. Stop!"

The sternum shattered under the force of Brightwell's blows. The skin on his knuckles and the back of his hand had been torn by the sharp bone, but he did not seem to notice. Instead, he reached into the hollow that he had created and explored it, his arm buried within the statue almost to the elbow and his face tensed with the effort, until his features suddenly relaxed and he withdrew his hand. There was a small silver box clutched in his fist, this one entirely unadorned. He opened his hand and displayed the box to Stuckler, then carefully removed the lid. Inside was a single piece of vellum, perfectly preserved. He handed it to Miss Zahn to unfold.

"The numbers, the maps," he said to Stuckler. "They were all incidental, in their way. What mattered was the bone statue, and what it contained."

Stuckler was weeping. He reached for a shard of shattered black bone and held it in his hand.

"You did not understand your own acquisitions, Herr Stuckler," said Brightwell. "'*Quantum in me est.*' The details lie in the fragments, but the truth lies here."

He threw the empty box to Stuckler, who touched his fingers to the interior in disbelief.

"All this time," he said. "The knowledge was within my grasp all this time."

Brightwell took the final piece of fragment from Miss Zahn. He examined the drawing upon it, and the writing above. The drawing was architectural in nature, showing a church and what appeared to be a network of tunnels beneath it. His brow furrowed, then he began to laugh.

"It never left," he said, almost in wonder.

"Tell me," said Stuckler. "Please, allow me that much."

Brightwell squatted, and showed Stuckler the illustration, then rose and nodded to Miss Zahn. Stuckler did not look up as the muzzle of the gun touched the back of his head, its caress almost tender.

"All this time," he said. "All this time."

Then time, what was and what was yet to be, came to an end, and a new world was born for him.

Two hours later, Reid and Bartek were walking back to their car. They had stopped to eat at a bar just south of Hartford, their last meal together before they were due to leave the country, and Reid had indulged himself, as was sometimes his wont. He was now rubbing his belly, and complaining that chili nachos always gave him gas.

"Nobody made you eat them," said his companion.

"I can't resist them," said Reid. "They're just so *alien*."

Bartek's Chevy was parked on the road, beneath one of a long line of bare trees that filigreed the cars beneath in shadow, part of a small forest that bordered green fields and a distant development of new condos.

"I mean," Reid continued, "no decent society would even con—"

A shape moved against one of the trees, and in the fraction of a second between awareness and response, Reid could have sworn that it descended down the tree trunk headfirst, like a lizard clinging to the bark.

"Run!" he said. He pushed hard at Bartek, forcing him into the woods, then turned to face the approaching enemy. He heard Bartek call his name, and he shouted: "Run, I said. Run, you bastard!"

There was a man facing him, a small, pie-faced figure in a black jacket and faded denims. Reid recognized him from the bar, and wondered how long they had been watched by their enemies. The man did not have any weapon that Reid could see.

"Come on, then," said Reid. "I'll have you."

He raised his fists and moved sideways, in case the man tried to get past him to follow Bartek, but he stopped short as he became aware of a stench close by.

"Priest," said the soft voice, and Reid felt the energy drain from him. He turned around. Brightwell was inches from his face. Reid opened his mouth to speak, and the blade entered him so swiftly that all that emerged from his throat was a pained grunt. He heard the small man moving into the undergrowth, following Bartek. A second figure accompanied him: a woman with long dark hair.

"You failed," said Brightwell.

He drew Reid to him, embracing him with his left arm even as the knife continued to force its way upward. His lips touched Reid's. The priest tried to bite him, but Brightwell did not relinquish his hold, and he kissed Reid's mouth as the priest shuddered and died against him.

Miss Zahn and the small man returned after half an hour. Reid's body already lay concealed in the undergrowth.

"We lost him," she said.

"No matter," said Brightwell. "We have bigger fish to fry."

He stared out into the darkness, as though hoping that despite his words, he might yet have the chance to deal with the younger man. Then, when that hope proved misplaced, he walked with the others back to their car and they drove south. They had one more call to make.

After a time, a thin figure emerged from the woods. Bartek followed the line of the trees until he found at last the splayed figure, cast aside amid stones and rotten wood, and he gathered the body to him and said the prayers for the dead over his departed friend.

Neddo was seated in the little office at the back of his store. It was almost dawn, and the wind outside rattled the fire escapes. He was hunched over his desk, carefully using a small brush to clean the dust from an ornate bone brooch. The door to his place of work opened, but he did not hear it above the howling of the wind, and so engrossed was he in the delicate task before him that he failed to notice the sound of soft footsteps moving through his store. It was only when the curtain moved, and a shadow fell across him, that he looked up.

Brightwell stood before him. Behind Brightwell was a woman. Her hair was very dark, her shirt was open to her breasts, and her skin was alive with tattooed eyes.

"You've been telling tales, Mr. Neddo," said Brightwell. "We have indulged you for too long."

He shook his head sadly, and the great wattle of flesh at his neck wobbled and rippled.

Neddo put the brush down. His spectacles had a second pair of lenses attached to them by a small metal frame, in order to magnify the piece upon which he was working. The lenses distorted Brightwell's face, making his eyes seem bigger, his mouth fuller, and the red and purple mass above his collar more swollen than ever, so that it appeared to be on the verge of an eruption, a prelude to some great spray of blood and matter that would emerge from deep within Brightwell, burning like acid everything with which it came into contact.

"I did what was right," said Neddo. "If only for the first time."

"What were you hoping for? Absolution?"

"Perhaps."

"'On earth they shall never obtain peace and remission of sin,'" Brightwell recited. "'For they shall not rejoice in their offspring; they shall behold the slaughter of their beloved, shall lament for the destruction of their sons, and shall petition for ever, but shall not obtain mercy and peace.'"

"I know Enoch as well as you, but I am not like

you. I believe in the communion of saints, the forgiveness of sins . . ."

Brightwell stepped aside, allowing the woman space to enter. Neddo had heard about her but had never seen her. Without foreknowledge, she might have appeared beautiful to him. Now, facing her at last, he felt only fear, and a terrible tiredness that prevented him from even attempting escape.

". . . the resurrection of the body," Neddo continued, his speech growing faster, "and life everlasting. Amen."

"You should have remained faithful," said Brightwell.

"To you? I know what you are. I turned to you out of anger, out of grief. I was mistaken." Neddo commenced a new prayer: "Oh my God, I am heartily sorry for all my sins, because they have offended thee . . ."

The woman was examining Neddo's tools: the scalpels, the small blades. Neddo could hear her working her way through them, but he did not look at her. Instead, he remained intent upon completing his act of contrition, until Brightwell spoke and the words died in Neddo's mouth.

"We have found it," said Brightwell.

Neddo stopped praying. Even now, with death so close, and his protests of repentance still wet upon his lips, he could not keep the wonder from his voice.

"Truly?" he said.

"Yes."

"Where was it? I would like to know."

"Sedlec," said Brightwell. "It never left the precincts of the ossuary."

Neddo removed his glasses. He was smiling.

"All of the searching, and it was there all along."

His smile grew sad.

"I should like to have seen it," he said, "to have looked upon it after all that I have heard and all that I have read."

The woman found a rag. She soaked it with water from a jug, then stepped behind Neddo and forced the material into his mouth. He tried to struggle, pulling at her hands and her hair, but she was too strong. Brightwell joined her, pushing Neddo's hands down into the chair, his weight and strength keeping the smaller man's body rigid. The cold of the scalpel touched Neddo's forehead, and the woman began to cut.

23

We flew into Prague via London, arriving late in the afternoon. Stuckler was dead. We had hired a car in New York and driven north to his house after our meeting with Bosworth, but by the time we arrived, the police were already there, and a couple of calls confirmed that the collector and his men had all been killed, and that the great bone statue in his treasury now had a hole in its chest. Angel joined us in Boston shortly after, and we left for Europe that night.

The temptation was to press on for Sedlec, which lay about forty miles east of the city, but there were preparations to be made first. In addition, we were tired and hungry. We checked into a small, comfortable hotel in an area known as Mala Strana, which seemed to translate as "Lesser Town", according to the young woman at the reception desk. Close by, a little funicular railway ran up Petrin Hill from a street named Ujezd, along which old trams rattled, their connections occasionally sparking on the overhead lines and leaving a crisp, burned smell in the air. There were cobbles on the streets, and some of the walls were obscured by graffiti. Traces of snow still lingered in sheltered corners, and there was ice on the Vltava River.

While Louis made some calls, I phoned Rachel and told her where I was. It was late, and I was worried that I might wake her, but I didn't want to just leave the country without letting her know. Her main concern still seemed to be for the dog, but he was safely housed with a neighbor. Sam was doing fine, and they were all planning on visiting Rachel's sister the next day. Rachel was quieter, but more like her old self.

"I always wanted to see Prague," said Rachel, after a time.

"I know. Maybe another time."

"Maybe. How long will you stay there?"

"A couple of days."

"Are Angel and Louis with you?"

"Yes."

"Funny, isn't it, that you'd be somewhere like Prague with them instead of me?"

She didn't sound like she found it funny at all.

"It's nothing personal," I said. "And we have separate rooms."

"I guess that's reassuring. Perhaps, when you get back, you'll come here and we can talk."

I noticed that she didn't say when, or if, she was coming home, and I didn't ask. I would go to Vermont when I returned, and we would talk, and maybe I would drive back to Scarborough alone.

"That might be an idea," I said.

"You didn't say that you'd like to do it."

"I've never had anyone tell me that we should talk and then come out of it feeling better than when I went in."

"It doesn't have to be that way, does it?"

"I hope not."

"I do love you," she said. "You know that, don't you?"

"I know."

"That's what makes it so hard, isn't it? But you have to choose what life you're going to lead. We both do, I guess."

Her voice trailed off.

"I have to go," I said. "I'll see you when I get back."

"Fine."

"Good-bye, Rachel."

"'Bye."

The hotel booked us a table at a place called U Modre Kachnicky, or the Blue Duckling, which lay on a discreet side street off Ujezd. The restaurant was heavily decorated with drapes and rugs and old prints, and mirrors gave an impression of spaciousness to the smaller, lower level. The menu contained a great deal of game, the house's speciality, so we ate duck breast and venison, the various meats resting on sauces made from bilberry, juniper, and madeira rum. We shared a bottle of red Frankovka wine, and ate in relative silence.

While we were still finishing our main courses, a man entered the restaurant and was directed to our table by the hostess. He looked like the kind of guy who sold stolen cell phones on Broadway: leather jacket, jeans, nasty-colored shirt, and a growth of beard that was frozen somewhere between "forgot to shave" and "hobo." I wasn't about to point any of this out to him, though. His jacket could easily have contained two of me inside it, as long as someone found a way to release its current occupier from it without tearing it apart in the process, because the leather seemed to be a little tight on him. I wondered if he was somehow related to the Fulcis from way back, maybe from when man first discovered fire.

His name was Most, according to Louis, who had apparently dealt with him before. Most was a *papka,* or father, of one of the Prague criminal brigades, related by marriage to the *Vor v Zakone,* the "Thief in Law" responsible for all homegrown organized crime. Criminal organizations in the Czech Republic were mainly structured around these brigades, of which there were maybe ten in the entire country. They dealt in racketeering, the smuggling of prostitutes from former Eastern Bloc countries, pandering, automobile theft, drugs, and weapons, but the lines of demarcation between criminal gangs were becoming increasingly unclear as the number of immigrants increased. Ukrainians, Russians, and Chechens were now among the main participants in organized crime in the country, and none of them were reluctant to use violence and brutality against their victims or, inevitably, against one another. Each group had its own areas of specialization. The Russians were more involved in financial crime, while the aggressive Ukrainians favored bank raids and serial robberies. The Bulgarians, who had previously concentrated on erotic clubs, had now branched out into auto theft, drug trafficking, and the supply of Bulgarian prostitutes to brothels. The Italians, less numerous, focused on purchasing real estate; the Chinese favored running casinos and illegal brothels, as well as people smuggling and kidnapping, although such activities tended to remain within their own ethnic groups; and the Albanians had a piece of everything from drugs to debt collection and the trade in leather and gold. The homegrown boys were being forced to battle for their turf against a new breed of immigrant criminal that didn't play by any of the old rules. Compared to the new arrivals, Most was an old-fashioned specialist. He liked guns and women, possibly both together.

"Hello," he said. "Is good?"

He indicated the deer medallions in bilberry sauce on Angel's plate, surrounded by a pile of spinach noodles.

"Yeah," said Angel. "It's real good."

An enormous finger and thumb plucked one of the remaining medallions from Angel's plate, and dropped it into a mouth like the Holland Tunnel.

"Hey man," said Angel, "I wasn't—"

Most gave Angel a look. It wasn't threatening. It wasn't even mildly menacing. It was the look a spider might have given a trapped fly if the insect had suddenly produced a small bill of rights and begun complaining loudly about infringements on its liberty.

"—eating that anyway," finished Angel, somewhat lamely.

"Way to stand up for your rights," I said.

"Yeah, well I don't know what you're looking so smug about," he said. "You're sharing the rest of yours to make up for it."

The big man wiped his fingers on a napkin, then stretched out a hand to Louis.

"Most," he said.

"Louis," said Louis, introducing Angel and me in turn.

"Doesn't 'Most' mean 'bridge?'" I said. I had seen signs on the streets directing tourists to Karluv Most, the Charles Bridge.

Most spread his hands in the gesture of delight common to all those who find visitors to their land making an effort. Not only were we buying guns from him, we were learning the language.

547

"Bridge, yes, is right," said Most. He made a balancing gesture with his hands. "I am bridge: bridge between those who have and those who want."

"Bridge between fucking Europe and Asia if he fell over," muttered Angel, under his breath.

"Excuse?" said Most.

Angel raised his knife and fork, and grinned through a mouthful of deer.

"Good meat," he said. "Hmmmm."

Most didn't look convinced, but he let it slide.

"We should go," he said. "Is busy time for me."

We paid the check and followed Most out to where a black Mercedes was parked on the corner of Nebovidska and Harantova.

"Wow," said Angel. "Gangster car. Very low-key."

"You really don't like him, do you?" I said.

"I don't like big men who throw their weight around."

I had to admit that Angel was probably right. Most was a bit of a jerk, but we needed what he had to offer.

"Try to play nice," I said. "It's not like you're adopting him."

We got in the car, Louis and Angel taking a seat in back while I sat in the passenger seat beside Most. Louis didn't look uneasy, despite the fact that he didn't have a gun. This was purely a business transaction for him. In turn, Most probably knew enough about Louis not to screw him around.

We drove over the Vltava, past bright tourist restaurants and little local bars, eventually leaving behind a big railway station before heading in the direction of the enormous TV mast that dominated the night sky. We turned down some side streets until we came to a doorway with an illuminated sign above it, depicting a figure of Cupid shooting an arrow through a heart. The club was called Cupid Desire, which made a kind of sense. Most pulled up outside and killed the engine. The entrance to the club was guarded by a barred gate and a bored-looking gatekeeper. The gate was opened, Most handed the car keys to his employee, and then we were descending a flight of steps into a small, grimy bar. Eastern European women, some blond, some dark, all bored and worn down, sat in the murk nursing sodas. Rock music played in the background, and a tall, red-haired woman with tattoos on her arms worked the tiny bar. There were no men in sight. When Most arrived, she uncapped a Budvar for him, then spoke to him in Czech.

"You want something to drink?" Most translated.

"No, we're good," said Louis.

Angel looked around the less-than-glorified bordello.

"'Busy time'," he said. "What the hell is it like when it's quiet?"

We followed Most into the heart of the building, past numbered doors that stood open to reveal double beds covered only by pillows and a sheet, the walls decorated with framed posters of vaguely artful nudes, until we came to an office. A man sat on a padded chair, watching three or four monitors that showed the gate to the club, what appeared to be the back alley, two views of the street, and the cash register behind the bar. Most passed him and headed to a steel door at the back of the office. He opened it with a pair of keys, one from his wallet and the other from an alcove near the floor. Inside were cases of alcohol and cartons of cigarettes, but they took up only a fraction of the space. Behind them was a small armory.

"So," said Most, "what would you like?"

Louis had said that we would have no trouble acquiring weapons in Prague, and he was right. The Czech Republic used to be a world leader in the production and export of armaments, but the death of Communism led to a decline in the industry after 1989. There were still about thirty arms manufacturers in the country, though, and the Czechs weren't as particular about the countries to which they exported arms as they should have been. Zimbabwe had reason to thank the Czechs for breaching the embargo on the export of weapons, as had Sri Lanka and even Yemen, that friend to U.S. interests abroad and the target of a nonbinding UN embargo. There had even been attempts to export arms to Eritrea and the Democratic Republic of Congo, facilitated by export licenses covering non-embargoed countries, which were then used to redirect their cargoes to their true destinations. Some of these weapons were legitimately acquired, some were surplus weapons sold to dealers, but there were others that came through more obscure channels, and I suspected that much of Most's inventory might well have been acquired in this way. After all, in 1995 the Czech national police's elite anti-terrorist unit, URNA, was discovered to be selling its own weapons, ammunition, and even Semtex explosive to organized crime elements. Miroslav Kvasnak, the head of URNA, was sacked, but that didn't stop him from later becoming the deputy director of Czech Army Intelligence, and later the Czech defense attaché to India. If the cops were prepared to sell guns to the very criminals they were supposed to be hunting, then the free market appeared to have arrived with a vengeance. If nothing else, the Czechs, flush with the newfound joys of capitalism, clearly understood how to go about creating an entrepreneurial society.

Against the far wall were racks of guns: semi-automatic weapons mainly, along with some shotguns, including a pair of FN tactical police shotguns that were clearly just out of the crate. I saw CZ 2000 assault rifles, and five 5.56N light machine guns mounted on their bipods and lined up on a table beneath their smaller brothers. M-16 mags and M-249 saw belts were stacked neatly beside each. There were also AK-47s and rack upon rack of similar Vz.58s. Beside them were two further racks of various automatic and semi-automatic weapons, and arrayed on a pair of oilcloth-covered trestle tables was a selection of pistols. Nearly everything on display was new, and a lot of it appeared to be military issue. It looked like half of the Czech army's best weaponry was being stored in Most's basement. If the country was invaded, they'd have to make do with peashooters and cusswords until someone cobbled together enough money to buy the guns back.

Angel and I watched as Louis checked his weapons of choice, working the slides, chambering rounds, and inserting and ejecting clips as he made his selections. He eventually opted for a trio of Heckler & Koch .45 pistols, with Knight's suppressors to reduce flash and noise. The guns were marked "USSOCOM" on the barrel, which meant that they were made originally for U.S. Special Operations Command. The barrel and slide were slightly longer than on the usual H&K .45, and they had a screw thread on the muzzle for attaching the suppressor, along with a laser-aiming module mounted in front of the trigger guard. He also picked up some Gerber Patriot combat knives, and a Steyr nine-millimeter machine pistol for himself fitted with a thirty-round magazine and a suppressor, this one longer than the pistol itself.

"We'll take two hundred rounds for the forty-fives, and I'll take three thirties for the Steyr," said Louis when he was done. "The knives you'll throw in for free."

Most agreed on a price for the guns, although his pleasure in the sale was dimmed a little by Louis's negotiating skills. We left with the guns. Most even gave us some holsters, although they were kind of worn. The Mercedes was still parked outside, but this time there was another man behind the wheel.

"My cousin," explained Most. He patted me on the arm. "You sure you don't want to stay, have some fun?"

The words "fun" and "Cupid Desire" didn't seem a natural fit to me.

"I have a girlfriend," I said.

"You could have another," said Most.

"I don't think so. I'm not doing so good with the one I have."

Most didn't offer girls to Angel and Louis. I pointed this out to them on the ride back to the hotel.

"Maybe you're the only one of us who looks like a deviant," suggested Angel.

"Yeah, that must be it, you being so clean-living and all."

"We should be there now," said Louis.

He was talking about Sedlec.

"They're not dumb," I said. "They've waited a long time for this. They'll want to look the place over before they make their move. They'll need equipment, transport, men, and they won't try to get to the statue until after dark. We'll be waiting for them when they come."

We drove to Sedlec the next day, following the highway toward the Polish border because it was a faster road than the more direct route through the villages and towns. We passed fields of corn and beet, still recovering from the harvest, and drove through thick forests with small huts at their edges for the hunters to use. According to the guidebook I'd read on the plane, there were bears and wolves farther south, down in the Bohemian forests, but up here it was mainly small mammals and game birds. In the distance I could see red-roofed villages, the spires of their churches rising above the little houses. Once we left the highway we passed through the industrial city of Kolin, the crossroads for the railways heading east to Moscow and south to Austria. There were crumbling houses and others in the process of restoration. Beer signs hung in windows, and chalk-written menus were displayed by open doors.

Sedlec was now almost a suburb of the larger town of Kutná Hora. A great hill rose up before us: Kank, according to the map, the first big mine opened in the city following the discovery of silver on the Catholic Church's property. I had seen paintings of the mines in the guidebook. They reminded me of Bosch's depictions of hell, with men descending beneath the earth dressed in white tunics so that they could be seen in the dim light of their lamps, leather skirts at their backs so that they could slide down the mine shafts quickly without injuring themselves. They carried enough bread for six days, for it took five hours to climb back to the surface, and so the miners stayed underground for most of the week, only coming up on the seventh day to worship, to spend time with their families, and to replenish their supplies before returning to the world beneath the surface once again. Many kept an icon of Saint Barbara, the patron saint of miners, upon their persons, for those who died in the mines did so without benefit of clergy or the speaking of the last rites, and their bodies would probably remain below ground even if they could be found amidst the rubble of a collapse. With Saint Barbara close by them, they believed they would yet find their way to heaven.

And so the town of Kutná Hora still rested on the remains of the mines. Beneath its buildings and streets were mile upon mile of tunnels, and the earth was mingled with the bones of those who had worked and died to bring the silver to the surface. This, I thought, was a fitting place for the interment of the *Black Angel:* an ancient outpost of a hidden hell in Eastern Europe, a little corner of the honeycomb world.

24

We hung a right at a big Kaufland supermarket and came to the intersection of Cechova and Starosedlecka Streets. The ossuary was on the latter, directly before us, surrounded by high walls and a cemetery. Across from it was a restaurant and store named U Balanu, and around the corner to the right was a hotel. We asked to take a look at the rooms, eventually finding two that gave us a good view of the ossuary, then went to take a look at the interior itself.

Sedlec had never wanted for bodies to fill its graves: what the mines, or plague, or conflict could not provide, the lure of the Holy Land fulfilled. The fourteenth-century *Zbraslav Chronicle* records that in one year alone, thirty thousand people were buried in the cemetery, a great many of them brought there specifically for the privilege of being buried in soil from the Holy Land, for it was believed that the graveyard held miraculous properties, and that any decedent buried there would decompose within a single day, leaving only preserved white bones behind. When those bones inevitably began to stack up, the cemetery's keepers built a two-story mortuary containing an ossuary within which the remains might be displayed. If the ossuary served a practical purpose by allowing graves to be emptied of skeletal remains and freed up for those more in need of a dark place in which to shed their mortal burden, it also served a spiritual purpose at least equally well: the bones became reminders of the transience of human existence and the temporary nature of all earthly things. At Sedlec, the border between this world and the next was marked in bone.

Even here, in this foreign place, there were echoes of my own past. I recalled a hotel room in New Orleans, the air outside still and heavy with moisture. We had been closing in on the man who had taken my wife and child from me, and coming at last to some understanding of the nature of his "art." He too believed in the transience of all human affairs, and he left behind his own *memento mori* as he traveled the land, tearing skin from flesh, and flesh from bone, to show us that life was but a fleeting, unimportant thing, capable of being taken at will by a being as worthless as himself.

Except that he was wrong, for not all that we tried to achieve was without value, and not every aspect of our lives was unworthy of celebration or remembrance. With each life that he took, the world became a poorer place, its index of possibilities reduced forever, deprived of the potential for art, science, passion, ingenuity, hope, and regret that the unlived existences of generation upon generation of progeny would have brought with them.

But what of the lives that I had taken? Was I not equally culpable, and was that not why there were now so many names, of both good men and bad, carved upon that palimpsest I bore, and for each of which I might justifiably be called to account? I could argue that by committing a smaller evil, I had prevented a greater one from occurring, but I would still bear the mark of that sin upon me, and perhaps be damned for it. Yet, in the end, I could not stand by. There were sins that I had committed out of anger, touched by wrath, and for those I had no doubt that I would at last be charged and found wanting. But the others? I chose to act as I did, believing that the greater evil lay in doing nothing. I have tried to make reparation, in my way.

The problem is that, like cancer, a little corruption of the soul will eventually spread throughout the whole.

The problem is that there are no small evils.

We passed through the cemetery gates and skirted the graves, the more recent stones often marked with photographs of the deceased inset into the marble or granite beneath the word RODINA, followed by the family name. One or two even had alcoves carved in the stone, protected by glass, behind which framed portraits of all of those buried beneath the ground sat undisturbed, as they might have done on a sideboard or a shelf when those depicted were still alive. Three steps led down to the ossuary entrance: a pair of plain wooden doors overlooked by a semicircular window. To the right of the entrance, a steeper flight of steps led up to the chapel, for the chapel stood above the ossuary, and from its window, one might look down on the interior of the ossuary itself. Inside the door, a young woman sat behind a glass display case containing cards and trinkets. We paid her thirty Czech koruny each to enter, or barely $4 between us. We were the only people present, and our breath assumed strange forms in the cold air as we looked down upon the wonders of Sedlec.

"My God," said Angel. "What is this place?"

A stairway led down before us. On the walls at either side, the letters IHS, for *Iesus Hominum Salvator*, or

"Jesus Savior of Humanity," were set in long bones, surrounded by four sets of three bones representing the arms of a cross. Each arm ended in a single skull. At the base of the stairs, two sets of parallel columns mirrored one another. The columns were made up of skulls alternated with what appeared to be femurs, the bones set vertically beneath the upper jaw of each skull. The columns followed the edges of two alcoves, into which had been set a pair of enormous urns, or perhaps they might have been baptismal fonts, again constructed entirely from human remains, and lidded by a circle of skulls.

I stepped into the main area of the ossuary. To my right and left were chambers containing huge pyramids of skulls and bones, too many to count, topped in each case by a wooden crown painted gold. Two similar barred rooms faced me, so that they occupied the four corners of the ossuary. According to the information leaflet thrust into our hands at the door, the remains represented the multitudes facing judgment before God, while the crowns symbolized the kingdom of heaven and the promise of resurrection from the dead. On one of the walls, beside the skull chamber to my right, there was an inscription, again inset in bone. It read:

F. RINT
Z ČESKÉ SKALICE
1870

In common with most artists, Rint had signed his work. But if Bosworth was right, then Rint had seen something while he was completing the reconstruction of the ossuary, and what he had seen had haunted him to such a degree that he had spent years re-creating its image, as though by doing so he might slowly begin to exorcise it from his imagination, and bring himself peace at last.

The other chamber, to my left, was marked by the coat of arms of the Schwarzenberg family, who had paid for Rint's work. Once again, it was made entirely from bone: Rint had even constructed a bird, a raven or a rook, using a pelvic bone for its body and a section of rib for its wing. The rook was dipping its beak into the hollow eye socket of what was supposed to be a Turkish skull, a detail that had been added to the coat of arms as a gift from Emperor Rudolf II after Adolf of Schwarzenberg had curbed the power of the Turks by conquering the fortification of Raab in 1598.

But all of this was merely a sideshow compared to the centerpiece of the ossuary. From the vaulted ceiling a chandelier hung, fashioned from elements of every bone that the human body could supply. Its extended parts were hanging arm bones, ending in a plate of pelvic bones upon which rested, in each case, a single skull. A candleholder was inset into the top of each head, and a ribbon of interlinked bones formed the suspension chains, keeping them in place. It was impossible to look upon it and not feel one's sense of disgust overcome by awe at the imagination that could have produced such an artifact. It was simultaneously beautiful and disturbing, a marvelous testament to mortality.

Inset into the floor beneath the chandelier was a rectangular concrete slab. This was the entrance to the crypt, within which were contained the remains of a number of wealthy individuals. At each corner of the crypt stone stood a Baroque candelabra in the shape of a Gothic tower, with three lines of seven skulls set into each, again with an arm bone clasped beneath their ruined jaws, and topped by angels blowing trumpets.

All told, the remains of some forty thousand persons were contained in the ossuary.

I looked around. Angel and Louis were examining a pair of glass cabinets, behind which were contained the skulls of some of those who had died in the Hussite campaigns. Two or three bore the small holes of musket balls, while others had gaping wounds inflicted by blunt force. A sharp blade had almost entirely cleaved away the back of one skull.

Something dripped onto my shirt, spreading a stain across the fabric. I looked up and saw moisture on the ceiling. Perhaps the roof was leaking, I thought, but then I felt a rivulet of sweat run down my face and melt upon my lips. I realized that I could no longer see my breath in the air, and that I had begun to perspire heavily. Neither Angel nor Louis appeared troubled. Angel, in fact, had zipped his jacket up to his chin and was stamping his feet slightly to keep warm, his hands jammed into his pockets.

Sweat ran into my eyes, blurring my vision. I tried to clear it by wiping the sleeve of my coat across my forehead, but it seemed to make matters worse. The salt stung me, and I began to feel dizzy and disoriented. I didn't want to lean against anything, for fear of setting off the alarms about which we had been warned at the door. Instead, I squatted on the floor and took some deep breaths, but I was teetering slightly on my heels and so was forced to put my fingers to the ground to support myself. They touched against the crypt stone, and instantly I felt a wave of pain break across my skin.

I was drowning in liquid heat, my whole body aflame. I tried to open my mouth to say something, but the heat rushed to fill the new gap, stilling any sound from within. I was blind, mute, forced to endure my torments in silence. I wanted to die, yet I could not. Instead, I found myself sealed, trapped in a hard, dark place. I was constantly on the verge of suffocation, unable to draw a breath, and still there was no release. Time ceased to have meaning. There was only an endless, unendurable now.

And yet I endured.

A hand was placed upon my shoulder, and Angel spoke. His touch felt incredibly cool to me, and his breath was like ice upon my skin. And then I became aware of another voice beneath Angel's, except this one repeated words in a language that I did not understand, a litany of phrases spoken over and over again, always with the same intonation, the same pauses, the same emphases. It was an invocation of sorts, yet one bound up entirely with madness, and I was reminded of those animals in a zoo that, driven insane by their incarceration and the never-changing nature of their surroundings, find themselves endlessly stalking in their cages, always at the same speed, always with the same movements, as though the only way they can survive is to become as one with the place in which they are kept, to match its unyielding absence of novelty with their own.

Suddenly the voice changed. It stumbled over its words. It tried to begin once more but lost its place. Finally, it stopped entirely, and I became aware of something probing the ossuary, the way a blind man might stop the tapping of his cane and listen for the approach of a stranger.

And then it howled, over and over again, the tone and volume rising until it became one repeated shriek of rage and despair, but despair now, for the first time in so long, leavened by hope. The sound of it tore at my ears, shredding my nerves, as it called to me over and over and over again.

It is aware, I thought. It knows.

It is alive.

Angel and Louis brought me back to the hotel. I was weak, and my skin was burning. I tried to lie down, but the nausea would not go away. After a time, I joined them in their room. We sat at the windows and watched the cemetery and its buildings.

"What happened in there?" said Louis at last.

"I'm not sure."

He was angry. He didn't even try to hide it.

"Yeah, well you need to explain it, don't matter how weird it sounds. We got no time for this."

"You don't have to tell me that," I snapped.

He eyed me levelly.

"So what was it?"

I had no choice but to answer him.

"I thought, for a moment, that I felt something down there, under the ossuary, and that it knew I was aware of it. I had a sensation of being trapped, of suffocation and heat. That's it. I can't tell you anything more."

I didn't know what to expect from Louis in response to this. Now, I thought. Now we will arrive at it. The thing that has come between us is wriggling its way to the surface.

"You okay to go back in there?" he said.

"I'll wear a lighter coat next time."

Louis tapped his fingers gently on the edge of his chair, in time to some rhythm that only he could hear.

"I had to ask," he said.

"I understand."

"I guess I'm getting impatient. I want this to end. I don't like it when it's personal."

He turned in his chair and stared at me.

"They'll come, won't they?"

"Yes," I said. "Then you can do whatever you want with them. I promised you that we would find them, and we have. Isn't that what you wanted from me?"

But still he wasn't satisfied. His fingers drummed on the windowsill, and his gaze seemed drawn again and again to the twin spires of the chapel. Angel was seated on a chair in one dark corner, carefully maintaining a stillness and silence, waiting for what divided us to be named. A sea change had occurred in our friendship, and I did not know if the result would bring an end to it, or a new beginning.

"Say it," I said.

"I wanted to blame you," said Louis, softly. He did not look at me as he spoke. "I wanted to blame you for what happened to Alice. Not in the beginning, because I knew the life that she led. I tried to look out for her, and I tried to make other people look out for her too, but in the end she chose her own path, like we all do. When she went missing, I was grateful. I was relieved. It didn't last long, but it was there, and I was ashamed of it.

"Then we found Garcia, and this guy Brightwell came out of the woodwork, and suddenly it wasn't about Alice no more. It was about you, because you were tied into it somehow. And I got to thinking that maybe it wasn't

Alice's fault, that maybe it was yours. You know how many women make their living on the streets of New York? Of all the whores or junkies they could have chosen, of all the women who might have gotten involved with this man Winston, why should it have been her? It was like you cast a shadow on lives, and that shadow was growing, and it touched her even though you'd never met her, didn't even know she existed. After that, I didn't want to look at you for a time. I didn't hate you for it, because it wasn't intentional on your part, but I didn't want to be around you. Then she started calling to me."

He was reflected clearly in the glass now, as the night drew in. His face hung in the air, and perhaps it was a flaw in the glass that duplicated his reflection, or maybe it was something more, but a second presence seemed suspended in the darkening air behind him, its features indistinguishable, and the stars were shining through its eyes.

"I hear her at night. I thought at the start that it was someone in the building, but when I went outside the apartment to check, I couldn't hear her no more. It was only inside. I only hear her when there's nobody else around. It's her voice, except it's not alone. There are other voices with it, so many of them, and they're all calling different names. She calls mine. It's hard to understand her, because someone doesn't want her calling out. It didn't matter to him at first, because he thought nobody cared about her, but now he knows better. He wants her to stay quiet. She's dead, but she keeps calling out, like she's got no peace. She cries all the time. She's afraid. They're all afraid.

"And I knew then that maybe it was no coincidence that you found Angel and me either, or that we found you. I don't understand everything that goes on with you, but I do know this: whatever happened was meant to come to pass, and we're all involved. It's always been waiting in the shadows, and none of us can walk away from it. There's no blame to be laid at your door. I know that now. Sure, there are other women who could have been taken, but what then? They'd have disappeared, and it would be their voices calling, but there would be no one to hear them, and no one would care. This way, we heard, and we came."

At last, he turned back to me, and the woman in the night faded away.

"I want her to stop crying," he said, and I could see clearly the lines upon his face and the tiredness in his eyes. "I want them all to stop crying."

Walter Cole called me on my cell that night. I had spoken to him before we left, and had told him as much as I knew.

"You sound a million miles away," he said, "and if I were you, I'd keep it that way. Just about everyone you've ever talked to on this thing is dead, and pretty soon people are going to start looking for you to answer some questions. Some of this you may not want to hear. Neddo's dead. Someone cut him up badly. It might have been torture in order to gain information, except there was a rag stuffed in his mouth, so even if he had something to give up, he wouldn't have been able to speak. That's not the worst of it, either. Reid, the monk who spoke with you, was stabbed to death outside a bar in Hartford. The other monk phoned it in, then disappeared. Cops want to talk to him too, but either his order is protecting him or they really don't know where he is."

"Do the cops think he did it? If they do, they're wrong."

"They just want to talk to him. There was blood on Reid's mouth, and it wasn't his own. Unless it matches Bartek's, then he's probably in the clear. It looks like Reid bit whoever killed him. The blood sample has been fast-tracked to a private lab. They'll get the results in a day or two."

I already knew what they would find: old, corrupted DNA. And I wondered if Reid's voice had now joined Alice's in that dark place from which Brightwell's victims called out for release. I thanked Walter, then hung up and returned to my vigil upon the ossuary.

Sekula arrived on the morning of the second day. He didn't come alone. There was a driver who waited behind the wheel of the gray Audi, and Sekula entered the ossuary in the company of a small man in jeans and a sailor's coat. After thirty minutes, they came out and took the stairs up to the chapel. They didn't stay there long.

"Checking out the alarm," said Angel, as we watched them from the hotel. "The little guy is probably the expert."

"How good is it?" I asked.

"I took a look at it yesterday. Not good enough to keep them out. Doesn't even look like it's been upgraded since the last break-in."

The two men emerged from the chapel and walked around the perimeter of the building, then headed back to the Audi and drove away.

"We could have followed them," said Louis.

"We could," I said, "but what would have been the point? They have to come back."

Angel was pulling at his lower lip.

"How soon?" I asked.

"Me, I'd get it done as soon as possible if the alarm wasn't a problem. Tonight, maybe."

It felt right. They would come, and then we would know everything.

There was a small courtyard beside the U Balanu store across the street from the ossuary that doubled as an outdoor area for the restaurant during the summer. It was an easy matter to gain entry to it, and that was where Louis took up position shortly after dusk the following evening. I was in the hotel room, where I could get a good overview of all that was taking place. Louis and I had agreed that we would make no move alone. Angel was in the cemetery. There was a small shed with a red tiled roof to the left of the ossuary. Its windows were broken, but guarded by black steel grates. At one time it might have functioned as the grave digger's cottage, but it now contained just slates, bricks, planks of wood, and one very cold New Yorker.

My cell phone was switched to vibrate. All was silence, apart from the distant growl of passing cars. And so we waited.

The gray Audi arrived shortly after nine. It made one full circuit of the block, then parked on Starosedlecka. It was followed minutes later by a second, black Audi and a nondescript green truck, its tires thick with accumulated mud and the gold lettering along its body faded and unreadable. Sekula got out of the first car, accompanied by the little alarm specialist and a second figure wearing black trousers and a calf-length hooded coat. The hood was up, for the temperature had dropped considerably that day. Even Sekula was identifiable only by his height, as a scarf covered his mouth and he wore a black knitted cap on his head.

Three people emerged from the second vehicle. One was the charming Miss Zahn. She didn't seem troubled by the cold. Her coat was open and her head was uncovered. Given the temperature of what was running in her veins, the night probably felt a little balmy to her. The second person was a white-haired man whom I did not recognize. He had a gun in his hand. The third was Brightwell. He was still wearing the same beige clothes. Like Miss Zahn, the cold didn't appear to bother him unduly. He walked back to the truck and spoke to one of the two men inside. It looked like they were planning to transport the statue if they found it.

The two men climbed down from the cab and followed Brightwell to the back of the truck. Once the door was opened, two more men climbed out, swaddled in layers of clothing for the cold journey in the unheated rear. Then, after a brief consultation, Brightwell led Miss Zahn, Sekula, the unknown individual in the hooded coat, and the alarm specialist to the cemetery gate. One of the hired hands followed them. Angel had locked the gate behind him when he was making his way to the hut, but Brightwell simply cut the chain and the group entered the grounds of the ossuary.

I took a brief head count. Outside we had the driver of the Audi and three of the truck crew. Inside the grounds there were six more. I buzzed Louis.

"What can you see?" I said.

"One guy now at the ossuary door, inside the grounds," he said quietly. "The driver, standing at the passenger door, back to me."

I heard him shift position.

"Two amateurs from the truck at either corner, keeping watch on the main road. One more at the gate."

I thought about it.

"Give me five minutes. I'll come around from behind the truck and take the corner guys. You have the driver and the man at the gate. Tell Angel he has the door. I'll buzz you when I'm ready to move."

I exited the hotel and worked my way as quickly as I could around the block. Eventually, I had to climb a wall and walk through a green field containing a children's play area, the cemetery to my left. I buzzed Angel as I entered the field.

"I'm in the field behind you. Don't shoot me."

"Just this once. I'm gonna move with you."

I heard a low noise from the cemetery as Angel emerged from the shed, then everything was quiet again.

I found a gate at the far end of the field. I opened it as quietly as I could. To my left I could just see the back of the truck. I kept to the wall until it began to curve toward the main entrance. The shape of the guard at the gate was clearly visible. If I attempted to cross the street, there was a good chance that he would see me.

I called Louis again.

"Change of plan," he said. "Angel's taking the door *and* the gate."

Inside the cemetery, the guard at the ossuary door lit a cigarette. His name was Gary Toolan, and he was little more than an American criminal for hire based in Europe. Mostly he just liked women, booze, and hurting people, but some of the people for whom he was now working gave him the creeps. They were different, somehow: alien. The guy with white hair, the looker with the strange skin, and most of all the fat man with the swollen neck made him very uneasy. He didn't know what they were doing here, but he was certain of one thing: he had their number, and that was why he had received payment in advance. If they tried anything, he had his money, he had a backup pistol, and the men that he had sourced for these freaks would stand by him in the event of trouble. Toolan took a long drag on his cigarette. As he dropped the match the shadows around him shifted, and it took him a second to realize that the falling light and the mutating darkness were unrelated.

Angel shot him in the side of the head, then moved toward the gate.

Louis checked his watch. He still had the phone to his ear. I waited.

"Three," counted Louis. "Two, one. Now."

There was a soft pop, and the man at the gate crumpled to the ground, shot from behind by Angel.

I ran.

The Audi driver immediately went for his gun, but Louis was already moving to take him. The driver seemed to sense him at the last minute, for he was starting to turn when Louis's bullet entered the back of his skull. Now one of the men at the corner was shouting something. He ran to the cab and almost managed to open the door before he slid down the side and tried to reach for the small of his back, where my first shot had taken him. I shot him again on the ground and took the last man as he loosed off a round. It blew out a chunk of crumbling masonry from the wall beside my head, but by then the man who had fired the shot was dead.

Louis was already pulling the body of the driver into the restaurant courtyard. He stopped when he heard the shot. Nobody emerged from any of the nearby houses to see what was going on. Either they had taken the shot for a car backfiring or they just didn't want to know. I pushed the bodies of the two men under their truck, where they would not easily be seen, then Louis and I ran to the ossuary. Angel was crouching at the door, casting quick glances into the interior.

"One more down inside," he said. "He heard the shot and came running. It looks like they've got the crypt stone up, and there's a light burning by the hole, but I don't think there's anyone else in there. I guess they're all below ground."

The heat inside the ossuary was intense. At first I was afraid that I was about to experience a return of the nausea that I had felt the previous day, thus confirming Louis's worst fears about me, but when I looked at Angel and Louis, they had both begun to sweat profusely. We were surrounded by the sound of dripping water, as rivulets ran from the ceilings and walls, dripping on the exposed bones and washing like tears down the white cheeks of the dead. The body of the alarm specialist lay inside the door, already speckled with moisture.

The crypt stone had been ejected from its resting place and now lay to one side of the entrance, beside which a battery-powered lamp burned. We skirted the hole, trying not to expose ourselves to anyone waiting below. I thought I could detect, however faintly, the sound of voices, and then stone moving upon stone. A flight of rough steps led down into the gloom, a trace of illumination visible from an unseen light source in the crypt itself.

Angel looked at me. I looked at Angel. Louis looked at both of us.

"Great," whispered Angel. "Just great. We should be wearing targets on our chests."

"You're staying up here," I told him. "Keep to the shadows by the door. We don't need any more of them arriving and trapping us down there."

Angel didn't object. In his position, I wouldn't have objected either. Louis and I stood just out of sight of the steps. One of us would have to go first.

"What'll it be?" I said. "Age, or beauty?"

He stepped forward and placed his foot on the first step.

"Both," he said.

I stayed a couple of steps behind him as he descended. The floor of the ossuary, which doubled as the crypt ceiling, was two feet thick, so we were almost halfway down before we could see anything, and even then half of the crypt remained in darkness. To our left was a series of niches, each occupied by a stone tomb. All were ornately carved with coats of arms or depictions of the resurrection. To our right was a similar arrangement of tombs, except that one of the stone coffins had been overturned and its occupant's remains spilled across the flagged floor. The bones had long since disarticulated, but I thought I could faintly see traces of the shroud in which the body had been interred. The niche, now empty, revealed a rectangular opening previously concealed by the tomb, maybe four feet high and as many feet across. I could see light filtering through the gap from behind. The voices were louder now, and the temperature had risen noticeably. It was like standing at the mouth of a furnace, waiting to be consumed by the flames.

I felt a breath of slightly cooler air at my neck, and in the same instant spun to my right, pushing Louis to one side with as much force as I could muster before I hit the floor. Something sliced through the air and impacted on one of the columns supporting the vault. I smelt a hint of perfume as Miss Zahn grunted with the shock of the crowbar's impact upon the stone. I struck out as hard as I could with my heel and caught her on the side of the knee. Her leg buckled and I heard her scream, but she whipped the crowbar instinctively in my direction as I tried to rise, striking me on my right elbow and sending a shock wave through my arm that paralyzed it immediately. I dropped my gun and was forced to scramble backward before I felt the wall at my back and could raise myself using my left hand. I heard a shot fired, and even though it was suppressed it still echoed loudly in the enclosed space. I couldn't tell where Louis was until I scrambled to my feet and saw him pressed against one of the tombs, locked in close combat with Sekula. The lawyer's gun now lay on the floor, but with his left hand he was keeping Louis's own gun away from him while his right scratched against Louis's face, looking for soft tissue to damage. I couldn't intervene. Despite her pain, Miss Zahn was limping around me, looking for another opportunity to strike. She had removed her jacket to allow herself some respite from the heat, and in the course of her attempts to strike me the buttons on her black shirt had popped. A shaft of light caught her, and I saw the tattoos upon her skin. They seemed to move in the lamplight, the faces twisting and contorting, the great eyes blinking, the pupils dilating. A mouth opened, revealing small, catlike teeth. A head turned, its pug nose flattening further, as though another living being inside her had pressed itself hard against her epidermis from below, trying to force itself through to the world outside. Her whole body was a teeming gallery of grotesques, and I could not seem to draw my eyes from them. The effect was almost hypnotic, and I wondered if that was how she subdued her victims before taking them, entrancing them as she moved in for the kill.

My right arm ached, and I felt as if all the moisture was being drained from my body by the heat. I couldn't understand why she didn't just shoot me. I stumbled backward as Miss Zahn feinted at me. I lost my footing, and then the crowbar was moving in a great arc toward my head when a voice said, "Hey, bitch!" and a booted foot caught Miss Zahn in the jaw, breaking it with a sharp snapping sound. Her eyes squeezed shut in shock, and in the shadowy light I thought that the faces on her body responded in turn, the eyes briefly snapping closed, the mouths opening in silent roars of agony. Miss Zahn looked to where Angel lay sideways upon the stairs, just beneath the level of the ceiling. His right foot was still outstretched, and above it he held the .45.

Miss Zahn dropped the crowbar and raised her left hand. Angel fired, and the bullet tore through the palm. She slid down the wall, leaving a trail of dark matter behind. One eye remained open, but the other was a black and red wound. She blinked hard, and once again all the tattooed eyes on her skin seemed to blink in unison, then her eye closed, the painted eyelids on her body drooping slowly in turn until at last all movement ceased.

As she died, the energy seemed to leave Sekula. He sagged, giving Louis the opening that he sought. He forced the muzzle of his gun upward into the soft flesh beneath Sekula's chin, and pulled the trigger. The noise of a shot reverberated around us once again, the sound finding material expression in the dark fountain that struck the vaulted ceiling. Louis released Sekula and allowed him to crumple to the floor.

"He stopped," said Louis, indicating Sekula. "I was under his gun, and he stopped."

He sounded puzzled.

"He told me that he didn't think he could kill a man," I said. "I guess he was right."

I sagged against the damp wall of the crypt. My arm ached badly, but I didn't think there were any bones broken. I nodded my thanks to Angel, and he returned to his post in the ossuary itself. Beyond us lay the opening in the wall.

"After you this time," said Louis.

I looked at the remains of Miss Zahn and Sekula.

"At least I might see the next person who attacks us," I said.

"She had a gun," he said, pointing at the pistol tucked into Miss Zahn's belt. "She could have just shot you."

"She wanted me alive," I said.

"Why? Your charm?"

I shook my head.

"She thought I was like her, and like Brightwell."

575

I stooped and passed through the gap, Louis steps behind me. We were in a long tunnel, with a ceiling barely six feet in height that prevented Louis from standing up straight. The tunnel stretched ahead into the darkness, curving gently to the right as it went. On either side were alcoves or cells, most of which appeared to contain nothing more than stone beds, although some had broken bowls and old empty wine bottles on the floor, indicating that they had been occupied at one point. Each had a kind of portcullis arrangement to close it off, the barred gate capable of being raised and lowered through a pulley and chain system outside the alcove. In nearly every case, the alcoves were unbarred, but we came to one on the right upon which the gate had been lowered. Inside, my flashlight picked out clothed human remains. The skull still retained some of its hair, and the clothing was relatively intact. The stench was foul from within.

"What is this place?" said Louis.

"It looks like a jail."

"Seems like they forgot they had a guest down here."

Something rustled in the closed cell. A rat, I thought. It's only a rat. It has to be. Whoever was lying in that cell was long dead. It was tattered skin and yellowed bone, nothing more.

And then the man inside moved on his stone cot. His fingernails dragged across the stone, his right leg stretched almost imperceptibly, and his head shifted slightly where it rested. The effort it took was clearly enormous. I could see every wasted muscle working on his desiccated arms, and every tendon straining in his face as he tried to speak. His features were buried deep in his skull, as though they were slowly being sucked inside. The eyes were like rotted fruits in the hollows of the sockets, barely visible behind his emaciated hand as he sought to shield himself from the light while simultaneously trying to see those that lay behind it.

Louis took a step back.

"How can he still be alive?" he said. He could not keep the shock from his voice. I had never heard him speak like that before.

Like the half-life of an isotope: that remained the only way that I could fathom it. The process of dying, but with the inevitable end delayed beyond imagining. Perhaps, like Kittim, this unknown man was proof of that belief.

"It doesn't matter," I said. "Leave him."

I saw Louis raise his pistol. The action surprised me. He was not a man known for conventional mercies. I laid my hand on the barrel of the gun, forcing it gently down.

"No," I said.

The being on the stone slab tried to speak. I could see the desperation in its eyes, and I almost felt something of Louis's pity for it. I turned away, and heard Louis follow.

By now we were deep beneath the ground, and far from the cemetery. From the direction in which we were heading, I believed that we were somewhere between the ossuary and the site of the former monastery nearby. There were more cells here, many with the portcullises lowered, but I glanced in only one or two as I went by. Those who had been incarcerated in them were now clearly dead, their bones long separated. They probably made mistakes along the way, I thought. It was like the old witch trials: if the suspects died, they were innocent. If they survived, then they were guilty.

The heat grew more and more intense. The walls were hot to the touch, and our clothing became so burdensome that we were forced to shed our jackets and coats along the way. There was a rushing sound in my head. Threaded through it, I thought, I could discern words, except they were no longer fragments of an old incantation spoken in madness. These had purpose and intent. They were calling, *urging*.

There was light ahead of us. We saw a circular room, lined with open cells, and a trio of lanterns at its center. Beyond them stood the obese figure of Brightwell. He was working at a blank wall, trying to free a brick at the level of his head, using a crowbar. Beside him was the hooded, jacketed figure, its head lowered. Brightwell registered our presence first, because he turned suddenly, the crowbar still in his hands. I expected him to reach for a gun, but he did not. Instead, he seemed almost pleased. His mouth was disfigured, his lower lip crisscrossed with black stitches where Reid had bitten him during his final struggle.

"I knew," he said. "I knew that you'd come."

The figure to his right lowered its hood. I saw a woman's gray hair hanging loose, and then her face was exposed. In the lantern light, Claudia Stern's fine bone structure had taken on a thin, hungry aspect. Her skin was pale and dry, and when she opened her mouth to speak I thought that her teeth seemed longer than before, as though her gums were receding. There was a white mote in her right eye, previously hidden by some form of concealing lens. Brightwell handed the crowbar to her, but he made no attempt to move toward us, or to threaten us in any way.

"Nearly done," he said. "It's good that you should be here for this."

Claudia Stern inserted the crowbar into the gap Brightwell had made, and strained. I saw the stone shift in its place. She repositioned the bar, then pushed hard. The stone moved some thirty degrees, until it was set perpendicular to the wall. In the gap revealed, I thought I saw something shine. With a final effort, she forced the stone away. It fell to the floor as she continued to work at the bricks, forcing them apart more easily now that the first breach had been made. I should have stopped her, but I did not. I realized that I, too, wanted to know what lay behind the wall. I wanted to see the *Black Angel*. A large square patch of silver was now clearly visible through the hole. I could pick out the shape of a rib, and the edge of what might have been an arm. The figure was rough and unfinished, with droplets of hardened silver fixed upon it like frozen tears.

Suddenly, as though responding to an unanticipated impulse, Claudia Stern dropped the crowbar and thrust her hand into the hole.

It took a moment for me to notice the temperature rising again, for it was already so hot in the chamber, but I began to feel my skin prickle and burn, as though I were standing unprotected in intense sunlight. I looked at my skin, almost expecting it to begin reddening as I watched. The voice in my head was louder now, a torrent of whispers like the rushing of water at a great fall, its substance unintelligible but its meaning clear. Close to where Stern was standing, liquid began to drip through holes in the mortar, sliding slowly down the walls like droplets of mercury. I could see them steaming, and I could smell the dust burning. Whatever lay behind that wall, it was now melting, the silver falling away to reveal whatever lay concealed within. Stern looked at Brightwell, and I could see the surprise on her face. This was clearly beyond her expectations. All of the preparations that they had made indicated that they had intended to transport the statue back to New York, not to have it melt around their feet. I heard a sound from behind the wall, like the beating of a wing, and it brought me back to where I was, reminding me of what I had to do.

I pointed my gun at Brightwell.

"Stop her."

Brightwell didn't move.

"You won't use it," he said. "We'll come back."

Beside me, Louis seemed to jerk his head. His face contorted, as though in pain, and he raised his left hand to his ear. Then I heard it too: a chorus of voices, their words raised in a cacophony of pleading, all coming from somewhere deep within Brightwell.

The silver drops had become a series of streams, seeping out through cracks in the walls. I thought I heard more movement behind the stones, but there was so much noise in my head that I could not be certain.

"You're a sick, deluded man," I said.

"You know it's true," he said. "You sense it in yourself."

I shook my head.

"No, you're wrong."

"There is no salvation for you, or for any of us," said Brightwell. "God deprived you of your wife, your child. Now He's going to take a second woman away from you, and a second child. He doesn't care. Do you think He would have allowed them to suffer as they did if they really mattered to Him, if anyone really mattered to Him? Why, then, would you believe in Him and not in us? Why do you continue to have hope in Him?"

I struggled to find my voice. It seemed as though my vocal cords were burning.

"Because with you," I said, "there is no hope at all."

I sighted carefully along the barrel.

"You won't kill me," said Brightwell once more, but there was now doubt in his voice.

Suddenly, he moved. All at once he was everywhere, and nowhere. I heard his voice in my ear, felt his hands on my skin. His mouth opened, revealing those slightly blunted teeth. They were biting me, and my blood was pooling in his mouth as he tore into me.

I fired three times, and the confusion stopped. Brightwell's left foot was shattered at the ankle, and there was a second wound below his knee. The third shot had gone astray, I thought, and then I saw the red stain upon his belly. A gun appeared in Brightwell's hand. He tried to raise it, but Louis was already on top of him, pushing it away.

I moved past them both, making for Claudia Stern. Her attention was entirely focused on the wall before her, mesmerized by what was taking place before her eyes. The metal was already cooling upon the ground around her feet, and there was no longer any silver to be seen through the gap in the wall. Instead, I saw a pair of black ribs encased by a thin layer of skin, the exposed patch slowly increasing in dimension around the area where her hand remained in contact. I grasped the woman's shoulder and pulled her away from the wall, breaking her connection with whatever was concealed within. She screamed in rage, and her voice was echoed by something deep within the walls. Her fingers scraped at my face and her feet kicked at my shins. I caught a flash of metal in her left hand just before the blade sliced across my chest, opening a long wound from my left side all the way up to my collarbone. I struck her hard in the face using the base of my hand, and as she stumbled away I hit her again, forcing her back until she was at the entrance to one of the cells. She tried to slash at me with the knife, but this time I kicked out at her, and she fell onto the stones. I followed her in, and removed the knife from her hand, placing my foot against her wrist first so that she could not strike out at me. She made an attempt to scramble past me, but I kicked her again and my foot struck home. She let out an animal sound and stopped moving.

I backed out of the cell. The silver had stopped bleeding from the walls, and the heat seemed to dissipate slightly. The streams upon the floor and wall were already growing hard, and I could no longer hear any sounds, real or imagined, from behind the stones. I went to where Brightwell lay. Louis had torn away the front of his shirt, exposing his mottled belly. The wound was bleeding badly, but he was still alive.

"He'll survive, if we get him to a hospital," said Louis.

"It's your choice," I said. "Alice was part of you."

Louis took a step backward and lowered his gun.

"No," he said. "I don't understand this, but you do."

Brightwell's voice was calm, but his face was contorted with pain.

"If you kill me, I'll find you," he said to me. "I found you once and I'll find you again, however long it may take. I will be God to you. I will destroy everything that you love and I will force you to watch as I tear it apart.

And then you and I will descend to a dark place, and I will be with you there. There will be no salvation for you, no repentance, no hope."

He took a long, rasping breath. I could still hear that strange cacophony of voices, but now its pitch had changed. There was an expectancy to it, a rising joy.

"No forgiveness," he whispered. "Above all, no forgiveness."

His blood was spreading across the floor. It followed the gaps in the flagstones, gradually seeping in geometric patterns toward the cell in which Stern lay. She was conscious now, but weak and disoriented. She stretched a hand toward Brightwell, and he caught the movement and looked to her.

I raised the gun.

"I will come for you," said Brightwell.

"Yes," she said. "I know you will."

Brightwell coughed and scraped at the wound in his belly.

"I will come for them all," he said.

I shot him in the center of the forehead, and he ceased to be. A final breath emerged from his body. I felt a coolness upon my face, and smelled salt and clean air as the great choir was silenced at last.

Claudia Stern was crawling across the floor, trying to resume contact with the figure that still stood trapped behind the wall. I moved to stop her, but now there were footsteps approaching from the tunnel behind us. Louis and I turned and prepared to face them.

Bartek appeared in the doorway. Angel was with him, looking a little uncertain. Five or six others followed, men and women, and I understood finally why no one had responded to the shot on the street, why the alarm had not been replaced, and how a last crucial fragment of the map had found its way from France to Sedlec.

"You knew all along," I said. "You baited them, then you waited for them to come."

Four of those who had accompanied Bartek stepped around us and surrounded Claudia Stern, dragging her back to the open cell.

"Martin revealed its secrets to me," said Bartek. "He said that you'd be there at the end. He had a lot of faith in you."

"I'm sorry. I heard what happened."

"I will miss him," said Bartek. "I think I lived vicariously through his pleasures."

I heard the jangling of chains. Claudia Stern started to scream, but I did not look.

"What will you do with her?"

"They called it 'walling' in medieval times. A terrible way to die, but a worse way not to die, assuming she is what she believes herself to be."

"And there's only one way to find out."

"Unfortunately, yes."

"But you won't keep her here?"

"Everything will be moved, in time, and hidden once again. Sedlec has served its purpose."

"It was a trap."

"But the bait had to be real. They would sense it if the statue were not present. The pretence of its loss had to be maintained."

Claudia Stern's screams increased in intensity, then were suddenly silenced.

"Come," said Bartek. "It's time to leave."

*　　*　　*

We stood in the churchyard. Bartek knelt and brushed snow from a headstone, revealing a photograph of a middle-aged man in a suit.

"There are bodies," I said.

Bartek smiled.

"This is an ossuary, in a churchyard," he said. "We will have no trouble hiding them. Still, it's unfortunate that Brightwell did not survive."

"I made a choice."

"Martin was afraid of him, you know. He was right to be. Did Brightwell say anything before he died?"

"He promised that he'd find me."

Bartek placed his hand upon my right arm, and squeezed it gently.

"Let them believe what they will believe. Martin told me something about you, before he died. He said that if any man had ever made recompense for his wrongs, no matter how terrible they were, it was you. Deserved or not, you've been punished enough. Don't add to it by punishing yourself. Brightwell, or something like him, will always exist in this world; others too. In turn, there will always be men and women who are prepared to confront these things and all that they represent, but in time, you won't be among them. You'll be at rest, with a stone like this one above your head, and you'll be reunited with the ones whom you loved and who loved you in return.

"But remember: to be forgiven, you have to believe in the possibility of forgiveness. You have to ask for it, and it will be given. Do you understand?"

I nodded. My eyes were hot. I dredged up the words from my childhood, from dark confessionals inhabited by unseen priests and a God who was terrible in His mercy.

"Bless me, Father, for I have sinned . . ."

And the words spilled out of me like a cancer given form, a torrent of sins and regrets purging themselves from my body. And in time, I heard two words in return, and Bartek's face was close to mine as he whispered them in my ear.

"Te absolvo," he said. "Do you hear me? You are absolved."

I heard him, but I could not believe.

V

Through these years I've seen days that I won't miss at all,
But then God knows I've been as high as the sun.
Through it all you kept me warm,
holding on to my hand,
but now you're on your own.

Pinetop Seven, "Tennessee Pride"

Epilogue

The days fall like leaves. All is quiet now.

The marsh grass is blackened, and when the wind blows from the southeast it carries with it the smell of smoke. Someone found the charred body of a mute swan floating in the water, and the burned remains of shrews and hares have been discovered in the charred undergrowth. The dog no longer likes to venture where the fire burned, and so the twin boundaries of his world are represented by events from the recent past: flames rising where no flames should have been, and a deformed man drowning slowly in a pool of bloodied water as a pregnant woman watches him die.

I traced the young prostitute named Ellen to Tenth Avenue, just a couple of blocks from Times Square. After the death of G-Mack, I heard that she'd been taken under the wing of a new pimp, a middle-aged serial abuser of women and children who called himself Poppa Bobby, and liked his girls to call him Poppa or Daddy. It was after midnight, and I watched single men hover around the street girls like hawks circling wounded prey. Natives drifted past the hookers, by now immune to such sights, while late-night tourists darted uneasy looks at them, the glances of the men perhaps lingering for a moment too long before returning to the street ahead or the faces of their partners, a little moisture falling softly and secretly upon the seeds of their discontent.

Ellen was different now. Before, she had maintained a veneer of toughness, and had carried herself with a confidence that, if she did not actually feel it in reality, was still a sufficiently strong counterfeit of the original to enable her to live the life that had been forced upon her. But now as I watched her stand on the corner, a cigarette in her right hand, she looked lost and fragile. Something had broken within her, and she appeared even younger than she was. I imagined that would have suited Poppa Bobby just fine, as he could then sell her to men with such tastes as a fourteen-or fifteen-year-old, and they would inflict themselves upon her with greater ferocity as a result.

I could see Poppa Bobby about halfway down the block, leaning against the window of a convenience store, pretending to read a newspaper. Like most of the pimps, he kept his distance from the women under him. When a john approached one of his "team", as he called them, the girl would usually commence walking toward Bobby, in part so as not to attract the attention of any curious cops who might be watching by carrying on a conversation with a stranger at a street corner, but also to allow the pimp to fall in behind, maybe eavesdrop on the negotiations to make sure the girl wasn't trying to rip him off. Whenever possible, Bobby preferred to have nothing to do with the clients themselves. It made them uneasy, he knew, to deal with a man, shattering whatever illusions they might have had about the transaction in which they were engaged. In addition, if the john turned out to be an undercover cop, then there was nothing to connect Bobby to the girl.

I watched a man casing Ellen from the subway entrance. He was small and pale, with a Dodgers cap pressed down low on his head. The cap failed to hide his eyes, instead causing the hunger in them to shine more brightly in the shadow of its peak. His right hand worried relentlessly at a small silver cross that dangled from a leather strap on his left wrist: a misguided offering from a priest or a therapist, perhaps, so that when he felt the urge upon him he could touch it and derive from it the strength to resist his appetites, except the touching of the cross had instead become an element of his preparations, the icon an extension of his sexuality, each stroke ratcheting his excitement up a notch so that sex and worship became inextricably bound together in a single act of transgression.

Eventually he decided to make a move on her, but I slipped past him and got to her first. He seemed about to say something, but I raised a finger to him in warning and, reluctantly, he backed away, melting into the crowds until he could find another outlet for his cravings.

Unseen by him, a dark figure detached itself from a wall and followed him.

It took Ellen a moment to recognize me. When she did, she tried to move around me, hoping to attract Poppa Bobby's attention. Unfortunately, Poppa Bobby was otherwise engaged. He was sandwiched between two large Italian-Americans, one of whom had a big gun pressed into Poppa Bobby's side. Tony Fulci was laughing. His arm was draped around Bobby's shoulder, and he had clearly just told Bobby to laugh along with him, because Bobby's mouth split reluctantly like a dropped orange. Tony's brother Paulie was behind the two men, with his right hand in the pocket of his leather jacket and his left clenched by his side, forming a fist like the business end of a sledgehammer. They led Bobby to a dirty white van, its motor running. Jackie Garner was sitting in the driver's seat. He nodded to me, barely perceptibly, before Bobby was hustled into the back and the van pulled away.

"Where are they taking him?" said Ellen.

"It doesn't matter."

"Will he be back?"

"No."

She looked distraught.

"What am I gonna do without him? I got no money, no place to go."

Her teeth worried at her lower lip. I thought she was about to cry.

"Your name is Jennifer Fleming," I said. "You come from Spokane, and you're seventeen years old. Your mother reported you missing six months ago. Her boyfriend has since been charged with assault, possession of a controlled substance with intent to supply, and sexual abuse of a minor based upon photographs found in the apartment he shared with your mom. The photographs were dated. You were fifteen when they were taken. Your mom claims that she didn't know it was going on. Is that true?"

Jennifer was crying now. She nodded.

"You don't have to go home yet, if you don't want to. I know a woman who runs a shelter upstate. It's pretty, and you'll have some time to think. You'll have your own room, and there are green fields and woods to walk in. If you like, your mom can come visit you and you can talk about stuff, but you don't have to see her until you're ready."

I didn't know what to expect from her. She could have walked away, and found shelter with some of the older women. After all, she had no reason to trust me. Men like G-Mack and Poppa Bobby had probably offered her protection too, and extracted a heavy price in return.

But she didn't walk away. She dried her tears with the back of her hand, and suddenly she was just a lost girl. The woman she had been forced to become disappeared entirely, and the child that she still was took her place.

"Can we go now?" she said.

"Yes, we can go now."

Her eyes moved sideways, looking past me. I turned to see two men approaching. One was skinny and black, with gold chains at his wrist and neck. The other was a fat white man wearing a red padded jacket and worn sneakers.

"Fuck you doing?" said the white guy. "Where's Bobby at?"

"Look over your shoulder," I said.

"What?"

"You heard me: look over your shoulder."

He did. It was a quick movement, like a dog snapping at a fly. Over by the subway, barely ten feet from us, Angel stood watching. Louis was just rejoining him. He dropped something into a trash can as he walked. It looked like a Dodgers cap.

Angel waved. Tubby tapped his buddy on the shoulder and the slim black man turned to see what the problem was.

"Shit," he said.

"If you don't walk away now, those men will kill you."

They exchanged a look.

"I never did like Bobby anyway," said the white guy.

"Who's Bobby?" said the black guy.

They walked away and I left with Jennifer, Angel and Louis staying with us until we had retrieved my car from the parking garage. We drove northwest beneath starless skies. Jennifer slept for part of the journey, then found a station that she liked on the radio. Emmylou Harris was singing Lennon and McCartney's "Here, There and Everywhere", one of those cover versions that most people had never heard but that most people should.

"Is this okay?" she said.

"It's fine."

"I like the Beatles. Their version is better, but this is good too. It's sadder."

"Sometimes sad is good."

"Are you married?" she asked suddenly.

"No."

"Got a girlfriend?"

I wasn't sure how to answer.

"I used to, but not any more. I have a little girl, though. I had another daughter once, but she died. Her name was Jennifer too."

"Was that why you came back for me, because we have the same name?"

She thought about the question. "If it was, would that be enough?"

"I guess. What will happen to Poppa Bobby?"

I didn't answer.

"Oh," she said, and she said nothing else for a time. Then: "I was there, y'know, the night G-Mack got killed. That wasn't his real name. His real name was Tyrone."

We were driving along the highway now, away from the interstate. There was little traffic. Ahead of us, red lights ascended into the air like fireflies as a distant car scaled a dark, unseen hill.

"I didn't see the man who killed him," she said. "I left before the police came. I didn't want any trouble. They found me, though, and they asked me about that night, but I told them that I wasn't with him when he died."

She stared out the window. Her face was reflected in the glass.

"I can keep a secret, is what I'm saying," she said. "I won't tell. I didn't see the man who killed Tyrone, but I heard what he said before he pulled the trigger."

She didn't turn her face away from the glass.

"I won't tell anyone else," she said. "Just so you know, I won't ever tell another soul."

"What did he say?" I asked.

"He said, 'She was blood to me.'"

There are still boxes in the hallway, and clothes on the chairs. Some of them are Rachel's, some are Sam's. They buried Ellis Chambers's son Neil today, but I did not attend the funeral. We save those whom we can save. That is what I tell myself.

The house is so very quiet.

Earlier, I walked down to the seashore. The wind was coming from the east, but I felt a warm breeze on my face when I looked inland, and I heard voices whisper to me in passing as the sea called to them, welcoming them into its depths, and I closed my eyes and let them wash over me, their touch like silk upon me and their grace momentarily resonating in some deep part of me before it dissipated and was gone. I looked up but there were no stars, no moon, no light.

And in the darkness beyond night, Brightwell waits.

I have been sleeping, seated in a wicker chair on the gallery, wrapped in a blanket. Despite the cold, I do not want to be inside, lying in the bed where, so recently, she too once lay, looking at the empty reminders of our life together. Now something has awoken me. The house is no longer silent. There is a creak from a kitchen chair. A door closes. I hear what might be footsteps, and the laughter of a child.

We told you that she would go away.

It was my decision. I will add no more names to the palimpsest of the heart. I will make reparation, and I will be forgiven my sins.

The wind chime in the hallway casts its song into the still, dark night, and I feel a presence approach.

But we will never leave.

All is well, all is well.

Acknowledgments

Much of the historical detail is this novel is based on fact, and the monasteries mentioned are all real. In particular, the ossuary at Sedlec is much as I have described it, although far more impressive visually than I could convey in words. Anyone interested can pay a virtual visit through my website (www.john-connolly.co.uk) but if you are lucky enough to find yourself in the Czech Republic, then Sedlec is worth a trip. I would like to express my thanks to the staff at the ossuary, to Vladímira Saiverová and Jarmila Palasová at the Philip Morris company, and to my Czech guide Marcela Kršková for their kindness and assistance in researching the Sedlec sections of this book. I am also grateful to the wonderful Luis Urrea, author of *The Devil's Highway*, for his help with matters of translation. As always, any mistakes are my fault, not theirs.

Finally, I would like to thank Sue Fletcher, my editor at Hodder & Stoughton, and Emily Bestler, my editor at Atria, for their kindness, advice, and support. Thanks also to Swati Gamble, Kerry Hood, Lucy Hale, Sarah Branham, Judith Curr, Louise Burke, and all the staff at both publishing houses who have done so much for my books; to Chuck Antony; to Darley Anderson and his staff, for looking out for me; to

Heidi Mack, my wonderful web maven; to my mother and Brian; and to Jennie, Cameron, and Alistair for, well, you know . . .

The following books and articles proved useful in my research:

Books

Altová, Blanka—*Sedlec Cistercian Monastery* (Hora, 2001)

Aries, Philip—*The Hour of Our Death* (Knopf, 1981); *Western Attitudes toward Death* (Marion Boyers, 1976)

Binski, Paul—*Medieval Death: Ritual and Representation* (British Museum Press, 1996)

Chlíbec, Horyna, Jirásek, Novák, Pinkava—*Memento Mori* (Torst, 1998)

Goodrick-Clarke, Nicholas—*The Occult Roots of Nazism* (Tauris Parke, 2004)

Heald, David and Kinder, Terry L.—*Architecture of Silence: Cistercian Abbeys of France* (Harry N. Abrams, 2000)

Henry, Mark R.—*The US Army in World War II* (Osprey, 2001)

Leroux-Dhuys, Jean-François—*Cistercian Abbeys: History and Architecture* (Könemann, 1998)

Levenda, Peter—*Unholy Alliance* (Continuum, 2003)

Link, Luther—*The Devil* (Reaktion, 1995)

Pagels, Elaine—*The Origins of Satan* (Allen Lane, 1995)

Prophet, Elizabeth Clare—*Fallen Angels and the Origins of Evil* (Summit University Press, 2000)

Tice, Paul (and Fra Poggius)—*Hus the Heretic* (The Book Tree, 2003)

Tobin, Stephen—*The Cistercians: Monks and Monasteries of Europe* (The Herbert Press, 1995)

Articles

Duffy, Peter—"Blitzkrieg Cabbie" (New York Press, March 24–30, 2004)

Gray, Jeffrey—"Code of Quiet" (Village Voice, June 25, 2002)

Prout, Jade—"Mayhem & the Maine-iac" (The Portland Phoenix, March 26, 2004)

Thompson, Ginger—"On Mexico's Mean Streets, The Sinners Have a Saint" (The New York Times, March 26, 2004)